# THE GUARDED ONE
## A FALCON FALLS SECURITY NOVEL

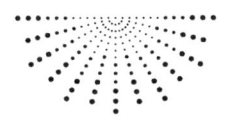

BRITTNEY SAHIN

EMKO MEDIA

*The Guarded One*

By: Brittney Sahin

Published by: EmKo Media, LLC

Copyright © 2022 EmKo Media, LLC

This book is an original publication of Brittney Sahin.

In accordance with the U.S. Copyright Act of 1976, the scanning, uploading, and electronic sharing of any part of this book without permission of the publisher constitute unlawful piracy and theft of the author's intellectual property. If you would like to use material from the book (other than for review purposes), prior written permission must be obtained by contacting brittneysahin@emkomedia.net Thank you for your support of the author's rights.

This book is a work of fiction. Names, characters, places, and incidents either are products of the author's imagination or are used fictitiously. Any resemblance to actual persons, living or dead, business establishments, events, or locales is entirely coincidental. The author acknowledges the trademarked status and trademark owners of various products, brands, and/or restaurants referenced in this work of fiction, which have been used without permission. The publication/use of these trademarks is not authorized, associated with, or sponsored by the trademark owners.

Chief Editor: Deb Markanton

Editor: Arielle Brubaker

Copy Editor: Michelle Fewer

Proofreader: Judy Zweifel, Judy's Proofreading

Cover Design: LJ, Mayhem Cover Creations

Image License (front): Serdar Kayabali / (back): iStock

Ebook ISBN: 978-1-947717-34-3

Paperback ISBN: 9798835133864

❦ Created with Vellum

*For the dreamers*

\* \* \*

*"Ask for what you want and be prepared to get it."*
-Maya Angelou

*"Once you make a decision, the universe conspires to make it happen."*
-Ralph Waldo Emerson

## CHAPTER ONE

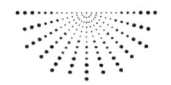

JUÁREZ, MEXICO

"Got a light?"

Beckett withdrew his attention from the only bit of calm he'd managed to locate, the heavens, and focused on the woman standing before him. Her bold red lips parted slightly as if anxiously awaiting the cigarette dangling between her two fingers. By his take, it was an act—and not a good one. She'd probably choke on the first drag if he had a light to offer.

*That really your best pickup line?* "I don't smoke." Beckett looked around the patio outside the club and tipped his head toward one of the men puffing away to his heart's content, calling her bluff.

The too-young-for-him blonde tucked her cigarette into a little metallic bag before propping the purse under her armpit. "Are you about to tell me why I shouldn't smoke as well?"

"Not my business, ma'am." Beckett exhaled sharply, his eyes moving back to the midnight-blue sky.

"Well then." Her dramatic breathy pause meant she wasn't going anywhere.

He inwardly groaned. Rejecting this girl tonight wasn't on his list of shit to do.

"What brings you to this side of the border? You from El Paso?" she pressed.

He wasn't from Texas, but El Paso was just over the border. And it was where he and his brother-in-law, Jesse McAdams, had rented a blacked-out Chevy Suburban before making the journey into Mexico an hour ago.

*What the hell am I doing here though?* Were the last three weeks of nearly sleepless nights the culprit? Was the lack of sleep to blame for why he broke a promise he made to his three brothers to never go on such a "hunt" again?

After the cutoff *"I'm in a lot of trouble, and I need your —"* voicemail he'd received three weeks ago, Beckett had told himself he wouldn't fall victim to that woman again.

And if she died one day from her reckless and irresponsible behavior . . . well, God rest her soul, if she ever had one, because she wasn't his problem anymore. Well, that'd been the plan, at least. *Yet here I am.*

Not that he was about to provide this girl with the truth. He wouldn't let her know his brother-in-law was currently doing an internal perimeter sweep of the club, calculating any potential problems for a mission Beckett wasn't supposed to be on.

A knot of guilt tightened in his stomach as he thought back to that morning when he'd looked his sister, Ella, square in the eyes and lied to her. Told her he was taking her husband away for a hunting trip in Texas.

He was hunting. Just not deer. And not in Texas.

*"A bonding trip,"* he'd lamely added while trying to stand strong beneath his sister's don't-bullshit-me gaze

while Jesse had still been blinking away the remnants of sleep.

"No answer, huh? Is the sky really all that more interesting than me?"

*A feisty one, huh?* He lowered his gaze and started to reach for his hat to tip it in apology, then remembered it wasn't the Stetson he usually wore. Instead, he flicked at the brim of the uncomfortable hat and drew a hand over the scruff on his jawline. "Why I'm here doesn't matter."

"Oh, come on, don't be so salty. You won't even tell me if this is a business or pleasure kind of trip? This place is pretty lit." She batted her false lashes. "And I'm here, so. YOLO, right?"

*Lit? YOLO?* Sweet Jesus, he was too old for this.

She was probably some rich girl from one of the schools in El Paso, looking for some "adventure" across the border on daddy's dime.

God help him when his daughter went away to college. More like help the men who'd be dealing with an overprotective father. McKenna was thirteen going on twenty, and that thought alone was enough to keep him awake at night.

"And if I say I'm not here for either, will you leave me alone?" He crooked his head, waiting to see if he'd offended her enough to send her on her way.

Her pout wasn't remotely subtle.

*Yup, a bored rich girl, for sure.* Not that he had anything against money. But some of the privileged women he'd come across back when he lived in Los Angeles may have been to thank for his quick assumptions about the perky blonde dressed like a 1920s flapper girl.

Of course, it was his job to size people up. Sheriff of his hometown, Walkins Glen, Alabama, after all.

"Do you really think you should be at a place like this?" Beckett couldn't help but switch to father mode. She didn't look more than eight to ten years older than his daughter. Was she even legally allowed to drink in Texas? *And good Lord, am I really going to be forty-two next month?*

"What makes it safe for you but not for me, aside from your Y chromosome and the amount of testosterone I feel just oozing out of ya?" Her icy blue eyes collided with his as if prepared to tango. And he didn't think it was to join those doing the actual tango on the dance floor of the 1920s-themed club.

He quietly studied her, hoping she'd give up and walk away.

No such luck.

She whipped her blonde hair to her back, and he caught a smell of what he assumed was her perfume in the process.

His eyes fell closed as he took his time to commit the scent to memory, trying to figure out why the smell of— *cherries?*—had him thinking about another blonde. *Sydney Archer.* "What perfume is that?" he asked instead of bothering to respond to whatever ridiculous question she'd posed.

"Oh, you like it? I swear I almost caught a smile from you. A nice change from your grumpy look."

He ignored her compliment-jab, opting to continue thinking about Sydney. He'd brushed past her at his friend's wedding reception last month in April.

The gorgeous woman, also a badass by what he'd learned, worked alongside Jesse at their security company, Falcon Falls. She was a single parent to a thirteen-year-old as well. Maybe that was the only reason he'd noticed Sydney? *Who am I kidding?* Every man had to have noticed her there.

"It's Tom Ford. Lost Cherry," she replied in a light, airy voice when he'd yet to speak.

Beckett nearly leaned in and took another whiff of her as if he were a K9 tracking a fugitive's scent.

"It's rather intoxicating, right? Makes me feel like a goddess, especially in this getup."

Beckett forced open his eyes, trying to understand why the scent had him losing his focus.

*Cherries.* He almost did smile that time. *At least I've still got it.* He'd been afraid he'd lost his ability to observe the minute details since he'd left the LAPD over a decade ago. But the smallest of things, right down to scent, had always helped him identify a suspect.

"So, anyway." She shrugged. "I'm here because I'm writing my senior thesis on the Prohibition Era. I go to school in El Paso." Her words snatched his attention her way. Or maybe he'd already been looking at her, but he hadn't actually seen her. Not with Sydney in his head. A woman he had no business thinking about, let alone remembering her sexy body in that backless dress she'd worn that night.

He'd brought a date to Savanna and Griffin's wedding. His first date in ages too. The night had been short-lived for them because one thing Beckett was, was a gentleman. And he wasn't about to take some woman home for a quick lay— even if it'd been far too long—when he knew he'd be picturing another pinned beneath his body instead.

Hell, he'd barely been able to look his date in the eyes during the reception after he'd found himself checking out Sydney. Every time he glanced her way, he'd imagine walking his fingers along the curve of Sydney's spine straight to that ass of hers.

"Wait, what?" Beckett blinked, forgetting where he was again. The magnetic pull of Sydney, a woman he barely knew, was damn strong if she could hijack his thoughts on a night like this. "You're here for a school essay?" *Not* what he'd been expecting, not that he'd asked her for that information.

"Mmhmm. One of my professors mentioned Al Capone used to cross the border into Juárez during that time to stock up on booze. And when I heard about this tourist trap of a location as a nod to that time period . . . well," she said, speaking almost too fast for him, "I had to come see for myself. Although, I have to admit I feel like we're two birds in a gilded cage here. We're in a luxurious nightclub in the middle of nowhere, but we don't have true freedom." Her big, blue, seemingly innocent eyes found his as she whispered, "Cartel and all."

He shuddered at the thought of his daughter ever doing something so insane. Did this girl's dad know her whereabouts? Would he lose his mind to learn his daughter was in one of the most dangerous neighborhoods on the continent, not far from a place nicknamed Murder Valley and controlled by narcotraffickers?

Fuck, the idea of McKenna ever doing something like that for the sake of an essay gave him more than just heartburn. He set a hand to his chest and did his best to find a deep breath.

"I think this place is really a front for money laundering or drug smuggling. Something equally as shady as what Capone used to do himself." She pointed toward the door leading into the club, and the sounds of jazz filtered out into the night air when it swung open and closed a moment later. "I mean, the club has framed images displayed from the St. Valentine's Day Massacre of twenty-nine. If that doesn't say it all."

Her two steps back gave him a chance to find that breath he'd needed.

"I heard a rumor that some billionaire has his eye on the

place though," she added. "Soooo, what was the *Great Gatsby* quote you used to get into the club?"

Wow, did this woman ever stop talking? He thought back to his research on the place. Along with adhering to the strict 1920s dress code, patrons could only gain admission by quoting one of the famous *Great Gatsby* lines. The bouncer had a list on an iPad he'd scrolled through to verify, all part of the intrigue to bring tourists there. He hardly doubted the bouncer truly gave a damn about *Gatsby*.

Beckett had cursed the Amazon purchases he'd made a few nights ago when he'd ordered his era-appropriate outfits in preparation for a trip Jesse had been unaware of at that point. Then he'd praised Amazon Prime delivery for getting the shipment out to their small town so quickly.

"'*Let us learn to show our friendship for a man when he is alive and not after he is dead*,'" Beckett repeated the *Gatsby* quote he'd provided the bouncer earlier. When he'd researched quotes, he'd latched on to that one.

Subconsciously, he knew he probably selected it because he'd been such a jerk to Jesse not too long ago, and he truly did want to make amends and be friends again. Right his wrongs with his brother-in-law.

Beckett had only fessed up the truth about the trip to Jesse an hour before crossing the Bridge of the Americas into Mexico. Of course, Jesse wasn't an idiot, so when Beckett had casually mentioned before they'd left Alabama to bring a passport just in case . . .

Maybe in Jesse's mind tonight would be a chance to pay Beckett back for the nightmare they'd all survived in January when both Beckett's sister and daughter had been caught in the crossfire of Jesse's past.

But to Beckett, Jesse didn't owe him anything, and *he* was now indebted to his brother-in-law.

"I chose a quote from Daisy Buchanan, of course." She painted on a smile. Possibly a legitimate one, but he was losing faith in his ability to read her. "'*I hope she'll be a fool. That's the best thing a girl can be in this world, a beautiful little fool.*'"

Yeah, this woman was a fool to be in a cartel-run club for the sake of a college essay, that was for damn sure.

"Will you do me a favor and dance with me? Do you know the foxtrot? I actually don't, but we can fake it til we make it, right? The music does sound pretty dope. And we look snatched in our outfits," she rambled. "I almost feel like we time traveled and are really in the nineteen-twenties." She opened her palm. "Will you help me write my paper? Give me a night of a lifetime I won't forget?"

"I'm twice your age. There won't be any night with me." He was tempted to remove his hat and show her his hair to reinforce that he was too old for her. Stress had done a number on him, and he now had a few silver streaks cutting through his brown hair at his temples.

"Mm." She tipped her head with an almost curious expression, not what he'd expected. "There's another cherry-scented-perfume-wearing woman you'd rather dance with, isn't there?"

*Sydney?* The idea of anything ever happening with that woman, outside his imagination at least, was crazy. They were from two different worlds. He'd have to settle for admiring her beauty from afar if she ever came back to his small town for work. "No, but now I feel like it's my duty to ensure you get back over the border safely." *Thanks for that.* Like he needed any more responsibilities tonight when he was there with one mission in mind. To find Ivy.

"Ah. A chivalrous gentleman, even for a grump."

Grump. Mr. Grumpy. That was his sister's nickname for

him. Maybe it was well-earned. *Sometimes. Fuck. Okay. Most of the time.*

"You're why older men are preferable to guys my age. They'd take advantage of me." She turned her open palm to the side as if a request for a handshake instead. "I'm Jennifer."

He zeroed in on her hand. No way could he leave Jennifer in Mexico alone. He'd never sleep at night wondering if she'd gotten herself kidnapped by the cartel. "Well, Jennifer, I won't be dancing tonight. But I'll do my best to keep an eye on you from inside the club. And to make sure you get home after you're done with your research."

She closed one eye as if contemplative. "You're a hero-type, aren't you? My grandfather was a cop in Boston, and you've got that vibe."

He almost laughed. She really was more perceptive than him tonight. Cherry perfume aside, those three weeks of no sleep had screwed him up.

"Let's just go inside." He ought to locate Jesse anyway. He'd been gone for too long.

Of course, Jesse could more than handle himself. After all, he was a former Army Ranger and CIA hit man.

Beckett slipped a hand to Jennifer's back and guided her into the club. The place really was a tourist trap, drawing mostly Americans, from what Beckett could tell, to spend money on an experience. The only thing calming his nerves was the fact the place would've long since stopped being a tourist hot spot if Americans kept going missing afterward.

"I'll be over there." He pointed to the only bar in the room, and she nodded a small thanks before wandering out to the dance floor near the live band currently playing a song Beckett's mother loved, "It Don't Mean A Thing" by the legendary Duke Ellington.

Beckett settled on an empty black barstool and removed his fedora. The fact he was wearing that was another example of his insanity. Same with the three-piece tweed suit, suspenders, and cap-toe Oxfords.

From the corner of his eye, he caught Jesse joining him at the bar. "I had to step out and call Ella. She's been texting nonstop with worry," he explained, and Beckett swung his gaze Jesse's way.

Jesse looked every part a 1920s gangster. If he weren't so worried about the outcome of this trip, he'd probably laugh at how they were both dressed. "And what'd you say to her?"

"I lied. Not happy about that. But the truth would keep my pregnant wife up all night, and she doesn't need the stress."

"I'm sorry," Beckett earnestly apologized. "The last thing I wanted to do was put you in this position." *But I knew A.J. wouldn't help, and my other brothers aren't equipped for this.* "I—"

"I'm glad you didn't come here alone," Jesse cut him off. "Remember, I do this kind of stuff for a living. *But* I'm not excited about going behind Ella's back because I promised I'd never keep secrets again."

"Shit, I'm really damn sorry about that. And I'm also sorry for the way I—"

"Please, if I hear one more apology from you, I'll kick your ass," Jesse said with a smirk. "I told the same to A.J. when he wouldn't shut up with the apologies too."

"Yeah, but we all treated you like shit in January, and you didn't deserve that. Sure, we weren't aware of the um, baggage, you were carrying at the time, but that doesn't excuse our behavior. You're family now, and I—"

"I would've reacted the same as you did if I'd been in

your shoes, and you know it." Jesse let go of a deep breath. "So, can we please bury this once and for all?"

"Fine," Beckett reluctantly agreed. *"But* I still owe you for breaking your promise and lying to Ella tonight. Ten times over."

"Just buy the drinks for the next few weeks, and we're even," Jesse said as Beckett checked to ensure Jennifer was safe and confirmed she appeared happily dancing.

"Deal." *And I can start tonight.* Beckett swiveled back on his seat and waved over the bartender *"¿Que le gustaría, señor?"* His gaze fell to the bartender's hands before him. Three black dots were inked between his index finger and thumb on his left hand.

He'd learned from his time as a detective with the Narcotics Division in Los Angeles years ago that those dots were often inked on ex-cons, meaning *mi vida loca*, my crazy life. Usually tattooed while serving time.

The bartender being an ex-con wasn't a surprise given their location and the fact Jennifer was right about her research. It was well-known the club had connections to the Sinaloa cartel, one of the most powerful drug trafficking organizations.

He'd had his fair share of run-ins with the Sinaloas because of their connection to MS-13 back in LA. And the memories left more than just a bitter taste in his mouth.

A broken nose. A fractured rib. Two gunshot wounds. And did the gaping metaphorical hole in his heart also count as a wound? Maybe that last one wasn't physical, but the pain seemed to last the longest for him.

*"Un tequila, por favor, y una cerveza para mi amigo."* Beckett slid the bartender a thousand pesos, equivalent to about fifty bucks, more than double the cost of the drinks.

The bartender tipped his head in respect and quickly

pocketed the six hundred extra pesos for his tip. "*Cómo no, señor.*"

"Careful," Jesse warned when the bartender went to retrieve tequila and a beer. "Show off too much money here, and we'll have bigger problems."

"Copy that," Beckett returned in a low voice. He was out of his element there. It'd been thirteen years since he'd been in LA doing any type of undercover work.

Back in his small town, crime wasn't an issue, which he was happy about, of course. It was one of the reasons he'd moved back home to raise his daughter there.

Jesse tugged at the lapels of his jacket. "You can put a man on the moon but me in this suit . . ." His voice trailed off when the bartender slid their drinks across the dark polished wood.

Beckett's attention swerved to another one of the bartender's tattoos. This one was of *Santa Muerta* on his neck. The queen of the underworld.

And maybe Jennifer was partly right in her gilded cage assessment. They were in a place gleaming with glitz and glamor. The art deco designs and geometric shapes screamed Jazz Age, but in reality . . . they weren't free. They were in the belly of hell. If they weren't careful tonight, they'd be swallowed right up. And they didn't have sidearms. Not even a replica of an era piece like a tommy gun to shoot their way out of the place.

*What if she's gone? What if I'm too late?* Beckett shifted the sleeve of his jacket and checked the time. *Still early.* Maybe her shift hadn't started yet. *If she even works here.*

His guilt further suffocated him as he thought about the disappointed expressions his family would point his way if they knew where he was and why.

His mother would be the first to slap him all the way back

to the actual 1920s for ever taking such a risk as leaving his daughter fatherless if shit went sideways.

*I'm an idiot. A sleep-deprived idiot.*

He shifted on his seat to put eyes on Jennifer once again. As he turned, his gaze collided with one of the servers walking by. She was wearing only a strand of pearls and heart-shaped tassels covering her nipples for her top. The woman paused to check if he was . . . well, interested in something beyond a drink. He shook his head, and she continued walking.

"If we're going to make a move, we better do it fast. I clocked three rival cartel members on my check earlier. Probably the Juárez gang not happy about the Sinaloas taking more and more ground here," Jesse informed him, keeping his mouth close to Beckett's ear so he could talk without shouting over the poppy melody of the song "Sing Sing Sing" now being played by the band.

*I have a daughter back home, and I'm here for . . .* Beckett released a heavy breath, letting that thought go.

"I do have a question." Jesse turned to the side. "Since you didn't go to A.J. for help this time, how'd you find out she was here? Who supplied your intel?"

Beckett parted his lips, prepared to summon a response when he saw her.

The *her* he was there for.

Ivy.

She was hard to miss, and the sight of her gave him the chills. Not the kind Sydney had managed to provoke at that wedding, when he'd spied her tanned back in that dress that dipped dangerously low to her ass, making a man want to commit all types of sins.

No, these were the shit-is-about-to-go-down goose bumps that covered his skin beneath his heavy clothes.

Ivy's dark hair was draped like a curtain over her shoulders, covering part of her gold flapper dress. She slowly descended the set of spiral stairs off to the side of the band, her eyes focused on the crowd. Was she searching for her next mark? Who was the vixen's target?

Beckett pushed away from the bar and rose, leaving his tequila untouched. "She's here." He'd clamped down on his teeth, nearly chewing on the words as he'd spit them out. "And she sees me," he announced as his eyes locked with hers, and she froze on the third step from the bottom.

"How are we playing this?" Jesse asked.

Ivy lifted her chin as some kind of directive. Where'd she want him to go?

"Jennifer," Beckett hissed at the realization she was gone from the dance floor.

"Who's Jennifer? Did I miss something?" Jesse asked.

"A new responsibility and I don't see her." He couldn't let some young girl die because of his mission, but he also couldn't lose his chance to talk to Ivy. He may not get another one. "Don't let Ivy out of your sight. I'll find you in a minute." Ivy was downstairs now, meandering through the crowd and advancing toward the exit. "She's leaving."

"I'm on it." The second Jesse started through the pack of dancers, Beckett began searching for Jennifer.

Why'd he have to meet that girl tonight? He didn't need the headache. But he also didn't need her death on his conscience.

Once at the center of the club, he looked around, hoping he'd just missed her out there, but there was no sign of her.

*Where are you, damn it?* He was near heart failure when he spotted a flash of blonde hair. His shoulders fell with relief as Jennifer exited the women's restroom. *For fuck's sake. Thank God.* He cut through the crowd to get to her.

"You okay?" She angled her head, appearing alarmed by whatever crazy look he must've been giving her.

"I have to step outside for a minute. Don't do anything to get yourself killed in the meantime, okay?" he demanded, his worried, harsh tone washed out by the music.

"Um. Yeah, sure." She shrugged, and that wasn't all that comforting of an answer, but he had to get to Ivy before it was too late.

He rushed for the front door, but a thick, muscled arm stretched before him as a blockade. "I wouldn't go out there if I were you," the bouncer warned in English.

When Beckett shot him a menacing look, a demand to let him continue, the guy lowered his arm.

"Your funeral." He folded his beastly arms and stepped clear, but Beckett didn't make it far.

Twenty or so meters away, Jesse was in the middle of fighting not one, but three men. And before Beckett could step in for an assist, Jesse had managed to remove a 9mm from one of the gangster-dressed men and popped off three quick precision shots.

All three fuckers fell like dominoes.

*Did I really just see that?* He didn't think those were kill shots, but damn, the way Jesse had dropped them so fast was eerily impressive. And it was also the first time he'd witnessed Jesse in action. Of course, he'd brought Jesse with him tonight for a reason.

Beckett stepped forward but stopped yet again when Jesse lifted a quick palm, signaling him to hold.

It didn't take Beckett long to figure out why. Ivy was nearby, standing alongside a vintage Cadillac with her hand over her mouth and a man at her side. He had to be cartel.

"You just took out the trash for me. Juárez gang." The suited man by Ivy approached Jesse.

Beckett hated standing in the shadows while Jesse handled whatever the hell was about to happen, but he'd trust his brother-in-law on this one and wait and see.

"They were trying to take her," Jesse said, probably for Beckett's benefit, to alert him to why he'd shot three people. Clearly, the suited guy had witnessed Jesse's heroic acts in saving Ivy.

"I'd like you to come with me." The man snapped his fingers, and several other men started for the moaning bodies on the ground. "Now."

Jesse quietly nodded, then stole one last look at Beckett before stepping into the back of the Cadillac while Ivy slid onto the front passenger seat.

Jesse mouthed what looked like the name "Carter" to Beckett before the car door shut.

Carter was one of Jesse's two bosses at Falcon Falls, so he assumed he was requesting an extraction.

*What in the hell did I just do?*

Beckett faced the bouncer, who, for whatever reason, had tried to save his life moments ago by keeping him from the fight. "The woman, is she—"

"She's Miguel Diego's," he grunted. "The owner's girl."

*Great.* Ivy was in bed with the cartel. Literally.

And now his brother-in-law was in cartel hands.

*My sister's going to kill me.*

## CHAPTER TWO

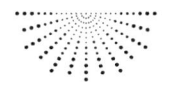

It'd taken Beckett a handful of seconds to learn Miguel Diego, the club owner, lived in a military-style compound in Murder-Fucking-Valley just outside Juárez. And he had to assume that was where he was taking Jesse.

Beckett's first instinct had been to tail the Cadillac, but he'd made a promise to deliver Jennifer to the border safely. Surprisingly, the bouncer had given him a *you didn't hear it from me* idea as to the whereabouts of Miguel Diego's compound. A good thing because Jesse's location on the tracking app they were using, on the off chance they got split up, had vanished moments after he and Ivy were whisked away. Jesse's phone was going to voicemail as well, which meant Miguel either demanded Jesse turn it off or it'd been destroyed.

After learning the club manager's name, Beckett had gone back in the club and quickly snatched Jennifer's wrist, demanding they leave right away.

Thankfully, she hadn't protested but instead scampered to keep up with his long strides. When they had burst through the door and stumbled on the three bodies being hauled away, leaving a trail of blood in their wake, the horrified look on her face caused Beckett to shelve the stern lecture he'd planned on delivering before tucking her into her car. He was pretty sure she'd be having nightmares after this, but at least she wouldn't come back.

Beckett huffed out a frustrated breath and grabbed his phone from the console of the rental as he waited in the parking lot near the border crossing and watched Jennifer's Tesla inch forward in the line of cars progressing toward Texas.

He'd followed her there and decided to wait until she'd safely crossed into the States before he took off. The way his luck was going tonight, he didn't want to take any chances. He'd also given her his number and asked her to text him when she made it back to her dorm.

"How in the hell did I let tonight happen?" he hissed while scrolling through his contacts, grateful he had Carter's number saved.

Beckett's only hope for Jesse right now was that he'd saved Miguel's girlfriend from three enemy cartel members. Miguel now owed Jesse, right? But in Beckett's experience from dealing with the cartel in Los Angeles, that didn't guarantee Jesse a get-out-of-death card.

"What happened?" Carter answered after the second ring.

"Jesse gave you a heads-up, didn't he?" Apparently, Jesse hadn't only called Ella on his perimeter sweep. *Smart man.*

"Yeah. And since *you're* calling me, it's safe to say something went wrong," Carter answered in a low voice.

*That's an understatement.* "Jesse and I got separated." He paused to let that sink in. "I don't know how much he told you, but I'm down here searching for a woman. I know her as Ivy Barlowe. Not sure her current alias." Beckett waited for a second, then went on to explain how the rest of their "hunting trip" had played out.

Although Carter Dominick and Gray Chandler technically co-ran Falcon Falls Security together, Beckett had a feeling Carter was the one ultimately calling the shots. And hell, he'd been the name Jesse had mouthed, so he had to assume Carter would help Beckett put together an extraction plan for Jesse if need be.

"I already called in the guys who were local to our headquarters," Carter shared the news. "Gray, Jack, and Griffin are with me now."

Their HQ was up in Pennsylvania, but Griffin and Jesse spent most of their time in Alabama since their wives were there. The fact Griffin was back in Pennsylvania meant he was there for a possible upcoming assignment. Well, hopefully, that operation could wait. They were down a man anyway.

"We'll need all hands on deck though," Gray spoke up from somewhere in the room, his voice loud enough to be heard but not close to wherever Carter had Beckett on speakerphone. "Oliver is in Miami. He just wrapped up a quick bodyguard gig for some fitness influencer."

"Those assignments pay the bills, ya know," Jack London chimed in as if feeling the need to explain why Oliver had accepted such a job. But from what little Beckett knew, the team wasn't hard up for cash. Carter seemed to have the finances more than covered. Well, that was what Jesse had alluded to over the last few months during their brief conversations back home between shooting at the range together or playing a game of pool at the local bar, The Drunk Gator.

"Can Oliver hop on a quick flight to me? And don't you have your own jet?" Beckett asked, still not sure if they would have enough people to storm a heavily armed compound and avoid collateral damage. The last thing Beckett wanted on his conscience was someone's death due to his own stupidity for going to Mexico in the first place.

"I texted my pilot a minute ago," Carter answered. "He's prepping the jet. You and Oliver will both need to fly into Cancun and make your way to Tulum, either on your own or together, depending on when you land. We need Sydney."

"Wait, slow down there. What am I missing? Why in the Sam Hill would I leave here?" Beckett stole a quick look at the line of cars to ensure Jennifer's Tesla was gaining ground in getting closer to the border. Good. Only four cars ahead of her. He could check off one problem in a moment.

"Sydney's in Tulum until Monday morning. A girls' getaway-slash-recruiting mission," Gray responded that time. "She specifically said she doesn't want to be disturbed. Only call she'll take is from her son."

"Pretty sure her exact words were, 'I don't care if you're bleeding out on the table, stitch yourself up. Don't call me.'" It was a coin toss if Jack was joking.

Beckett's sister had remarked with awe quite a few times that Sydney reminded her of the Marvel character, *Black Widow*. Not just partly in looks but in her overall ability to cut an enemy down without hesitation.

"So, why in the hell do you want me to go to Tulum? Send Oliver if she really won't take your calls." Beckett highly doubted that was the case though.

"Because this is your problem. Your mess to clean up." Gray's words were cutting. And true.

*Fuck. He's right. But still, something doesn't add up.* "Why do I get the distinct feeling you're sending me to Tulum to actually keep me out of danger?" he challenged. "You don't think I can hang with the big boys in helping extract Jesse? So, you're going to assign Oliver to keep me out of your way until the job is done?"

"Not at all," Carter quickly reassured him, but he didn't continue, so what was that supposed to leave Beckett to think?

"You really could use backup if you're going to pull Sydney from her getaway. Oliver will have your six." More humor from Jack. Jesse had mentioned Jack was the team's resident comedian, always ready to defuse a situation with humor. Surely, he was exaggerating the level of annoyance this unexpected interruption to her vacation would provoke from Sydney.

*Backup, huh?* Did they really think he couldn't find his ass with both hands in his pockets? "I'm not sure if you've pegged me as some slow-talking country sheriff, but that's—"

"It's not that." And yet, no further explanation from Carter. What was his game plan, and had he already come up with a contingency plan in the event shit went sideways after Jesse called him earlier?

"I'm not leaving here without Jesse. So, you either clue me in on what you're really thinking, or I end the call and find another way to get Jesse."

The line went quiet for a moment. They'd most likely muted the call while Carter spoke to the rest of his team there.

*I need them,* Beckett reminded himself. He couldn't take on a cartel compound alone, and his brother A.J., a former Navy SEAL, was somewhere overseas at the moment. So, he had to play by Falcon's rules whether he liked it or not.

"We have an idea, and it does involve you going to Tulum. No guarantee what might happen or how this will all play out, but we need to trust Jesse to control the narrative while he deals with the Sinaloa cartel and go from there," Carter finally came back on the line and revealed.

"Go on," Beckett requested. "You've got my attention."

"The Sinaloas will now be indebted to Jesse. That much is obvious," Carter began. "They may even attempt to recruit him after witnessing his skills in taking out three men. But they'll also be suspicious of a plant and want to make sure Jesse isn't undercover for the DEA or a rival gang."

Beckett spied Jennifer's Tesla safely crossing the border checkpoint. Now that she was safe, he left the parking lot. "They'll test Jesse," he agreed. "Some fucking reward."

"In their minds, offering Jesse a seat at their table, or even scraps like a dog, *is* a reward for what Jesse pulled off earlier," Carter pointed out, and Beckett had to agree based on his work with Narcotics in Los Angeles. "We need eyes on that compound for their next move, but Jesse is smart. He knows how to handle this. He'll find a way to get to a new location, one we have better access to. And make Miguel or whoever is running the show over there think it's their idea."

"Jesse was onto you before the plane even left Alabama. He knew this weekend was never intended to be you two bonding and braiding each other's hair," Jack jested. "He used one of his aliases when y'all crossed into Mexico earlier."

Beckett hadn't exactly flipped open Jesse's passport to peek at the details before he'd handed it to the border agent. But it'd make sense Jesse wouldn't want to enter a foreign country using his real name, given his past with the CIA. *I should've told him everything from the start. This is my fault.*

"Also," Jack went on, "knowing Jesse, he'll find a way to lead Miguel to Tulum since he knows Sydney is already there. If he can't swing that, they'll most likely travel somewhere in Mexico. *Regardless*, he'll get out of there one way or another. He knows we can't storm a heavily fortified cartel compound on short notice without a few of us dying, or at least, making international headlines."

Not an option. Either outcome. And Jack was right. Now that Beckett knew the real Jesse, not the version Jesse had let everyone believe him to be all those years, the man was more than capable of dealing with the cartel.

"He won't walk out the front door even if they offer that option, not without Ivy. Not knowing who she is. So, Jesse will make sure the plan involves her leaving too," Beckett rationalized. "You think he can get word out to us even if they take his phone?"

"We have protocols in place if any of us ever get separated or stuck in a dead zone–type area for cell service. Just leave the communication issue to us," Carter informed him, and Beckett did his best to allow that news to lower his blood pressure.

"Regardless of what happens next, I want you in Tulum," Gray instructed. "We'll need to bring Sydney into the mix before she hops on a flight back to D.C. on Monday anyway."

"I have a friend in El Paso with a plane and access to weapons." Of course Carter did. Money talks. "He'll be your ride to Cancun. Get to Tulum, make contact with Oliver, and wait for the next steps."

"Sydney's not going to love us crashing her weekend getaway and turning it into an operation." Jack really wanted to drill that point home, didn't he? But to Beckett, pissing off Sydney was the least of his worries.

Of course, if he was being honest with himself, he wasn't thrilled about facing the only woman who'd inspired any type of fantasies for as long as he could remember.

"I'll secure a hotel room for you at Sydney's resort," Carter said a moment later, then added, "And I'd hold off on calling your sister until we know more. She's pregnant, and telling her Jesse is with—"

"She'll be expecting a goodnight text from her husband, and if she doesn't get one, I wouldn't put it past that woman to come looking for Jesse herself," Beckett grumbled.

"Then text her. Tell her Jesse passed out by the campfire," Jack quickly responded. "This hunting trip was your idea. I'm assuming you didn't tell Ella you were hunting for a woman in a club run by the cartel, right?"

"Copy that," is all Beckett offered for an answer, pissed at himself for this whole mess.

He ended the call once they'd finalized a few more details, then slammed the heel of his hand against the steering wheel.

Damn that cutoff voicemail three weeks ago.

Damn her plea for help.

Damn McKenna's mom.

## CHAPTER THREE

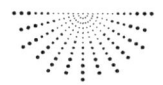

WASHINGTON, D.C. – THIRTY HOURS EARLIER

"I don't know what to say or why I'm even calling, but . . ." Sydney paused, contemplating what message to leave today.

She was on her third cup of coffee that afternoon and jittery, not her norm.

"Levi's been closed off the last few weeks," she finally went on. "Something's bothering him, and he doesn't want to talk about it." Sitting on her king-sized bed, Sydney smoothed her palm over the gray waffle-weave cotton duvet cover, her latest *forced* purchase from Pottery Barn.

Her mother had popped down from New York for a quick and unexpected visit, and she'd insisted they spend a few hours shopping together. Not Sydney's favorite thing to do by a long shot.

"Mom, you in there? I'm home from school." When her son lightly tapped at the bedroom door, she ended the call, tossed the phone on the bed, and jumped up.

Clearing her throat to brush away the emotions besting

her today, she walked over and opened the door. "How was school?" she asked, joining her son out in the hall on the second story of their home.

Levi shrugged. "It was school." He attended a private school in Arlington, Virginia, where his father lived, less than twenty minutes away from her condo in D.C.

Sydney resisted the urge to reach out and brush the too-long strands of dark hair away from his face to see his eyes.

"I may go to Grady's tonight instead of Dad's. Maybe even stay at his place all weekend since you'll be gone."

*Right. My trip.* She was leaving for Tulum in the morning in hopes of recruiting a good friend of hers to join Falcon Falls Security, but she was also looking forward to two uninterrupted days of lounging beneath the sun with a cocktail in hand. "Well, that's up to your dad since it's his weekend with you."

"He's been busy, so he'll be fine with it." Levi turned, most likely on his way to hide in his bedroom to play video games. The norm lately, and she hated the distance growing between them. Working for Falcon required a lot of travel, which wasn't ideal for a divorced mom of a teenager, so when she was home, she wanted to spend as much time with her son as possible. But he'd been avoiding her lately, and she had no idea why.

"What's he been busy with? Work stuff?" Her ex worked at the Pentagon but never on the weekends, so she was curious as to what was taking him away from their son.

Levi faced her again, allowing his backpack to fall to the floor, but he kept one strap loose in his grip. Another shrug from him as a response meant he was keeping secrets from her, and damn, they had to do with his dad, didn't they?

"When are you going to tell me what's going on?" She

leaned her shoulder against the wall, careful not to knock into one of the framed photos of her son.

She did her best to pull off casual and friendly. Less "warrior-like" since Levi liked to joke that she only had two modes: mom or fighter. And sometimes, weren't they one and the same? Helping rid the world of evil also helped keep her son safe.

But her "fighter-warrior" mode also intimidated a lot of Levi's friends, especially those of the opposite gender. Her son was handsome, smart, and kind. She couldn't risk a girl, or anyone for that matter, taking advantage of him. His grandparents' fortune ensured he was recognized as the richest kid in his school.

"Are you and Lucy okay? Did you break up?" She was one of the few girls who'd made it past all of Sydney's grilling stages and hadn't been scared away.

Levi shook his head. "No, Lucy and I are fine. Taking things slow."

God, she didn't want to know what "slow" meant for a thirteen-year-old boy, but she hoped he was at the hand-holding stage only and nothing more.

How old was she when she lost her virginity? *Eighteen, right.* "So, what is it? Please. I promise I won't, um."

Her son's lips curled into a brief smile. A smile was promising, she supposed. A smile meant whatever was bothering him wasn't earth-shattering. "Won't what?" And when he spoke with a teasing tone, that helped her heart a little too.

It couldn't be that bad since he was now brushing his fingers through his hair to expose his light green eyes, a match to her own. His dark hair, the opposite of her light blonde, was a gift from his biological dad. But his cheekbones and jawline, as well as eyes, were all hers.

"I'm . . . well, I'll be okay." He let go of the strap to his bag and narrowed the space between them. He was already taller than her. She was just over five-six, and her teenage son had stretched to nearly six feet practically overnight last summer. "It's you I'm worried about."

"Me?" She immediately shoved away from the wall. "Are you concerned about my work? I know leaving the family business last year was a big deal, and I—"

"You're much happier being a badass saving the world than you were working for Grandpa." He gave her a shit-eating grin, likely knowing that she wouldn't comment on his language when he was complimenting her. "I'm proud of you, Mom. No, that's not what I, um . . ."

Ah, he was just like her sometimes. Had trouble spitting out his thoughts. And she didn't want him to take after her in that respect.

Truth be told, he was one of the rare few who saw her loving and caring side. But then, Levi made it easy for her to be that person.

"I'm tough. Whatever it is you're holding back, I can take it." She tipped her head and reached for his shoulder, giving it a gentle squeeze.

"You are tough, Mom. But you have a big heart. I don't know why you keep that hidden from people." He smiled. "Except me and Aunt Mya."

Mya wasn't technically family, but she was the closest thing to a sister for Sydney. It was Mya who Sydney hoped to recruit to Falcon Falls Security that weekend, and with any luck and some heavy persuasion, she'd get her way.

When Levi's focus fell to the floor in her silence, he added, "I don't think it's my place to tell you. You should talk to Dad."

*Oh shit.* And now she knew what was bothering him. But

she wasn't sure why that would be such a big deal for him. It wasn't like his father hadn't dated since they split. "It's been four years. I know your dad sees other women. You don't need to worry about me." Or maybe it was because . . . "And if you like this woman he's seeing, you don't need to feel bad about that. I want you to like whoever your father ends up with. She'll be in the house, so." Her stomach did a little sickening flip at the thought of another woman helping raise her son, but it was a reality she'd eventually have to face.

"It's *who* he's dating that I'm not, well, happy about, and you might not be either," he slowly spat out.

She did her best not to close her eyes and sink back into the painful memories of Seth's affair four years ago. To think back to the night Levi caught his father making out with Sydney's only other close friend at a holiday party. The year of therapy Levi went through after that night . . . damn Seth for that.

"*Her?*" Sydney kept her voice as steady as possible for the sake of her son, but internally, she was on fire.

Levi lifted his green eyes to meet hers. And the look there said it all. He found out because he caught them again, didn't he? And she wanted to kill the son of a bitch for doing that to their son, *again*. After everything he'd put Levi through with that affair, he was back with *her?*

Sydney's fingers curled into her palms at her sides. No way did Seth know Levi had caught him with Alice. He would've speed-dialed Sydney to do damage control afterward. Offer her a briefing of the instance like she was a colleague at the Department of Defense.

He'd give her an AAR—after-action report—to detail what the hell had gone wrong, same as he'd done four years ago.

Try and talk his way past the disaster of his own making.

*Alice.* Her best friend. Her *former* best fucking friend.

Sydney, Alice, and Mya had been like sisters. Close-close friends. And since Mya was the youngest of them, really, Sydney had spent more time with Alice. *Too much time, apparently. Because she fell for my husband.*

Was it crazy she'd been more hurt by Alice's betrayal than her husband's? Because maybe Seth had been right, and her love for him wasn't enough.

"Enough" had been his favorite word back then. Sydney hadn't given him enough attention. Not enough sex. Not enough passion. Not enough love. And Alice had filled in for her.

But after the affair and Levi needing therapy, her ex ended things with Alice for his son's sake. And she'd thought Alice moved back to New York.

Levi lifted his chin. "See, it's that look in your eyes that has me worried."

"I won't hurt him." *Just in my head.* "Or Alice," she promised. "You know I only go after the bad guys."

"And I think what they're doing is bad, so . . ."

"I won't be going all Hawkeye on them, don't worry," she said, doing her best to lighten the tone of the conversation. Not that Levi knew how many lives she'd taken with the bow and arrow. But she'd taught her son to shoot with one, and he knew her skills were well above par. She was Sydney Archer, after all. Her last name derived from famous archers in England, from what her grandfather had always loved to tell her.

"Maybe head to a kickboxing class after I go to Dad's?" Levi suggested, her son knowing her all too well. He reached for his bag from the floor. "But don't tell Dad I saw," he began around a swallow, "anything."

Her lips remained sealed in a tight line. She'd do anything

for her son. Always. "I'll be back in town on Monday. If you need me, call, okay? Your number is the only one getting through to me. I'll check on you while I'm there, of course."

He let go of his bag again and looped his arms around her waist, pulling her in for a hug like he was the parent consoling her. Did she deserve him? This amazing kid? God, she hoped so. She needed him. He was her everything. Her reason for being.

"Kickboxing sounds like a great idea," she said when he pulled back, forcing a smile.

"Or the gun range." He brushed his hair away from his left eye to wink.

All she could think about was how her son had removed a heavy burden from his shoulders by finally confiding in her, which was all that mattered. He didn't need to carry the weight of his father's sins. Or hers, for that matter. Because maybe she hadn't been "enough" for Seth, but she'd be more than "enough" for Levi. No matter what.

Levi grabbed his backpack, then narrowed his eyes as if searching for a memory he couldn't quite put his finger on. She knew that look because she was guilty of doing the same thing from time to time. "You haven't been inside Dad's place lately, right?"

She shook her head, trying to make sense of his question.

No, she avoided stepping into Seth's home at all costs. The last thing she needed was an assault to her senses to trigger memories she didn't feel like confronting. She didn't need to walk into his home to remember the way the aroma of his imported coffee drifted around when brewing in the morning. Or to walk into his office and see his collection of rare war biographies that she swore smelled like they'd been dipped in formaldehyde. And his cologne. She'd never date a man who wore Jean Paul Gaultier ever again.

The memories of their marriage didn't hurt, but they were a reminder of her failure in Seth's eyes to be the wife Seth needed. And honestly, maybe she wasn't meant to ever marry again. In fact, she had no plans to settle down in the near future. She'd focus on being the mother Levi needed and the "warrior" he saw her as working for Falcon Falls.

No, she didn't need love. She didn't need all the hassle that came with it either.

"Why do you ask?" she finally pressed.

"I just . . . well, maybe wear a new perfume?" he suggested, then abruptly darted to his room.

She waited for his door to click shut before heading into her bedroom to grab the bottle of Tom Ford from her vanity. "Wearing my signature scent, too, are you?" She let out a string of creative expletives, then chucked the bottle into the trash. She'd worn that perfume for years, and Alice knew that.

Sydney went back to her bed and peered at her cell phone.

Making that call, leaving that voicemail . . . it'd become a habit.

But it was pointless.

Those calls were always pointless.

And Levi was right—if she didn't go hit something, she might do something she never did, something she hated.

Hell, she might cry.

## CHAPTER FOUR

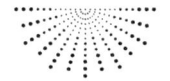

TULUM, MEXICO

"White sand beneath our feet, turquoise water lapping the shore, and mimosas in our hands. What more could we ask for?"

Sydney slapped a palm to the top of her floppy sun hat when a sudden breeze threatened to whisk it away, spilling a few sips of her drink in the process, and laughed at her friend's singsong praise of their surroundings. She and Mya were relaxing on wicker chaise loungers on the beach at their resort, the Caribbean Sea their current view and not a cloud in sight.

After sightseeing the Mayan ruins yesterday afternoon, they'd opted to spend their Sunday doing nothing but soaking in the sun. Aside from a little beach yoga after breakfast that morning, this had to have been the laziest Sydney had been in months.

"Well," Sydney began, fighting a smile and resting her arm back on her lap once the breeze had died down, "you know what I'd add to the mix to make this day totally perfect."

Mya turned her head toward Sydney and playfully kissed the air. "I'll give you my answer before you leave tomorrow, I promise."

"Before *I* leave? Are you staying longer?"

"Maybe. I might need an extra day or two in the sun." Mya looked around as if ensuring no one could hear what she planned to say next. But then nothing came.

Something was up with Mya. She'd had her head on a swivel the entire time they'd explored the Mayan ruins yesterday, and she doubted it had to do with Mya's fear of snakes or the uptick in recent saltwater crocodile attacks at the lagoons.

"I know you want to talk about the prospect of my fabulous self working with Falcon Falls." Mya sighed and turned to face the Caribbean Sea. "But let's just be two hot women on a beach with no worries in the world for a little bit longer."

"And you're *sure* there's nothing to worry about?" Sydney repeated the question she'd asked her friend three or four times yesterday.

Of course, Sydney had her own list of worries she didn't plan to share, and at the top was how her son was going to handle his father and Alice dating.

Mya brought the rim of her champagne flute to her lips and sipped. "No. We should drink more. Get baked. Not from pot." She smiled. "From the sun. You know, just chill. You were the opposite of relaxed yesterday, so let's not repeat that."

"Ditto," Sydney said under her breath. She hadn't told Mya about Seth and Alice yet because she didn't want to spoil Mya's mood. Alice had been like a sister to her as well.

Although Sydney never asked her to, Mya had ended her friendship with Alice after learning of the affair. That loyalty still meant the world to her.

Sydney finished her drink and discarded the empty glass on the little wicker table sandwiched between their sunbeds. It was only May, but the sun was already beating down on them, and her skin hadn't seen much in the way of Vitamin D in the last few months. They'd need to open the umbrella for some shade because, sunscreen or not, she'd get more than baked. She'd be fried. "Okay, well then, how's Mason?" She bent her knees and drummed her fingers on her thighs.

"That's work talk," Mya shot back.

"Mason is also your go-to for sex, so I think the subject is fair game."

Mya placed her glass on the table and switched to her side, propping her head up and staring at Sydney for a few beats. "Fine." There was an eye roll behind those sunglasses, Sydney was sure of it.

She'd known Mya and Alice for as long as she could remember. Basically forever. Their fathers had all gone to Yale at the same time. Mya's dad was now a prominent judge in New York City. Alice's father was a senator. And Sydney's father? He ran one of the most successful defense companies in the world. Built it from the ground up with a small loan and nothing more. Her dad had been happily telling his own Bezos-Amazon-in-a-garage nothing-to-something story long before Amazon even existed.

Maybe she was being unreasonable wishing the affair had been enough for her father to cut ties with Alice's family. It hurt knowing her dad still vacationed with the Morrisons, and Alice was often on board the yacht or at whatever island they were visiting.

The fact that the Archer–Morrison outings doubled in

frequency since Sydney left the family company to work for Carter and Gray at Falcon Falls had her wondering if her old man was playing dirty. Payback for disconnecting herself from the Archer empire.

*"You're heir to the throne. If you don't take over, then it's up to Levi,"* her dad had said on her way out the door last year, and she knew that was a threat.

She loved the man, but he loved his company more. And no way would she budge on her decision and go back to the family business regardless of how many games her father played. She'd never let him get to her son and force him into a life he didn't want the way he'd once done to her after she'd left the Army.

Sydney reset her focus on the topic at hand. "Well, are you going to follow up after your 'fine' comment?" She faked a pout. "Come on, give me something juicy since my love life is beyond repair, and neither of us want to talk about the only thing I do well. Work."

Mya grunted. "You do a lot of things well. You just don't let anyone know there are more sides to you than the all-business-don't-mess-with-me version people see."

Sydney waved a hand in the air. "Oh, Miss Investigative Reporter, you're so good at changing the subject. But no, back to you. To the handsome Mason Matthews."

Sydney knew Mason, and his older brother, Connor, as well. Not in the way Mya knew Mason, of course. Absurdly rich people often knew other absurdly rich people, and that was the case with the Matthewses and the Archers. Before Mason and Connor's father died, he'd worked in a similar industry to her family.

"I'm not a journalist anymore," Mya reminded her.

Okay, that was technically true, but her research and investigative skills, combined with her incredible ability to track people around the world, were the skills Sydney was interested in for Falcon. And it would be nice to have another woman out in the field since she was surrounded by a sea of testosterone on a regular basis. Story of her life though since West Point, she supposed.

"Yeah, you gave up journalism to work with Mason to hunt human traffickers." Mason and Connor had been Marines before entering the private security sector, now doing similar work to Falcon Falls. Not that they were competitors since they were both trying to do good in the world, but she had no problem stealing Mya away from the Marines to the Army side.

"Believe me when I say nothing serious has ever happened or will ever happen with Mason," Mya was quick to say. "We used each other for sex when we were horny. That's it."

*Horny.* Yeah, Sydney had realized she was horny and then some last night when alone in her hotel suite.

"I need to stop sleeping with Mason. Nothing is going to come from it. I'm ready for the new me. No more sex with that man." She dug into her beach bag and showed Sydney her current read. "I'm trying to learn to break my bad habits at least."

Sydney had brought her own book, but it was far from a self-help one.

Mya flicked a finger at the cover. "You should read this when I'm done. This author, Joe Dispenza, has some pretty riveting ideas about manifesting and the universe. I love it." She tucked the book back into her bag before relaxing on the lounger again.

"I'm sure he does." Sydney smiled. "So, uh, this new you . . . is that why you dyed your hair? Went from blonde to brunette?" The color did look great on her best friend.

Technically, Mya had never been a natural strawberry blonde anyway.

"It was that or cut it all off. I opted for a color change." She casually shook her head. "All I know with one hundred percent certainty is that sleeping with Mason also screws my chance of ever finding someone to love."

"And you don't love him?" Honestly, Mason was another reason she believed her friend should work at Falcon Falls.

If Mya truly wanted to change the dynamics of her relationship with Mason, she needed to put a little space between them. Stop working together for a bit. It'd be a win-win for both Sydney and Mya if she joined the team.

"We love each other like friends who also have sex," Mya said with a laugh. "But not the passionate and intense kind of love that makes your stomach hurt when you're not together. I don't actually know if I've ever experienced that before."

"Love that hurts?" Sydney grimaced. "Shouldn't it do the opposite?"

"I don't know." She dramatically tossed her arm into the air. "We haven't had sex in months. A few close calls, but I resisted. Gave myself an orgasm instead." Mya leaned over the side of her sunbed and combed her fingers through the sand before reaching out to snatch something from Sydney's bag this time. "You brought a book too, huh?" She grinned. "And whaaat? *You* reading a romance novel? I don't believe it." She sat upright once again and positioned her legs on each side of the sunbed while studying the book.

Sydney didn't bother to budge from her fixed position since she decided she really did feel lazy. Crazier things had happened. Like starting that book last night, which had sent her libido into overdrive. She hadn't needed much of a push since it'd been so long since she'd been touched. Not even by her own hand.

"Okay, for as long as I've known you, the only things you've read are biographies and Sun Tzu's *The Art of War*–type stuff. Not something with a badge-wearing cowboy on the cover." Mya pushed her shades into her hair and brought the book closer as if needing a better look.

"The book wasn't my idea." It was the truth, but now Sydney was kicking herself for not reading a book like that sooner. Damn, that author could write a sex scene. Maybe it'd turn her "not good enough in the bedroom" situation into "more than enough."

*Why am I thinking about Seth? He sure as hell wasn't who I was thinking about last night. Screw that man.*

"So, it fell into your bag, huh? You brought it to the beach, so you're not trying to hide it from me if you were planning to read it here." Mya casually flipped through a few pages.

"I don't get embarrassed. I couldn't care less about who sees me reading a romance novel. The guy on the cover could be naked for all I care." She paused, knowing that wasn't the answer Mya wanted, then changed the subject. "You know Griffin Andrews from Falcon?"

"The hot one?" Mya smiled. "Wait, they're all hot. The one with the Southern accent?"

"I think they're all Southern. Well, originally, at least. The one who married Savanna."

"Oh. Savanna's the one who, um, lost her Navy SEAL husband years ago? Yeah, I remember him now." Mya's tone was soft, a gesture of respect for Savanna's loss.

"Well, back in January, my team was working an op in France, and Savanna came along." Sydney shook her head when Mya opened her mouth to no doubt ask why. "It's too complicated, so don't ask. The point is during that trip, I learned that Savanna loves to read romance novels. So, the last time Griffin and I worked an op, he gave me a stack of books. Said his wife wanted me to have them. I think she got the idea that I'm lonely and sad. Maybe she thought I needed some fictional heroes to keep me company. I don't know."

"Huh." Mya continued to thumb the pages of the novel. "Wherever would she get that idea? I mean, surely, she also witnessed your badassery?"

As a matter of fact, yes. Both Savanna and Jesse's wife, Ella, had witnessed Sydney kill a few bad guys in France. Not that Sydney was happy about it, and she wasn't sure if she'd define her actions that night as anything other than just doing her job and protecting Savanna and Ella. Badass? Hardly.

*Anyways.* She didn't want to think about that operation. It'd been a tough one, but with a happy ending since it had brought Ella and Jesse together finally. And now they were going to have a child.

"Griffin must have blushed when he gave you the books." Mya chuckled. "And did your former college beau have anything to say about it?" She lifted the book as a reminder of what she was talking about.

"Gray knows better than to comment." Sydney had dated Gray Chandler, who co-ran Falcon Falls, when they were both at West Point. But that was a long time ago. She was thirty-seven now, and she hadn't even been legally allowed to drink when they'd been together.

"Do you think Gray hopes there's still a spark there? You two were quite the scandal back at West Point from what I remember," she teased.

"The only scandalous thing about our relationship was that he was a Firstie, and I was a Plebe. Against the rules." Seniors, known as Firsties at West Point, weren't allowed to date Plebes, aka freshmen. *Not that I was great at following rules back then.* "He thought I was Sydney Bowman. He didn't even know that I'm an Archer until our paths crossed again last year. Not the best way to start a relationship, right? You know, with a lie. So no, there's no spark between us anymore." Gray had been a great guy in college, and he still was, which was why she wanted to work with him at Falcon. But he hadn't been *the one*. *There is no "the one" for me though. Screw it.* "I'd rather talk about fictional men. Or *work*. Not my love life."

"Fictional men it is," Mya responded. "I spend most of my time reading reports on human trafficking, so I think I should switch things up. You bring any other books with you? I don't want to take the cowboy sheriff away from you."

"I have another," Sydney confessed with a sly smile. And maybe she didn't want Mya taking away the cowboy now that she had a soft spot for that fictional man.

"I happened to watch two seasons of *Bridgerton* last week. I think the show is based on a book series, and let me tell you, those men make me want to go back in time and be properly courted." Mya winced a beat later. "Well, aside from losing women's rights and all. And having my father offer a dowry to a dude to take me off his hands is grotesque *and* something he'd probably support even now."

"Your dad worries about you, but he loves you."

"My dad is a lying, cheating ass."

"Wait, what?" Sydney blinked in surprise. This was news to her. How long had Mya been keeping that bit of information to herself? But why'd she get the feeling that wasn't the reason Mya had been on guard for the last twenty-four hours when they were there to relax? *Unless the idea of working with me makes her nervous?*

"I don't want to talk about it, but my parents are separated. It seems my dad has been sleeping his way through New York." Mya lightly patted the top of the book. "I'm going to need another mimosa." She frowned. "How about you tell me about the hot cowboy in this book." She lifted one hand like a request to let go of the topic of her dad. Discussing cheating wasn't exactly Sydney's favorite thing anyway, and Mya knew that.

"Well, okay. Yeah, I'd say the cowboy delivered."

"Who'd you picture for your man candy while reading since his face is hidden on the cover?" Mya grinned, her mood lightening up again. "And damn, woman, I really do need to take up reading if it's got you blushing right now. A rare sight to see."

"It's the sun," she lied. "But if I were to blush, you'd probably be the only one to ever witness it happen."

"Okay, so spill. Who'd you fantasize about when reading about the good sheriff?" She shifted her sunglasses back in place. "Or was he bad? Wink wink."

"I think you're actually supposed to wink, not say that." At least they were both smiling again.

"Right, right. So . . .? I need answers because based on your absence of speech, the guy you have in mind is someone you know." Mya sat taller with excitement.

"The only men who hit on me lately want something called a situationship. Hell if I know what that means. Not together but together?" She shrugged. "*Or* they call me a MILF. Right to my damn face." What happened to a real man? A gentleman? Someone who treated a woman right. Took her out on dates and asked her questions with the purpose of getting to know her, not just getting her in the bedroom. "And these guys are babies. Barely thirty. I swear I don't understand the new trend of these young guys wanting an older woman. While men my age want younger women." *Alice is my age. She's thirty-seven. Seth chose her. Damnit, don't think about them right now.*

"You're stalling. Borderline blabbering, which is so not your norm. Which means you don't want to fess up about the real man who played the cowboy sheriff in your head last night." Mya opened the book and began skimming pages again. "I'll find a hot scene and read it aloud until you tell me his name. You know I'll do it."

"Is that supposed to scare me?" Sydney laughed, reaching for her glass, having forgotten it was empty.

"Oh, this part is spicy." Mya traced one of the lines with her finger, her lips tipping up into a smirk. "*'That's quite the penal code you have there, Sheriff,' she said as he unsheathed his weapon.*"

Sydney held her stomach while laughing, her ab muscles a little sore from the intense core-dominant yoga session that morning. "It does not say that," she finally managed. "And you didn't even use 'penal code' correctly."

"I made you laugh, though, so let's call it a wash. But this part here about the handcuffs is more than intriguing. Maybe I do need this book when you're done."

"No, the sheriff's mine." She hadn't meant to react so quickly, but well, the words had come out. Sun and mimosas to blame. For sure.

Sydney squeezed her thighs together at the memory of the scene from the book she'd mentally role-played after reading last night. And the leading man *had* been someone she knew. A Southern, cowboy-hat-wearing sheriff with espresso-brown hair and the most incredible brown eyes she'd ever seen. They were a near match to how the author had described the sheriff's eyes in the book. What had she called them? An antique cherry brown? Or maybe it was mahogany. Hell, some type of light wood.

*But . . . damn. Beckett Hawkins, and the hands on that man too.*

She'd done her best not to stare at him when he'd reached for an appetizer from a serving tray by her at Savanna and Griffin's wedding last month, but the immediate image of his hand wandering over the slope of her ass cheek popped into her mind anyway.

And so last night, it only made sense for it to be Beckett she thought about. Wishing it was his fingers, not hers, coaxing her into orgasm.

"He's a sheriff in real life, which is probably why I thought of him," Sydney confessed when she'd only meant to think that thought.

"Oh?" Mya lowered the book to her lap and pivoted her way. "The sheriff with a daughter you mentioned meeting back in Alabama? That hot hunk of a man?"

"How do you know he's hot?" Sydney challenged, knowing she'd never describe a guy that way.

"You blushed when mentioning him. Remember, you don't do that often and only around me, so . . ."

Ah, damn Mya for that. But she was probably right.

Beckett had made an impression on her. He was a single parent like her. And maybe everyone called him grumpy or moody or whatnot, but she understood his protectiveness. They were alike in that regard as well.

"So, you pictured him while you got yourself off, huh?" Mya was loving every minute of this.

"I know what you're thinking, and nothing will ever happen between us. I only thought of him because he's the only small-town sheriff I know who also wears a cowboy hat. It made sense."

Sydney sat up, an idea coming to mind. One that Seth had teased her about over the years, insisting she'd never do something as thrilling and shameless as tossing her top on a beach that *wasn't* a nude one.

She was a totally different woman now than when she was married to him though. A "warrior," right? Bold. Fierce. *Enough.*

So, Sydney went for the knot of her bikini top at her back and untied the strings.

"Topless, huh? Might draw attention to us." Mya stowed the book back in Sydney's bag as Sydney allowed the little black triangles to fall to her lap.

"Eh, let them look. Who cares, right?"

Mya pursed her lips for a moment as if she was on the verge of sharing whatever she was keeping from Sydney. "Sure. I mean, if we're going to truly relax, I guess we go big or go home?"

# CHAPTER FIVE

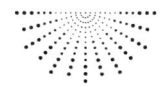

"Dad, can I ask you something?"

Beckett held the phone to his ear as he opened the terrace door of his hotel suite and was greeted by harsh heat, a shocking contrast to the air-conditioned room. "Yeah, baby girl?"

"Daaaad, I'm not a baby anymore. Officially a teenager." Like he needed the reminder.

"You'll always be my little girl. The apple of my eye." He let go of a somber breath, his thoughts gliding back to the past as he moved out farther on the terrace.

*"I'm going to be a father,"* he remembered announcing to his dad over the phone almost fourteen years ago. *"I'm dealing with gangs and the cartel. Lowlife assholes."* His voice had been shaky. And not from the bourbons he'd tossed back. He'd been truly terrified about bringing a kid into the world, especially given his job and the shit he'd witnessed. *"I—I don't know how to raise a child."*

*"You're not alone. You two will figure it out. I mean, you could always come back home. The sheriff is looking to retire, but he won't do it without someone worthy to replace him."*

His father had been mentioning that fact for years, and never in his wildest dreams had Beckett believed he'd accept the position and move back home.

But he never believed he'd be raising his daughter alone either.

Beckett blinked, pulling himself from that small nine-hundred-square-foot apartment in LA and back to his current reality. A sunny but shitty one at that.

And it really was sunny. Obnoxiously so, given the reason he was there.

"Sorry, sweetie, you wanted to ask me something? What is it?" Beckett made his way to the railing, gripping the too-hot metal and squinting from the sunlight as he waited for his daughter's reply. Too bad he hadn't brought sunglasses on his trip.

But one thing he did have now was a Glock 22 tucked into the waistband of his pants, hidden beneath his shirt. Carter's pilot friend had arranged for a buddy of his to meet up with Beckett when he'd arrived in Tulum an hour ago to supply him with weapons. He sure as hell hoped he wouldn't find himself in any trigger-pulling situations.

Shortly before Beckett worked up the courage to call home and face the music for the bad news he needed to deliver, Oliver had texted that he was almost to the hotel.

"McKenna?" Beckett prompted, wondering why she was still quiet. As far as she knew, he was in Texas with her uncle, and she shouldn't have a worry in the world. No way could he tell her the truth, despite the fact the questions about her mother had been more frequent in the last few years. The truth was complicated. "Is there something bothering you?"

"Maybe," she finally answered, and that *maybe* just about broke his heart. Not a good sign from his straight-shooting daughter who never beat around the bush. Probably learned that from him.

"When you took me to visit Elaina in D.C. last week, she said something, and well, I tried to let it go like she asked me to, but I have a bad feeling in my stomach now."

"What'd she say? Why didn't you say something sooner?"

"Elaina begged me not to say anything. She hadn't even meant to tell me, but her words just tumbled free and then she slapped a hand over her mouth. She told me not to worry about it, but I know about her abilities. You know she's basically prophetic, right?" A shaky breath cut through the line. "You took me to D.C. because you wanted to talk to her dad, right? It wasn't so I could visit with one of my best friends. It was a work thing, huh?"

*Fuck.* This was not how he wanted to tell McKenna about what was going on with her mom. But maybe he should have known this day would come after his unusual encounter with Elaina last week.

Beckett's brother, A.J., worked with nine other former Navy SEALs, doing some type of clandestine work he wasn't privy to, and one of them had a daughter close to McKenna's age. The girls had grown close, so Beckett took McKenna to visit Elaina whenever possible. She was right though. Their last trip was more for his benefit than his daughter's because he'd needed a favor from Elaina's parents, Liam and Emily.

The day he and McKenna planned to fly home after staying at Liam and Emily's house for the weekend, Elaina bumped into Beckett in the narrow hallway and lifted her hands as if in surrender, staring at him with big, confused brown eyes. Then she groaned as if in pain and abruptly took off for her bedroom.

"She had a vision?" Beckett asked for clarification. "And it had to do with me?"

Elaina's "visions" were still a question mark for Beckett. He wasn't sure if he believed in that kind of supernatural stuff. But from what he'd learned, Elaina's biological parents were super-geniuses. Her birth mother had a hunch about Elaina's unusual gifts and conducted experiments on her as a child to confirm her theory.

Liam and Emily had adopted Elaina a few years ago, and they were trying to give her a healthy and stable life, but from time to time, Elaina seemed to just "know things."

"I think she had a vision about you. And maybe, um . . . about my mom."

A string of profanities cut through his thoughts at that last part. *How could Elaina know that?*

"She wasn't specific. She mumbled something, and that's when she cupped her mouth," she quickly explained. "But you don't believe in her abilities, do you?" McKenna let go of a heavy, frustrated breath.

Beckett released the railing and turned toward his hotel suite, trying to wrap his head around the fact a twelve-year-old had experienced a vision about him.

"Sweetie." He lifted his ball cap and readjusted it on his head, trying to figure out what to say to keep McKenna level-headed and panic-free. "If I were in danger, Elaina would've told me. She would have said something to me or her dad, right?" The best he could do right now was calm his daughter's fears. It certainly wasn't the time to tell her that her mother had left him a voicemail asking for help, that he was in Mexico, and her uncle was currently at a cartel compound. "And she asked you not to say anything."

McKenna remained quiet for a moment before

whispering, "I guess. But you'd tell me if something was going on, right?"

His heart couldn't take this. The lies. This wasn't just an "of course, Santa is real" white lie he'd told her as a kid—this was so much more than that. He hadn't divulged the full story about why her mom wasn't in the picture because he didn't need to destroy the image of the woman who gave birth to her.

"Hey, is that your dad?" he overheard Ella ask. She was babysitting McKenna at their family's ranch that weekend, and now, it'd be for longer. His daughter was smart enough to realize when he told her he wasn't coming back from his hunting trip on time that he was full of shit. And that Elaina and her eerie visions were possibly right.

"Can you put your aunt on the phone, baby girl?" he asked in a gentle tone and pulled the terrace door closed, needing the air-conditioned room to cool down his overheated body.

"Yes, if you promise me one thing. If you promise me you'll come home alive from wherever you're really at."

Beckett closed his eyes and hung his head. Part of him was proud his daughter wouldn't let anyone pull the wool over her eyes. The other part just wanted her to be a kid. But also a kid with a mother who hadn't fucking abandoned her.

"I promise," was all he managed, doing his best not to allow his tone to waver.

"Beckett?" Ella called out, and it was her turn now. He'd more than likely get one hell of a verbal lashing when he came clean to his sister, and it'd be well-deserved.

"I need you to get out of earshot of McKenna before we talk," he warned, listening to the heels of her cowgirl boots click across the floorboards. When the background noise on her end went quiet, he admitted, "We're in Mexico. But Jesse and I are currently split up. And he can't contact you at the moment."

"Mexico?" Her tone was steady. Calmer than he'd anticipated. This wasn't her first time dealing with her husband in danger, but it was the first time since the addition of that gummy bear–sized baby in her belly.

"I'm sorry I made Jesse lie to you. I needed someone to have my back, but I didn't expect things to go down last night the way they did." He tried to get the truth out as quickly as possible. Rip the Band-Aid off fast.

"McKenna's mother," Ella whispered. "That's the only thing I can think of that'd have you needing Jesse's help." He heard the pain in her tone and knew there were tears in her eyes. "And he's in danger now, isn't he?"

"I'm here because of her, yes." He finally parted his lids and saw little white dots in his vision for a moment. "Jesse's at one of the Sinaloa cartel's compounds. He *willingly* went with them, and in a weird twist of fate, they're indebted to him. He's not in immediate danger. He's trying to help me."

"I don't understand," she said softly, her voice most likely not working at normal levels as she tried to wrangle her emotions and process the news. "Isn't that the same cartel El Chapo used to run? I—I saw a documentary about him."

He didn't want to add fuel to the fire, so he deflected the best he could. "Carter and a few of his guys are in Mexico and watching the compound. Plans are in motion. I know telling you not to worry is a waste of time, but I won't let anything happen to your husband. We'll come back home together."

"My husband can handle himself. He's not some fictional character from a movie. He's the real deal. A badass that bad guys are afraid of . . . and I know my man, he won't die on me. He won't leave me and the baby." Despite her strong words, her voice trembled. "But you, Beck, you promised you'd never go after that woman again. No matter what she told you. And I won't have her be the death of you. I just won't have it. She doesn't deserve you or McKenna."

"I know," he said, gripping the back of his neck with his free hand. "And you're right. Jesse will be fine." He needed his sister to hang on to that thought, to not stress and worry. To stay tough. "And I will be too. But can I be the one to tell A.J. about this?"

He didn't want his situation distracting A.J. while on a mission. "I'll tell him when he's back home." *Whenever that might be.* "I have to go," he added when he heard a knock on the door, assuming it was Oliver. "I love you, sis. And tell McKenna I love her too." He ended the call before she had a chance to say more because his stomach and his heart wouldn't be able to tolerate a response.

On his way to the door, he dialed up Elaina's mother, Emily, assuming her husband was also working the op with A.J., and he didn't want to disturb him.

Beckett opened the door and stepped aside so Oliver could enter as the call went to voicemail. "Hey, Emily, it's Beckett. We need to talk. Call me when you get a chance."

"Everything okay?" Oliver asked while heading straight to the bed, his eyes focused on the heavy-duty black case there.

Beckett pocketed his phone as Oliver opened it up and retrieved a 9mm and a mag. He chambered a round and inserted the standard magazine of 15 rounds into the weapon, so it was fully loaded. "I just spoke to my sister. She seems to be more worried about me than her husband despite the fact he's the one in a cartel compound."

Oliver pivoted to face him, tucking the weapon at his back in the waistband of his jeans. He was dressed nearly identical to Beckett, minus the cowboy boots. He had on military-style black lace-up boots instead.

"That's because Jesse is Jesse. And you, well, I guess you'll need to prove your skills to all of us before we decide if you can hang with the big boys." Oliver flashed him a quick smile, clearly not worried about his teammate, which should have put Beckett more at ease. "But first, you'll need to survive a confrontation with Sydney." He flicked the brim of his plain black ball cap as if to say, *Good luck.*

*Sydney. Great.* Another tough woman he needed to deal with. "Any updates from Carter and Gray?" he asked once they left the hotel suite and were alone in the stairwell. His room was only two flights away from Sydney's.

"They're positioned outside the compound, but they can't get into any overwatch positions. It's in the middle of the desert. And putting up one of our small drones during daylight hours to try and spot Jesse on the inside would be stupid. So for now, the boys are on standby."

Beckett had to trust Jesse and his instincts. He chose to get in that Cadillac last night. He knew what he was doing.

"They're probably by the pool or at the beach," Oliver suggested after they'd located Sydney's room and their knocking went unanswered.

Beckett nodded, and they headed outside in search of the two women. "So, how well do you know this woman Sydney is with?" he asked once they'd determined they weren't at the pool.

Oliver tossed him a quick look from across his shoulder, a smirk meeting his eyes. "You looking for the Cliffs Notes or the unabridged version?"

"You pick." Beckett shielded his eyes from the sun as he scanned the nearby beach and found himself slowing his pace, not all that eager to tell Sydney what he'd gotten her teammate tangled up in.

"Short version," Oliver decided. "After the Army, but before joining Falcon, I was a bodyguard for a real estate mogul in Dubai. My boss was, well, thrown from a building, and I was set up as his attacker. Accused of killing him."

Beckett stopped in his tracks. The short version of the story was a fucking doozy already. He couldn't imagine the long explanation.

Oliver faced him and shrugged. "Mya and I have mutual friends, and she assisted in a roundabout way to ensure my name was cleared so I wasn't"—he ran his thumb across his throat—"executed."

"Well, that's, uh, quite a story."

Beckett blinked in shock when Oliver added, "Your brother and his SEAL buddies helped save my neck too."

He supposed he wasn't all that surprised. A.J. tended to save the world a lot, from what he'd learned. Even post-military. But A.J. had made it clear he'd never help Beckett go after McKenna's mom again, not even if she called from her deathbed. A.J. hated the woman, but how in the hell was Beckett supposed to let McKenna's mother die?

"Small world, I guess," Oliver added as they began walking the boardwalk to approach the loungers set up near the water. "Mya happens to be friends with Sydney as well, and Sydney's interested in Mya's talents. She was a journalist in New York before joining a security team of former Marines who hunt down human traffickers. She's great at finding people. Top-notch research skills."

"And Sydney wants to poach her from the Marines?" Beckett was surprised by the unexpected smile on his lips that he quickly erased with the back of his hand.

"Or at least borrow her from time to time. I think she

wants another woman on the team. Maybe serve as a buffer between her and Gray." Oliver chuckled, but Beckett wasn't clued in on the joke. "Gray and Sydney dated back at West Point, and I swear, the way that man still looks at her when we operate . . ."

*Ah, enough said.* Not that he ever planned on making a move on Sydney, but he wouldn't let her occupy his thoughts again when he needed to relieve some tension. She may have been who he'd imagined a few times since Savanna and Griffin's wedding last month, but he wouldn't think about another man's woman.

"There they are." Oliver pointed, and Beckett clenched his jaw at the sight. "Not awkward at all, considering they're topless. We should take our shirts off so they don't feel uncomfortable," Oliver teased as they neared the two women.

Beckett advanced with slow steps and looked around, taking in the other sunbathers. "I don't think this is a nude beach." He hadn't meant to say that aloud, or for that to be the first thing Sydney heard.

Sydney turned her head to the side and put eyes on the two of them. Her glasses shielded her gaze, so he couldn't tell if she was surprised or pissed to see him and Oliver there. She casually sat upright, and it took every ounce of willpower for Beckett to keep his gaze above her breasts, but they were perfectly fucking perfect and right there.

"You going to arrest me, Sheriff?" A smile briefly flitted across her glossy lips. "I think we're outside your jurisdiction."

"*He's* the sheriff?" Beckett overheard Mya ask, but he still couldn't rip his eyes free from Sydney's face despite the fact Mya seemed to know of him, for whatever reason.

"Hey, we paid good money for these. Gotta show them off. It was a two-for-one special." He had no clue if Mya was joking, not that he cared. He believed a woman ought to do whatever she wanted with her body if it made her happier or more confident. He wasn't one to judge.

Not that he didn't want McKenna to love and accept herself, which he was certain she did, but . . . *why am I thinking about this right now?*

Sydney reached for her top and secured the two little black triangles over her breasts.

Part of him wanted to thank God she was covering up, but the larger, more throbbing part of him begged the devil to have the breeze blow the fabric into the Caribbean.

"Good to see you again, Mya," Oliver piped up, his tone low and almost growly. Had seeing Mya topless done a number on his brain?

"Oliver," Mya softly responded and stood alongside Sydney, both their tops now securely in place. "Happy to see all of your . . . body parts still intact."

Beckett was pretty sure the light laugh from Oliver was borderline flirty, but before Oliver could say more, Sydney spoke up, "I can guess why *you're* here." She pushed her sunglasses into her hair while settling her gaze on Oliver. "But not you." She reached for a black, see-through wrap thing and circled it around her hips, tying it into a skirt.

Beckett did his best not to clock every inch of her exposed skin. But he noticed what looked like a tiny scar above her belly button, which had him wondering if she'd had a navel piercing at one point. And he couldn't help but observe the way her cleavage popped out of her top as if her breasts preferred to be free again.

"Did something happen to Jesse?" Sydney asked Beckett, cutting straight to the point. "That's the only reason I can think of as to why you'd be here. And I'm also going to assume you're somehow to blame for what's happened."

*Smart woman.*

"Jesse's currently inside one of the Sinaloa cartel's compounds in Juárez, but we're hoping he'll use his newfound popularity to lead them here to Tulum, or somewhere close by," Oliver announced, maintaining his casual and worry-free tone when Beckett had yet to explain.

"And you're right, it's my fault," Beckett confessed, his gaze fixed on Sydney's gorgeous light green eyes. Her blonde hair settled in waves over sun-kissed shoulders, and she brushed her hair to her back as she studied him.

"The Sinaloas?" Mya whispered after a slight gasp, her reaction making it clear she'd heard of the cartel. Considering she was once a journalist, that made sense.

But then Mya abruptly looked toward the sea, her chest rising and falling with deep breaths, and Beckett couldn't help but wonder if her knowledge of the cartel was more than just an occupational hazard.

"This is about a woman, am I right?" Sydney's question caught him off guard. How in the hell did she know that?

Beckett took what he hoped wasn't a noticeable gulp. "Why do you say that?"

"Women are often the reason men do stupid things," Sydney responded.

*Ain't that the truth.*

"And your brother-in-law wouldn't be where he is right now if someone hadn't screwed with your head. So, who's the woman? And how in the hell did she manage to get my teammate into such a precarious situation?"

Beckett exchanged a quick look with Oliver. "I was looking for my daughter's mother."

Sydney tilted her head at his confession, genuine surprise crossing her face this time. Or was that sympathy? Empathy? He couldn't think of the right word at the moment, not with her looking at him like that. Like she somehow understood his dilemma and his pain.

Maybe Jack was right, and Beckett did need backup when facing her, but it wasn't for the reasons he'd suggested. No, it was because this woman could break down his fucking walls and make him forget he was a gentleman, all without breaking a sweat. She *was* dangerous. And the last thing he needed was another dangerous woman in his life who'd have him throwing reason out the window.

"Did you find her?" Mya asked, breaking the silence. Sydney had yet to look away from Beckett, those green eyes of hers still peering straight into his soul.

"No, but I found the woman who taught McKenna's mother everything. The woman who showed her how to be a con artist and manipulate people." Beckett paused for a beat, taking a moment to cool his rising anger. "If anyone will know where my daughter's mother, Cora, is . . . it's Ivy, McKenna's aunt."

## CHAPTER SIX

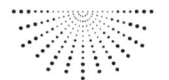

SYDNEY'S EYES LANDED ON THE LARGE, VIBRANTLY COLORED photo of a cenote that hung over the king-sized bed as she removed her bikini top and bottoms. She and Mya had visited the jungle area of Tulum yesterday, and Sydney had been captivated by the beauty and history of the cenotes, which she'd learned from their tour guide was pronounced "seh-no-tays."

The Yucatan Peninsula was home to thousands of these natural limestone sinkholes. As the only source of freshwater, they were sacred to the ancient Mayans. It was believed Chaac, their god of rain, resided at the bottom of the cenotes, and sacrifices were commonplace to please the deity.

Their guide had invited them to join one of the small snorkel tours, but Mya had chickened out. "*Swim around in an underground hole that is connected to hundreds of other underground holes? With my luck, I'd somehow get sucked under and be the next sacrifice.*"

Mya could chase down human traffickers but getting into a body of water that wasn't crystal clear was somehow out of the question.

Sydney pulled her attention down to the cerulean-blue comforter, a match to the sea, and her thoughts drifted to last night. To that romance novel and the fictitious images of Beckett's warm body heating hers.

*And now he's here.* Mya would call that serendipitous or something as colorful.

"Sydney?" a voice she recognized asked from outside her door. She'd planned to meet everyone at the beachfront bar after she and Mya went to their rooms to change, so she wasn't sure why Beckett had decided to drop by.

"Yeah, one second," she responded, quickly searching for anything to put on. There was no way in hell she was answering the door naked, even though a tiny part of her wanted to do just that and see how Beckett responded.

After securing a white silk robe from the closet, she knotted the tie at her waist and swung open the bright blue door.

Beckett was a far cry from the vest-wearing suits she'd dated here and there in the last several years, but he made an impression in all the right ways. He gave off a badass *Walker, Texas Ranger* vibe, a reminder of the Chuck Norris show she'd watched as a kid with her grandfather. Not that Beckett looked like good ol' Chuck, but damn. She'd noticed Beckett's swagger the first time on New Year's Eve at Jesse and Ella's wedding.

At six feet, probably two inches, and she'd guess even taller with his cowboy boots on right now, Beckett smoothed a hand over his five o'clock shadow, wordlessly studying her. Taking in the sight of her from her bare feet on up to her beach-wavy blonde hair.

She was guilty of the same, cataloging every inch of the man before her.

A white tee hugged his broad shoulders and muscular

biceps, and she knew if he turned around, his ass would look oh-so fine in those well-worn jeans. Were they Wranglers? Weren't those a cowboy-type brand?

Beckett fidgeted with his black ball cap. She had a feeling he was far more comfortable wearing a cowboy hat, but he'd draw a lot more attention to himself donning one of those at the resort. And she doubted attention was what he was going for, given the circumstances.

"Hi," he finally managed, breaking the silence first. Sydney had to blink away the salacious thoughts that'd popped into her head courtesy of the fictitious world she'd happily lived in beneath the bedsheets last night.

"I was hoping we could start over." He cleared his throat and, likely inadvertently, let his gaze flick down to her chest before meeting her eyes once again.

"Oh?" She leaned into the doorframe, keeping the door propped open with her shoulder. "I thought we got off to an excellent start."

"Yeah, see," he began, closing his eyes for a brief moment, "I can't tell if that's sarcasm or not, but I reckon it is." That Southern drawl of his had her stomach doing a weird little flip. "But I do apologize for seeing—"

"My breasts?" she tossed out. "I wouldn't have been topless on a beach if I weren't comfortable with my body. And now I'm naked beneath this robe, so we've come full circle."

Beckett reached for the brim of his black ball cap and tipped it as if that were a gentleman's way of saying *I'm sorry*.

"Let's just not make it a habit of you seeing me partially clothed, and we should be all set." She stepped back into the room, and he caught the door with his palm before it shut.

"Oh," she began, arching a brow, "was there more you wanted to say?"

He looked over her shoulder, his eyes landing on her bed as if being alone with a woman unsupervised was somehow against the rules. Were they on that *Bridgerton* show Mya had been talking about? Not that Sydney had watched it, but she could imagine what life was like for a woman in the 1800s and thanked the universe she hadn't been born then.

"You don't smell like cherries."

Sydney's gaze fell to the hardwoods beneath her bare feet, hating that her thoughts had landed on Alice and how she'd hijacked Sydney's favorite cherry-scented perfume. Memories of that woman and everything she'd taken from her, including their friendship, pummeled their way through her mind all over again.

The news from Levi on Friday was far too fresh. But she'd never let that interfere with her job and safely extracting Jesse from the cartel. She'd learned to bury her thoughts and feelings when need be, which was ninety percent of the time. Give or take.

When she looked up, she wasn't expecting to see his full lips curving into the slightest of smiles, one that had crinkles forming around his brown eyes. "You have a good memory and an excellent sense of smell." She left the entryway to snatch her new bottle of perfume from the vanity and came back to find his palm still propping the door open, but he'd yet to cross farther into her suite.

She shook the little bottle of Tom Ford, Black Orchid, between them. "I used to wear a cherry-scented one. I decided I needed a change." She had no clue why, but instead of handing him the bottle, she offered her wrist as if he might want to sniff her.

*What did they put in those mimosas?* Maybe it was the

combination of the drinks and the sun? Because *this* was not like her.

Beckett lifted her wrist to his nose and closed his eyes, breathing her in. When their gaze met once again, the look in his eyes was raw, almost primitive. Like a man doing his best not to succumb to . . . desire?

With his eyes locked with hers, and his hand still wrapped around her delicate wrist, she'd swear his thoughts were becoming as derailed as hers. It was as if he were mentally untying her robe to part her thighs to check if she was wet for him.

*It's that book. And maybe the mimosas,* she rationalized, remembering a scene from chapter thirteen. The sheriff had asked the woman if he made her wet, and she'd been stubborn and defiant and told him no. And to call her bluff, he asked her to touch herself. Prove it. She'd boldly lifted her skirt and caressed her sex, but when she removed her hand, her fingers were coated in her arousal. Within a minute, he had her on her back and was inside her. Pounding her hard.

"It's nice." Beckett freed her wrist and stood upright, his gaze cutting away from her as if feeling guilty for having dark, erotic thoughts given his brother-in-law's situation.

*Or maybe it's just me with those ill-timed thoughts.*

"You're not what I expected," he said as she turned and tossed the perfume bottle onto the bed.

"And what'd you expect?" *Cold-hearted with bone-chilling icy walls? Dangerous and deadly with a bow?* She rattled off a few more possibilities in her head as she waited for him to respond.

"Well, Jack warned me you'd be pissed I ruined your weekend. I guess he was giving me a hard time."

"I've had a few mimosas. It's entirely possible the *me* you expected will show up once I have some food in my stomach to counteract the alcohol." She was only partially kidding. She really had no clue why she'd allowed her guard to slip even for the few hot seconds they shared as he breathed in her perfume, even if it was one-sided.

"I should let you get to it now." His focus landed on the bed again. "You know, get dressed."

"Sure." She nodded and started for the en suite, assuming he'd leave without another word. But when she looked back, he was still standing there, eyes on the floor as if there was something else he wanted to say or ask.

"Jesse *will* be okay," she noted in case that concern dominated his thoughts, which was more than likely the case. "I wouldn't be standing here so calm if I didn't believe he could handle himself." And that was the truth—no sugarcoating needed, not that she knew how.

"If your son's father was in danger, and he wasn't the greatest person on the planet . . . would you do the same? Would you try to help him?"

Ah, the pieces of the puzzle were coming together.

Beckett said McKenna's mother was a con artist, so he was likely questioning the sincerity of Cora's request for help. Was he being conned again? How many times had this happened before? And why'd she leave him and McKenna in the first place?

"I would do anything for my son even if I hated my ex. He'd want his dad alive, which means I would help him."

Beckett nodded and faced the door, and it was only then she spied the shadow of a bulge at the back of his waistband.

"How'd you get a weapon over the border? They let you fly armed because of your badge?"

He twisted back around. "No, a friend of Carter's friend?" It came out more like a question as if he didn't quite understand Carter's network of influence. "I have a piece for you too. I can get it to you after we're done at the bar."

"Hopefully, we won't need weapons here, but it's nice to be packing just in case." She forced a small smile, then spotted Mya in the hall a second later.

"Oh, I didn't expect you to be here." Mya quickly brushed past Beckett to enter the room. "Can we meet you at the bar? I need a few seconds with my friend." She set her hands on Beckett's chest and gently nudged him toward the hall as if he might resist.

*Only Mya.*

"Of course." Beckett had barely left the room before Mya tossed two fisted hands in the air by her face and mimed explosions with them.

"That's your cowboy sheriff," she whispered. "You know I don't believe in coincidences. We were talking about him, and now he's here. This is Joe Dispenza's theory of manifestation in action. The universe placed the four of us together in Tulum for a reason. And the fact that his daughter's aunt and Jesse are with not just any cartel, but with the Sinaloas—"

"Mya, you're rambling." Maybe there really was something in those drinks?

"I'm just a little shocked, I guess."

"Sure it has nothing to do with the other guy here?" Sydney angled her head, remembering the way her friend had said Oliver's name at the beach. Flirty, for sure.

"If we work together, I promise Oliver won't become Mason two-point-oh."

"So, you like him?" Sydney smiled. "Hmm, now I'm not sure if Oliver will be your reason for *not* joining Falcon or your reason *for* joining."

Instead of answering, Mya's gaze flitted around the room,

landing on the photo of the cenote hanging over Sydney's bed, and there was a moment where Sydney wondered if Mya regretted not taking the leap—changing her habits, starting with her fear of swimming in water other than pools. But then she blinked a few too many times as if her nerves were settling in, claiming control of her thoughts.

*Habits die hard.* "What's going on? There's something you're not telling me, and it has nothing to do with whether you're attracted to Oliver." Sydney folded her arms and waited for her friend's full attention.

"Maybe." Mya nodded. "Okay, yes." She tipped her chin, her eyes cutting to the ceiling. "I may have chosen our trip to be in Tulum for a reason. Girls' weekend while you convince me to join your team," she went on, her gaze finally moving back to Sydney's, "and for a small mission, one I didn't tell you about because it's not until tomorrow after you've already left. And I don't need backup."

"Mya," Sydney hissed and reached for her friend's forearm. "And Mason and the others don't know the real reason you're here either, am I right? If Mason knows, that means he's somewhere on overwatch keeping tabs on you right now."

Mya frowned. "No, he doesn't know. He'd lose his mind."

Sydney released Mya and turned her back, angry at her friend for potentially placing herself in danger. "Can't swim in a river, but you can chase bad guys on your own. Perfect." The effects of the mimosas were quickly leaving her system now. "If Mason would go apeshit for you doing whatever it is you planned to do tomorrow, then it's not a simple mission, and you do need backup. You should have told me." She spun back around, doing her best not to explode at her best friend.

In truth, she'd do the same in Mya's shoes. Hadn't she

done the same in the past? But Mya wasn't a trained operative. She'd never served in the military or on the front lines like Sydney had. Mya was a valuable asset with her research skills, but she wasn't equipped to go out into the field. And the idea of losing her friend . . .

"I'm sorry. It's not a big deal. Mason's just a worrier. He didn't like the idea of me even coming to Tulum. Gave me every worst-case scenario for a single woman in Mexico."

"But he *let* you come, huh?"

She smiled. "Once he knew it was you I was traveling with, he wasn't so worried."

Sydney fidgeted with the knot at the front of the robe, tightening it a bit more as she figured out her next steps. She refused to let Mya stay in Mexico alone tomorrow for a "mission," but what if Jesse needed an extraction before then? "This is why you've been looking over your shoulder the whole time we've been here?"

"More like I was worried Mason didn't trust me and would show up in true wet-blanket fashion." Mya opened her palms as if that made perfect sense.

Sydney supposed her best friend would've given her the heads-up if she'd been on edge because she'd been concerned their lives were at risk.

"You know how I said everything happens for a reason . . .?" Mya's sentence dangled in the air a bit as if there was more she wanted to say but wasn't sure how to express it.

Sydney knew exactly what Mya was about to share. Whatever mess of a situation Beckett had found himself in, as "fate" or whatever Mya wanted to call it, was connected to why Mya was in Tulum.

"The reason I'm here, my source, well, he's from the—"

"The Sinaloa cartel," Sydney finished for her after an exasperated sigh.

## CHAPTER SEVEN

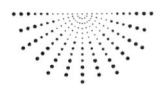

*This is paradise.* And yet, it felt anything but.

With his back to the beach, Beckett observed the guests crowded around the rectangular-shaped bar beneath a white canopy-style tent that offered some shade. A few lights that looked more like upside-down baskets hung from the center of the tent.

The three "mixologists," as he'd learned they were called instead of bartenders, were busy crafting colorful cocktails, making the guests smile and laugh with a few Tom Cruise, *Cocktail*, moves.

Only one of the tables that circled the expansive bar was occupied. Two people were sitting on the area's beachside, staring lovingly into each other's eyes while sharing a bright blue drink so big you could take a damn bath in it.

"Guess we gotta deal with the heat," Oliver commented while joining him. "A table should be private enough." He motioned to one at the far end of the bar with a view of the jungle that surrounded the hotel. ATV-style golf carts were transporting guests back and forth between the beach and jungle. Probably tour guides.

Beckett sat opposite Oliver to keep his attention on the bar. It always made him feel better to clock every person in a public space. Get a read on his environment. Force of habit? Probably, but it'd kept him alive once or twice back when he'd worked in Los Angeles, and he needed to be on guard to help Jesse and Ivy.

Four bachelor-types were shooting tequila, attention laser-focused on three unaccompanied brunettes at the bar. And by Beckett's count, there were eight couples there. No red flags, though it looked like one of the husbands was going to get a drink to the face if he didn't stop checking out the blonde across the bar from him. Or maybe he'd get decked by the girl's boyfriend, who appeared to work out for a living based on the size of his biceps.

A server approached their table with open arms and a welcoming smile. "*Bienvenidos al Pueblo Mágico.*"

Beckett lowered the brim of his ball cap to shield the bright noon sun from his eyes as it washed over them, then he scooted his chair to steal some shade from the palm tree.

"*Pueblo Mágico,*" the man repeated to Beckett and Oliver as if they hadn't heard him the first time, but Beckett was too preoccupied wondering what was holding up Sydney and Mya to pay much attention to anyone or anything.

"Magic Town," their server translated. He must've assumed by their lack of response that they didn't speak a lick of Spanish. That wasn't true. He was fluent, but his thoughts were too jarred, and his body was still on edge after his brief encounter with Sydney.

"You're here in paradise, and it's full of mysticism and wonder," the man went on. "Extraordinary things happen to people here."

*Extraordinary, huh?* Was that the word Beckett would use

to define whatever had happened to him in Sydney's room? No, more like possessed. *By desire.*

The man pointed toward the thick line of trees. "Lush Mayan jungle there." He tossed a thumb over his shoulder toward the water. "A gorgeous beach full of beautiful women." His grin was downright infectious, but there was only one specific gorgeous woman that came to Beckett's mind.

"We're not tourists, so you don't need to sell us on the city's greatness, but we appreciate your enthusiasm," Oliver responded in a respectful tone.

"Ah, but there's no need for me to sell anything. This place sells itself, yes?" The man pointed to a female server heading their way with a tray of cocktails alongside a basket of chips and a side of tempting guacamole. "I had these drinks whipped up as a welcome when I saw you two take a seat." He set down two small martini glasses, filled with frothy, pale-yellow cocktails that were garnished with pineapple wedges.

Beckett had no intention to drink today, but he didn't want to insult the man, so he took a hesitant sip, and Oliver did the same.

"When Prohibition began, many of the best mixologists fled to Mexico and created what we like to call a cocktail renaissance," the man continued with pride, and Beckett's stomach dropped at his words.

*Prohibition?* After his experience at Capone last night, the last thing he wanted to think about was anything 1920s. He'd prefer to stay in the *twenty*-twenties, damn it.

As if sensing Beckett's dissatisfaction, the man offered, "How about a Mayan mule then? Little vodka, sour orange juice, ginger syrup, and tonic water. In a nice ice-cold copper mug with a touch of mint."

"We have two more joining us. I think we're all mostly hungry," Oliver told him. "So, maybe you could bring us an assortment of your most popular dishes? Some tapas too?"

"Ah. *Por supuesto.*" *Of course.* The man reached for the menus and tucked them under his arm. "So, if you're not tourists, are you here for business?" He tipped his head toward Beckett's Ariat leather cowboy boots as if he didn't believe they were businessmen either.

"Something like that." Beckett peered around the bar again, counting two more men sitting at the bar alone. Mid-thirties. One appeared antsy, looking around as if wondering whether he'd been stood up.

"Well, life cannot be all business. Must have some pleasure too, right? Just don't go too deep into the jungle for an adventure without a guide. Ghosts haunt those grounds."

*Mayan ghosts?* Beckett expected the man to toss in a joking wink, but it never came. Before he could follow up with a question about the so-called ghosts, merely out of curiosity, his gaze jumped straight to Sydney and Mya heading down a boardwalk leading to the bar.

Sydney had on black shorts, black sandals, and a white tank top. Her blonde hair lay in soft waves over her shoulders, but a mild breeze blew a few strands in front of her face, and she quickly swept her hair to her back. No purse on her, unlike Mya.

Mya's clothes were flip-flopped from Sydney's. White shorts. Black tank. White sandals. He hadn't paid much attention to what Mya had been wearing earlier in Sydney's hotel room, too hung up on what Sydney *hadn't* been wearing beneath her robe. And hell, his dick stirred in his jeans at the memory.

"Ah, I see you have the pleasure part covered." The man

must have followed Beckett's line of sight to spot Sydney and Mya.

Beckett wasn't sure if the strange swell in his chest was relief they'd finally joined them or nerves. His daughter would blurt, *You're acting weird, Dad,* if she were there with him.

"I'll come back with that food soon. And four Mayan mules." The man tipped his head and left.

"You ready for them?" Oliver asked. Beckett could hear the smile in his tone, but he didn't peer his way to confirm it. He was too preoccupied with the scene before him.

One of the "bachelors" he'd pegged earlier had stood from the bar and blocked Mya and Sydney's path. Sydney was waving Mya off as if telling her, *I got this.* Mya gave Sydney a hesitant look and then started for where Oliver and Beckett were seated.

When the man turned to the side and snatched Sydney's wrist, Beckett quickly pushed against the table to stand, unintentionally sliding it into Oliver in the process. "Sorry," he mumbled, eyes back on his target. No way in hell would Beckett let any man like that near his . . .

He let go of that thought as Mya said, "Oh, she's got this. Let her do her thing." But Beckett was already on the move, spinning his ball cap backward en route.

Sydney freed herself from the man's grasp, planted a palm on the guy's chest, and shoved.

"You're drunk. That's the only reason I'm not breaking your arm," Beckett heard Sydney warn, but the idiot didn't get the message.

Worried the idea of a challenge would only turn this guy on even more, Beckett moved in next to Sydney and hissed, "Back off."

"Who are you? Her sugar daddy?"

*Okay, I'm not that old. And Sydney's the rich one.* Well, according to his sister, she was the daughter of a billionaire. "Go back to your buddies," Beckett offered the same chance Sydney had given him. He was far outside his jurisdiction, so maybe he could slug the guy without losing his badge?

The twenty-something man-child looked back and forth between him and Sydney before lifting his hands in the air in surrender. He headed back to the bar, and a loud cry of boos cut through the air from the other idiots in his entourage.

"What is it with these young guys wanting an older woman?" Sydney asked with a shake of the head. He had no clue what she was talking about, but he knew she wasn't that old. Younger than Beckett, yes, but . . . "I know you didn't need saving. I wasn't trying to undermine—"

"I *didn't* need saving," she cut him off. "*But* that doesn't mean I don't appreciate you having my back." Her light eyes captivated him for one long second before his gaze traveled to her lips, which transformed into the most beautiful smile he'd seen on someone other than his daughter. "Also, chivalry doesn't have to be dead."

She turned toward their table and walked that way, and Beckett cupped a hand to his mouth as he watched her delectable backside. Sydney wasn't that tall. Maybe five-six or so. But the woman was all legs. And damn, could he envision those shapely legs wrapped around his hips as he plunged inside her.

As Beckett tossed a look back toward the bar to ensure the tequila-shooters were behaving, the group of single brunettes waved at him, motioning him over. *Yeah, no, thank you.* He ignored them and joined Sydney and the others, opting to stand and catch some shade from the palm tree. He needed to cool off. He still wanted to go punch that guy.

"Not going to sit?" Did Sydney know how much power those green eyes held as she pointed them his way?

"I think I'll stand for a minute." Not only had he nearly gotten into a bar fight, something he wouldn't normally do, well, not since he was younger . . . the fact he'd pretty much SNIFFED Sydney in her room meant his head was practically up his ass.

His attraction to Sydney was like nothing he'd ever experienced. Not even with McKenna's mother, Cora. He'd never met a woman he'd had such an intense, almost primitive-like, reaction to before.

Earlier in her room, his thoughts had gone wild in the space of a heartbeat as he'd held her wrist, drawing his nose to the sensitive part of her skin.

Images of him peeling her robe from her body had planted roots in his mind. Palming and worshipping those creamy-white breasts he'd seen earlier on the beach. Flicking his tongue across her light pink nipples, their color a match to her luscious lips.

"You do plan on telling us everything, right?" Mya asked, her voice breaking through his thoughts.

Beckett's attention briefly snagged on Sydney's white tank top that fit like a glove as he moved his focus to Mya and answered, "Of course."

"Okay, good. Well, should we order something first," Mya suggested, reaching for a chip and dipping it into the guac. "I might think better with food in my stomach instead of just the alcohol already there."

"I ordered more food for the table. Asked them to bring their specials. Hope you don't mind," Oliver announced. "Those drinks weren't our idea."

"Oh, some woman at the bar sent them your way?" Mya teasingly asked, twisting in her seat to look toward the bar that was getting increasingly crowded, to the point Beckett had lost track of everyone there.

"Nah, just our uber-friendly waiter," Oliver shared with a smile. "So." Oliver flicked the brim of his ball cap. "Why don't you tell them what you know?"

Beckett nodded, his back going straight as he eyed Sydney. Her attention was on Mya, her lips tight as if she were concerned about something other than the situation at hand. Not that he knew her well enough to get a read on her.

When Sydney shifted her focus to Beckett, his arms tensed. Her gaze lingered on his mouth, which was distracting as hell.

How much should he tell them? These people were practically strangers. Did he want to get into the gritty details of his past right away? What was "need to know" information?

"Three weeks ago," Beckett began, deciding he'd start there, "Cora, McKenna's mother, left me a voicemail. Well, her message was cut off, but she was in trouble." He thought back to her message, to the fear in Cora's tone, unlike any other time before. "At first, I thought it was a trap. A way to, um, get money from me." He lowered his eyes to the table. "But she didn't call back. If it were another one of her schemes, she'd have made sure I could find her. Given me more clues, I mean."

"I take it this isn't the first time she's done this to you?" Sydney asked, her tone a touch sympathetic to the hell McKenna's mother had put him through in the past.

His entire relationship with that woman had been a lie from the start. Conned from day one. The only pure, innocent part that had come from his time with her was McKenna being brought into the world.

"Yeah, which is why I was hesitant to believe her. And

why I didn't do anything at first, because like the times before, I expected another call to come." Beckett held Sydney's eyes, doing his best to reveal the uncomfortable truths he never talked about. "I hadn't heard from Cora in nearly six years."

"So, when the call didn't come, you decided to find her sister? See if she could help?" Mya asked, and Beckett gave her his attention.

"I couldn't ignore her message." Beckett cleared his throat and coughed into his fist. "I was worried, so I reached out to a contact to see if they'd have better luck tracking down Cora," he explained, then set his eyes on Oliver.

"You didn't ask A.J.?" Oliver asked in surprise, because yeah, that'd make the most sense to go to his Navy SEAL brother, who had access to an abundance of contacts, including the FBI, the CIA, and every other alphabet soup agency.

"A.J. wants nothing to do with helping me find Cora. He made that clear after the last time Cora reached out," Beckett admitted, his eyes going to the sky this time. "I went behind his back, something I'm not proud of, and asked someone he works with for help. Liam Evans. Well, actually, I asked his wife, Emily, for help."

"Ah, right. Emily works for the Attorney General," Oliver said, making the connection. "She has access to criminal records and the like."

Beckett lowered his gaze once again and nodded. "Cora and Ivy both have records, and I was hoping Emily could reach out to her government agency contacts for me. Use their facial recognition software programs to scan for Cora's last whereabouts."

"No matches for Cora, I take it? Just a match for Ivy."

Sydney most likely now understood how Beckett had wound up in Mexico.

"Right. One of Emily's contacts got a hit on Ivy's face in Juárez, and after a bit more of a refined search in that area, they were able to place her at the club, Capone, on a few different occasions. The alias she used to originally enter Mexico, well, I doubt it's the one she's going by now." He paused to let the information sink in. "I figured Ivy worked at the club and was searching for a new mark, someone to con," Beckett shared. The guilt at sidestepping his brother and asking someone else to lie for him, like he'd asked of Jesse, nagged at him.

He knew asking Emily for help and keeping that from A.J. was beyond a big ask, that it was straight-up wrong. But Emily was understanding of the situation in a way A.J. wasn't. She'd do the same for her daughter if Elaina's biological father ever found himself in a jam. Emily and Liam would do anything for Elaina. Take any risks.

Beckett owed a lot of apologies when this was over.

"Do you think it's possible that if Cora's really in danger, she called her sister too?" Sydney asked. "That Ivy was working at the club as a way to find Cora? Maybe there's a connection."

Beckett closed his eyes, memories of the past attacking him. Assaulting his senses. Taking over.

Cora connected to the cartel? *No. Not a chance in hell.*

Beckett adamantly shook his head and freed himself of the past so he could open his eyes and focus. "Cora would never go near the cartel. Not any cartel, for that matter."

"Why?" Oliver folded his arms and leaned back.

Before Beckett could offer a response, his phone vibrated in his pocket.

It was Emily. He wasn't prepared to have the conversation

about what Elaina had shared with McKenna there in front of everyone, so he'd have to call her back.

He quickly pocketed his phone as their friendly server returned with a tray of bottled waters as well as the Mayan mules in the copper mugs.

"*Gracias*," Beckett thanked him, knowing they wouldn't drink them.

Sydney lazily circled her index finger around the rim of the mug as if her thoughts were whirling. Maybe brainstorming possibilities as to why Ivy had really been at that club.

"So, you were saying?" Oliver prompted, but Beckett wanted to get back to explaining how Jesse ended up separated from him last night.

"Jesse and I went to the club. You, uh, have to dress like you're in the Roaring Twenties to get in," he hurried out, "and some rival gang members tried to abduct Ivy before we had a chance to talk to her. Apparently, she's dating the club owner." *Another oddity.* Why would Ivy date anyone in the cartel, even for money, knowing her sister's past? It didn't make sense. Maybe he wasn't thinking clearly, given his deep involvement in the whole situation, not to mention his lack of sleep . . . so was Sydney right? If Ivy was at that club, was she trying to find a way to Cora through the cartel? Had Cora really found herself in trouble with the Sinaloas?

"Let me guess, Jesse saved Ivy, and the owner of the club was grateful for Jesse's help," Sydney deduced. "Jesse went willingly with these cartel guys because he believed it was the only way he could get to Ivy without trying to abduct her too. And you stayed behind to get word out to Carter?"

*Damn, she's good.* "That about sums it up."

"The club owner is Miguel Diego. Ever heard of him?"

Oliver tossed out, his focus landing on Mya as if she might have come across his name before in her line of work.

But Mya's attention was now fixed on her phone. Her brows drew together in a tight line, and she looked back over her shoulder toward the bar.

"He sounds vaguely familiar," Sydney responded when Mya didn't speak up. "I assume we're waiting for our next steps, right? Hoping Jesse can find a way to leave the compound with Ivy so we can get to them easier?"

Beckett nodded, then looked at Oliver. "Is Falcon planning to help me find Cora too?"

Oliver and Sydney exchanged a quick look, but it was Mya's flushed face as she turned back to the table that had Beckett worried.

"I should probably mention the fact I'm in Tulum because of the Sinaloa cartel as well," Mya dropped the unexpected news, and Beckett nearly lost his footing at her quick admission.

"I'm sorry, what?" Oliver rasped, clearly rattled.

"I have a source within the cartel." She looked back over her shoulder again, and fuck, was her source the twitchy guy in the ball cap at the bar? The one now staring at Mya?

"We've worked together before. I trust him." Mya winced as if that were hard to say. "I know that sounds weird because he's still with the cartel, but he's trying to take them down from the inside. He's against human trafficking, and lately, the cartel has been utilizing their drug trade routes for trafficking people." She kept her voice low even though they were out of earshot of the other guests.

"Are you kidding me right now?" Oliver asked, his tone laden with disbelief and shock. "Do you have backup here? Mason and the others, are they on the hotel grounds?" When

Mya remained quiet, he removed his sunglasses and glared at her.

"Your contact is at the bar by the asshole who bothered Sydney," Beckett commented. "And he knows what you look like, right?" He pointed to Mya's phone resting on top of her purse on the table. "And he just texted you?" He peered at Sydney to see her mouth opening a touch as if this was news to her. Or, at least, *some* part of this was new information.

"I didn't come to Tulum with backup. And I only told Sydney ten minutes ago that I planned to meet my source here tomorrow for some new intel." Mya didn't look back at the bar to confirm Beckett's theory, but Beckett swore Oliver's jaw was about to snap from worry. "Yes, that's him at the bar. He just arrived, and he didn't expect to see me here today. But now, he thinks we should just go ahead and get it over with."

"And what was the plan for tomorrow? Or well, what's the plan now?" Beckett asked, doing his best not to make it obvious when he checked Mya's source again.

"I was supposed to meet him here tomorrow at four, set my phone on the bar, and he'd stand next to me. Our phones would sync, mine would download the information, and then he'd leave. That's it. That's how it's always worked in the past."

"How many times have you . . ." Oliver let his question hang in the air, still shocked by the fact Mya pulled similar moves in the past and, from the sounds of it, alone.

She was brave. And Beckett assumed that was another reason Sydney was looking to recruit Mya to Falcon Falls.

"Text him that I'm meeting him at the bar instead." Oliver abruptly stood. "A sniper can pop off two headshots before I count to three in Spanish. What if he was followed?"

"Are you mad at me?" She scoffed and folded her arms,

staring up at Oliver. "I'm always careful. But women are being sold like cattle. Kidnapped from their families. He's offering me the trade routes the cartel uses to do this, *risking his life,* and you expected me not to come?"

"I expected someone from your team, *several* someones, in fact, to have your six," Oliver bit out, his voice taking on a bit of a growl. "Mason doesn't deserve you if he'd let you just . . ." Oliver closed his eyes.

"You're kidding me, right?" Mya stood, her nostrils flaring a bit.

There was more to the story between Oliver and Mya, but it wasn't Beckett's business, nor was it the time to figure it out.

"I'm not going to let you risk taking a bullet because of me." Mya reached across the table and poked Oliver's chest.

"Oh, so you think that's a possibility, yet you planned to show up here tomorrow by yourself." Oliver's hands balled at his sides.

Sydney joined everyone on their feet just as Beckett spied three new guests from his peripheral vision, and damn it, they were armed. "Get down. Gunmen. *¡Al suelo! ¡Tienen pistolas!*" he shouted as loud as possible to be heard over the pulsating music, then motioned for Oliver to move and flipped the table on its side.

Beckett circled his hands around Sydney's waist and pulled her down for protection as gunshots rang out. Oliver did the same with Mya, and both men drew their weapons. "There are three of them."

Screams erupted as the music was cut out, and the shooters began yelling orders in Spanish for everyone to be quiet and not move.

Was this some random holdup or were they looking for Mya?

Beckett quickly stole a look around the overturned table and spied Mya's cartel source slumped over the bar, a bullet hole in his head. Another sweep of the area revealed the man-child who'd hit on Sydney groaning in pain from a stray bullet to the shoulder.

"Your guy is down," Beckett whispered, and Mya closed her eyes for a moment—either in mourning or shock. Probably both.

"They're looking for you, Mya," Sydney announced.

"And I think they found us," Oliver hissed. "On my count?"

Beckett nodded and held up two fingers to let Oliver know he'd get the two gunmen coming their way from his left side.

"Roger that," Oliver mouthed, then counted back from three.

In one fast movement, they darted into action, surprising their would-be assailants. Keeping low to the ground, they shifted to the side and popped off kill shots.

Guests screamed as chaos ensued. "Tangos down," Oliver commented while rising to his full height and burying another bullet in each of the three guys to ensure they were down for good. Something Beckett would have lost his job over back in the States, but this was different.

"There are probably more guys on the way," Sydney said as the guests' cries continued to echo around them.

Beckett looked toward the jungle in search of the ATVs he'd seen come and go earlier, checking for security.

A hundred or so yards away, he spotted three of the all-terrain vehicles fast approaching. His gut told him they sure as hell weren't the security crew or brave tour guides looking to earn their hero badge. "I'm pretty sure more *are* coming."

"Let's get out of here before they kill everyone just to be

sure they got me," Mya whispered. "I won't let innocents die because of me."

"The other two were pissed at the shooter for taking out Mya's source before he met with her," Beckett quickly translated what he'd heard before they'd taken the men down.

Beckett focused back on the three approaching recreational vehicles. Ten guys by his estimates, heavily armed, coming straight for them. He doubted the police would be en route if they learned this was a cartel-related hit, not until the situation was no longer an active one. "*Salgan de aquí. Vamos!*" he yelled toward the frightened guests, and they began fleeing the bar.

"We need to get them to chase us away from the resort," Mya suggested, taking sharp breaths. "It's the only way to keep everyone at the hotel safe."

"The jungle is our best option," Beckett said, breathing heavily as he calculated the odds. "But we need to use another entry point since they're coming from there now."

"We have to draw their fire." Sydney walked toward the edge of the bar on the jungle side, and Beckett joined her while they waited for the vehicles to get within shooting range.

"Ready?" Sydney asked as Oliver stood alongside Beckett.

"Yeah," Beckett answered. He and Oliver shot off a quick round, catching the closest driver, and the vehicle veered to the side and hit a palm tree.

"Well, we got their attention," Oliver said while facing them, and he motioned for Sydney and Mya to move. "And now would be a good time to run."

## CHAPTER EIGHT

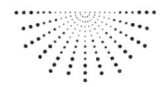

"I NEED TO GRAB MY CONTACT'S PHONE." MYA SPUN IN THE opposite direction, but Sydney quickly hooked her by the arm and swung her back around.

"Hell no. You can't save anyone if you're dead," Sydney bit out. "And also," she began, pulling Mya along, "the cartel most likely tracked your contact here using his phone. We don't need to lead those assholes right to us."

Sydney tossed a quick look over her shoulder to see Oliver and Beckett running closely behind them, acting like human shields.

"That way." Sydney pointed to a narrow outdoor hallway between two buildings that would provide some cover and prevent the ATVs from following.

They could gain some ground before showing themselves near the jungle, luring the men away from innocent bystanders. The archaeological ruins and other tourist sites were north of their hotel, so they'd have to do their best to avoid any heavily populated areas like those as well.

"Turn your phone off," Sydney instructed Mya while running alongside her, grateful they'd both worn flat shoes instead of wedges to lunch. "They don't know who you are yet, but if they manage to track your contact's messages back to you, then—"

"I'm so sorry," Mya rushed out as they entered the open-air hallway, passing the empty fitness center on their left.

Word of the active shooter situation traveled fast.

"Just stay alive today, and we'll be good." Sydney grabbed hold of Mya's arm and came to an abrupt halt, then slowly poked her head beyond the cover of the hallway to ensure it was clear.

Beckett sidestepped Sydney and announced in a tone that brooked no argument, "Stay here, I'll check." He kept his back to the white stucco wall and peeked around the corner.

"Will the police come?" Mya asked, and honestly, Sydney had no answer for her.

"Let's just assume we're on our own for now," she responded, her eyes landing on a row of what looked like archery targets in the distance.

"It's clear from what I can tell, but I hear engines out there somewhere." Beckett faced her, and she reached for his arm on instinct. His gaze briefly cut to her hand before moving up to her face.

"I need a weapon," she said after swallowing, unsure why her heart was playing some weird game with her right now. Pitter-freaking-pattering because of how he was looking at her? At a time like this. *Really?* Pissed at herself, she let go of his arm and shook her head to focus. "I can grab a bow from over there." She pointed toward the archery center. From the looks of it, golf clubs had been abandoned on the ground when guests fled the scene after hearing shots fired.

She started to exit the hallway, but Beckett snatched her wrist, taking her breath right along with him. "Let me check again," he said in a steady voice, and she didn't resist.

Maintaining his grip on both his Glock and her, he edged out beneath the exposed overhang. "We're good. I'll lead. Oliver, you stay behind them."

*Human shields again?* She didn't argue, *but* he would need to let go of her at some point.

An uneasy look crossed Beckett's face, a flicker of fear flashing briefly in his eyes. Was he worried she might die out there? Hell no. Leaving her son motherless was *not* an option. *He doesn't know me*, she reminded herself and slowly pulled her wrist from his embrace.

With that, he wordlessly took off as planned, and she hung close behind.

*This should work.* She snatched a discarded learner-level recurve bow from the ground near the archery target. There was a quiver full of arrows nearby as well. *A right-handed one, at least.* "Let's go." She slung the quiver's leather strap across her body and to her back, then gripped the bow and began running again.

"We have company," Beckett warned as they neared the thick bank of trees parallel to the dirt pathway meant for horses and ATVs.

Sydney pivoted to the left, catching sight of an armed tango waiting near the edge of the woods, less than half a football field away.

The man began waving, and she twisted to see the three all-terrain vehicles tearing up the driving range a hundred yards back. Looked like they'd recovered the vehicle that crashed into the tree and found another driver.

"Move!" Oliver yelled as if Sydney had any intentions of chilling for a quick sunbath.

They continued their zig-zagged style of running to dodge incoming fire from both directions, but Beckett stopped a few seconds later, taking Sydney by surprise. He dropped to one knee, pivoted, and took down the asshole on guard by the woods.

"Nice shot," she said, probably too low for him to hear. They'd successfully made it to the jungle, and the bad guys were officially taking the bait and leaving the hotel grounds. "Don't head north. Too many tourist spots that way," Sydney alerted them at the memory of their travels in the jungle yesterday.

They shifted off the designated pathway and took a sharp turn, whacking tree branches out of the way as they ran. It was obvious by the thick vegetation that this area wasn't meant for tourists—there was a minefield of obstacles in their way as they worked to put distance between themselves and the thugs behind them.

A few minutes later and deeper into the woods, Beckett stopped running. "Time to move quietly now," he suggested, and Sydney agreed.

They were too noisy at a high-speed pace, and in danger of getting hurt by Mother Nature in the process. It'd be feather-light and cautious steps from that point on, so they could pick off the men one by one.

"Re-enacting *Hunger Games* was not on the hotel's activities list," Mya surprised Sydney with a joke. Then again, the way Mya leaned forward, clutching her side and trying to breathe, she might not have been kidding.

The last thing she wanted was for her friend, who lacked military training, to be in any situation even remotely close to the *Hunger Games* books her son loved reading.

Sydney motioned to Mya to rest her back against one of the reddish trees behind her. "Catch your breath for a second before we continue." The break would give them a moment to think and plan. To listen to the jungle and see how close they were to the enemies. But then . . . "Shit. The security cameras," she remembered. "If they send someone back to the hotel to check the cameras, it won't matter if we kill everyone out here—the cartel will figure out who we are anyway."

"What about calling in Gray's sister to help? She handles the same kind of stuff you do for us," Oliver proposed, and she started to phone Gray with her Apple watch before he finished talking.

Sydney lifted her wrist near her mouth and cupped her hand behind her watch to prevent Gray's voice from carrying when he answered the call.

Gray's sister, Natasha, worked for the CIA. She also worked with her husband's "off-the-books" SEAL Team that ran ops for the President. She wasn't sure if Beckett knew the truth about what A.J. did for a living as part of that same team.

Sydney closed her eyes and continued to listen to their surroundings while waiting for the call to connect.

There was still the faint sound of an engine in the distance, but she had to assume most men coming after them were now on foot. At the moment, she only heard birds singing nearby. Possibly squirrels jumping between trees or a spider monkey spying on them.

"Sydney, everything good? I take it you spoke to Oliver and Beckett?" Gray finally answered.

"We have a situation," she whispered. "I need your sister to delete all hotel security footage for the entire resort starting yesterday morning. And have her change our names on the hotel booking database. I can't explain, but we're dealing with the cartel, and we need an assist."

"Fuck, okay," was all the response she needed.

"Gotta go." Sydney slapped a hand over her watch and ended the call before he could ask any questions. A fallen tree branch or the crunch of leaves nearby meant they wouldn't be alone for long. Someone was out there. Possibly waiting for backup or to carry out a surprise attack. "I've got this," Sydney mouthed to Beckett, realizing he'd visually tracked the sound as well.

As she crossed in front of Beckett, he circled a hand around her waist, stopping her to issue a quick order, "Be careful."

Sydney nodded as he released her, but the feel of his touch lingered on her side. She focused on the gray-barked trees in her line of sight, searching for her target. She turned sideways and relaxed her shoulders, notching an arrow onto the bow and raising it.

The bow wasn't the right size for her frame, but she'd have to make do. Loosening her grip so it wasn't too tight, she sent the arrow flying as soon as the man moved into her line of sight.

Without missing a beat, she rushed in his direction, knowing the arrow wouldn't be a kill shot regardless of where it struck him.

The man dropped his weapon in surprise as the arrow pierced his right shoulder. Before he could make sense of what was happening, she hooked her leg around his and brought him to the ground. Flipping him beneath her, she grabbed the knife she spied strapped to his leg, and finished him off in one fast, clean movement.

"Nice shot." She overheard Beckett repeat what she'd said to him earlier, but when she twisted around to look his way, it was Mya's look of shock that stole her attention.

"Holy shit, Syd," Mya cried, a hand over her mouth.

She didn't have time to calm her friend over the dead body. She removed the man's rifle and offered it to Mya.

"You think you can use this? It's easier to shoot than a pistol. But heavy."

Oliver stepped forward, shaking his head. "No, I'll take that. She doesn't need to kill anyone."

"Unfortunately, she might need to, but okay, take it." Sydney slid the bloody knife back into the leather sheath and handed it to Beckett. "Come on. Where there's one, there will be more."

They began moving again, navigating the woods at a slower pace, sticking to the shadows as much as possible. They didn't get far before Beckett halted them, throwing an arm straight across Sydney's chest so abruptly that her steps faltered.

She followed his pointed finger up a few inches from their heads to see a red snake twisted around the branch, its tongue flicking curiously. Beady black eyes right on her.

"Yeah, let's not survive these assholes only to get eaten by the jungle," Oliver said while shifting Mya behind him.

"Or attacked by a Mayan ghost," Beckett muttered. She had no idea where that thought had come from, nor had she expected a joke from him, but—

"It's a red coffee snake," he interrupted her thoughts. "Larger than normal. Looks like a coral snake but not venomous. If we back up, it'll leave us alone."

"*Looks* like a coral snake?" Mya whispered. "Or *is* a coral snake?"

"I grew up on a ranch, and no, we don't have these snakes there. But my father made me memorize nearly every damn snake known to this side of the hemisphere." Beckett's arm still stretched across Sydney's chest as if that would somehow halt the snake from darting down. "We'll be good. Just back up slowly. It may not be able to kill you, but it can still leave a mean bite."

"Roger that," Oliver remarked.

Beckett slowly lowered his arm only to hook it around Sydney's waist again, this time in a protective manner.

"We're clear, thank God," Mya rasped once they were far enough away from the snake.

"Hold on," Sydney said before they started moving once more, noticing a text flashing on her Apple watch. She read the message quickly, then faced the others. "Natasha's fast. She must have already watched the security cameras and saw what happened because Gray's instructing us to find somewhere to hide and wait."

"Wait for an extraction? They can't get to us in time," Oliver commented, scanning the terrain, 9mm still in hand. The rifle hung across his chest.

"No, Gray said Carter has contacts here. He called in a favor. But he said Carter's friends were already aware of our situation and en route. They're here somewhere." She did a three-sixty, feeling a chill creep up her spine.

"Weird," Mya said while copying Sydney's moves.

"Gray will ping my watch to get a location when it's safe, and he said these guys will escort us back to the hotel," Sydney added after reading Gray's next text.

**Gray:** *Confirm transmission.*
**Sydney:** *Copy.*

"Carter sure as hell has a lot of contacts all over the place," Beckett said as she looked up from her watch. "Lucky for us, I guess."

Before Sydney had a chance to respond, she twisted around to follow where Beckett's gaze had jumped, narrowly missing a bullet before he tackled her to the ground.

Three more shots followed, and Beckett remained on top of her a few seconds longer. He had his forearms on each side of her, and he lifted the weight of his crushing chest from hers so she could breathe before twisting to the side in one fast movement. Once on his back, he took two shots, and Oliver announced, "Tango down. But there's probably more guys on the way."

Beckett shifted into a crouched position and offered Sydney his hand to help her up.

"Thank you," she murmured, a bit stunned she'd overlooked that shooter.

"Uh, yeah, we're going to need to pick up the pace and run," Oliver stated the obvious when shots rang out again, and they started in a new direction, heading east.

Beckett cleared the way for her by staying in the lead, which was helpful and not necessary. She could handle herself.

"I think I know where we can hide," she announced when an idea hit her. *Cenotes. There are a few thousand smaller ones, so we have to come across one of those sinkholes soon.* Without losing speed, she switched her watch to waterproof mode so she didn't destroy her line of communication with Falcon.

"Please tell me it doesn't involve a hole in the ground," Mya said while trying to keep up with Sydney's pace.

"You gotta face your fears at some point, right?" It was their best option. "We can hide underground. And if it's possible, use the rivers down there to swim to a new location and find dry ground while we wait for another text from Gray," she explained once the shooting had ceased, which meant they'd placed enough distance between themselves and the gunmen.

"There, you see that?" She pointed toward a slight clearing in the woods up ahead. "I think that's one of the cenotes."

"Yeah, I think so," Beckett confirmed after jogging ahead of the rest of them.

She came up alongside him and peered down the hole. It was more like a jagged dirt circle in the ground. Wide enough for two adults to squeeze in at the same time. Nothing nearly as big or touristy as the ones she and Mya had viewed yesterday.

Beckett crouched to get a better look and tossed a small rock into the opening. A faint splash followed a second later. "There's water there. Maybe a thirty-foot drop."

Sydney turned and held her hand open, inviting Mya to jump with her. "The water will cushion our fall. You've got this."

Mya stared at Sydney's palm and took a hesitant step backward. "And if they follow us down into the hole?" Panicky brown eyes met hers a beat later.

Jumping into this pit frightened her more than the men chasing them. Only Mya.

"Then we pick them off one by one as they drop in. We'll have the advantage," Oliver calmly said.

"I can't." Mya started to back up even more. Sydney shot Oliver a quick look, a silent message of what she needed him to do.

Oliver gave her a slight, barely noticeable nod, then tucked his gun into his waistband, and shifted the sling of the rifle so the weapon went to his back.

Their weapons would suffer water damage if submerged for too long and more than likely shoot like shit or misfire, but it was a chance they'd have to take.

"I'm sorry," Oliver said just before grabbing hold of Mya. One arm around her waist and a hand over her mouth, having the foresight to muffle her screams, he forced her into the hole with him.

"You ready?" she asked Beckett. He extended his palm, offering to hold her hand while they jumped.

And for whatever reason, she took it. She let him take the lead once again.

*Guess I'm getting my way after all. I wanted to swim down here*, she thought with a shake of her head, right before they jumped.

# CHAPTER NINE

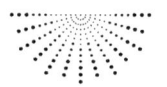

"They're up there, I can feel it." Mya's voice was soft and shaky as she huddled against the limestone wall inside the cenote while Oliver stood at her side, looking somewhat annoyed. Sydney was pretty sure he was still pissed off that her friend had risked her life and, by extension, all of theirs, by agreeing to meet with her cartel contact on her own.

Sydney looked away from the two of them and fixed her attention on the opening they'd all jumped through five minutes earlier. Soaking wet and utterly exhausted, they were lucky to have found a small ledge of dry land off to the side of the river while they waited to see if they'd be followed.

"Maybe it's not them up there," Oliver whispered, keeping his voice quiet to prevent any echoing inside the cave. "It could be those Mayan ghosts Beckett mentioned earlier."

Sydney was in a lunge-like position, bow in hand, prepared to send an arrow if anyone dropped through the hole. The idea of shooting a weapon while treading water was less than ideal, but at Oliver's joke, she stole a look at him from over her shoulder.

Was Oliver looking to usurp Jack's position as comedian of Falcon, or simply using comic relief to cut through a tense situation like she'd witnessed a lot of the guys do during her time in the Army?

*Yeah, that's probably it. In his own weird way, Oliver's trying to calm Mya.* Especially given that their current situation was at least an eight out of ten on the whiskey-tango-foxtrot meter—military-speak for WTF.

As Sydney swiveled her gaze back to the hole, she couldn't help but think of Levi. He knew she hated hearing him curse, so whenever they had a disagreement, rather than saying the acronym, he'd protest, *whiskey-tango-foxtrot, Mom.* She shook her head and smiled as she pictured her son. He knew damn well it was hard for her to keep a straight face and be upset after that.

"What do you think? Is it the baddies or our ghosts?" Oliver asked playfully, wiggling his fingers toward Mya.

"Don't be a dick," Mya warned. Sydney didn't look back again, but she knew her friend was more than likely elbowing Oliver in the ribs. "I know you're mad at me. And I deserve it."

"One second," Sydney interrupted whatever back-and-forth the two of them were about to engage in. "They're leaving." Relief settled the butterflies in the pit of her stomach, and she repositioned herself alongside Beckett, sitting with her legs over the ledge.

"Thank God," Mya replied as Sydney rested her bow on her thighs.

"Either they don't believe we'd ever jump down here," Oliver began, "or they're more afraid of this place than Mya."

Mya huffed out a frustrated breath, which could have been for any number of reasons, but the most likely contender for the top spot? Oliver Lucas.

"In all seriousness," Beckett spoke up, "if you had met with that guy alone tomorrow as planned, you would have died." He certainly wasn't one to sugarcoat things. But for whatever reason, when he'd spoken, his gaze was fixed on Sydney, not Mya.

"I can't even begin to imagine if you'd . . ." Oliver let his words trail off, all traces of humor disappearing as genuine concern settled in his tone.

Sydney had read Oliver wrong. He wasn't using comedy to cut through tension or piss off Mya. No, it was because he'd have lost his shit just thinking about what might have happened if Mya had been alone for the meeting with her cartel contact.

"I chose Tulum because it's relatively safe," Mya revealed. "Aside from an uptick in carjackings between here and Cancun, I thought I'd be fine." She shrugged. "This would have been our fourth meeting in Mexico, and clearly, I'm still alive."

"Yeah, you were lucky those first three times," Oliver hissed.

"And lucky again this time, I guess." Mya released a shaky breath, which had Sydney twisting around to check on her. "But you should never have been in danger because of me. I'm sorry."

"Mya, this is what Oliver and I do. This is normal for us." Sydney shot her teammate a quick look, unable to read his expression in the dim lighting. "But I don't want this to be the norm for you. Whether you work with Falcon or stay with Mason and his guys, you're not a field agent. Or an operator."

"I was a reporter. I get it." Mya's shoulders fell as she covered her face with her palms. "And I'm sorry. I won't do something like this again." She lowered her hand to focus on Sydney, "You have my word."

"All that matters right now is that you're safe," Sydney responded softly, doing her best to tap into the part of her brain that she reserved for her son. The emotional side. "Well, we're almost out of the woods."

"Figuratively. And hopefully soon, literally," Oliver piped up.

Sydney faced the water again, curious what Beckett was thinking about since his only contribution to the conversation had been lecturing Mya about how she would have died tomorrow were it not for . . . *well*, what happened today. And thank God they'd been there with her.

Could Mya have been right with all her talk about the power of thought earlier on the beach? Who was that author she was talking about?

"So, what's the plan?" Mya asked, followed by the sound of a hard slap as if Mya had swatted Oliver.

Sure enough, when Sydney checked on the two of them, Mya was on her feet but crouched so she didn't hit her head, and Oliver was in the same position but with his hands in the air in surrender as if saying, *Okay, okay. You don't need me.*

"Should we swim until we find a place we can exit?" Mya asked, moving to where Sydney sat next to Beckett.

"That'd be my choice, but it'll depend on whether the throughway is high enough for decent airflow so we can keep our heads above water as we swim," Beckett said while Oliver removed the magazine from the rifle along with the round in the chamber. "We won't know until we try."

"Right, makes sense." Mya peered at Oliver, who was now discarding ammo into the river before chucking the rifle in as well. "What are you doing that for?"

"I don't think we need this," Oliver responded. "As much as I hate littering, it's preferable to some adventurous kids discovering this thing sitting here on the ledge."

Beckett nodded in agreement and then, without another word, dove headfirst into the water. After a couple of seconds, he popped up to the surface, swiping one hand through his hair. He'd lost his hat at some point on their run, same with Oliver. "Only about fifteen feet deep right here. I assume that will change at some point," he shared while treading water to remain afloat, "but I doubt we'll be doing any standing in this river."

"Okay." Sydney turned to Mya and set a hand on her forearm. "You good?" Her friend was a strong and confident woman, and Sydney didn't mean to treat her like a child, but Mya was out of her element.

"I'll keep hold of you," Oliver offered, and Sydney waited for the objection to come.

"I can swim. Thanks," Mya quickly responded. "I just prefer to see what's around me in the water. And there have been a few attacks by saltwater crocs in recent years, so it's a legitimate concern."

"Wait, wait." Oliver held both palms up and peeked over the ledge toward Beckett. "Crocs?"

"There are no crocodiles in there." Sydney rolled her eyes. "And Oliver's not scared. He's just being an asshole."

"Let's go." Oliver held his hand out for Mya, but she knocked it away.

"Not your greatest fan right now," Mya said as Sydney jumped in, clutching her bow tightly in the process. "You didn't need to put your big, filthy hand over my mouth when we jumped," Sydney heard Mya add once she'd risen back to the surface and neared the edge, waiting for Mya to jump into the lukewarm water.

"I'll hold that for you," Beckett offered. Sydney looked his way, deciding whether to be insulted or grateful.

"I'm good," she decided. Sticking with stubbornness.

"All right. I'm going in. So, if you want to stay on the ledge alone while we swim, go for it." Oliver jumped into the water, and Mya grumbled something before swinging the shoulder strap of her purse around to position the bag at her back. Sydney was surprised she'd managed to hang on to that thing the entire time.

After a few quiet minutes of swimming and, thankfully, enough oxygen and light to keep them moving, Mya rasped, "Oliver, tell me that's your leg touching me."

"Not my leg," Oliver returned, and Mya squealed, launching herself straight at him, dragging them both below the surface for a moment.

Sydney swam in place, waiting for them to come back up. She was more fatigued from a few minutes of swimming than the days she hit the gym back home.

*I need a vacation from my vacation.* Well, she supposed, she was technically working now.

"Damn, Mya," Oliver sputtered when they resurfaced, Mya's chest tight to his, her arms tangled around him, clinging on for dear life. "I was joking."

Mya hissed and leaned back enough to gently whack him on the chest before pushing away completely. "Jerk." She started to swim again, and Sydney found herself exchanging a quick eye roll with Beckett as though they were the only two adults down there.

Once Oliver and Mya were ahead of them, Beckett swam next to Sydney and whispered, "Were those two ever . . . a thing?"

"No, but I think they're attracted to each other," Sydney stated what felt like the obvious.

"That's your definition of attraction, huh?" A light laugh from this growly-grumpish man, while in a cave and running for their lives, was the last thing she'd expected.

"It's not the kind *I'm* used to, but I think it's Mya's style. The love-hate thing." She took a moment to shake out her arm, tired from holding the bow while swimming, and before she could continue moving, Beckett snatched it from her hand.

"If you insist on keeping this with you, then it's my turn to carry it." He lifted his chin, a silent directive to keep swimming and not argue.

Sydney didn't usually tolerate men bossing her around, nor did it often happen, but for whatever reason, she kept her mouth shut. Because her arm really was fatigued, and her fingers were cramping.

"How'd you become so proficient with the bow, anyway?" Beckett peeked back at her while swimming. "Last I checked, they're not standard issue in the Army."

She thought back to the first time she'd held a bow at the age of nine, and how she'd been a fan from the moment her first arrow struck the target. "My ancestors were, well . . . I come from a long line of archers. My grandfather wanted to ensure he passed along the skill to me before he," she said around a swallow, "died."

Beckett stopped swimming for a moment to peer back at her and frowned. "I'm sorry."

"Don't be. He lived a long life." She smiled at the memory of her grandfather. She'd give anything for him to have seen Levi grow up. He'd been a hardworking and energetic man. Always saw the good in people. Looked for the silver linings in all aspects of life. He would've made a great role model for Levi. Not that Seth was a bad father, but . . .

Shit, were there tears in her eyes? She dove under the water to hide the emotions that had pushed through at such an inopportune time, and when she rose to the surface, she motioned for him to continue swimming.

Beckett hesitated as though waiting for her to add more to the story, so she swam up alongside him and added, "My grandfather didn't come from money. Not like me, I should say. But if it weren't for his influence and how he raised my father, I highly doubt my dad would've turned an idea into a multi-billion-dollar business."

"Your grandfather sounds like he was a good man."

"He was," she softly said.

"Hey, I see light." Mya's words had Sydney tucking away her memories so she could focus again.

"As long as you don't mean *the* light, as in the staircase to Heaven, then we're good," Oliver joked. He was a battle-hardened paratrooper from the 82nd Airborne, but right now, he reminded her of her son.

*Boys.*

"You think these vines can be used as a rope to climb out?" Mya asked.

"Tug on them and see. If you fall, I'll catch you. Promise." Oliver swam beneath the beam of light pouring in from the large hole above. No visible ladder, so she doubted this was one of the cenotes visited by tourists.

"Smartass." Mya grabbed a handful of vines and tugged. "Seems secure, but you may want to check, Syd."

"That can be our way out, then." Sydney swam over to check the vines. It appeared to be about a twenty-five-foot climb up the wall. "We can wait here until Gray texts. He should be able to reach us, but I'll message him to double-check."

"We can wait on that dry ground over there," Beckett announced as Sydney grabbed on to a handful of vines and braced the soles of her sandals against the rock wall.

Hoisting herself up, she channeled her rock-climbing know-how.

With multiple vines clutched in both hands and a firm grip, she ascended the wall despite the less-than-ideal slippery footing, lifting her chin toward the light overhead. The jungle wasn't nearly as dense around this cenote, so she didn't want to remain visible much longer and risk being seen.

"This should work." Sydney faced the wall again, realizing something was wrong. *Felt* wrong, at least. And it wasn't the cramping in her fingers from carrying the bow. A shiver rolled over her spine at the realization red ants—*fire ants*—were currently crawling from the vines to her right hand, and when she dropped her focus to her tank top, she saw that a few had already made their way to her chest. *How the hell did they get there so fast?* "Just great," she grumbled, ignoring the stinging sensations on her hands.

She quickly let go of one fistful of vines and freed the quiver from her body.

"What's wrong?" Mya called out from below, an undercurrent of panic in her tone.

"I'm about to fall. Move," Sydney warned just before letting go with her other hand and falling backward into the cenote.

Once fully submerged by the water, Sydney quickly peeled her tank top off before rising to the surface. "Are they gone?" She tossed her top out of the way and brushed a palm over her exposed skin to rid herself of any stragglers.

"What the hell happened?" Mya asked as she swam over.

"Fire ants," Sydney answered once she confirmed all the stinging bastards were gone. "Fastest way to get them off me."

With that issue solved, she began looking for her

discarded tank top and realized that her breasts were on full display, her sheer, nude-colored bra offering absolutely zero coverage since she was soaking wet.

*Let's just not make it a habit of you seeing me partially clothed.* Her words from only hours ago rang through her mind as she spotted Beckett crouched on the dry ground, forearms resting on his muscular thighs and her top dangling from his fisted hands. A slow, sexy smirk lit up his face, and she knew exactly what was on that man's mind.

In a nearly husky voice, his eyes wandered to her chest as he said, "It seems we've come full circle."

## CHAPTER TEN

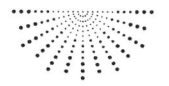

"This is becoming a habit with you, Miss Archer." During the past few hours, Beckett had seen this woman topless, in a silky robe with nothing beneath, and now in a nude see-through bra. What would happen if they spent any significant amount of time together?

Sydney didn't bother to respond as she quietly swam toward where he stood. Once she reached the ledge, he extended his arm to offer an assist.

Instead of taking his hand, she reached for the ledge off to his side, attempting to hoist herself up the slippery rock wall.

He didn't budge, curious how many times she'd keep at it before finally accepting his help. *Stubborn.*

A battle of frustration warred in her eyes after each failed attempt. Not only was she headstrong, but she was clearly not used to failing.

Beckett pulled his focus away from the struggling blonde beauty cursing under her breath to where Oliver propelled himself up the steep ledge on the second try, and surprisingly, Mya allowed him to help her up.

"You two have a height advantage," Sydney mumbled as if still needing to defend her failed attempts.

He crouched a bit more, still holding her wet top, and peered into her eyes. They were ringed by her smudged black mascara and eyeliner, only making her look even sexier, in his opinion.

With her thick mass of blonde hair slicked back, showing off her high cheekbones and full lips, she looked like a supermodel in a travel commercial for Tulum.

"Does that mean you'll take my hand if I give it to you?" Beckett smiled when her green eyes pierced him like one of her arrows. That dark but borderline seductive look shot him straight in the . . . well, not the heart. Right now, it was a different organ driving the show with her breasts lifting and falling from deep frustrated breaths. "Ma'am?" He arched a brow, opening his hand, doing his best to remain gentlemanly before his thoughts veered into caveman-like territory.

"Don't call me ma'am," was all she said before slapping a hand over his forearm and squeezing, taking control of her assist. Doing his best to maintain his footing despite the slick surface beneath his wet boots, he leaned back and pulled her onto the ledge.

But damn it . . . he slipped and went backward, landing on his ass with her on top of him. Straddling him, her hands planted on his wet chest as she caught her breath, she studied him with a sharp intensity that had him curious as to what was going on in that beautiful mind of hers.

"Sorry about making you fall," she whispered, and then she shifted to the side and stood, offering him *her* hand this time. Opting not to be a stubborn ass, he took it.

Their palms connected, and a wave of heat traveled from his fingertips and spread up and into his arm.

He swallowed and released her hand once on his feet,

nearly forgetting they weren't alone. When he swiveled his gaze to see Mya and Oliver sitting with their backs to the wall and focusing squarely on them, all they were missing was their movie theater popcorn for the show.

Both he and Oliver had seen Sydney topless on the beach earlier, so why'd it bother him Oliver could see Sydney's breasts as her nipples strained against the fabric of her nude, sheer bra?

"Your shirt," Beckett offered, anxious for her to cover up for more than one reason now.

"She seems more comfortable without one today," Mya said, catching everyone by surprise given how nervous she'd been that afternoon.

"Funny," Sydney said while shaking her top out as if worried more ants might be clinging to the fabric.

"You should get some aloe vera for your chest and hands. A little red," he noted, doing his best to discreetly eye the small welts from the fire ant stings near her cleavage.

Sydney followed his gaze to check for herself before pulling her top on. "I'm sure the hotel gift shop has some," she softly commented, then slowly stepped closer to Oliver and reached for the quiver he must have snatched from the water after Sydney had tossed it.

"Lost a few arrows down the river," Oliver noted, nudging his chin toward where Beckett had set the bow.

Sydney sat against the wall alongside Mya and rested the bow and quiver on her lap before tapping at her watch, most likely checking to see if Gray had received her earlier text. "Message went through. He says it shouldn't be much longer."

"Wow, that's good news," Mya said as Beckett leaned against the wall. "But while we wait, I do have to ask something." Mya focused on Sydney as she twisted her blonde hair into a side braid, the tail hanging a few inches below the curve of her left breast.

Beckett doubted her hair would stay like that for long without a hair tie. And he only knew this because he'd learned several different ways to braid hair over the years for McKenna's sake. Things he'd never thought he'd do in his life. But worth it to see his daughter smile.

"Yeah?" Oliver prompted when Mya's words seemed to get stuck in her throat.

Mya twisted to face Oliver this time. "Do y'all still want me on your team after all of this? My recklessness got us into this situation."

Sydney let go of her braid and stretched out, repositioning the bow and quiver farther down her legs.

"You're brave. Smart. Intuitive. And clearly great at finding sources that will be putty in your hands and give you intel. So yes, I still want you working with us," Sydney said, her tone resolute.

Mya winced. "My source is dead because of me."

"He's dead because he joined the cartel in the first place," Oliver quickly reminded her. "But maybe he'll have better luck in the um, afterlife, for trying to do the right thing in the end." He lifted his palms to the air. "I agree with Sydney. You should join us. We wouldn't let you come down here alone like your *other* team did."

"They didn't know that's why I came to Tulum. I lied about why I'm here," Mya defended before dragging a hand down her face.

*Yeah, I can relate to that.*

Mya let go of a deep breath, her shoulders slumping slightly in the process. "If I work with you guys, then consider this," she said while twirling her finger in the air, "a trial run. Which means I need more information from you, Beckett, if I'm going to help find Cora."

Beckett pushed his back away from the wall at what she was implying. He knew what this former journalist would want from him. And although she didn't rub him the wrong way like the reporters back in Los Angeles always had, he wasn't sure if he was ready to unzip his lips and open up like this was some him-on-a-couch therapy session. Talk about feelings? Hard pass, as his daughter liked to jokingly say when she didn't feel like doing chores. Of course, he wasn't joking.

"You do realize you have to share what you know at some point, right?" Mya pressed, reading his thoughts.

Or maybe reading his face. He'd probably turned on his "grump look" as his sister teased. Scowling. Furrowed brows. Etcetera. Etcetera.

"We have time," Mya continued as he remained quiet. "We're sitting here waiting for a rescue. Why not share what you know so that when we leave here, we can get started right away? The sooner we find your ex, the better."

"Right now, my concern is for Jesse." Beckett folded his arms, the back of his skull hitting the hard surface behind him.

"And Jesse's safety might very well be tied to Cora's now." Mya didn't need to remind him of that possibility. Beckett had been plagued by that thought ever since Jesse had stepped inside that Cadillac last night.

*I'm the reckless one.*

"I know it may not be easy to talk about this woman if she hurt you in some way, but I can't help if all I have to work with is a blank page. Maybe start with how you and Cora met?" Mya suggested, her tone soft like butter on his mother's homemade biscuits.

Damn, the woman was good. He couldn't blame her for tapping into her arsenal of interview skills to try and bait him into opening up. But that didn't mean he wanted to pour his feelings out and write his life story to fill up that blank page of hers either.

They'd have to settle for the bullet point version of his life.

Beckett exhaled an uneasy breath and freed his arms from their locked position across his chest.

"Did you meet her in Los Angeles when you were a cop?" Oliver chimed in, throwing Beckett a softball to help ease him into this conversation.

They didn't need to hold his hand through this, but why'd he find himself gripping the back of his neck where the bundle of nerves there seemed to twist?

"You were a cop in LA?" That piece of information had Mya's interest piqued. "*So*, before you were a sheriff in Walkins Glen, you worked in California?" Her question came across more like a statement in search of confirmation.

He mussed up his hair as he considered the words he'd be comfortable sharing. "I always planned to go into law enforcement. And I wanted the opposite of my small town. I chose LA because I hate the cold, so New York City was out of the question," he finally revealed. "After I graduated college, I joined the academy in LA. Seeing all the problems with gangs and drugs, I decided I wanted to work my way into the Narcotics Division and become a detective." *Okay, that's enough backstory there.*

"Oh." The little sound slipped from Mya's lips as if she were already filling in the rest of his story herself.

Beckett shifted his focus to Sydney, and why was this next part so hard for him to share? Was he worried she'd think he was an idiot for allowing a woman to con him? *Just get it over with.* But he couldn't seem to look away from her as he spoke. "I come from a music-loving family. In my free time, I'd go to a few jazz and blues clubs on the weekends." *There's a point to this, I swear.*

"I remember Jesse telling us your hometown was named after your dad and another guy there. Walker and Hawkins combined, right?" Oliver spoke up. "Walkins Glen. Except there's no actual glen in your town," he added with a light tone, and Beckett looked his way to see him smiling. "Your dad was a musician after the military . . . and then took over running the ranch."

Beckett nodded. "Like I said, music is in my blood. So, I used to hang out at one specific place regularly, and that's where I met a singer."

"Cora," Mya whispered.

Beckett's throat grew tight, his heart rate climbing now that he'd reached this part of his story—a story that'd suddenly gone from bullet points to full-blown detail. "One night, a couple of guys were trying to mug her outside the club, and I stepped in to help. After that, we started dating." He thought back to that night and the sight of Cora standing next to her red Civic, trying to shove away the two men harassing her, demanding money. It was all an act. "She pulled the whole damsel-in-distress thing on me as a way to con her way into my life."

Beckett turned and set a hand to the wall, bracing himself as he prepared to share the part of the story that always dismantled him. He'd loved that woman with everything he had, and in turn, she'd ripped his heart out and destroyed him. Destroyed his ability to ever trust or allow himself to love another woman again. But as much as Cora had hurt him, he wouldn't change a thing. She'd given him McKenna.

"You can stop." Sydney's hand landed on his shoulder. "You don't need to do this now. Not down here."

He shifted away from the wall, her hand slipping away in the process. "It's fine. I'm fine. You should sit."

She angled her head and continued to study him as though she understood the scope of his pain. Maybe she did?

"I'd rather go ahead and get it over with." *I've come this far, so why not finish?*

"She chose you as her mark because of your job, didn't she?" Mya, the quick study, asked.

Beckett faced her, unable to get through the next part of this conversation while finding himself lost in Sydney's gaze. "More like MS-13, the gang, did. She owed them a favor. Cora was always getting involved with the wrong people. And I was someone the gang couldn't buy. They couldn't put me on their payroll. So, they found another way to get to me," he confessed, feeling foolish all over again.

"What happened?" Mya was on her feet now, her reporter brain most likely working overtime, possibly plotting the potential outcomes of how his story went.

Uncomfortable, he attempted to shove his hands into his pockets, forgetting he was still soaking wet from their dive into the cenote. So instead, he crossed his arms once again, trying to get control of his emotions. To fight off the demons of his past that were more real than the "ghosts" in the jungle.

"Six months into our relationship, she accidentally got pregnant. I proposed, thinking that was the right thing to do. We never got married though." He paused for a breath to collect himself. "And then, a few days before McKenna was born, I caught her going through my work computer at our apartment." He swallowed the lump down his throat. "She tried to lie her way out of what she was doing, but then she broke down and confessed."

He resisted the urge to close his eyes, to travel back in time to that night. In truth, he didn't want to relive that moment. But more times than he could count, he did relive memories just like that one. How could he have been so blind to miss the signs she was using him to relay information to MS-13?

"Cora said they'd kill her if she didn't trick me into dating her and then worm her way into my life. But then she said she fell in love with me. I know, she's a con artist, so why believe her?" Beckett shook his head. He still had no clue if Cora ever truly loved him, but it didn't matter. "I didn't know what to do. She was about to have our child. And I needed time to figure out how to handle the news. Part of me wanted to throw her in jail. But how the hell could I do that?" His stomach turned at the memories piling one by one in his mind.

"What happened?" Mya softly asked.

Beckett blinked a few times. "Two days after McKenna was born, Cora disappeared. She left a note saying goodbye."

"She just left?" Mya rasped, and yeah, it was a hard pill to swallow. Even for Beckett thirteen years later.

"Her note said McKenna would be safer without her in our lives. And she assumed the cartel would believe she betrayed them by leaving, so she'd need to go into hiding for a bit." He closed his eyes this time, hoping his body didn't betray him and show any physical signs of the emotional beating his memories gave him.

"Did you try to find her?" Mya asked.

"Of course." Beckett opened his eyes to see Mya taking careful steps to not slip into the water as she sidled up alongside Sydney. "Not that I knew what in the hell I'd do if I found her. Fuck, she used me for months to help drug dealers and murderers. I decided it'd be safer to move back to

Alabama and raise McKenna there." He uncrossed his arms only to tighten his hands into fists at his sides. "I didn't find Cora after that, but she found me. She'd call for help or show up from time to time. Never saw McKenna though. She just did her best to manipulate me to get what she needed. *Money.*"

"And you helped her?" Oliver asked in surprise as if he wouldn't have done the same. But Oliver didn't know what it was like to be a parent. It wasn't so simple.

"She's the mother of his child," Sydney whispered before facing Beckett. "What else could he do?"

"You said earlier you haven't heard from Cora in years, though, right? Three weeks ago was the first time in a while?" Mya reiterated.

"Yeah, nearly six years." He'd seen Ivy since, but not Cora. "That last time she showed up I warned her if she ever contacted me again, I wouldn't help her. And shockingly, she listened. Well, up until recently."

"So, that's why you don't think Cora would be involved with the cartel now," Mya said in understanding. "And I assume her sister knows Cora's story, so she wouldn't want to get mixed up with the Sinaloas either."

"Right, but like I said, Cora was always great at accidentally getting herself mixed up with the wrong people. I guess it's not inconceivable to think Cora's in trouble now because someone from the past connected to MS-13 or the Sinaloas has found her. Many of her old crew were arrested not long after she fled town, and they probably blamed her for it." But Cora was also great at remaining invisible. Hell, even Emily's contacts couldn't find her with their facial recognition software. How would anyone from her past be able to find her? "Bad luck, maybe?"

"I take it the cartel never knew Ivy back when Cora was

in LA, or she wouldn't risk going to that club in Juárez?" Mya asked.

"No, Ivy never lived in LA while Cora was there, and she had no connection with the cartel from what I know . . . well, once I learned the truth, that's what Cora told me."

Before Beckett could share more, Sydney's gaze dropped to her watch and she announced, "They're coming now."

"Who?" Mya stepped closer to Oliver. "Good guys or bad guys?"

"Good guys," Sydney answered as Beckett listened for signs they weren't alone.

Within a minute, a deep voice called out, "Sydney Archer, Carter Dominick sent us. Let's get you all out of there."

## CHAPTER ELEVEN

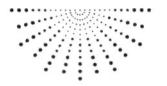

"Don't get me wrong, I'm grateful," Beckett began once the four of them were above ground, "but how is it that you happened to get here so fast? Didn't Carter call less than an hour ago?"

"Happened to be in the neighborhood?" Oliver tossed out sarcastically as he joined Beckett to face the strangers before them.

Beckett stole a quick look at Sydney standing alongside him. She was assessing their surroundings, as well as the six guys that screamed former military, from their all-black clothes to the black and green paint streaked across their faces.

"We were gearing up when Carter called." One man broke from the pack, and the way he moved and spoke screamed "leader." Confident but not cocky. "We heard about the shooting at the hotel. I live ten mikes out. We fast-roped into the jungle from my private helo."

*Mikes. Helo. Fast-roped. Yeah, you're a veteran.*

The man in charge lifted his chin when the sound of a chopper flying over the canopy of leaves came into earshot.

His men had most likely handled the cartel members on foot after dropping in and then advanced to their location after Gray pinged Sydney's watch. Relatively quickly too.

"Well, we appreciate your help," Mya chimed in, stepping forward to offer her hand.

"You're not police. Or active-duty military," Oliver said as he shook the man's hand next. Beckett and Sydney quietly followed suit out of respect. "So, who are you?" Oliver followed up. "And how do you know my boss?"

The man's lips tipped into a smile before he tossed a look over his shoulder at his men, who mirrored his amused look. "I'm Martín Gabriel." He opened his palms to the sky. "But my men and I are known as *los fantasmas*."

"Ghosts," Beckett finished for him. "So, you're the ghosts of the jungle we were told about." Now it made sense. Sort of.

"Ah, okay," Oliver said. "Let me guess, vigilantes? If you were gearing up to take out these thugs before Carter called, you must handle this type of situation on a regular basis. Independent of the police, right?"

"Someone must, *sí*? The *policía* can only do so much without endangering the lives of their families if they get involved in cartel business." Martín stowed his hands into his pockets and angled his head, then pinned Beckett with a knowing look, possibly sensing he was law enforcement.

Unfortunately, because of his time working in LA, Beckett understood the gravity of Martín's words more than he cared to admit. Had he stayed in town, McKenna's life may have been in danger at some point because of his work.

"And you're not afraid of the cartel?" Mya asked, sounding a bit mystified by the man.

"*They* should be afraid of *us*, and I think they're

becoming so. We are developing an intricate network across Mexico to combat these men who try to destroy our country."

"Brave of you," Oliver said. "I assume you met my boss through your dealings with the cartel?"

Martín nodded. "Let's say my head is still attached to my body because of him." He motioned for them to begin walking, and Beckett was more than happy to oblige. He was waterlogged. And although walking in wet boots wasn't his idea of a good time, the lure of a hot shower and clean clothes compelled him forward.

"Stupid question because you wouldn't be here otherwise, but are all the bad guys dead?" Mya asked, rooted in place.

Martín turned back toward her. "*Sí.*"

Mya closed the space between them. "If you're hunting down the cartel, there's something that may help you." She quickly explained all about her inside source and the cell phone that contained information about the human trafficking routes.

"My men will locate his phone. And I can promise you" —Martín stopped and set a hand over his heart—"that I will personally help destroy that network. And we shall offer our support if you find yourselves facing the Sinaloas again."

Beckett wasn't usually quick to judge people, but Martín not only saved their asses, he gave off good vibes. Beckett's gut told him the guy was more than worthy of his trust. And he'd take all the help he could get to save his brother-in-law and McKenna's mother and aunt.

"Carter has requested that the four of you spend the night at *mi casa* to err on the side of caution for now," Martín explained as he resumed walking, keeping pace with Beckett while his men followed closely behind.

"We'll take you back to your hotel so you may collect your things. *Policía* are not on the hotel grounds yet. We've instructed them to wait for my word before coming." Martín and his team clearly had the pull and respect from local law enforcement to bow to his requests. Better they deferred to Martín than the cartel though. "A car will pick you up and take you to my home. Not enough room in my bird for all of us, I'm afraid."

Beckett briefly caught sight of the helicopter through an opening between branches overhead. It appeared to be following along, which made Beckett feel a bit better to have eyes in the sky as they navigated the woods back to the resort.

Sydney remained relatively quiet while walking until Martín turned his attention to the bow she'd decided to bring back with her. "You come from a long line of archers, *si*?"

"How could you possibly know that?" Sydney asked, more than a hint of speculation coming through her tone.

From the corner of his eye, Beckett spied Martín smiling. "Call it a feeling. My ancestry can be traced back to the Mayans who once ruled this very land. They were excellent archers."

"Are you sure you don't mind us staying with you tonight?" Sydney asked after a quiet moment had passed. "I'm sure we'll be okay at the hotel. We shouldn't be identified. My team handled the security cameras."

"I'd feel better if you stayed with us. *Mi casa es su casa*," Martín replied without hesitation. "Besides, my wife, Valentina, loves any excuse to host a dinner party. You'll make her happy. And a happy wife means a happy life. You must agree, *si*?" He peered at Beckett and tipped his head in Sydney's direction. "You two are married?"

"*Us?*" Beckett stopped walking, trying to understand how this man with his excellent read on people thus far had drawn such a conclusion. "We barely know each other," he explained as his eyes connected with Sydney, who stood still as well, quietly staring back at him.

When Beckett focused back on Martín, his brown eyes gleamed as if he knew something they didn't. "*El corazón no miente.*" Martín grinned. "Neither do the eyes."

*El corazón no miente? The heart doesn't lie. Hell yes it does. Over and over again.* And his relationship with Cora was proof of that.

Beckett cleared his throat and checked for a reaction from Sydney, but she was already on the move again. Instead, it was Oliver he'd discovered looking his way with a smile parked on his face.

Beckett waved his hand, motioning for Oliver to lose that stupid grin and walk.

As they followed Martín back to the hotel, he shared a few more details about the Mayans and their history.

Once they exited the jungle, Martín looked up at the helo still chopping the air, signaled something, and then the helo veered off in another direction.

"If you would like to get your belongings and meet my driver out front in fifteen minutes?" Martín suggested once they were by the archery targets. The grounds were still eerily quiet, and he assumed guests and staff were lying low until the bodies were removed, and they trusted the danger was gone. "Is that enough time?"

"Sure." Sydney set the bow and quiver down on a table nearby as if she hadn't used it to shoot a man not long ago. Her clothes appeared to be drying in the heat, same as his, but when she faced him, he spied her nipples through her white top, and he had to gulp and look away.

"See you soon, then. And glad you're all okay," Martín said before sharing the driver information for their pickup.

Then he twirled his finger like a helo blade to rally his team to part ways.

"Did this really happen?" Mya looked around in disbelief once they were alone. "Is this a regular day at Falcon Falls? I mean, I know what Mason and the guys do is dangerous, but I've never been in the field to see it, so."

"At least Mason has some sense," Oliver mumbled, which earned him a scowl from Mya.

"I wouldn't say this is a regular day," Sydney answered a moment later as Mya opened her purse and dug around, probably looking for her phone to see if it survived their swim.

Beckett was fairly certain his phone was dead since it'd been in his pocket the entire time. He'd need to call McKenna and Ella from the phone in the hotel room before they left.

*Shit, scratch that.* If the cartel traced any outgoing calls to try and figure out their identity . . .

"Sydney, your cell phone is in your room, right?" he asked, remembering she'd only had her Apple watch when joining them at lunch.

"Yeah, you can call your daughter from it if you'd like," she answered, reading his mind.

"Let's get a move on." Oliver set his hand on Mya's back, motioning for her to walk, and Beckett and Sydney quietly followed them toward the hotel. Not a single guest, staff member, or police officer in sight yet.

The bar area emerged on their left as they neared the main part of the hotel by their suites, and Oliver tugged at Mya's arm. "Don't look," Oliver warned at the sight of the bodies still lying on the ground. "I'll walk you to your room so you can grab your things," he offered Mya once they were inside the main building. Still no sign of life. "And don't argue."

Beckett waited for the two of them to part ways, then

followed Sydney up the back stairs to her room, neither speaking a word, which suited him just fine.

Once in her suite, he let go of a heavy breath, trying to wrap his head around the last twenty-four hours. From the 1920s club to being saved by "ghosts." He was pretty sure no one would believe the story even if he tried to sell it to the *Enquirer*.

"At least the keycard still worked." She set the piece of plastic on the dresser in front of the mirror and began untangling her hair, working the strands loose from the braid that had miraculously stayed in place. "I could use a quick shower before we go. You?"

He looked down at his dirty, mostly dry clothes. He'd love nothing more than to wash off the craziness of the day.

"Not together," she tossed out as if worried he may misinterpret her words.

Of course, after feeling like a pinball getting whacked around every which way today, sex *shouldn't* have been on his mind. And yet . . . thoughts of Sydney straddling him in that cave earlier pounded his exhausted mind.

"I can be alone. You don't need to babysit me. Plus, I think you've seen me partially naked enough for today." That bit of humor, or maybe it was sass, had him smiling.

"I'd feel better if we stick together." He shoved a hand in his pocket in search of his keycard, assuming his would work since Sydney's had. "I can go grab my bag and come back."

"Okay." She handed him her keycard. "Take this in case I'm still naked"—she briefly squeezed her eyes closed—"I mean in the shower when you get back." She pointed to the bed where her phone was and gave him the four-digit passcode to access it. "Feel free to call home when you return."

"Thank you." He waited for her to disappear into the

bathroom before heading to his own suite. He locked the firearm into the weapons case and collected the rest of his belongings before making his way back to her room.

After discarding his bags by the door, he removed his boots and socks and let out a sigh of relief before grabbing her phone.

He listened to the running water from the bathroom while waiting for the call to connect with his sister, doing his best not to imagine Sydney naked in there.

"Sydney?" Ella answered, and Beckett forgot she'd most likely have Jesse's teammate's number saved. "Did something happen?"

"No, it's me. Everyone's fine." He walked toward the terrace and shifted the curtains to the side to check for movement down below.

The resort was still a ghost town. Literally. *Los fantasmas.* Beckett spied two of Martín Gabriel's men who'd rescued them earlier walking the beach as if standing guard.

"I had a weird afternoon, and my phone took a swim in a river, so that's why I'm calling from Sydney's line," Beckett finally shared.

"Jesse-type weird?" AKA, killing bad guys?

"Just weird." She didn't need the details. No one did, for that matter. "I need a favor, and then I just want to hear McKenna's voice."

"She's riding with Caleb. She wanted to be on her horse. Get her mind free from her worried state."

McKenna was in good hands with his brother, and he'd calm her. But still. He missed his daughter. "I don't want her stressed out." He let go of the curtains and faced the room, picturing his daughter's long dark hair, a gift from Cora, blowing behind her while riding her horse.

"Just worry about getting home alive right now. We'll

take care of McKenna. And I called out from work tomorrow." Ella was an elementary school teacher, but she also designed clothes on the side as a hobby. A hobby that was now paying off. But he was grateful she'd been around so much over the years to step in as a motherly figure for McKenna. She had a better grasp of the younger generation than Deb Hawkins, their mom. "So, what's the favor?"

Ella not asking about Jesse meant she'd already phoned Griffin or Gray for regular updates. He'd expect nothing less from Ella.

"I need Emily's number. I don't have it memorized."

"Liam's Emily? Why would you need her number at a time like this?" A pause and then, "Nooo, Beck, you didn't," she drawled. "You went to Emily since you knew A.J. would turn you down, didn't you? Not sure how A.J. will feel about that."

"One problem at a time. I'll deal with that issue and the guilt that comes with it after I get your husband free from the cartel." He did his best to ignore the knot of pain in his abdomen at such a conversation. "Her number, please." He held the phone to his ear with his shoulder and snatched the notepad and pen from the nightstand by the bed.

"Fine." Ella was quiet for a moment and then rattled off the digits.

He huffed out a deep breath. "Ella," he spoke before she had a chance to yell at him again, "I'm really fucking sorry." And then he hung up.

Beckett pocketed the piece of paper with Emily's number on it, deciding he'd call her later once they set up at their next spot.

He was about to toss the phone onto the bed when it began ringing. *Not* Ella. Gray's name popped up. He eyed the closed bathroom door for a moment and hesitantly accepted the call. "Hey, it's Beckett."

"Sydney okay?" Gray's tone came across as more surprised it was Beckett on the line than worried.

"Yeah. I didn't want to leave her alone after everything that's happened, so I'm in her room," he explained, realizing he'd soon have to share why she didn't answer herself and had no clue how that would go over with Sydney's ex.

"Sydney doesn't need a babysitter," Gray quickly commented.

"She said the same thing," Beckett recalled. "I'll have her call you back."

"Where is she?"

"The shower."

When the line went quiet, Beckett could almost hear the wheels in Gray's head turning. He either didn't believe Beckett's answer or didn't know how to process it. But what was abundantly clear by Gray's pause was that he still had feelings for Sydney. Beckett couldn't blame him. He barely knew Sydney, and he was losing his mind around her.

"Do you want to wait to have Sydney fill you in on why we were being chased in the jungle today, or . . .?"

"Yeah, have her call me when you get to Martín's." No small talk before he ended the call.

"Annnd he's pissed." Beckett chucked the phone onto the bed. Like he needed any more problems.

Not sure what to do with himself while he waited for Sydney to finish showering, he wandered around the room, finding himself drawn to a few books on the other nightstand.

He doubted the books came with the hotel since there hadn't been any in his room. But he was expecting Sydney to have books more about "how to kill someone with one hand behind your back" than a romance novel. These were more up his friend Savanna's alley.

And they were romance books, right? The men on the covers appeared to have lost their shirts, so either romance or thrillers about hunting a clothes thief.

He chose one of the three to flip through, unsure if any man aside from his brother, A.J., really had abs that fucking defined in real life.

Beckett thumbed the pages, maybe to distract himself from the fact Sydney was wet and naked in the other room, then stopped halfway through and read a few lines. He was more of a *Lee Child* or *Dean Koontz*–type reader himself.

A lump rose in his throat when his attention dropped to the next paragraph on the page, a sex scene, and he found himself reading every line out of curiosity.

*"You've been naughty. Really fucking naughty all week," he growled out, imprisoning my body beneath his hard, muscular frame. He stared deep into my eyes as I lifted my hips, begging him to fill me. To ease the aching pain there.*

*"I know. And it took you long enough to make a move," I whispered, my heart thrashing in my chest with anticipation for what was to come. He was my bodyguard. Assigned to protect me. Given orders not to touch me.*

*"You know I'll lose my job for this," he hissed as the head of his cock nudged my wet sex.*

*"No one will find out, but if you don't give it to me now, I'll lose my mind." I dug my nails into his shoulders, clinging to him as I stared into his eyes, letting him know how desperately I needed him, even if I'd spent the last week acting as if I hated him. God, that was the furthest thing from the truth.*

*He leaned in and brought his mouth to my ear, and my*

*nipples pebbled with his breath there. "You're a bad girl, aren't you, baby?"*

*"Yessss," I cried, dragging the word out as he plunged deep inside me and—*

"Savanna thought I could use some love in my life."

Beckett flinched and dropped the book at Sydney's words. He hadn't heard the water shut off or the door open, too engrossed by the erotic words on paper.

"Not sure why I just admitted that," she added as he bent down to pick up the book and then strategically held the thing across his crotch, hoping she didn't discover the book Savanna had given her had also given him wood.

*Fuck thriller novels.* Why wasn't he reading these? *Because I can picture . . . You.*

All thoughts of the call with Gray went out the window as his gaze journeyed up the length of Sydney standing there in a colorful V-neck dress that stopped mid-thigh. Her hair was wet from the shower, and she had a hairdryer in one hand, the cord dangling on the ground.

She'd put a touch of mascara on from what he could tell. A little lip gloss. And that was it. Damn, the woman was beautiful. And this situation did not ease the blood flow rushing to his dick.

"Have you read any of the books she's given you?" *Why'd I ask that?*

Sydney's attention fell to the book he was still using as a fig leaf, and that thought almost had him laughing. What an absurd situation to be in, especially given the day they'd all had.

"I may have read one. It's not my usual genre." She began coiling the cord of the hairdryer around her hand. "I was surprisingly engrossed by the book though. A nice escape. And the sex, well"—she smiled—"was hot. *But* I guess my question is, don't these women ever pee afterward? Aren't they afraid of getting a UTI?"

His lips broke into a smile too, and he wasn't exactly sure what to say, but damn.

"I guess that wouldn't be sexy to write for the author." She lifted her shoulders and looked to the ceiling with a playful expression crossing her face. "How about this, '*After having her third back-to-back orgasm from the Sex God, she hurried to the bathroom to pee so she didn't get an infection.*' Yeah, I think that'd kill the mood." She lightly laughed.

But he was hung up on the "third orgasm" part. "Three orgasms, huh?" He lifted the book, hoping his erection would obey his command and go down. He flicked the cover while adding, "Sounds—"

"Impossible for me." He lost her green eyes to the floor, and some part of his brain wanted to snatch that up as a challenge. "Anyways. I'll, um, dry my hair out here while you shower since we're short on time."

And that reminded him . . . "Gray called. I didn't want to worry him, so I answered."

Sydney set the hairdryer on the bed and folded her arms, her gaze cutting to the phone.

"He didn't seem all that thrilled when I told him you were in the shower and you'd have to call him back." He went to tip his hat in apology and realized it was gone. Lost to the jungle when they'd been running.

"Who I shower with isn't his business," she said, not with bitterness, more like a basic fact. Yet, a touch of blush rose up her cheeks as her eyes slowly walked up the length of his body to find his face. "You know what I mean."

He nodded, unsure of what to say. She had a past with Gray, and he needed to remember that. "I'll just shower." *And forget about what I read in that book.*

He hadn't meant for his body to brush against hers while en route to the bathroom, but that slight touch was all it took for his brain to detour back to that sexy scene, and his dick to disobey orders.

Damn it to hell, what was wrong with him? They weren't two characters in a book, throwing caution to the wind and giving in to their mutual desire. They were real-life people dealing with the real-life cartel in Mexico. And they both had baggage. So, he'd need to flush any idea of multiple-damn-orgasms with this woman down the drain. And pronto.

Sydney was off-limits for a hell of a lot of reasons.

And he reckoned he'd better remind himself of that.

Over. And over. And damn over again.

# CHAPTER TWELVE

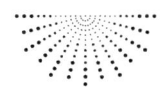

Sydney turned off the hairdryer and set it on the dresser with a thunk as her eyes locked on the reflection in the mirror. Beckett stood in the bathroom doorway, his muscular frame clad in a fluffy white towel that clung perilously low on his hips and revealed those two delicious V-lines.

"I don't know," she mused, "I think I may rock the whole topless look better than you." She chewed on her lower lip with blatant intent, unable to stop herself from toying with him for whatever insane reason. "But I'll admit, you're giving me a run for my money."

Beckett set his palms to the doorframe, his muscles going taut with the action, readying himself to join her in the room. *Or* trying to hold himself back. "Now, you see . . . no matter what I say next is bound to get me in trouble."

She arched a curious brow and leaned her hip against the dresser. "Oh really?" *Go for it. Get yourself in trouble*, was on the tip of her tongue, dying to slip free.

After the day they'd had, she needed to offset the drama with a little humor. *Or is this flirting?*

"You definitely win in that department." His voice lowered an octave while he fixed her with a smoldering gaze. So, he'd decided to go for the ballsy answer, admitting he'd enjoyed seeing her topless twice that day.

"Now that we've cleared that up," she said with a smile, "why are you parading around in only a towel?"

And why did it have her heart hammering? Sure, she worked with a group of special operators who were ripped enough to belong on a book cover, but she'd never found herself gawking when they removed their shirts. There was something about Beckett though. His incredible physique gave an entirely new meaning to the term "dad bod," and she couldn't tear her eyes away.

"Left my suitcase out here." With a lift of his chin, he looked toward his luggage sitting by the main door.

Instead of following his gaze, Sydney's eyes journeyed from the smattering of chest hair on his golden-tan body over to the vein in his left arm that cut down his bicep.

"Oh." The word was little more than a puff of air as her attention fell to where she swore his dick had just twitched behind that towel, certain he was working up to an impressive hard-on. So . . . he hadn't taken care of himself in the shower. *What the hell, Sydney? Of course, he didn't jerk off in your shower.* "Would you like me to get your bag for you? Wouldn't want to risk that towel falling off," she teased while going for his duffel bag.

Beckett remained in place, hands still glued to the interior doorframe of the en suite.

"Thank you," he muttered through clenched teeth when she dropped the bag just outside the bathroom.

*My goodness, Sheriff, what's got you all worked up? Was it the book? Did it make you as horny as the other one made me last night?* But unlike earlier, when she'd caught him absorbed in the romance novel, he wasn't trying to hide his arousal behind a book. Well, she was pretty sure that was what he'd been doing.

"Do you need help putting your clothes on too? Did you sustain an injury during our jaunt through the jungle I don't know about?"

A sexy laugh rumbled from his chest and hit her in the solar plexus. "We define *jaunt* a little differently where I'm from." His lips tipped into an easy smile that further knocked her off guard as he slid his palms up the doorframe, then pushed away. "In my opinion, that excursion was less than pleasurable." That deep, husky tone of his was as spine-tingling as his laugh.

Taking a step forward, he stopped and slowly slid his gaze over her body before reaching down for his bag and brazenly tossing her a wink as he did so. Another surprise. Wow, this man.

Then just like that, Beckett stood, retreated to the bathroom, and shut the door before she was able to utter a word in response.

*What the hell is wrong with me?* She spun away and tried to get a handle on her emotions, which was proving to be difficult around him.

Men, no matter how good-looking, never rendered her speechless.

The sight of shirtless men never caused her panties to become soaked.

And good-looking, shirtless men, even those sporting six-pack abs, sure as hell never caused romance-novel-level butterflies to take flight in her stomach with a mere wink.

*Whiskey-tango-foxtrot.* Sydney unplugged the hairdryer, deciding to let the rest of her hair air dry. She needed to pack up her stuff so they could get a move on as soon as Beckett was clothed.

She grabbed the cowboy-sheriff romance book from her beach bag and tossed it into her luggage along with the other books from the nightstand. Why on earth had she packed all the ones Savanna had given her? No clue. Even if Beckett and Oliver hadn't crashed her vacation that morning, she'd never have had time to read them all.

Sydney huffed out an exasperated breath after she finished packing, then zipped her suitcase and set it next to Beckett's boots by the door.

As she waited for the sheriff to get dressed, her attention paused on her reflection in the mirror above the dresser. The skin along her cleavage had faded from angry red to pink— the fire ant bites almost forgotten. But what tugged at her mind from their time in that cenote was what Beckett had shared. After learning what Cora had put him through, Sydney realized he had as many layers as she did. Maybe more.

Beckett emerged from the bathroom wearing a fresh pair of faded jeans and a plain white tee. His dark hair, shorter on the sides than the top, was still wet but slicked back as if he'd combed it with his fingers. And the touch of silver at his temples gave him a distinguished look she found incredibly hot.

Even the frown directed at his boots, soaking wet from their "jaunt" in the jungle, was sexy. Whenever she heard that word in the future, she'd always think of Beckett with a smile.

"You hate wet boots as much as every operator I know, huh?"

"I do." Beckett crouched and searched his bag, pulling out a pair of wide-strapped black flip-flops. "Not my usual style of footwear, but I bought them at the airport in Cancun as if I somehow knew I'd need them."

"Fate." She chuckled as he tucked his boots into his bag.

"I'm beginning to think so." Beckett's serious tone hinted that his comment wasn't just about his footwear.

Sydney cleared her throat, trying to loosen the odd swirl of emotions that had appeared the moment she set eyes on him at the beach that morning, and had thrown her for a loop ever since. "We should go."

Beckett gestured toward the door and snatched all the bags, except for her purse.

Deciding not to be stubborn and protest, she quietly retrieved her phone and followed him from the room.

Tossing one last look at the framed photo of the cenote over the bed, she wondered if Mya was right when she declared words held power.

Sydney had gone from wishing she could swim in the underground river that morning to jumping right into one in the afternoon. *Yeah, talk about fate. Something along those lines,* she supposed.

She closed the door behind her, shutting out the rest of her thoughts along with it, and they silently made their way to the hotel entrance.

Mya was sitting shotgun in a blacked-out Chevy Suburban, and Oliver stood with his back resting against the vehicle waiting for them. "Finally," he said while checking his watch.

They were at the most five minutes late. Worth it for the showers and change of clothes. Mya and Oliver had clearly decided to wait, given they were still in the same outfits from before.

Oliver opened the side door for Sydney to climb in while Beckett stowed the bags in the trunk, and she found herself in the middle between the two guys. Not the bucket-type seats she preferred, so they were sandwiched together.

"Let's roll." The driver pulled away from the hotel, taking a turn a bit sharply when exiting, which knocked her into Beckett, and Heaven help her, her palm landed on his crotch.

Sydney quickly yanked her hand back and mumbled an apology. As she righted herself in the seat, she caught Oliver smirking. *Jerk.*

"You good back there?" Mya twisted to look back as Sydney tugged at the thin material of her dress, trying to cover a bit more of her thighs.

"Great," Sydney lied with a tight smile, shifting side to side to try and get comfortable between the muscular arms pinning her in place.

Any more bumps in the road, and she'd wind up flashing everyone her panties, so she lifted her purse from where it was wedged between her feet on the floorboard and set it atop her thighs.

Within a second of doing so, her ex's name popped onto the screen of her Apple watch. She was tempted not to answer at all. She'd spoken to both Seth and Levi before she'd gone to the bar earlier to let them know she was extending her stay. *But what if something's wrong? What if something happened to Levi?*

Sydney fished her phone from her bag, accidentally elbowing Beckett in the process, and brought it to her ear. After a quick "sorry" to Beckett, she answered, "Seth?"

Mya looked back at her once again, alarm in her eyes. Her thoughts must've settled on the same idea that something was wrong for him to be calling. He *never* called unless there was a problem.

"We need to talk," Seth cut straight to the point.

*Great.* He was using his "Major" voice. His authoritative

military tone. No bullshit, just the facts, ma'am. She hated when he talked to her like she was one of his officers. They'd never served in the Army together, but he'd always treated her like he was her commanding officer during their marriage. "Bad timing," she responded, focusing her attention out the front window of the SUV.

More bumps in the road and another sharp turn jostled her against Oliver this time. The middle seat was hell.

"You need to hear this from me before Levi tells you," Seth announced as the driver hit a pothole. The phone tumbled from her lap, landed on the floor, and somehow activated the speakerphone. *Shit.*

"Levi confessed he saw Alice and me together, so I decided to tell him the truth," Seth rattled on. Her heart climbed into her throat as she scrambled to find her phone on the floor, almost bumping heads with Beckett, who dove in to assist in the search.

"Hold on, let me take you off speaker," she quickly called out, hoping he'd realize others were listening and keep his mouth shut for a damn minute. Whatever bomb he was about to drop on her . . . well, she didn't want everyone else in the vehicle hearing.

"Alice and I are getting married," Seth revealed just as Beckett set the phone in her palm.

# CHAPTER THIRTEEN

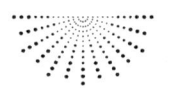

*"I'M DONE. WE'RE DONE. WE'VE BEEN DONE LONG BEFORE this thing with Alice. And honestly, Sydney, did you ever even love me? Are you capable of love?"* The words Seth had thrown at her the day she'd learned of his affair with Alice four years ago echoed through her mind at his news, so instead of switching Seth off speakerphone, she ended the call, having no desire to continue the conversation right now.

Sydney leaned back in her seat, her thighs sticking to the leather, and wondered why the heck the driver hadn't turned on the A/C because the breeze streaming through the open windows was a soup of hot and humid air. She tucked her phone back into her purse and put on her best poker face to keep from revealing how she felt about Seth's news. But when she looked up, Mya was still watching her, a mixture of sadness and pity on her face. Now her best friend knew why Sydney had been "off."

The crazy thing? She couldn't care less if Alice and Seth got married or even wanted to start a family and have a house full of babies. It was Levi's reaction to it all and how he'd handle the new dynamic that she was worried about. God, he was still trying to get used to high school as the youngest freshman there, and now this?

"I'm so sorry," Mya silently mouthed to Sydney.

Just that morning, Mya admitted she'd learned of her father's string of affairs, and the last thing Sydney wanted was for Mya to worry about Sydney's problems too.

Oliver patted her knee twice before she could respond, making her flinch. "You okay?" he asked.

Stuck between Beckett and Oliver, her arms pinned at her sides and her hands set on her purse, Sydney was trapped like a sardine in a can, unable to even squirm without elbowing both men. She did her best to remain still, trying to act as if she were unaffected by Seth's phone call, and lied, "A hundred percent."

"I've never known you to be anything less than a hundred and fifty." Oliver was doing his best to comfort her. He was better at dealing with feelings and emotions than her, but not by much.

Most of the team tended to keep their thoughts under lock and key. It kept them focused on the job, and it was safer for everyone if they didn't allow their personal lives to get in the way during missions.

*Like I am now.* The rest of the drive was painfully quiet. Even the beautiful scenery wasn't enough to distract her thoughts, to keep her past from needling her in the ribs, poking and prodding much too close to her heart and threatening to crack the defenses she'd erected years ago. *Not enough.* Seth's constant refrain aimed at her and her competence as a wife and lover, as Levi's mother, and even her professional life had been what turned her into an even harder and colder person. *Was I really that bad before though?*

"We're here," the driver abruptly announced, hitting a

massive pothole in the dirt road just before driving through a gated entrance.

"Sydney?" Oliver prompted as if still waiting for her to overturn his concerns and prove she was as "okay" as she'd clearly failed to let on.

She peeked at him from over her shoulder and found him studying her with a worried look. He knew Seth was her ex, but he didn't know the dark and gritty details of why they'd divorced.

But Sydney was familiar with the look in Oliver's light brown eyes. Part sympathy and part "want to kill a guy" for upsetting a teammate. He was becoming like a brother, and as an only child, part of her had always wanted an overprotective sibling.

She'd hoped for a lot of "brother-types" in the Army, but it took time to earn their trust. Even as a cadet at West Point, women were still heavily outnumbered.

Eventually, while serving, she'd found her tribe. Found a group that had accepted her. Let her into their circle. And then . . .

"I'm good," she promised. *I will be. As long as Levi's okay, I'll be fine.*

"The Gabriel *hacienda* is pretty far back in the woods," Mya piped up, breaking the awkward tension. "We're pretty much in the jungle."

"Señor Gabriel purchased this property two years ago. It's quite the place. We call it *El Gimnasio de la Selva*." The driver caught Sydney's eyes in the rearview mirror. "The Jungle Gym," he translated as they neared the front of the sprawling estate. "There are twenty bungalows on the property as well. We have set up four for you all. Unless you are couples and wish to share?"

"No, four rooms, *por favor*." Sydney spotted a helo pad

off to their right and noticed Martín's helo had yet to return. "Is Martín still at our resort?"

"*Sí.* He's asked me to bring you to your rooms to relax and freshen up. He will meet you back here for dinner in the courtyard with his wife," he informed them as they rounded the circular driveway in front of the pinkish-hued stucco home, which Mother Earth appeared to have partially reclaimed with vines winding up the front. The architecture had a Spanish colonial feel to it, but she doubted the place was very old.

The moment Oliver exited the vehicle, Sydney scooted across the seat and stepped out, desperate for a breath of fresh air. Beckett retrieved their luggage from the trunk, while Oliver did the same for himself and Mya. But when the driver began walking and motioned for them to follow, Sydney couldn't move a muscle.

Beckett set the bags down and approached her, shielding his eyes with his hand to keep the bright, beating sun free from his face. There was a narrow opening between the leaves overhead, and the light seemed to strike him step by step as he closed the gap between them.

Sydney set a hand to her abdomen, trying to wrap her head around whatever strange sensations seemed to be attacking her. A tingling feeling in her hands. A tremble in her stomach. Her heart racing. A tightness in her chest. Was this a panic attack? Levi had described the same sensations after he'd had his first one shortly after he'd learned of the affair, and . . . *is this one? Why now?*

"I'm coming." She waved Mya off, feeling her friend's eyes on her without looking her way. "Go ahead. Be right behind you."

Sydney focused on Beckett quietly standing before her,

his hand at his side now that they were in the shade, but he didn't say a word.

*You were betrayed too. You know exactly what I've been through.* She frowned at that fact because she hated the idea of others suffering, but she knew Beckett had gone through hell too. And he recognized the last thing she needed was pity.

She wasn't sure how long they simply stood there staring into each other's eyes. A handful of seconds? A minute or two?

But the tightness in her chest lost its hold beneath his steady brown gaze. The comfort he managed to offer her from his quiet but strong presence helped pull her back together. Helped remind her she was tough.

*You're a badass warrior, Mom.* She decided to replace Seth's words with her son's, and more of the painful sensations in her body seemed to drift free.

"Let's go," she said softly and tipped her head in thanks for what he'd done for her, quietly being there for her, knowing what she'd needed. "I'm ready."

He retrieved their bags once again and hung behind her as they traveled through the massive double-door entranceway.

Oliver, Mya, and their driver stood in the foyer discussing the history of the property.

"Hey." Mya gave her an easy, sweet smile, an invitation to join in on their conversation.

Sydney wasn't up for talking, so she was happy Mya peppered their driver, now their tour guide, with questions about the estate as they navigated the gorgeous property.

Sydney barely noticed the beautiful details and design inside the home or the jungle setting once they were back outside either. And had Beckett not warned her, she would have tripped over an iguana lounging on the path leading to their bungalows.

"Here we are." Their guide stopped and opened his palms near four structures—two buildings on each side of the wider part of the trail, surrounded by trees. Hammocks of brightly woven material hung on the small front porch areas of each bungalow.

"What are they made of?" Mya asked, pointing to the bungalows while they approached.

"Mostly chukum stucco. Chukum bark is all over the Yucatán Peninsula. The bark's color is what gives the exterior that earthy, natural color. And the thatched roofs are made of dried palm leaves. The bungalows don't have AC units, but there's a fan over each bed. And a small outdoor shower attached at the side."

Sydney's attention swerved toward Beckett to discover him scrutinizing her intently, but not in the same way he'd looked at her in the hotel room. No, that blaze of desire from earlier had been replaced with something else. Concern?

"Well." The man slapped his palms together and rubbed them. "Can I get you anything else?"

"We're all set." Sydney thanked him and watched as he walked toward the main house, then quickly lifted her eyes toward a rustling sound in a nearby tree and swore she spotted a spider monkey spying on them. So much for the option to have a private shower. This little guy would creep on her for sure.

"I'll set your stuff down in one of the bungalows." Beckett tossed a look back at her. "Matter which one?"

"Any. Thank you." She pivoted her gaze to Mya. "Give me a minute, and then we can talk?" She knew Mya was anxious to have the official, *Are you okay?* conversation after Seth's call.

"Okay." Mya retreated to her bungalow, and Oliver did the same, leaving Sydney out there alone and so deeply mired in her thoughts that she slammed into a wall of muscle as she entered the doorway of her bungalow.

"Shit, sorry." Beckett grabbed her arm like she might lose her balance.

"No problem. Thanks for dropping off my bag." Sydney managed a small smile that apparently did nothing to convince Beckett she was fine because he kept hold of her arm and tilted his head, studying her once again. She tensed when he took a small step closer, lifted his other hand, and skated the pad of his thumb across her cheek, wiping away a tear she hadn't known was there.

"The wind," she sputtered. "It must have made my eyes water." *I don't cry. Not over Seth. Hell no.*

Beckett's brown eyes narrowed as he replied, "Of course," before backing up to allow her inside the room.

She quickly wiped her fingers across her cheeks before turning to find him still standing in the doorway.

"My son didn't take the divorce well." The words fell from her lips before she could catch them. And now she'd have to add more to that sudden drop of information. "I'm worried how he'll feel about his father remarrying. Seth's not his biological father, but he raised him and so . . ." *Why am I telling you this?*

Beckett took one step forward.

Just the one.

But it was enough to send her back two.

"I guess I just gave you the bullet point version of my life. Minus a few major, um, bullets." She gently set a hand across her throat, willing herself to shut up. Mya was right earlier when they were on the beach. It wasn't like Sydney to ramble. Babble. Blabber. Whatever.

"Bullet points," he said in almost a whisper as if those words meant something to him. He drew a hand across his mouth before gently stroking his jaw. "I'll take any bullets you want to send my way."

"Literally?" She arched a brow to break whatever spell she'd seemingly fallen under. Was the jungle enchanted? Because right now, an intimacy stretched between them that went beyond the physical. "Or just figuratively?"

"I would have taken a bullet for you in that jungle if need be, yes. Without hesitation."

She was the one taking a step closer to him this time. "I wouldn't have let you." She erased the last bit of space between them, tempted to set a hand to his heart. To try and ease the burdens he was carrying because she knew how heavy hers were, and she could see the suffering burning in his eyes.

Well, something was burning there. Maybe it wasn't just mental anguish?

She gathered in a small breath when his hands framed her body. "I'm going to hug you right now. Just giving you a heads-up so you don't—"

"Hurt you?" She sent him a nervous smile, and he nodded. "And if I'm not the hugging type?" For a guy whose sister referred to him as Mr. Grump, he was throwing her off yet again.

"Then permission to hurt me when I go in, but I'm gonna do it anyway." His resolute tone was surprisingly comforting.

"I guess a hug is better than a bullet," she whispered, a bit unsure, but she let him do it anyway.

He gently pinned his chest to her body, and his hands traveled around to her back. "Thanks for not—"

"Kneeing you in the groin," she cut him off again, unable to stop her mouth from running away like always in these situations. Because she really didn't know how to do this. But she was trying. For whatever reason, she found herself wanting to try.

"Precisely."

She took her cue from the tone of his voice and willed her body to relax, to let the stiffness melt away. It'd been so long since she'd allowed anyone to comfort her that she felt out of practice.

Had she ever let Seth just hold her like this?

She released the thought, not wanting to think about him right now.

So, she turned her cheek and closed her eyes, listening to the sound of Beckett's strong, steady heartbeat.

He quietly held her there like that, one hand softly stroking up and down her back. Caressing and calming her for a few minutes.

"I clearly don't do this," she admitted without pulling away.

"Do what exactly? Hug?"

"Show weakness." Her confession had him easing back, and he freed his arms from her body but then tipped her chin with a fist, guiding her eyes to meet his.

"I'd hardly call this weakness. But it's not something I'm so great at doing myself, if I'm being honest."

"Hugging or?" she whispered as he opened his fist and slid his palm along her cheek.

"Opening up." He tilted his head, eyes focused on her mouth as if he wanted to kiss her.

And she doubted she'd resist. The pull between them was strong.

She didn't have to decide whether to stop him or encourage him because Gray's name suddenly popped up on her watch at the same time her phone began ringing, causing them both to freeze.

Did Gray have news?

She had no idea how she'd found herself caught up in this man's arms, with her heart on her sleeve. That was way more Mya's thing. It was for the best that Gray interrupted.

Beckett roped a hand around the back of his neck, his eyes still trained on her watch, and then she remembered that he'd answered Gray's call on her cell earlier while she'd been in the shower. Ah, she hadn't filled Beckett in on *those* particular bullet points from her life at West Point with Gray. And while there was nothing between them now, he was still protective, so no telling what Gray had said to Beckett.

She supposed it didn't matter. There couldn't be any more almost-moments between her and Beckett. For too many reasons to list.

"I should, um, take that," she said before answering the call over her Apple watch.

"Hey, you at your new place?" Gray asked when the call connected.

"Yeah, we're here." She stole a quick look at Beckett, his jaw clenched as if he were struggling with the same thoughts she'd just had. The *what did I almost do?* kind.

"Are you alone right now?" The thinly veiled hint of reproach in Gray's voice said it all.

"You hear from Jesse?" she deflected, hoping for a subject change for all their sakes.

The line was quiet for a moment before Gray shared, "Jesse made contact via our protocols. I won't get into the details, but he's safe."

"Next steps?" she asked, checking Beckett's reaction to the news and finding the obvious signs of relief in every square inch of his body.

"He said to hang tight. Working on a plan," Gray responded. "But in the meantime, we're running a few leads as to how Cora may possibly have a connection to this club Capone. Or why her sister was there in the first place." At the mention of Cora, Beckett looked toward the door as though he might bolt. "But what I'd like to know is what in God's name happened today?"

Sydney quickly explained the details involving Mya and her inside man at the cartel, and Gray quietly listened.

"She knows she can't go rogue like that if she joins our team, right?" Of course, that'd be by-the-book Gray's reaction.

"Obviously."

"Okay, well, I'm glad you're all safe. Good thing Oliver happened to be there to have your six," Gray continued. "And Carter's friend, Martín, too." He paused for a moment, and Sydney didn't fail to notice he'd purposely left out Beckett's name. "Well, call me if anything changes."

"Did you tell Ella?" Beckett asked, taking her by surprise, announcing his presence and that she was *not* alone.

Silence hung in the air for a moment before Gray said, "She was the first call we made. Your sister insisted on that during our last talk." A pause before, "I, uh, have to go. Talk soon." And then the call ended.

She didn't need this attitude from her teammate. *Please tell me you don't still have feelings for me, Gray.* Her focus landed on the only piece of furniture in the room, the bed with a simple black comforter on top. Most likely, the rooms were normally used for the guys on Martín's team.

"I told you we didn't need to worry about Jesse. He'll be fine," she finally managed while turning to face Beckett.

He nodded. "I'm sorry about Gray. I hope I haven't

caused any problems for you two by being here now, or well, the whole shower thing earlier."

"There's nothing between us," she quickly explained.

That didn't mean there could be anything between her and Beckett, but the man didn't need extra guilt on his shoulders, thinking he'd almost kissed a taken woman. And they *had* almost kissed. She didn't think she'd imagined that moment, even if she was hungry and a little dehydrated.

Beckett dragged his gaze to her face, but why in the hell did he not seem convinced by her answer? *Ah, Cora.* He had trust issues. And sadly, she could relate. "I'm going to take another shower," she decided to let him know for whatever ridiculous reason. *Like there isn't enough tension with us? Sure, go ahead and tell him you're getting naked again. Perfect.*

But she really did need to get her head back on straight, and usually, a cold shower helped shock her system.

She had no clue if it'd be enough to help her forget the Seth and Alice news. Or the possibility that Gray may still have feelings for her.

But she most definitely had to stop whatever was going on with Beckett.

Her walls needed to go back up. She had to go back to defense mode.

Because she knew without a doubt that she'd never survive another broken heart, even if her asshole ex didn't think she actually had one to begin with.

She did.

The problem right now . . . it sure as hell felt like it was beating for a stranger.

## CHAPTER FOURTEEN

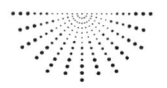

"Mom, I asked him to wait until you were back to tell you." Levi's voice was brittle. Broken. And Sydney could kill Seth for doing this to him again.

She set her back to the wall alongside the bed, needing support while she summoned the right words. The last thing she wanted to do was lie to Levi, but she didn't want him worrying about her. "How are you?" she asked instead. "You were at Grady's when we talked this morning. What happened?"

Levi was quiet for a moment before murmuring, "I came home earlier than Dad expected."

*Oh, for the love of God, Seth. Did he catch you again?* Her fingers curled into her palm at her side, and she took a slow, deep breath, fighting the desire to catch a plane and punch the man. "And that's when they told you they're getting married?"

More silence before a soft, "Yes. She had a ring on, and I noticed it."

*I don't know what to say.*

"I don't want to live with them. She was . . . she was always Aunt Alice, and then she hurt you so bad, and I . . ."

"Levi," she cried, tears gathering in her eyes, her voice breaking this time. "I wish I could fix this. You know I would if I could."

"You can't fix everything, Mom. I know you try, but some things just, well, they suck." She heard him swear under his breath, and she had no intention of calling him on it. "This just sucks." His voice nearly broke at that, and she knew he was fighting like hell to keep the tears at bay, to not show weakness.

*Like me.* "Hey," she said while wiping at her cheek with her free hand, "we're going to get through this. We're Archers, right? We're badasses."

She heard the half-laugh through the phone. "You think I'm a badass too?"

"Hell yes." She pushed away from the wall. "Stronger than me. So much stronger." Her lip quivered as she resisted allowing more tears to flow. "We'll get through this, okay? You and me. We've got this. It may feel like it's us against the world sometimes, but I'd rather you in my corner than anyone else on the planet." And shit, she was crying again, so she pulled the phone away from her face a bit to try and catch her breath.

Once she blinked away the rest of the tears, she brought the phone back to her ear as he said, "Mom?"

"Yeah, sweetie?" she whispered.

"You're the only one I'd want in my corner too." He was quiet before adding, "I love you, Mom."

"I love you so much," she cried.

"Promise me you won't let this interfere with your job. I need you to come home safe." Levi knew she was officially on work business in Mexico now. She'd promised her son that she'd never lie or sugarcoat things with her new job. When she'd revealed her trip was extended after Beckett and Oliver had first shown up that morning, she'd been honest with him. Well, as honest as she could without revealing too many details. He didn't need to know about the cartel.

"I'll promise as long as you promise to call me if you need me. No matter what."

"Deal," he answered. They exchanged a few more words before she ended the call as Mya knocked at her door.

Tossing her phone on the bed, she did her best to shake free her emotions before letting Mya in.

"First order of business, are you okay?" Mya cut straight to it. "And second, hot damn, woman, you look stunning."

Sydney did what she did best—locked her emotions up in a steel cage and tried to change her mood to get through the night.

She swept her hands down her sides, turning this way and that like a showroom model, flaunting the gift that had been delivered to her room twenty minutes ago—a dress with instructions to wear it to dinner. She was exhausted and not in the mood to dress up, but she didn't want to be rude and decline their host's generosity.

And even though her mood was still off despite her best efforts to fake it, Sydney lightly laughed and complied when Mya twirled her finger, motioning for Sydney to spin.

The dress wasn't anything she'd choose for herself, but it was beautiful. The dark blue skirt, decorated with panels of embroidered flowers, was set off by a bright orange sash around her waist, and embroidered flowers adorned the white off-the-shoulder peasant-style blouse. Sydney had let her light blonde hair air dry for a "beachy" look, and it fell in soft waves over her shoulders.

"Damn," Mya repeated, her eyes bright.

"Back at ya." Sydney smiled when Mya took her turn to spin, holding out the sides of her skirt. Their dresses were identical except for the color of the sash. Mya's was red, the bold color fitting for her friend's personality. Spirited. Sexy. Confident. Take charge.

Mya was able to win over everyone—from cartel thugs to New York suits—and in the process, had them confiding their deepest secrets, armed with only a defiant lift of her chin and a sharp gaze.

But she was also kind. Vulnerable. Sensitive. Willing to share her emotions, *unlike* Sydney.

They were both alike in some ways. And yet so, so different at the same time.

"Beckett's going to lose his mind." Mya's words had Sydney playfully scowling.

"And Oliver?" Sydney teased. "Has he seen you in your dress?"

"Not yet. And he can pour on the flattery, but I refuse to forgive him for slapping a hand over my mouth and yanking me into that hole. Even if that was all your doing." Mya's smile had Sydney wanting to call bullshit on her supposed "animosity" for Oliver. "I still can't believe this day happened. I mean, we went from relaxing on the beach to the bottom of a cenote to escape cartel shooters. And everything else since then." Mya walked past her and sat on the bed.

Sydney lifted the skirt of her dress slightly before heading toward Mya.

"So, are you okay?" Mya repeated. "I swear, I could kill Alice. Well, not actually kill her like"—she made a fist and mimed stabbing a knife at her chest—"stabby-stabby. But you know, I'm just . . . pissed."

Sydney let go of the skirt while shaking her head and

smiled because only Mya's cheeky sense of humor could lighten her up at a time like this.

She needed to stitch herself together after talking to Levi, and she had no desire to pull at a thread and find herself unraveled again. "I'm okay. You know me, I don't care about Alice or Seth. Just Levi."

Mya frowned. "When did the Seth-and-Alice thing start up again?"

"I don't know. Levi saw them together a few weeks ago, but he didn't say anything to me until the other day." *And then he saw them again today.* "But Seth's ill-timed and 'important'"—Sydney made air quotes—"phone call makes me think Levi confessed the same news to Seth just today." The achy sensation in her stomach returned. "Levi was so mad at Seth after the affair. It took him a long time to forgive his dad, and I just don't know what this will do to him. Seth promised him that it'd been a mistake four years ago, and he'd never meant for anything to happen with Aunt Alice. Well, that's how Levi referred to her back then."

"He calls her the She-Devil now when he mentions her to me," Mya said with raised eyebrows. "Levi is strong, and he's older now. Plus, he has you."

"Yeah, except I'm here working, and I should be there with him and—"

"Stop." Mya jumped up and gestured with her hands, calling up her Italian ancestry. "Levi loves the work you do. He admires you so much, and I don't think you see that because Seth-the-fucktwat is always in your head."

Mya's spot-on assessment had chills crawling up Sydney's spine, and it felt like she was wearing a corset that had been cinched too tight. Fuck, it hurt more than she cared to admit, but only because her pain was for her son.

"Levi just wants me to focus on being careful during this

job." She pointed to her phone on the bed. "We just talked. He's doing his best to pull himself together, but I know if he thinks I'm falling apart, it'll be harder on him."

"You don't fall apart. So, no worries there." Grabbing hold of Sydney's forearm, Mya continued in a softer tone. "But honestly, ever since you left your dad's company, Levi has been happier. I think he saw how much you hated working at Archer, and he knew it wasn't what you wanted. You know, he thinks of you like you're a Marvel comic book hero in the flesh. He knows you'll get through this new challenge, and he will too."

Sydney set her free hand to her abdomen as a tingling sensation fluttered across her skin.

"Everything will be okay. I promise." Mya lightly squeezed her arm. "I jumped into the . . . well, more like I was *forced* into that cenote today. And if *I* can do that, anything is possible." She winked playfully, trying to lighten Sydney's mood. Something few people could do. "Fate. The Universe. The Cosmos. Whatever you want to call it. Something bigger than us is going on right now, don't you think?"

Sydney nodded, a bit spellbound by her friend's new outlook on life. That book by Joe-something-or-other had really made an impact.

"Let's look at the facts," Mya said, sliding into journalist mode, and began counting by slapping her fingers against her open palm as she listed evidence to defend her stance. "I chose Tulum to meet with my Sinaloa contact." Slap. "Beckett happened to trace his ex's sister to Mexico, and she's connected to the same cartel." Another slap. "Then, while we were on the beach talking about that hot hunk of a cowboy sheriff, he shows up." Slap, slap, slap.

*Hot hunk of a cowboy sheriff?* Sydney smirked as the

image of Beckett wearing only a towel had her pulse pounding. *And that hug. And the almost-kiss.*

"And then, to top it off, this crew of vigilante hotties saves us. Their leader, Martín, happens to know your boss and owes him a favor. And it's his mission to take down the same freaking cartel we're after." Mya opened her palms and lifted her chin to the ceiling as if she had a direct line straight to the Big Man in the sky. "Someone is pulling our strings, leading us on this path."

"When you put it that way . . ."

Mya lowered her gaze to meet Sydney's. "What if this is also fate's way of bringing you and a certain someone together? Have you considered that?"

Before Sydney could respond, there was a knock at the door. "It's us," Beckett announced.

Mya waggled her brows as if to say, *Mmhmm, and here that certain someone is now.* "Shit." She set a hand to her forehead. "My Botox is wearing off if I can do that."

Sydney chuckled. "You're too young for that," she tossed out while starting for the door.

"Hey, it's preventative. Just planning ahead."

Sydney looked back and smiled before opening the door.

Beckett and Oliver stood on the porch, and it appeared Martín had provided them with new clothes as well. Unlike the traditional Mexican dresses she and Mya were wearing, they wore khaki linen pants, button-down shirts—Beckett in black and Oliver in blue—and loafers.

Sydney swallowed as her gaze connected with Beckett's a moment later. They remained quietly studying each other, and it took Mya nudging Sydney in the back to "get a move on" for Sydney to budge.

"Hm. I guess you're capable of cleaning up nicely," Mya commented, joining Sydney on the porch. She had to assume

Mya was teasing Oliver, but how could Sydney look anywhere other than at Beckett?

She freed herself from his eyes only to trail them down the column of his tan throat to where the top two buttons of his shirt were open.

"And did you even bother to shower?" Oliver jabbed. "Looks like you've still got some river mud on your neck there."

Oliver reached toward Mya, then laughed when she swatted his arm away.

"I guess we should head to dinner," Sydney forced out when her attention resettled on Beckett's dark, incredibly piercing gaze.

"Right," Mya said in a cheery tone, then stepped off the porch, leaving Oliver behind.

Sydney and Beckett stood locked in place, staring at each other as if a Disney fairy godmother had cast a spell over them.

*What is wrong with me?*

Beckett blinked and drew a hand over his sexy, scruff-covered jaw. "You're . . ." He cleared his throat and brought that masculine hand around to the back of his neck. "Absolutely beautiful." The sweet sincerity of his tone did nothing to overshadow the dark, hungry look in his eyes that said he wanted to make her *his*.

She smiled her thanks. "You look quite handsome yourself." That was an understatement, and it was taking everything in her not to walk her fingers up the buttons of his shirt and free them one by one.

"Are you ready?" O*r we can stay here staring at each other, knowing we have insane sexual chemistry we shouldn't act on?*

He nodded and offered her his hand. *Ladies first.* She'd

grown used to and was okay with things like opening doors for herself. The days of genteel manners were long gone for the most part, and she'd forgotten what it was like to be treated like a lady. Beckett was proving to be a true Southern gentleman. *A gentleman who could hopefully turn savage in the bedroom.*

She joined Beckett on the trail, and they walked side by side, hanging ten or so feet back behind Oliver and Mya, who were arguing about sports. Of course. Why not? *Only Mya.*

"Football is big in Alabama, right?" Sydney asked Beckett, trying her hand at small talk.

He peeked over at her, an easy smile on his face. "That's one way of putting it."

"Thought so." She returned his smile before looking ahead. The sun hadn't quite set, but the canopy of towering trees cocooning their path made it seem darker.

"And you grew up in . . .?" he asked.

"Born in Danbury, Connecticut. Bounced back and forth between Connecticut and New York City as a kid. I met Mya and . . ." *Alice.* She cringed at the thought. *Levi and I will be okay,* she reminded herself. "I met her in Manhattan. Our dads went to school together."

"You don't have a city accent," he commented. "Not really."

"I guess it's because I traveled a lot growing up. Summers in Europe usually." *And stop there.* She didn't want to remind him she came from wealth. She wasn't sure why it'd bother her if he thought of her as some snob. She was far from it. Hell, she barely owned any brand names, it wasn't her thing. "LA didn't erase *your* accent, I see."

"Ha. Yeah, no, I guess there's no getting rid of the Bama in me."

"And you would probably never want to leave Alabama

again?" Beckett's steps slowed at her question, and she realized maybe it sounded as though she'd asked him, *Would you leave your home for love?*

"I, um."

"You two okay back there?" Mya called out, turning to the side while still walking, preventing Beckett from having to answer.

"We're good," Sydney responded as Oliver snatched Mya's elbow to keep her from falling when she tripped on her dress.

"They're better than you." Oliver chuckled as Mya faced forward.

"To answer your question," Beckett began a moment later, "I don't know."

Sydney kept her focus on the path ahead, unsure if she could look at him right now without tripping. Physically falling. Mentally too, maybe. "Oh."

"So." That one word from Beckett filled the bit of quiet between them after she'd dropped that uncomfortable "oh" into the night air. "You, uh, went to West Point. How was that?"

Quick subject change. And a conversation she wasn't quite sure how to navigate either. "It was okay, I guess. I owed the Army five years after I graduated, but technically I only served four." She had no intention of going into the hows and whys, at least not tonight.

"And Gray?"

*Ohhh. That's where you want to take this?* "He was in his last year there when we met. Pretty sure he proposed because of pre-deployment jitters."

"He *proposed*?"

## CHAPTER FIFTEEN

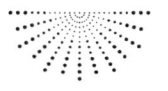

Beckett stopped in his tracks, momentarily stunned by Sydney's rather offhanded comment, and his pulse skyrocketed in anticipation of what she might say next.

*A marriage proposal?* And while nearly two decades had passed, it was pretty damn clear Gray was still hung up on her. Who'd blame the guy?

"I turned him down," Sydney clarified. "Back then, Gray knew me as Sydney Bowman. I didn't want anyone at West Point knowing about my family." She wet her lips and dropped her eyes to the skirt of her dress. "He had no idea."

He understood withholding the truth from her classmates, he supposed. But from a guy she dated? Why not come clean? It wasn't his place to ask her, though, so he kicked at a stone with the toe of his loafer and tried to wrap his head around what this new information meant. What would he do with it?

"Gray still has feelings for you," he found himself admitting aloud. "I saw how he looked at you at Savanna and Griffin's wedding last month." Like he'd wanted to rip her dress off and devour her—same as Beckett. But until Oliver had spilled the news, he sure as hell hadn't known she and Gray had a history. "And I know what you said, but—"

"But what?"

He returned his attention to her, pausing at her luscious lips for a moment before journeying up to her bold green gaze.

He'd nearly kissed her back in the bungalow before Gray had called. *But we didn't go through with it, which means we're on the same page.* He shouldn't worry about her past or who she'd once shared a bed with. Nor who she might share a bed with tomorrow or the next day.

So, then, why'd it feel as though they were both standing there wanting to do a lot more than just breathe in the same air?

"Nothing." He opened a palm, an offer to continue walking, but she remained in place. Quietly studying him as if waiting for him to expand on whatever thoughts he'd chosen not to share.

*No, sweetheart, you don't want to hear them. Because they all center around you in my bed, and that's a place we sure as hell can't be.*

"Hey, you two coming?" Oliver hollered, and Beckett forced a smile and nodded.

"Yes," Sydney returned and began moving. Beckett gave her a head start, sensing they needed some space to process whatever awkward moment passed between them.

He trailed behind her, hating the knot forming in his throat and the tight fist-like feeling in his chest. Upon reaching the courtyard, he found Mya and Oliver off to the side of the pool, the skirt of Mya's dress billowing around her as she twirled in a circle and took in the majestic setting.

Maybe years ago, Beckett might have fallen under the

romantic spell of this place, but romance had been dead for him for a long damn time.

He swung his focus to Sydney, in his mind a much more beautiful sight than the tropical flowers surrounding the courtyard and pool.

Standing at the head of a long, rectangular table, she shook the hand of a woman Beckett assumed was Martín's wife, Valentina. He slowly crossed the paver stones to greet their hosts. "*Hola*," he said as he reached to take Valentina's offered hand.

"Nice to meet you," she responded. "Not under these circumstances, of course." After firmly shaking Beckett's hand, she motioned toward Sydney, who now stood at Beckett's side. "Your wife here was just telling us that—"

"We're not married," Beckett and Sydney replied simultaneously, and he peered at her, finding a touch of red inching up the column of her throat. A nervous smile played across her lips before she refocused on their hosts.

*Shy? Really? Hmm.*

"Ah, that's right." Valentina clapped her hands together in front of her face. "How could I forget? My husband already told me that." She reminded Beckett of a younger version of his mother. Already playing matchmaker two seconds into the conversation.

And that reminded him . . .

His mom had flown to LA the day McKenna was born and had disliked Cora from the moment she met her. Honestly, if his mom hadn't been by his side when Cora took off, he probably wouldn't have survived it. He'd been young then, young for a detective at least.

*And I'll be forty-two in June. Damn.*

"You two would make beautiful babies, though, if you

don't mind me saying," Valentina added when neither Sydney nor Beckett had spoken.

"Forgive my wife. She watches too many bachelor reality shows." Martín came up behind Valentina, wrapped his palms over her shoulders, and kissed the top of her head. "I think she secretly wants to leave me for a younger man, and all the men in those shows are in their twenties." He laughed, obviously trying to cut through any awkwardness his wife's comment had created.

"I would never leave him, and he knows that." Valentina looked over her shoulder at Martín and patted his hand. "But he's always busy saving the world." She opened her palms to the sky now and shrugged. "I get bored, what can I say? I have to occupy my time somehow."

"Mmhmm. With young bachelors, eh?" Martín teased while motioning toward the long table, waving over to Oliver and Mya.

Beckett pulled out a chair for Sydney, which seemed to give her pause. She tossed an unsure look his way, squinting her eyes a little as she studied him.

"This isn't chivalry," he said, pitching his voice low enough for her ears only. "Just manners."

"Thank you," she said, allowing him to scoot her chair in farther.

He cleared his throat while rounding the table to sit opposite Sydney, still feeling a bit rattled by Gray's proposal to her years ago.

"Sorry for the circumstances once again, but we're so happy to have guests wearing nice clothes to dinner instead of holstered weapons." Valentina was blunt, and yup, she'd fit in just fine back home at his family's ranch. "Well, I assume you're not carrying a weapon beneath your clothes tonight, are you?" Her gaze met Beckett's from where she sat two seats away from Sydney.

"No, ma'am." He graciously smiled, and they all took turns thanking them again for their hospitality.

"Ah, here's the food," Martín beamed as several members of his staff approached carrying large trays.

Beckett's stomach growled in appreciation at the sight of the dishes placed down the center of the table. Fruit and cheese platters. Beef and pork dishes. Small tapas. A beautiful array of local cuisine. "Thank you for all of this."

Martín gestured to the food. "*Buen provecho.* Dig in."

Oliver didn't hesitate and eagerly began piling up his plate.

"You can always get seconds. You know that, right?" Mya jabbed, but Beckett was too preoccupied with Sydney to inspect Oliver's leaning tower of tapas.

Her plate was empty, eyes zeroed in on the cherries her hand hovered over.

*Cherries?* He thought back to the hotel when she'd told him she'd swapped her cherry-scented perfume for a different one. What was the story there?

She blinked as if emerging from a daze, snatched some grapes and cheese, then busied herself with adding a little of everything to her plate. A woman with an appetite was his kind of girl.

"Not hungry?" she asked, licking her lips as she peered at Beckett's empty plate and picked up her fork. Oh, he was hungry alright, but not for food.

"Starving," he promised, hoping the desire that'd reared up again wasn't too obvious as she popped a grape into her mouth.

Yeah, he wanted to kiss those perfect lips.

No, he *needed* to kiss her.

Every part of her.

He wanted to lay her out on the table and fucking devour her. Feast on every inch of that perfectly silky skin before sliding between her legs and—

"You may not be married, but you two are lovers, no?"

And just like that, Valentina's question shocked him back to the fact he and Sydney weren't alone. And he'd been living in an *If things were different* alternate reality in his head.

But things weren't different. He was still a small-town sheriff living in Alabama, a single dad raising his daughter while managing a cargo hold's worth of baggage. And he was in Mexico because of said baggage.

"I'm sorry, what?" He set the black linen napkin on his lap and placed his hand on top of it, trying to will his dick down, then focused on Valentina.

Valentina lifted a brow. "If you don't mind me speaking so candidly?"

"She will anyway." Martín smiled and reached for a bottle of wine. "Apologies in advance."

"Well," Valentina began despite the fact neither he nor Sydney had acquiesced. She accepted a glass of wine from her husband before continuing, "I know passion when I see it. You look at that woman the way my husband looks at me. Like you want to . . . well, you know."

"Like I said, apologies." Martín chuckled as Beckett chanced a look at Sydney.

He had no clue what to say, and Sydney's silence suggested she was in the same boat, so he reached for his bottled water and gulped a few heavy swallows.

"How about we eat, *mi amor*? And leave them alone about their personal lives," Martín suggested.

"What? Talk about the cartel instead?" Valentina sighed. "He is obsessed with them. In taking them down, I should say. He's also not allowed to work on Sundays—God's day of rest. But I allowed him to make an exception when we learned of the situation. Plus, Carter Dominick called, and when that man calls . . ."

"You've met Carter?" Oliver asked before taking a bite of food, and Beckett finally worked his heart rate down to normal levels to get some food on his plate as well.

"*Claro que sí.* Carter is a unique man. He reminds me a bit of my husband. A wild card and not much of a rule follower." Valentina smiled before taking a sip of her wine.

"Carter is that," Oliver remarked.

The bottle of red made its way down the table, and Beckett decided he'd have a small pour. Maybe it'd help ease his nerves. Jesse and Ivy were safe for now, so he felt a little less guilty about enjoying a nice meal. Plus, Martín saved their asses earlier, and he told himself it'd be disrespectful to decline their generosity.

"And you all work with Carter?" Martín sliced his pork chop with a sharp blade. The meat was drizzled in a dark sauce, and it was calling Beckett's name, so he finally added a serving to his own plate.

"Just the two of us." Oliver motioned to Sydney before focusing on Mya across from him. "She may join our team as well."

"Ah, I see." Martín fixed his attention on Beckett as if waiting to hear the reason he'd accompanied the others.

Valentina set her eyes on Beckett as well when he remained silent. The woman was as curious as Mya. "I'm, well, here for . . ."

"He's helping us track the cartel," Sydney spoke up. "He has some inside sources."

Beckett's shoulders fell at her words, and he shot her a small nod of thanks for having his back.

Thankfully, Martín changed the subject and began talking about his ancestors and the history of the Mayan people.

Twenty or so minutes later, music began to pour from the speakers positioned around the courtyard area, and Valentina stood and twirled her finger in the air. "Time to dance. I love to salsa, but my husband doesn't like the exchanging-partners aspect of that dance. He's a bit possessive that way. Perhaps tonight we just dance however our bodies feel like it?"

"I'm not really up for dancing." Oliver patted his stomach as if being full was why he had no interest in dancing. Doubtful.

"It will help you rest later," Valentina insisted while taking her husband's hand. "Dancing frees your mind so you can think better tomorrow when it's a new day. Every tomorrow is a chance for new beginnings, *si*?"

*New beginnings?* God, he'd give anything for that. But he was still haunted by his past. By Cora and the damage she'd left in her wake.

"Maybe one or two dances, then?" Mya politely smiled at Valentina. "I don't need a partner."

"Oh, don't be silly." Valentina shook her head and began looking around the courtyard. "There are plenty of men here that would love nothing more than to help you free your mind if you'd prefer not to mix business with pleasure by dancing with Oliver," she added.

"No, that won't be necessary." Oliver was at Mya's side before she could object. Mya may have driven him nuts, but it seemed he didn't want her driving any other man crazy either.

"That's what I thought." Valentina winked. "And now, you two?"

"Us?" Sydney pointed at her chest as she slowly rose from the table, leaving Beckett the last to stand. "As in us-us?" she added while tipping her chin in his direction.

"Prove me wrong." Valentina smiled brightly. "As Sasha Azevedo said, '*To dance is to be in tune with the steps of life.*' If you two are not in sync," she added with a shrug, "then perhaps you really have no chemistry."

*Chemistry isn't our problem.* That fact, that *reality* was a kick in the nuts because he'd never wanted a woman this badly in his life. He'd never felt anything so visceral, so raw and downright primal before. The savage need to gather Sydney in his arms . . . *and* at a time like this? What the hell was happening to him?

*Pueblo Mágico,* he recalled the man's words from the bar before they'd been shot at earlier. *It's just a magical place*, he rationalized. No other explanation.

When his eyes locked with Sydney's again, he called bullshit on himself. It wasn't merely the magic of Mexico. *It's her.*

He circled the table and offered Sydney his hand, deciding to let her choose whether she wanted to dance. She accepted his palm without hesitation, and her warm skin against his already hot flesh quickened the beats of his heart.

They silently walked toward the open area at the side of the dining table where Mya and Oliver were already dancing.

He was more of a country, jazz, or blues fan, but when he set his hands on Sydney's hips, he realized they could be in complete silence, and he wouldn't notice. He'd still move with her.

"You good?" he asked as she draped her forearms over his shoulders, inching closer.

"I think so." She wet her lips, and the heat glowing in her green eyes obliterated all rational thought.

"Jesus." The word slipped free as he pulled her tighter against him.

"I'm Sydney, actually," she whispered against his ear,

lingering for a moment before gently gliding her cheek against his to meet his gaze once again.

Unsure of what to say—because every ounce of blood in his body was on a journey south—he slid his hands around her back and eased them into a slow, sensual dance. On instinct, he bent his knees and pulled her closer so when she swiveled her hips, her sex rubbed against his. It was torture. Sweet, hot torture.

Her hands slipped from his shoulders to his biceps, her short nails digging into him as she arched back and tipped her head heavenward to peer at the starry sky.

Beckett took the opportunity to skate one palm along the smooth column of her throat down the center of her body while supporting her lower back with his other.

She clutched his biceps for support when she shifted upright, staring at him breathlessly. They stayed like that for one quiet moment, both locked in place, and he did his best not to kiss her right there in front of everyone.

She finally began moving again, and they did a piss-poor job of proving Valentina wrong.

Sydney gathered the fabric of her skirt in one hand, and he couldn't stop himself from hooking her leg and pinning her knee to his waist, drawing her body even tighter against his. He kept hold of her back as she dipped, and he stared at her tits that strained against the dress in the process.

He had no idea how long they danced, but at some point, the music stopped, and they were both breathless and sweaty.

Without letting go of Sydney, he swiveled his gaze to find Valentina at his side, an amused expression on her face. Oliver and Mya were gone. To bed? *With each other?* He doubted that.

"I would say you two found dance partners in each other. You dance beautifully together," Valentina commented, then chewed on her lip a little as if she were watching a reality show come to life in front of her. "It's getting late. Maybe you two get some sleep, *sí*? Your friends left a few minutes ago, not that you noticed."

He released his hold on Sydney as he replied, "Thank you for dinner and your hospitality."

"Yes, thank you," Sydney said, her voice strained.

Valentina simply winked, set a hand on his shoulder, and patted twice before leaning in and whispering, "She's special. I can tell. Don't lose her."

"What'd she say to you?" Sydney asked once Valentina and her husband left them alone in the courtyard.

Beckett faced her. "Nothing you don't already know."

Sydney's cheeks were flushed, and she swiped a hand over her collarbone, damp with sweat. "How long were we dancing?"

"I have no clue." He stole a look at the dinner table, finding it already cleared. He really had been lost to everything and everyone around them while they'd danced.

And he sure as hell had never danced like that before.

"Shall we?" He opened his palm, gesturing toward the path.

They walked the trail in silence, no small talk. *Or* heavy talk.

But his thoughts were racing. Body still on edge with need.

When they reached her small porch, he followed her to the door. *Just say goodnight and go.*

Sydney opened her door, then turned around, keeping the door propped open with her back. "So."

"So." He smiled and pocketed his hands, worried he'd reach for her, and he had no excuse to touch her again. No music. No Valentina pushing them to check if they were in sync.

"Tonight was unexpected." Her soft, sweet tone did nothing to stamp out the burning lust coursing through his veins.

"I'd say today, overall, has been . . . well, it's been unique."

She angled her head, eyes journeying over his chest. "You're hot."

He chuckled. "Am I?" But he knew she was referring to his linen shirt clinging to his frame from sweat. "I need another shower before I sleep, but I'm worried about Cha Cha."

"Cha Cha?" Her beautiful smile had his heartbeat pounding harder and harder.

He removed a hand from his pocket to point to the trees. "He's the little spider monkey I named earlier, and he was creeping on me through the window."

"And you named him Cha Cha?"

"That's the sound he makes with his teeth." He shrugged. "Anyways, there's no roof over the shower, so I get the feeling Cha Cha will be watching me. Not a fan of that idea."

Sydney laughed and folded her arms as if she were chilly, which wasn't possible, but . . . "There goes my shower." She captured her lower lip between her teeth for a second, and realizing what she'd done, quickly freed it. "Goodnight, then."

She expelled a deep, heavy breath and started to turn. Before thinking twice, he withdrew his hand from his pocket and circled her wrist, drawing her back around.

Her gaze fell to where he held her just before he gently pulled her against him, and her door clicked closed.

"I'm going to kiss you now." His tone was harsher than he'd meant, his body driven by insane need.

"Telling me so I don't kick you in the balls?"

"Mmhmm." He released her wrist, captured her cheeks between his palms, and slowly drew himself closer to her.

"Okay, then." And at that, he guided his mouth to hers.

They shared a breath as her lips parted and she offered her tongue, and fuck, he took it.

Her hands went to his chest before sliding around to the back of his neck, and he deepened the kiss even more.

Every part of him was on fire, their tongues dancing as erotically as their bodies had moved out in that courtyard.

He broke free from their kiss to trail his lips to the shell of her ear, sliding a hand down to cup her breast at the same time. She gasped as he gently rolled her beaded nipple between his fingers, and fuck if that sound didn't go straight to his dick.

"More," she pleaded, grinding against his painfully hard erection.

"Not yet," he admonished, nipping at her earlobe, unable to hold back the drops of precum as she moaned in pleasure.

He silenced her with his mouth, kissing her fervently again, and she walked backward, hitting the door.

Breathing hard, he let go of her breast and set both palms on the doorframe, resting his forehead against hers.

"Sydney," he whispered. "We should—"

"I know," she cried in return. "We shouldn't," she added in a defeated voice. "I know."

That was *not* where he was going to go with his sentence. But he channeled his control and gathered his strength so he could pull away from her. If she wanted to stop, then so be it.

He tenderly kissed her mouth one more time before pushing away from the doorframe.

She was panting a little, and so was he.

He needed to corral the animal inside him. *Walk away. Go.* "Goodnight, Sydney," he said in a gravelly voice.

"I wish . . ." She shut her eyes.

He tipped his head, waiting for her to finish.

When she remained quiet, he forced himself to leave, knowing he had a date with his dick in that outdoor shower.

Damn, did he wish things were different.

## CHAPTER SIXTEEN

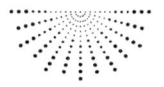

"What is that man doing to me?" Sydney murmured as she stared at her reflection in the bathroom mirror, her heart still racing from their kiss.

No man had ever made her feel so sexy. So desired. So *enough.*

She combed her fingers through her blonde hair, then lifted it off the back of her neck with one hand and fanned her skin with the other. Between the humid jungle air and the steamy dances with Beckett, she was "glistening," Mya's word for sweating.

Glancing over at the shower to her left, images of a naked Beckett standing beneath the spray, eyes closed in pleasure while stroking his cock, played through her mind.

She'd need to get herself off tonight, or she'd never get to sleep. She dragged a palm down her face because who was she kidding? No amount of touching herself would alleviate the unbearable ache between her thighs. Not while the man she wanted to handle that job was right next door.

She smoothed her palm along her collarbone, remembering the feel of his hands on her body when they'd danced. The way that man moved was sinful. But the way their bodies moved together was something altogether inexplicable. Valentina had been right about them being in sync. She and Beckett danced as though they'd done it thousands of times, like their bodies were made for one another, which was crazy.

Insane or not, she couldn't deny it. *Then why am I fighting it? I deserve even a piece of happiness, don't I?* And after the call from Seth and his news . . .

Every molecule in her body demanded she run to Beckett and surrender herself to him completely, something she'd never done with another man. But no one had ever made her feel like this before. Seth had *never* made her heart race like Beckett had done with just one sensual look.

*Can we have one night? Can I be that wild, reckless girl I once was?* She shook her head at her thoughts. Being with Beckett didn't feel reckless though. It felt *right*.

Before she knew it, Sydney was standing outside his bungalow and knocking on the door. The only answer was the sound of running water in the outdoor shower. She assumed he'd locked the door to the shower, but she told herself if he'd left the front door unlocked, it was fate, or whatever Mya wanted to call it, and she'd go inside.

She closed her eyes and set her hand on the knob, hoping for fate to be on her side as she slowly turned the handle.

*Fate.* She heard Mya's voice in her head as the door swung open. She removed her sandals and stepped inside, locking the door behind her before padding across the room toward the outdoor shower. A privacy wall separated it from the bedroom, so she couldn't see him yet, but the sound of running water let her know he was still out there.

She removed the sash and unzipped her dress, allowing it

to fall to the floor. The breeze from the overhead fan sent tiny chills across her exposed flesh.

*Beckett's already seen me topless. Twice*, she reminded herself, hoping to calm her nerves. This was the least dangerous thing she'd done that day, so why did it feel like the most? *Because you're putting your heart on your sleeve, and that's not something you've ever done.*

She rounded the privacy wall in nothing but her underwear, fully unprepared for the sight before her.

Beckett stood beneath the spray with his head hung low, hands braced against one of the wooden exterior privacy walls. The position gave Sydney a moment to inconspicuously admire his toned frame, from his broad shoulders down to his unbelievably delicious ass. He was one hundred percent cover model-worthy. Yet, there he was in the flesh. Golden and sexy before her.

"Beckett," she called out in a breathy voice.

His back muscles flinched and drew taut at the sound of his name. Without freeing his hands, he slowly turned his head, but she wasn't in his peripheral view, so she walked into the doorframe to get closer.

Once she was in sight, he quietly pushed away from the wall but didn't yet turn to face her. He tore his hands through his dark hair, slicking the wet locks back before reaching for the shower knob and turning off the water.

"It's only fair I get to see you since you've seen me partially naked so many times today," she said, hoping like hell he still wanted her as much as she wanted him.

"I'm more than partially naked. You sure you want me to face you?" She heard the deep rasp in his tone and noticed his hand was still on the shower knob as if it were anchoring him in place.

"Would it be better if I'm fully naked too?" she suggested.

"Sydney." The way he'd said her name wasn't a, *Are you sure you want to do this?* He seemed to recognize the kind of woman she was and that she'd never do something she didn't want to.

No, his "Sydney" was more of a warning of what was to come. That he was hanging on the edge, and once he faced her, he'd struggle to walk away like he'd done after their kiss.

But something about him reassured her that he could be on the verge of an orgasm, and if she said stop, he'd listen.

"Turn around," she commanded, hooking her thumbs at the sides of her lace panties.

He brought both hands to his sides before turning in place to face her fully. She dropped her gaze to his feet and worked her way up his toned legs and to . . .

She gulped as she took in his fullness. The sheer girth of the man coupled with his size sent a wave of heat to her core, and she clenched her thighs in anticipation. When she finally managed to focus on his face, she realized why he'd yet to budge.

He was waiting for her eyes. For her permission.

"Fair is fair," she finally managed while turning her back to give him a view of her ass since she'd had a long look at his moments ago.

She slid the nude-colored sheer panties down her thighs before bending forward a bit to unhook them from her ankles and toeing them to the side.

"Are you sure you want me to turn around?" she teased, catching his eyes from over her shoulder once upright.

He cocked his head to the side, a nearly dangerous look burning in his eyes. "You know I do," he murmured darkly.

She barely had time to face him again before he came at

her full force. Within seconds, he had her back inside the bungalow against that privacy partition, arms pinned over her head, wrists linked together in his firm grip.

He kneaded his fingers in her flesh before sliding his palm up and down the back of her thigh. His touch was electric, each stroke of his hand a reminder he was running the show. And just when she thought she'd have to beg for more, he hooked her leg around his hips, drawing her pussy right against his flesh.

With a tight jaw, his fierce gaze connected with hers, he said, "I don't have protection, sweetheart."

*Ohhhh.* Now she understood his hesitation to continue.

"But—"

"I can't get pregnant. Tubes tied," she interjected. "And I promise you I'm clean." She hadn't had sex without a condom since her divorce, but the idea of it happening with Beckett had her pulse fluttering even more.

"And *I* can't get you pregnant," he said, dropping the surprising news on her while maintaining his semi-firm grip on her wrists and leg. "I'm clean as well."

"You don't want more kids either?" This was not the sexiest conversation to have, but she didn't go around having unprotected sex, so this was also uncharted territory.

His brows slanted as he leaned in closer to her face, his chest tight to hers, and she shimmied, the friction of their close bodies making her ravenous for this man to fill her. "Well, I don't want another *baby.*"

*How about a thirteen-year-old teenager?* Her thoughts almost shocked her into asking him to release her so she could run. Because where had that come from? *This can only be about sex.*

But there wasn't a chance in hell she would run. She needed him right now.

"So, we're good." She parted her lips as an invitation, and this time he didn't hesitate.

He brought his mouth to hers, making her feel . . . complete?

Her wild need had her yanking her wrists against his grasp, and he let her go without resistance. She gripped his shoulders and hoisted herself up, wrapping her other leg around his hip and grinding against him as he pinned her against the wall.

Beckett kept one hand firmly beneath her ass and set the other against the wall over her shoulder, leaning in to whisper in her ear. "There's something I've been thinking about doing to you since last month."

*Since April? Since Griffin's wedding, really?*

He lowered her feet to the floor, then surprised her by whirling her around, pinning her chest to the wall. She set her palms alongside her body as he trailed a hand over the curve of her spine before cupping her ass with both hands and sinking down to his knees. Her eyes closed in anticipation, and a moment later she felt his lips along her backside while he worked one hand between her legs and up her sex.

"You have a beautiful body," he murmured against her skin, rubbing his fingers against her clit in tiny circles before thrusting them inside her. She clenched at the intrusion, milking his fingers as if they were his cock, desperate to have him fill her. To let him take her however he wanted.

"I'm thirty-seven going on thirty-eight," she cried between moans with each deep plunge. She wasn't insecure, but she knew she wasn't a young co-ed either. She was a mom with stretch marks and . . . "I'm—"

"You're fucking perfect," he finished before grabbing hold of her hips and urging her around.

He looked up at her from his knees, leaned forward,

parting her sex with his tongue, and she nearly saw stars as he flicked against her sensitive spot.

Her hands fell to his shoulders, desperately needing the support as her legs grew weaker with every stroke of his tongue over her flesh. She'd gotten a Brazilian wax in preparation for her trip, and her smooth skin heightened every nip, lick, and suck as he devoured her pussy.

*Holy hell.*

She tipped her head back and buried her short nails into his shoulders as she cried in ecstasy, coming harder than she ever remembered before. A wave of pure bliss washed over her, and she nearly collapsed to the floor.

Beckett slowly stood and cocked his head. "Now about the other two orgasms."

"Other two?" she whispered, feeling a bit drunk.

"Three 'impossible' orgasms," he repeated what she'd nearly forgotten she'd said back in the hotel.

He surprised her by scooping her into his arms and carried her to the bed, then gently set her at the center. But he didn't join her. He remained standing there, slowly running his hand along his length while watching her.

She brought her hands to her breasts and teased her nipples, letting her knees fall open in the process, and his nostrils flared. "Why are you waiting?"

"Giving your body time to recover before I make you come again," he said, his tone low and deep.

Her eyes fell to his cock. "Then let me taste you."

She started to sit, pinning her knees together, but he shook his head and commanded, "No. Stay there." A smile formed on his lips. "I'm waiting for number three. And, sweetheart, if you wrap those lips around me, I will fuck that mouth of yours and come down your throat."

Her body recharged at his dirty words, at the prospect of more.

"Demanding, aren't you?" But damn, did she like it. In the bedroom, this man could control her all he wanted, and she'd let him. All day. Every day. Forever.

*Forever?* She inhaled sharply at the thought and quickly lost track of her wild ideas when Beckett went to her discarded dress and retrieved the orange sash.

He slid the silk between his hands and tugged, probably testing its strength, as he approached, and she quivered with anticipation of what he might do with that sash.

Beckett prowled onto the bed, muscles flexing as his powerful body straddled her. Raising the sash, he arched an eyebrow, silently asking her permission.

"Yes, please," she whispered.

Her hands raced over his chest, and she smoothed a palm over the bit of hair there. But he stole her wrists within a moment and began to bind them to the headboard.

*This is new.* And who would have thought her chivalrous gentleman liked to . . . *Okay, well, he is a sheriff. I'm sure he could restrain me in more ways than I can count.*

Once he checked her hands were secure, he leaned in and pressed his mouth to hers, and she tasted herself on his lips. Another first.

"You okay?" he asked, his eyes momentarily turning from dark to caring.

"More than okay," she promised while arching her back as a request for him to touch her.

He smiled and set another sensual kiss on her lips before leaning back on his heels, but he managed to keep his weight from crushing her. His dick was so close to her pussy that if she just shifted a little, she could have him now. No waiting.

She gasped when he leaned in and nipped at her tit,

swiping his tongue around the sensitive flesh before giving her other breast the same treatment.

Beckett took his time with her nipples before he began trailing his lips down her body, shifting his weight in the process as his lips traveled farther south. He kissed her everywhere but where she wanted, leaving her aching and begging for more.

"Please." She tugged at her restraints with overwhelming need as he dragged his scruff along her inner thighs.

He surprised her by lifting both her legs and tossing them over his shoulders, sinking his mouth onto her flesh, chasing after orgasm number two.

Chills coasted over her body as she gave herself to this man. Every piece of her. Gave him her trust by surrendering to him. *Submitting.* Something that should've been unnatural, and yet, in this moment, it was anything but.

As he worked her over again with his mouth, delivering one pleasurable sensation after another, her fingertips curled into her palms, desperate for their bodies to connect as one.

"Beckett, I've never begged anyone for anything in my life," she said between breathy moans as he kept punishing her in the best possible way, "but please, for the love of God, fuck me."

He went still, and she looked down, witnessing his full lips hovering near her sex, a wild look in his eyes.

"Please," she nearly cried again, tugging at the headboard. "I need to feel you."

He must've heard the emotion choking her voice because he nodded, and her body trembled with relief that he was giving in to her plea.

Beckett shifted on top of her and pulled at the knot of the sash, freeing her hands. When she reached between their bodies and slid her hand along his length, he let out a low, guttural sound.

"You'll destroy me if you keep touching me like that," he hissed while looking her in the eyes. Still holding his weight over her, his biceps flexed.

"What do you think you've been doing to me?" She nudged the head of his cock at her center.

His eyes locked with hers, his jaw still strained. And then he did what she'd begged for him to do.

He thrust deep inside her.

# CHAPTER SEVENTEEN

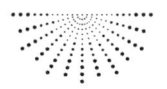

Beckett filled Sydney in one swift movement, not expecting such an intense reaction to strike him the moment their bodies connected. He held his body against hers, letting go of a shaky breath while giving her time to adjust.

She clung to his biceps and remained motionless as well. Not shimmying or moving. Not begging him to take her harder.

They stared at each other in silence, time stretching out. He'd never believed in the idea of soulmates, but he swore something inside him, something woven into the fabric of his being, felt familiar with Sydney the moment their bodies joined as one. It was as if they shared the same energy. The same heartbeat. The same breath. Always had.

*What in blazes is wrong with me?* He pumped his hips once, making sure she was ready for him, and at the sound of her responding moan, he let loose.

They quickly found their rhythm, and she gave as good as she got, clamping her pussy around him so tightly it was borderline painful. But that only triggered him to fuck her harder, the bedframe squeaking with each snap of his hips. He snaked a hand around her ass to steady her body and keep her head from colliding with the metal headboard.

He was teetering on the edge of his control when she arched her back, lifting it off the bed, chanting broken versions of his name.

The need to claim her, to mark her as his and pour himself into her tight little body was going to destroy him if he didn't slow down soon. He shifted his hand and dragged it up her torso, quickly pinching her peaked nipple to the point of pain, and the moment her eyes shot open, he let go, allowing the pleasure to wash over her body. Judging by her gasp and the flutter of her eyelashes, she more than enjoyed it.

How was it possible for this woman to have such a hold on him after so little time? Yet, he knew without a shadow of a doubt Sydney Archer had wrecked him for anyone else. There could be no one else after her. Anyone else would just be a sad imitation of her perfection.

Her eyes glistened as if she were on the same emotional page as him, and she was hanging on to her control, not yet ready to give in to ecstasy.

Without breaking contact, he guided them into a seated position, her legs firmly around his body and her tits pressed to his chest as she began rocking up and down, claiming his cock.

He leaned in and sucked her bottom lip as she worked herself on his hard length, taking control to find her climax. And when she began breathing hard and fast, he knew she was about to come.

"Right there. Oh God, yes, that's it." Up and down. Up and fucking down this woman went. Harder and harder. Slamming down on his cock.

He did everything in his power not to come as she cried and moaned from the pleasure, coming all over him. When her breaths finally began evening out, he cupped her chin and drew her mouth to his.

"Your turn," she whispered, easing off him in one fluid motion. She briefly positioned herself on all fours before lowering her chest to the bed and sliding her hands up to her ass, giving him the perfect view of her glistening pussy.

*Mine.*

One hand pinned her wrists together at the base of her spine while the other gripped her hip, and he slammed inside her. She cried out at the contact, her moans muffled against the comforter. He made it about sixty seconds before she fell to pieces, that third orgasm hitting her in record time, and thank fuck for that because he couldn't hold back any longer.

"I'm going to come inside you, Sydney," he rasped as his hips began to stutter. "I'm going to fill this pussy up with my cum and watch it run down your legs. That's what you do to me." He quickly brought both hands to her hips and thrust into her one final time. "Fuuuck."

His body went lax after he came deep inside her, barely able to see straight as he tried to rally his thoughts and get his breathing back on track.

Beckett bent forward and set a kiss to the skin between her shoulder blades. He pulled out forgetting they'd leave a sticky mess all over the bed. She cupped herself, trying to keep the mess at bay. He hadn't thought this through.

"One second." They didn't need Valentina to see physical proof she'd been right about them.

He grabbed a hand towel and rushed back to the bed, surprised to hear Sydney chuckling. "I bet this part doesn't make it into romance books."

"Or the fact I lasted less than two minutes," he said, laughing now too.

"Aw." Sydney stood and cleaned herself with the towel.

"You lasted longer than that. I did ride the hell out of you before we switched positions." She sauntered to the bathroom to discard the towel and freshen up.

When she came around the privacy wall, her stunning body striding toward him . . . did she have any clue how sexy she looked?

"Well, that was . . ." She joined him on the bed and rolled to her back, setting a palm on her abdomen, and he shifted to his side next to her.

"Next time, we'll go for four," he said, pulling her closer.

"You really do like a challenge, don't you?" she teased.

"I just like you." He closed one eye at the realization of what he'd allowed to spill free. The truth. A truth he hadn't quite understood.

"I wouldn't have guessed." She smiled and playfully chewed on her lip, purposely taunting him.

"I can show you just how much soon." He smiled, loving *this* feeling. Not quite definable, but a hundred percent perfect. "But I'm over forty. And *not* a romance novel hero," he added. "I'll need more time before I can get it up again. But that doesn't mean I can't pleasure you in the shower first."

## CHAPTER EIGHTEEN

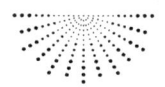

BECKETT DRAGGED A PALM DOWN HIS FACE, TRYING TO WAKE himself up. "Did I actually sleep?" he murmured, grateful to see Sydney still lying next to him. She had one leg wrapped around the black sheet, covering only part of her lower body, but her breasts were on display. The sight of this beautiful woman in his bed had him thinking maybe they'd go another round. Because damn.

"Are you surprised? After the night we had?" Sydney turned to her side, untangled her legs from the sheet, and draped it over her body. He was buck naked on top of the bedding; it was too hot to be covered by anything.

He fluffed his pillow and slid one arm under it as he faced her. "I guess you were the cure I needed for my insomnia." *But what about tonight? Tomorrow night?* He wasn't sure what would happen next between them, and he was kicking himself for thinking about that given the reason they were in Mexico.

"Well, I've heard people usually sleep better after sex, so I'm not sure I can take all the credit." The somberness in her tone took him by surprise. "Of course, I haven't exactly been testing that theory . . ."

"Good." He hadn't intended to say that out loud, but the thought of her in bed with another man didn't sit well. "It's been quite a long time for me," he shared, because at that point, why not?

They now knew every intimate detail of each other's bodies. And she was the first woman, outside of his family, to know the sordid details about Cora. He'd given her a lot more than the bullet point version of his life, and she hadn't run away. She was still there in his bed.

She lifted her gaze toward the orange sash still hanging loosely from the headboard behind them. "You surprised me with that."

"Surprised myself." He remembered her eyes wide and on him while he carefully bound her wrists before covering her body in kisses.

"Don't tie people up often, I take it? Not that it's any of my business." Her surprisingly shy tone of voice and dilated pupils betrayed a hint of nervousness. She was lying. She did care. And for whatever reason, he liked that she cared.

"Only those I arrest, so no, not in the bedroom." *That was new for me.* "You're the first, and I guess I got lost in the moment."

"So, um, what happened with your date from the wedding, then? If you haven't had sex in a while." She rolled her lips inward and shook her head as though chiding herself. "Not my business again."

"I think it is," he answered with a firm nod, reaching out to lightly caress her arm. "After the night we shared, I think whatever you want to know is very much your business."

Normally, he was a closed book. Even after spending the night with a woman. No bacon and eggs for breakfast and certainly no deep conversations over coffee or in the bed. But there he was, wanting to do anything and everything with Sydney, even if that felt like an impossibility.

As she remained quiet, probably considering his words, he circled his finger over the soft skin around her belly button, skimming back and forth along a faded scar above her navel, and then realized he hadn't yet answered her wedding date question.

"It was our first and last date. Because I saw you there in that backless dress, and you took my fucking breath away. I wasn't about to screw one woman while thinking of another." Maybe he'd overshared, but Sydney deserved the truth.

"Ohhh? And do I know this mysterious other woman?"

"You may know her, yes. And I happened to spend some time between her legs where she seemed to get to know God too."

She laughed and tossed him a quick, sexy look before her attention returned to the thatched roof ceiling. "I have a confession, then."

"Well, this should be good."

She faced him again, laying her head on the pillow. "One of those books Savanna gave me was about a sheriff. And I may have pictured you while reading it. And possibly while touching myself *after* reading." Her sexy tone and the way she looked at him had his body waking again.

The idea of this woman fingering her clit while imagining them together even before he'd shown up to Tulum . . .

*Damn.*

A few seconds passed before his gaze returned to her belly button. "How long ago did you have this pierced?"

She touched her navel and smiled.

"There's a story there, I take it?"

"Perhaps." Her smile dissolved though. "You really want to know?"

"I do," he was quick to answer. "Please."

"And if it involves another guy?" Her nose wrinkled adorably.

"Go for it, sweetheart. I can handle it."

"Keep in mind that you have a teenage daughter, so this story might strike a nerve." She raised a palm in warning between them, and he playfully glared at her before reaching beneath the sheet to set a palm on her hip. Not satisfied with just that simple touch, he reached around and gripped her ass, drawing her body closer to him.

"Stop stalling and just rip off the Band-Aid already," he told her while squeezing her firm ass cheek a bit harder. The memory of pounding her like an animal last night cut through his mind, and his morning wood was harder than hard.

"Okay." She slid her tongue between her lips, clearly trying to distract him, the little temptress. "A week after my eighteenth birthday, my bodyguard's son took my virginity."

She bit into her lip as his hand slid between her legs, hidden still by the sheet. His finger played over the lips of her pussy, fighting the ridiculous urge to demand *Mine*. "And then what?" He lazily smoothed the pad of his thumb along the seam of her sex, and the sheet dropped a little from a heavy breath, exposing her tits.

"You're distracting me," she whispered. "You've been doing that since last night, but I needed it." She moaned when he applied a little more pressure. "I really, really needed it."

He had a feeling her need had more to do with the phone call from her ex than their "jaunt" in the jungle, but he didn't want to think about that asshole. Or the fact he'd ever shared a bed with this beautiful woman and had been stupid enough to lose her.

*My gain*, he supposed, then internally winced. Her ex hurt her, and he'd rather Sydney have never been hurt, even if it meant last night wouldn't have happened.

"So, continue," he requested, his tone a bit deeper than normal. "Continue making me jealous."

"Jealous? This story is from twenty years ago." She planted her lip between her teeth and sucked her bottom lip when he cupped her sex with his palm.

"You're in bed with me right now. Naked. Soaking wet." He plunged two fingers inside her, and she arched her back, her nipples pebbling. "So, thoughts of any other man going near you, now, then, tomorrow . . . drives me a bit crazy. I can't help it." *Or explain it.* But he also didn't seem to have a mute button to hide his feelings. To stop himself from oversharing. "So, continue."

"I'll try my best with you touching me like that."

"The bodyguard's son," he prompted. "How old was he?"

"Twenty-two." She paused and looked at him, waiting for a reaction.

His hand went still. "Your dad kill him? How well did he hide the body?"

"You're funny."

He cocked his head. "I'm serious."

She rolled her eyes and playfully swatted his chest, but he captured her wrist with his free hand. "The point of this story is my belly button ring."

"I have yet to hear a connection between this too-old-for-you guy and your belly button ring." If his daughter had been in the same situation . . . no, he couldn't wrap his head around that idea.

"Ah, is this the sheriff or the father talking?"

"No distinction at the moment." He tipped his head, a request to continue.

"My dad walked in on us. He fired my bodyguard, and he gave me the silent treatment for a month. So, I rebelled. Got my belly button pierced to piss him off. To try and get him to talk to me."

Silent treatment? Fired the guy's dad? *That* was her father's reaction to his daughter losing her virginity to her bodyguard's son? *Yeah, I'm nothing like him.* "Did it work? Did he talk to you?"

"Eventually. The damn thing got infected and left a scar after I removed it." She shrugged. "I guess I was always a bit of a rebel. But I still feel guilty I got someone fired because of my stupid need for my father's attention."

The downside of being rich, he supposed. Busier parents? Was that the issue? He'd always done his best to be present in McKenna's life as much as possible, but he wished she had a mother there too. Sure, his mom and sister had stepped in, but no one could truly replace a mother's love, could they?

Beckett moved his hand up to Sydney's abdomen, feeling wrong about touching her after what she'd shared.

"How else were you rebellious? Jesse's dad forced him to join the Army to quote, unquote, straighten him out. Was that the case with you?" Of course, back then, Beckett hadn't known that Jesse's *dad*, not Jesse, needed straightening out. That news had only recently been revealed.

Sydney smiled. "Ha. No. I joined the Army because my dad *didn't* want me to."

"Surprised he didn't find a way to stop you."

"Oh, he tried, but I was stubborn. Although, I did give in to his request that I attend West Point first." She smoothed her hand over the dusting of hair on his pecs as if lost in thought. "And then I pissed him off by breaking a school rule the first semester."

"Which was?"

She lifted her gaze to meet his eyes. "I dated Gray. He was a Firstie, a senior, and it's forbidden for Firsties and freshmen to date."

The news Sydney and Gray had not only dated but Gray had also proposed was still a hard pill for Beckett to swallow. But it went down a little easier knowing she turned him down.

"I don't regret my act of rebellion in joining the Army because it turned out to be the best decision I ever made. I wouldn't have Levi if I hadn't, um . . ."

*Hadn't what?* He wasn't sure if she planned to finish her sentence, but based on the forlorn look in her eyes, he knew she was recalling painful memories this time.

"Anyways." She shrugged as if relieving herself of an emotional burden that'd momentarily pressed down on her shoulders. "My father offered to fund a new weapons program for half the usual fee and got me honorably discharged after serving four years instead of the five I owed the Army after West Point. I was so pissed, but . . . money talks. And the next thing I knew, I was working for him. He won."

He knew there was more to her story she was choosing to leave out, and those parts were hurting her now. Sensing she needed a hug but wouldn't ask, he urged her to shift, and he pinned her back to his chest and held her.

He couldn't help but calculate the difference between her age and her son's, assuming that was the part she was choosing not to share right now—Levi's father.

She'd said Levi wouldn't exist if it weren't for her serving in the military, so who was his dad? Had he been in the Army? What happened to him?

Sydney turned in his arms, and when she faced him, there were tears in her eyes. "All you did was ask me about my belly button scar, and somehow the conversation got so . . . deep."

Her body tensed, and he smoothed his thumb along the contour of her cheek, catching a tear there.

"See." She frowned. "My, um, book cover doesn't match the inside. Not now, at least. I'm not as strong as everyone thinks."

"You are strong. The strongest woman I've ever met. And I come from a family of tough women, so when I say that," he said around a hard swallow, his voice cracking from unexpected emotion, "I mean it."

"Most days, it's an act," she whispered.

"It's not an act. It's true." He gently cupped her chin, demanding her attention. "Look at me.

"Who made you think you're not strong? Was it *him*?" The idea her ex-husband had made this strong, beautiful woman feel inadequate and weak filled Beckett with rage.

Before she could answer, there was a knock at the door, followed by a voice he really didn't want to hear. "It's Gray. I'm looking for Sydney." A pause. "Let me in."

## CHAPTER NINETEEN

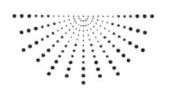

SYDNEY FROZE. WHY IN THE HELL WAS GRAY LOOKING FOR her in Beckett's bungalow? And why'd she feel like her dad was about to barge in and catch her with a guy in her bed, just like when she was eighteen?

"One second," Beckett called out, scrambling to snatch his linen pants from where he must've tossed them before his first shower last night.

Sydney eyed her dress on the floor and decided it would take entirely too long to put on. She considered hiding in the outdoor shower, but that didn't feel like the right thing to do.

*Gray's just a friend now. My team leader. It'll be fine.*

Beckett tossed her his linen shirt as if sensing her dilemma, then started for the bathroom while she fumbled with the buttons, knowing she was lying to herself and that things would, in fact, not be fine.

"Here," Beckett mouthed, handing over the panties she'd discarded near the outdoor shower last night.

"She's in there, isn't she?" The strained tone of Gray's voice had her heart sinking to the pit of her stomach.

"Am I opening up?" Beckett whispered as he spun toward her, wearing only his pants.

His attention swept over her body, stopping at her breasts. Sydney looked down to discover that the fabric was nearly sheer enough to display her nipples, and the bottom hem of his shirt covered barely enough to be decent.

She fastened the last buttons, then tightened her arms over her chest, hiding her breasts the best she could before nodding her okay.

Beckett swiped a palm over his face, then reached for the handle. "Yeah, Sydney's in here," he answered before opening up.

Gray's gaze cut straight to the rumpled bedsheets before meeting her eyes with a deep frown, his lips pressed together in a hard slash. She wished what was shredding him right now was anger, but she knew him too well.

"What are you doing here?" She walked toward him, telling herself she had nothing to be ashamed of, keeping her head held high.

Gray remained still and silent, his eye twitching slightly after a few seconds. Then he faced Beckett, let go of a few quick, shallow breaths like he might throw down with him, and wordlessly turned and left.

Sydney shot Beckett an apologetic look, knowing he had to be uncomfortable as hell, and then chased after her team leader. "Gray, would you stop? Please."

He was a few feet ahead of her, clutching his leg and walking slowly. Her heart plummeted at the sight he was hurting in more ways than one.

*Why? Why do you still care about me like that?*

Not too far from Beckett's bungalow, she caught up and grabbed his arm.

"Damn it, Sydney," he rasped, swinging around and pulling his arm free from her grasp. "For the love of God, just give me a second to process this." He cupped his mouth, eyes focused on the ground.

"I'm sorry. I know Beckett is technically a client, and it's an unspoken rule, but—"

"You think that's what I'm upset about?" He placed his hands on his hips and squared his stance. "You and I broke the rules at West Point, didn't we?"

God, she'd just shared that bit of truth with Beckett, and now here the man was in the flesh.

"I might be a hard-ass with everyone at Falcon," Gray continued, his deep voice thick with emotion, "but when it comes to you, I'd never tell you what to do."

"So, what are you upset about?" But staring into his eyes, seeing a world of hurt there, how could she not know the answer?

But she needed to hear it from him, to be absolutely sure she wasn't putting words into his mouth. She'd hoped they could be friends again when she joined Falcon, but lovers? No. She wasn't the person he fell in love with back in college. Not even close.

Gray hung his head, his bladed jaw tightening beneath his trimmed beard.

"Why are you even here?" she repeated.

"The whole team is here." Looking up, he slid his eyes over her shirt, his disapproval loud and clear. "Carter and the others are in the main house now."

"Why didn't you give us a heads-up?" *You wouldn't have found me in his bedroom if you'd bothered to call first.*

"Jesse reached out just after midnight. He's leaving Mexico with Miguel Diego and Ivy today," he shared. "There was no point in waking you up. We needed to come get you anyway. The pilot that brought Beckett here isn't allowed to fly to where we're going, so that's why we're picking you up."

"Oh." She processed the new information. "Where are we going?"

"Santiago, Chile."

"That's unexpected. I figured they'd stay in Mexico."

"Yeah, well." Gray raked his hands through his hair. "Get packed. We roll out in an hour." He turned to take off, but she couldn't leave things like this. It'd be awkward for everyone.

"Wait, I don't want things to be—"

"Too late," he hissed but quickly dropped his shoulders as if angry at himself for yelling. The man looked beaten. Deflated. Like he'd been kicked while already down.

*And I did that to you.*

"I don't want to do this here, Syd. I *can't* do this here."

"Do what?" She wasn't sure she could handle any more emotional hits after Seth's marriage announcement. "Gray, we were together a long time ago." She couldn't beat around the bush, and she needed to clear the air. They'd all need to work together, keep things professional and focused.

Gray tipped his head to the side, studying her mouth as if remembering the way she'd tasted. "I've spent twenty years searching for someone I could love as much as I loved you. Twenty years wasted. Because there's no replacing you. You get that, right? I've spent my life hoping our paths would cross again, and we'd get another chance."

"Gray." She reached out, her heart breaking for him, but he flinched and stepped back.

He tossed both hands in the air, a request to keep her distance. "Did you know about my accident when it happened?" Where was this coming from? Shit, just how much had this man kept bottled up inside?

"I knew, yes." She thought back to the day she'd learned Gray's helo had crashed, remembering the phone call from her friend in Military Intelligence who knew she and Gray had dated in college.

*"There's been an accident,"* Michelle had told her. *"Gray survived, but they had to amputate part of his leg."*

"I visited you," Sydney confessed. "I stayed until I knew you were in the clear. I visited when your parents, sister, and friends weren't in the room."

He closed his eyes and lifted his chin toward the blue sky overhead, unobstructed by trees on the open walkway.

After a few painfully quiet seconds passed, he tossed out, "Your ex was a moron for cheating on you. The stupid son of a bitch threw you away. How could he not see who was right in front of him? Who he had?" Gray worked his eyes back to hers.

"Wait . . ." *How do you know?* Who told him about Seth's cheating?

When Gray abruptly shifted his gaze over her shoulder, she turned to see Beckett disappearing into the bungalow. How much had he heard?

She spun back around as Gray dropped a string of curses under his breath. "I'm not supposed to know about Seth's affair."

"No, you're not." So how in the hell was it possible? It wasn't like Gray was teeing off with her dad on Sundays, and her dad spilled the news. And Mya would never betray her.

"Seth," he dropped the bomb on her. "I ran into him at the Pentagon when I was visiting my dad."

Right, Gray's father was the Secretary of Defense now. But still . . .

"Seth recognized me and stopped me in the hall," he explained. "Apparently, he took it upon himself to do background checks on all the guys at Falcon when you joined the team."

"And he told you we got divorced because he cheated?" How the hell did something like that come up in conversation?

"Honestly, he just kind of spilled it during the course of threatening me to stay away from you."

"He threatened you?" This wasn't the Seth she knew. Seth didn't give a damn about her. He'd repeatedly said she wasn't enough for him. That was his reason for cheating. And now he was marrying Alice, so why would he care who Sydney dated?

"He said to keep my hands off you." He let go of a gruff breath. "I'm guessing you told him we dated at West Point."

She must have mentioned it at some point, but it wasn't recently. "I'm still just . . ." *In shock.*

"And before you ask, no, I didn't hit him. I was at the Pentagon, and they frown upon that kind of behavior, especially from Admiral Chandler's son." He held his palms in the air. "But did I want to?" He leaned in a bit closer. "Hell yes, I did."

Sydney did her best to swallow the news. "I don't know what you want me to say."

"You don't need to say anything," he responded, his tone a touch defeated again. "Just pack. We leave for Santiago in an hour." And this time, when he turned, she let him go.

She covered her eyes with her hand, willing away the tears. She thought she was all cried out after her call with Levi yesterday.

"Sydney." Her hand fell at the sound of Mya's voice, and she peered over to see Mya on her porch waiting for her.

Sydney chanced a look at Beckett's bungalow, knowing they needed to talk, but where to begin? First, though, she needed a few minutes to pull herself together.

As soon as Mya shut the door behind them, she spun around and set her hands on Sydney's shoulders. "I couldn't help but overhear some of that. Are you okay? And are you wearing Beckett's shirt? What happened?"

Sydney eased away from her friend and sat on the bed. She pinned her knees together and cradled her head in her hands, elbows on her thighs.

"You weren't in your bungalow, so Gray stopped by searching for you. I'm sorry. If I had known, I would have distracted him," Mya rambled.

Sydney tore her hands through her bedhead hair and sat in silence while Mya waited for her to speak.

"In answer to your question about what happened . . . I slept with Beckett last night. Also, Gray informed me that he ran into Seth at the Pentagon a while back and, while threatening Gray to keep his hands off me, told him we got divorced because he cheated. Oh, and to top it off, Gray still has feelings for me. Serious from the sounds of it," Sydney finally revealed, her voice breaking.

"Well, for once in my life, I'm almost speechless. And, um, did Beckett hear any of that? And how do you feel about Beckett? And Gray?"

"I don't know if Beckett heard anything. God, I hope not." Sydney sighed before continuing, "I care about Gray, of course, but only as a friend and teammate." *How will we work together after this?* "Beckett, though, I don't know what I'm doing when it comes to him. I wasn't really thinking last night."

"Sometimes the best things happen when we just let go and stop thinking."

"That from the book?"

"I think it's a common expression." Mya shrugged. "Are you going to be okay? Will this be weird now? Beckett and Gray together on Carter's jet?"

"Gray already told you about Chile?" she asked, ignoring Mya's question.

And yeah, the flight would be awkward and uncomfortable for all of them. Not to mention they'd be working together to find Beckett's ex.

*What the hell? There's complicated, and then there's this.*

"Yeah, when he came looking for you. He told me the team had arrived and if I was still interested in joining Falcon, at least for this mission, to hurry and get dressed. I need to call Mason and tell him what happened before we head out." She lifted a hand. "Don't worry. I'll stick to the story involving my source. Nothing about Beckett."

Sydney had nearly forgotten about Mason. If Mya didn't return home when expected, he'd swoop down there immediately. "How do you think he'll take the news that you're working this op with us?"

Mya frowned. "Not well. He'll want to help, but I think that's one too many cooks in the kitchen, and I'm betting Carter will say no anyway."

*That he would.*

"Maybe I'll talk to Martín before we leave. See if he'd be open to Mason and his teammates coming to assist in taking down the cartel's human trafficking operation." Mya jumped at the sound of a sharp knock on the door. "But I won't tell Mason where we're going. He won't be able to resist showing up."

"It's us," Oliver announced.

"Why do I get the feeling a Mason-Oliver confrontation would be almost as awkward as . . ."

"Gray and Beckett?" Mya whispered. "It shouldn't be. But who knows with men," she grumbled before opening the door.

Sydney stood when she spotted Beckett and felt her cheeks blush. He was dressed in jeans and a black tee, hands in his pockets, hanging back with their other teammate, Jack.

"Hey." Jack sounded uneasy, obviously sensing the thicker-than-thick tension in the group. Not that Gray would've told him what had gone down.

*But shit, I'm still in Beckett's shirt.* She quickly folded her arms across her chest. "What's wrong?" She looked at Beckett, his face drained of color. Something far more serious than what he overheard her and Gray talking about had happened.

"Liam's wife called Gray because she couldn't reach Beckett," Jack shared. "She's who helped Beckett track Ivy to Mexico."

*Right, I remember.* And Emily couldn't reach Beckett because his phone died after their swim in the river.

"Emily insisted on speaking to Beckett, so I brought the phone to him a few minutes ago," Jack went on, standing alongside Oliver now while Mya remained on the porch.

"She and her daughter, Elaina, are at the airport about to catch a flight to Santiago. They'll arrive there late tonight," Beckett shared, his voice rough with worry. "Elaina woke Emily up at four a.m. and insisted they go to Chile. That it was a matter of life and death. Emily said she's never seen Elaina so shaken up. She didn't know what to do, and . . ." He shook his head as if still processing the news. "Elaina's a genius, a prodigy, and she has visions. I'm not sure. I was at their house last week, and she accidentally bumped into me in the hallway. Apparently, it caused her to see something. About me. Or Cora. I—I don't know the details."

"And Emily agreed?" Mya snapped her fingers. "Like that?"

"You don't understand. When Elaina sets her mind to something, if she thinks someone is in danger, there's no stopping her." Beckett palmed his jawline, his gaze on the trail. "Emily's parents rushed over to babysit Jackson, Elaina's little brother."

"There's no way Elaina would know we're headed to Chile unless she really can see things, right?" Oliver asked.

"I don't see how," Beckett responded. "Liam's overseas, so Emily left him a message about what's going on." Guilt clung to his every word. "Fuck," he said, dragging both hands through his hair now. "It's bad enough that I put Jesse in danger, but now a twelve-year-old and her mom are caught up in this."

Sydney looked beyond their group and saw Martín and Valentina headed their way alongside Carter.

"I just got a call from Liam Evans," Carter announced. "He's stepping away from his current assignment and catching the next flight to Chile. He'll meet us there."

Valentina stopped before Sydney. Their lighthearted hostess, who just last night would have winked and commented about Sydney's lack of clothing, was gone. In her place stood a woman who looked as though she was bearing terrible news.

"What is it?" Sydney peered at her boss for answers, but Carter tipped his head, deferring to Martín.

"The man your friend, Jesse, is going to see in Chile is a billionaire businessman. An eccentric man but . . ." Martín was quiet for a moment, his hands going into his pockets. "He's dangerous."

"And around these parts, he's known by another name,"

Valentina said, her eyes meeting Sydney's. "He's known as *El Vigilado*."

Sydney translated the words in her head before whispering them aloud, "The Guarded One?"

## CHAPTER TWENTY

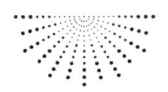

"How are you holding up?"

Beckett peered at Griffin Andrews as they stood inside Martín and Valentina's home, unsure how to answer the question. Because at the moment, he was barely standing upright. Hell, he had to lean against one of the pillars in the living room to support the weight of his damn problems.

"I'm . . ." Beckett shut his eyes and thought back to his call with Emily ten minutes ago, feeling the need to replay their conversation before he could answer what should have been a simple question.

*"You're really taking her to Chile just because she says she needs to go?"* Beckett had asked Emily, in shock because he couldn't imagine giving in to such a demand from McKenna, visions or not.

*"What choice do I have? You know Elaina."* Emily's voice had broken while talking. *"The fact we're going back to Santiago where she was raised . . . what if this is personal for her somehow?"*

*"I'm so sorry. I never should have come to D.C. and asked for your help. This is all my fault."*

*"I have a feeling Elaina would've been pulled into this one way or another. That's what my gut is telling me, so please, don't feel bad. But her headaches are getting worse. And they won't go away until whatever is wrong is stopped,"* she'd shared the heartbreaking news.

*"What do you mean?"*

*"Lately, she gets more distinct visions. Much more information than in the past. But she has to get closer to the problem. And if she doesn't, the pain in her head gets worse. That's what she finally admitted. Before Liam spun up, there was that hostage situation at a bank . . ."* she'd reminded him. How could he forget? Liam had been with his teammate, Knox Bennett, the President of the United States' son that day. The robbery attempt had been all over the news. *"Elaina sent Liam to that bank."*

*"I don't know what to say."* And he still didn't know what to say, not even to Griffin patiently waiting for him to talk right now.

*"I left Liam a message, and he's going to be so pissed when he finds out we didn't wait for him."* Choked up, she'd continued, *"But Elaina's in so much pain, and I . . ."* Beckett had nearly fallen to his knees at her words.

*"And she didn't share more? Or tell you why she never said anything to us sooner?"*

*"She told me that if she'd said something to you sooner, then you wouldn't be where you are now, and someone would have died. A woman. Dark hair. Brown eyes. That mean anything to you? Or maybe it's yet to happen."*

Beckett had been stunned into silence before sharing, *"Elaina was right. Someone here may have died if Oliver and I hadn't arrived when we did."*

*"Which means she's going to be right about Chile, and so, I need to go. I can't wait for Liam,"* Emily had said while

sniffling. *"Have you talked to A.J. yet? Does he know you're there?"*

"No. But he'll find out from Liam, I'm sure."

Beckett opened his eyes and let go of a shaky breath as Griffin swiveled his ball cap backward, eyes on Beckett, waiting for him to talk. The man had yet to press Beckett to share, which he appreciated.

"I'm okay," Beckett finally managed, doing his best to avoid eye contact with Gray, who was talking to Jack and Oliver.

"You're a shitty liar. You know I won't push you, but if you need to talk about something, even if it doesn't involve the case, I can try and channel my wife and be a good listener." Griffin's slight smile at the mention of Savanna had Beckett nearly cracking one as well.

Savanna had always been a good listener. She was also the one who'd given Sydney those romance novels. And that thought brought to mind the situation between Gray and Sydney.

Beckett had only heard a handful of words exchanged between them outside the bungalow, none of which boded well for the relationship Beckett had with Gray. Not that they knew each other *that* well, but Beckett liked to think of Gray as part of A.J.'s family, so by extension, part of Beckett's.

*And now?*

"I'll take your continued silence as a hard pass on my offer to have a feelings conversation." Griffin said "feelings" as if he'd chewed on the word and spat it out. He was a former Delta Force guy and, married to a sweet Southern woman or not, he was still a gruff operator.

Beckett pushed away from the pillar, testing his ability to stand beneath the world's weight on his shoulders without support. "I can't get the call with Emily out of my head," he took a chance and shared one burden. "Being in Chile is going to be hard on their family."

"Elaina's birth mother is from Chile, right?" Griffin asked, closing his eyes briefly as if trying to catch hold of a memory.

"Elaina was born in Texas, but she grew up in Chile. Her mom worked at a university in Santiago, and she was the level of smart that made international headlines. Same with Elaina's birth father," Beckett explained. "Elaina's mom died in a car accident four or so years ago in Santiago, and then Elaina was abducted not long after that. The rest of the story is a bit need to know, even for me, so I don't have all the details."

"I can see why it might be hard for Elaina to return to Chile, then." Griffin scrubbed a hand along his jawline. "Have Elaina's visions always been correct?"

"From what I know, yes. And Elaina just told her mom that a woman with dark hair and eyes would've died had I . . ." *Mya.* He was still a bit stunned at that revelation.

"Damn." Griffin blinked a few times before he tipped his head, and Beckett turned to see Carter gesturing for everyone to gather.

"I want to make sure we have our facts straight about this *El Vigilado* guy before we head out," Carter said, standing between Martín and Sydney.

Beckett spied Gray hanging off to the side of the group, just outside of the circle, and he wasn't sure how they were all going to work together now. But they had to find a way.

"Who is this 'The Guarded One'?" Griffin asked, using air quotes around the nickname. "His real name, I mean."

"Jorge Rojas," Martín revealed before Carter could. "He's a businessman. He inherited his fortune from his father, an oil tycoon from Venezuela who passed away almost six years ago. It was all over the news because Jorge's older brother died from a mysterious poisoning the day after their father did, making Jorge the richest man in South America."

"So," Beckett began, "we're dealing with a guy who killed his own brother to be the sole inheritor of the fortune." *Not a total surprise.*

Martín nodded. "Jorge lives in Chile, where his mother was originally from, and he recently had a mansion built there. One resembling something from the 1900s."

"If he's already rich, why resort to criminal enterprises? I'm assuming he's a bad guy, aside from knocking off his brother, or we wouldn't be having this conversation," Beckett commented. "Does it have to do with his nickname?"

Martín turned his attention to Beckett. "Some people collect blackmail on others to coerce them to do what they want. But in this case, secrets are willingly given to Jorge."

"Yeah, you're going to have to spell it out for me because I'm not following," Jack chimed in.

"Secrets are like a commodity," Martín answered. "And what do you offer a man who already has everything if you want something in return, such as a favor? You can't sell him your soul, but you can offer something more valuable. Your dirty secrets."

"He's considered The Guarded One because he's a protector of secrets from all walks of life," Valentina clarified for Jack. "From politicians who wish to be re-elected to businessmen needing to hide an office scandal or whatnot. He'll help anyone if the secret is worth it to him."

"What does he get out of it?" That was the part Beckett didn't understand.

"He's a man who has everything. An eccentric. A bored billionaire," Carter joined the conversation this time, as if he knew a thing or two about being rich and using the money in more interesting ways.

"These secrets are offered in exchange for something. I don't know exactly how it works. I'm not entirely sure what happens if they don't hold up their end of the deal. Maybe he destroys their lives. I don't know," Martín explained. "But I get the sense it's mostly a game to Jorge. From what I've heard, he's obsessed with games and theatrics, in general."

"I'm not too familiar with the man," Carter noted, "but Jorge is turning forty-five on Friday, and he's hosting a lavish party. Not sure about the details, but Miguel is most likely a guest. And now Jesse too."

"So, do you think Miguel sold a secret to Jorge, and that's how they know each other?" Mya asked. Beckett turned from the room, searching his mind for a memory . . .

"No," Beckett answered before Carter could. "You said he had his home built like it belonged in the 1900s? What specific time period?" He faced the room. "The 1920s? *Gatsby-like?* This ring a bell?"

Martín nodded. "Yes, he's obsessed with that time from what I have heard. Of course, he goes through phases. It could be the Gold Rush Era next year, who knows with that man." He opened a hand. "Bored and rich, so."

Beckett ran his palm along his jawline, eyes on the floor. "Jennifer said she heard that a billionaire was trying to buy Miguel's club, Capone."

"Who's Jennifer?" Sydney asked.

"Some college kid from El Paso I met at the club. She was researching the place for her thesis," he quickly explained, and his stomach dropped when it all came together. "I think I know how this all connects to Cora." He switched his focus to Carter. "Cora only ever contacted me when she needed money, and I hadn't heard from her in nearly six years when she called me three weeks ago. I'd hoped she'd finally found someone rich enough that she didn't have to bother me anymore."

"Someone she'd learned in the news had become the richest man in South America, perhaps," Oliver said, following his line of thought. "The timing fits."

Beckett set his hands on his hips, considering the possibility. "You say Jorge is obsessed with the nineteen-twenties and Al Capone. Maybe he's the billionaire Jennifer heard wanted to buy the club. If Cora is his mistress, wife, girlfriend, whatever . . . she was probably with him when he visited Capone." It was a stretch, but it was the only thing that made sense. "And knowing Cora and her bad luck, someone from her past recognized her there. That's why Ivy got a job at the club—she was trying to find a way to get to Cora and help her."

But was Cora still alive? She hadn't made contact since that call three weeks ago.

"Why wouldn't Ivy just come to you for help? If she knew her sister was in trouble, that seems like it'd be the easier option instead of infiltrating a cartel-owned club," Carter asked.

It was a fair question and one that had a simple answer. "Because two years ago, I arrested her."

# CHAPTER TWENTY-ONE

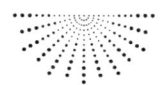

Beckett wasn't sure he had it in him to share more of his past. Unearthing memories he'd worked his ass off to bury deep down in the belly of hell where they belonged only pissed him the fuck off.

It'd taken months for him to get a good night's sleep after Ivy had shown up two years ago, but as time passed without incident, he stopped anticipating one of the Barlowe sisters barging into his life and creating chaos. At least until three weeks ago when Cora shot his peace to hell.

Beckett expelled a deep, exhausted breath, aware that everyone in the room was waiting for him to share the Ivy arrest story.

He considered offering the bare minimum to end the conversation quickly and stole a look at Gray, now leaning against a pillar.

The snippets of Gray and Sydney's conversation he'd heard earlier outside the bungalow moved through his mind in slow motion. *"Your ex was a moron for cheating on you. The stupid son of a bitch threw you away."*

Beckett wished a thousand times over he hadn't left the

bungalow to check on Sydney at that exact moment. At the time, he wasn't sure if the shocked look on her face was due to his presence or Gray revealing he knew Seth had cheated on her. His guess was both. Sydney didn't strike him as the type to go around telling people, Gray included, that her ex had been having an affair.

But Gray's further comments confirmed Beckett's theory about her asshole ex—that he'd more than likely instilled some insecurities in her, ones she guarded well.

"Care to share more?" Carter's deep voice drew Beckett's attention.

"Yeah, sorry." Beckett forced his shoulders to relax. "Two years ago, Ivy showed up on my doorstep late one night. She said she was there for McKenna. That she wanted to get to know her niece." He cringed at the memory and the anger he'd felt at the sight of her. "I told her to get off my property and never come back."

"You didn't ask her about Cora?" Mya quickly asked. "Weren't you curious?"

"I asked her the next night when she returned." Ivy had been a persistent pain in his ass. Far more than just a burr in his saddle. "She said Cora was happy and safe. That she had a new life, and that life didn't include Ivy. Not sure why she chose to avoid seeing her sister, but Ivy said although she and Cora spoke regularly, they hadn't seen each other in person in years. Not since the last time I saw her, apparently."

He'd considered them lies at the time, but now he had to believe that part of Ivy's story. Otherwise, Ivy was jeopardizing her life by going to Chile with the cartel if someone from Cora's new life might have recognized her.

"And then," Beckett went on, "Ivy launched into a story about recently learning she couldn't have children of her own, which was why she desperately wanted to meet and get to know McKenna."

Despite the time crunch, the team remained quiet, allowing Beckett to unravel his twisted past at his own pace, and he appreciated that.

"I didn't trust her, so I told her if she wanted a family, go visit her sister. To leave us alone." He gripped his temples with his thumb and forefinger.

"She clearly didn't heed your warning if you arrested her," Mya said.

"No, I came home from work and found Ivy on the front porch talking to McKenna's babysitter, trying to con her to get to McKenna. My babysitter was smart enough not to let a woman she didn't know inside my house with my daughter." He set his fist to his chest as he shared the bitter memory. "But when I saw her there, I was so pissed. I was in the process of slapping cuffs on her when my daughter came outside."

"I take it McKenna never learned who she was?" Sydney asked.

Beckett looked her way and shook his head. "No, I didn't want her to know." He opened his fist, realizing he was letting his memories trigger him too much. "Once I took Ivy to the station to question her, to learn her real motives, she claimed Cora asked her to get an update on McKenna because she couldn't come herself. To text her some new pictures. Details about her."

"Why would she suddenly want to know about her daughter after so much time had passed? Doesn't make sense," Mya pointed out, which had been Beckett's question too.

"Ivy said it wasn't the first time Cora sent her to Walkins Glen for an update about McKenna. The damn woman had spied on my family for her in the past. She showed me old images on her phone. But this trip was the first time she'd decided to try and talk to her." Beckett shoved away from the pillar, his back ramrod straight. "She said Cora was too afraid to ever come herself, worried she'd want to make contact if she saw McKenna in person." The thought made him physically ill. "And Ivy said Cora's new situation didn't allow her to visit anyway."

"Guessing her new situation has to do with this Jorge Rojas guy," Carter noted. "Well, if Ivy was even telling the truth."

"Yeah, hard to tell with those sisters." Beckett shook his head. "I warned Ivy if she ever came around again, I'd put her behind bars next time."

Before anyone else could say more, Gray stepped forward. "Your brother is calling me. I'm guessing he wants to talk to you." The world of pain Beckett had seen in Gray's eyes earlier had been replaced by a darker, graver look.

"Anything else you need to share about Ivy's visit before you take that call?" Carter asked, glancing at his watch. Beckett shook his head and started toward Gray. There was nothing left to say. "Fine. Five minutes and we roll out. We're flying direct, so we'll be in the air for about nine hours. In case your brother wants to know, we should arrive in Santiago tonight by seven local time."

Beckett acknowledged Carter with a lift of his chin. At least they'd arrive in time to meet Emily and Elaina at the airport.

Gray held the phone out in front of him as Beckett neared, and he saw that Gray had already answered it. An uncomfortable band of tension stretched between them as he accepted the phone.

*This is going to be fun.* Beckett turned away and said, "Hey, A.J., it's me."

"Liam told me what's going on," A.J. began as Beckett started for the glass doors to get outside. His heart was on a collision course with his ribs, pounding furiously with each step, as his body and mind prepared for what was sure to be a dressing-down by his brother. "He's obviously not fit to operate here given the circumstances, and of course, he wants to be with his family."

Beckett opened the door and stepped outside into the courtyard where he and Sydney had danced last night. "I'm so sorry," was all he could manage as he paced along the length of the rectangular pool.

"This kind of recklessness from you only happens when that damn woman is involved. Only then."

"Things are different this time." And he vowed to keep that promise.

"How? How are they different?" A.J. rasped. "Cora's still fucking with your head. Manipulating you to get whatever she wants. She's the devil, brother. The devil. And yet, she seduces you into her trap, and you help her each time."

"She's not going to seduce me." Beckett tossed a look to the wall of glass, hoping to catch sight of the only woman capable of seducing him right now.

Sydney's back was to him as Valentina spoke with her.

"When it comes to Cora, she says jump, and you'll ask how high."

"I haven't helped her in six years," he reminded A.J.

"Only because she didn't call you during that time," he shot back.

"She's still McKenna's mom," he defended, clinging to what felt like a flimsier excuse by the second.

"Sharing DNA with McKenna doesn't make Cora a mother."

Beckett turned back to the pool, the harsh sun reflecting off the water. And in that blinding light, it was hard not to face the fact he had screwed up.

But he reminded himself if he hadn't come to Mexico looking for Cora, Mya would've met her cartel contact today, and she may have died.

"Everything happens for a reason," he found himself mumbling, unsure if A.J. would buy into that.

"Not only is our pregnant sister's husband in danger, but do you have any idea what that voicemail from Emily did to Liam? Your actions are sending his family to Chile and—"

"I'm sorry," he repeated, doing his best to keep calm, to not let guilt cut him in half. He needed to keep it together to push through and figure out what in the hell was really going on.

"You promised me you'd never see Cora again. That you'd never let her get to you. No matter what."

"I know, and Cora may not even be alive."

"Regardless, you should have come to me. *I* should've been the first one you called."

"And if I had, you would have refused to help. You would have talked me down. And Mya would be dead." No matter how Beckett looked at it, there was someone alive because of his pursuit for McKenna's mother. "We have to trust Elaina on this." Was he crazy for putting his faith in a twelve-year-old? Yesterday he would've said yes. After his call with Emily, not anymore.

"Mya *Vanzetti*?" A.J. paused to let it sink in. Beckett forgot A.J. didn't know all the details of what had happened since Beckett had arrived in Mexico. A.J. had most likely gotten a bullet point version from Liam, who'd gotten it from

Carter. Fucking bullet points. "*She's* there with you? I'm confused."

Beckett quickly filled him in, then pointed out, "You see what I mean? It's fate or whatever you want to call it."

"Liam didn't tell me about Mya or what happened to you all yesterday. I assume he doesn't know. He was just in a panic to leave here for the airport."

"And where are you now?"

"By the Black Sea. That's all I can say," A.J. shared.

*Ukraine? Turkey?* Somewhere around there, Beckett assumed, doing something important.

"I'd be on that plane with Liam if I could, but we're down a sniper now. The second our mission is done, you know I'm on my way."

"You don't need to explain. Or come. We'll be okay." *We have to be okay.*

"Gray's sister will use her Agency contacts to try and find out what she can about this billionaire. Natasha will send you what intelligence she can find as soon as your jet reaches Chile. And knowing her, before your wheels touch the ground," A.J. added, and Beckett was grateful they had a connection to the CIA for help. "How's Ella?"

"Ella's Ella. She's tough. More worried about me than Jesse."

A.J. huffed a laugh. "Sounds like she and I are on the same page." He paused. "And are *you* okay?" Another pause. "I should have led with that, I'm sorry." A somberness filled his brother's tone this time.

"I'm trying to be." When he looked back inside, Sydney was peering his way, and his chest constricted as they made eye contact. *But I'm pretty sure I'm about to get my heart broken again.*

## CHAPTER TWENTY-TWO

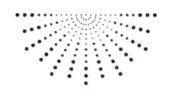

IN THE AIR

"Do we know where Jesse is staying in Chile?" Beckett asked Oliver, sitting next to him on Carter's luxury jet. "I assume he won't be staying at the billionaire's mansion."

"Probably a hotel in the city, but we'll track him down. And Carter will do his best to book us rooms at the same place," Oliver shared.

Beckett turned his attention toward Sydney, alongside Mya, at the other side of the cabin near the cockpit. Their seats faced his way, but Sydney and Mya were studying something on an iPad. Most likely researching their new target, The Guarded One.

Oliver must've followed his gaze because he said, "Wouldn't surprise me if Mason Matthews tracks Mya's phone to Chile and shows up unannounced." He cursed under his breath. "I'm still pissed he ever let her go to Tulum in the first place. Girls' trip or not."

"If you were in his shoes, you think you could stop a woman like Mya from doing what she wanted?" Beckett figured she was a hell of a lot like Sydney in many ways. For one, risking her neck to make contact with a cartel member if it saved others' lives. However, based on her actions in the jungle yesterday, it was clear she had no real training, military or otherwise.

"I don't know," Oliver grumbled, tossing his hands in the air. "That woman aggravates me to no end. Not sure how I'll work with her."

"Mmhmm. I'm sure it'll be unbelievably hard," Beckett deadpanned. When Oliver narrowed his eyes and pinned him with a WTF look, Beckett added with a wink, "I'm sure you'll figure out a way to handle it." Oliver mumbled something and rolled his eyes.

Oliver nudged him with his elbow. "Why don't you talk to Sydney? You can have some privacy in Carter's bedroom." Ah, he was playing dirty now.

Oliver knew exactly why he and Sydney couldn't disappear into the bedroom.

Gray Chandler.

"Why would I need to talk to her?" The plane had reached cruising altitude, so Beckett unbuckled his seat belt.

Oliver did the same, then stood and braced a hand overhead, peering down at Beckett. "Gray's a big boy. He'll be pissed for a bit, but he'll get over it."

*You don't get over a woman like Sydney.* "And Mason, you know him, right? Will he get over Mya working with Falcon for this op? Or joining the team on a more permanent basis?"

"He's also a big boy. When he doesn't have his head up his ass allowing Mya to make reckless decisions like taking a solo trip to Mexico," he growled and swung his focus Mya's way again. If the guy's jaw were any tighter, it'd snap.

"She was with Sydney. Mason knew that," Beckett

reminded him, defending a guy he didn't even know. "But yeah, I'll talk to Sydney when we land. *If* there's time."

"Well, that bedroom has seen plenty of action from our team," Oliver said when resetting his focus on Beckett. "Griffin and Savanna. Jesse and—"

Oliver let go of his words when Beckett scowled.

"Riiiight. Ella's your sister." Oliver grinned. "So, we'll just pretend I didn't mention that bedroom, and I'm going to walk away now." He tossed a thumb over his shoulder and retreated in that direction.

*Good idea.* Beckett stood a moment later and decided to use the bathroom adjacent to the bedroom rather than the one near the cockpit, which would require him to walk past Gray.

The moment he opened the door and caught sight of the bed, Beckett was slammed with the memory of Sydney's moans and sighs as he worshiped every inch of her naked body, bringing her to orgasm three times mere hours ago.

"Can we talk?"

His pulse kicked up at the sound of Sydney's soft voice from behind him. Better that than his dick standing at attention.

He turned to see her leaning against the interior doorframe.

"Should we wait until we land?" Beckett's focus cut over her shoulder to Gray talking to Carter, but Gray's back was to him at least.

"It's a long flight, and we haven't had a moment alone since . . . Gray."

He supposed it'd be okay to talk briefly if they kept the door open. "I didn't eavesdrop, by the way. I stepped out of the bungalow for a quick second to make sure you were okay."

"Well," she began, "I did see Cha Cha spying. He has no

shame." A tiny smile formed on her lips, and damn if it wasn't contagious.

"And?" He smiled and arched a brow.

"You were right about Gray's feelings," she whispered, lowering her gaze to the floor between them. "I wish he hadn't seen us together like that. You know, half-naked. But what's done is done." Sydney pulled her gaze back to meet his eyes.

She didn't mention the part Beckett had overheard—Seth's cheating. And it wasn't his place to bring it up. She'd tell him when or if she trusted him enough to share.

"But we shouldn't let it happen again while working together. Gray's a friend, and I don't want to hurt him." She drew in a deep breath as if needing to convince herself she was doing the right thing. "Plus, we have to put all our focus on the job, especially now that Elaina's involved."

He agreed one hundred percent, but that didn't change the fact he wanted to draw her into his arms and hug her right now.

"Okay," he said, finally working the word free. "Just friends, then." *Friends?* After last night—well, technically this morning—how the hell was he supposed to do that?

The regretful look on her face said she wished things were different too.

When she looked up at him and pressed her full lips together, he wanted to lean forward and suck on that bottom lip before sliding his tongue into her mouth and tasting her one last time.

*Friends, sure . . .* He didn't want to have sex with his friends. No, scratch that. He didn't want to *make love* with his friends.

"We can do this, right?" Another slow, deep breath sent his eyes to her breasts. "We can control ourselves?" she added as if struggling the same as him to get a handle on her desires.

Beckett reached out and gently grasped her forearm, hoping her body blocked the others from seeing his touch. "We have no choice." He stared deep into her eyes, his entire body going taut. Every damn inch of him tensing. "But, sweetheart," he rasped, bringing his mouth dangerously close to hers, feeling her sweet breath on him, "it's going to be really fucking hard for me to behave."

\* \* \*

SEVEN HOURS LATER

"Were you just checking out my ass?" Mya accused, looking back and giving Oliver the stink-eye.

Beckett dragged a palm over his mouth to hide his amusement and watched the show playing out before him. He'd managed to get a few hours of sleep, and now he and Oliver were sitting next to each other mid-cabin.

"Well." Oliver lifted both hands and mimed eyeballing the width of something. "It's hard to miss. You're literally standing right in front of me."

Mya whipped around, grabbed Oliver's wrists, and narrowed the space between his palms. "My ass isn't that big, by the way."

Oliver twirled his finger. "Maybe spin back around so I can take another look." He winked, and she knocked the brim of his ball cap down over his eyes before shifting into the aisle.

"You're nothing like—"

"Mason?" Oliver pushed his hat up, his tone switching from teasing to serious in the space of a heartbeat.

Beckett took that as his cue to bail and stood. Slipping past Mya, he looked around in search of the others. Griffin and Jack were asleep in the rear of the cabin near the bedroom. And Sydney?

"She's in the shower." Gray's words had Beckett gripping the seat to his left as if preparing for turbulence. "My sister, Natasha, sent us some intelligence," he added. Beckett turned to face Gray, who stood near the cockpit with Carter.

"And?" Beckett directed the question to Carter. It was clear Gray was still struggling to see Beckett as anyone other than the man who'd slept with Sydney. "Was she able to locate Cora in Chile? I assume having Jorge Rojas's name and location would make it easier." Ever since Emily's contact had come up empty, they'd been searching for the proverbial needle in a haystack. With any luck, Gray's sister had found something solid.

"Natasha got a hit. It's not much. But according to CCTV footage taken eight weeks ago, we can confirm Cora was in Santiago," Carter stated. "Either she's pretty damn good at avoiding CCTV cameras, or she's no longer there."

Proof of life eight weeks ago wasn't confirmation that she was still alive.

"Natasha tracked Jorge's private jet to Juárez three times in the last two months," Carter continued. "But terminal footage showed him accompanied only by men."

"So, if Cora never visited the club, then—"

"Miguel and four of his men visited Jorge in Chile three weeks ago," Gray interrupted Beckett. "I'm assuming Jorge invited him to Santiago to discuss the sale of the club."

"The timeline matches up." Beckett scrubbed a palm over the scruff on his cheek. "I don't know Miguel, nor was he on my radar when I worked undercover in LA, which means someone traveling with him had to have identified Cora when he visited Jorge in Chile."

"That's what we're thinking," Carter began. "Natasha's working to obtain the names of the passengers on board Miguel's flight to Santiago." When Carter's eyes shifted toward the rear of the jet, Beckett turned and followed his gaze. Sydney had just exited the bedroom wearing fresh clothes, her previous outfit bundled tight to her chest.

*Gray's behind me*, he cautioned himself, then returned his attention to the team leaders. "So, what's the next step?"

"I phoned my contacts in South America to see if any were near Chile. Camila, an old friend of mine, happens to be working on a case in Santiago right now. She agreed to wait at the airport for Miguel's plane, which arrived an hour ago," Carter explained. "Camila texted me that Miguel and his men, including Jesse, checked into a hotel in the city."

"Any chance Jesse will be able to use the phone if he gets his own room?" Beckett asked, eager to talk to his brother-in-law himself this time instead of through whatever cryptic channels Jesse and Carter communicated.

"I'm sure Jesse is still working to earn Miguel's trust, and outgoing calls from a hotel room can easily be traced. Miguel, or maybe even Jorge, will have someone doing that," Carter said. "Camila has offered us the use of her safe house outside the city, along with her weapons stash. But we should get a few rooms at the hotel too."

"How is it you have a friend with a safe house and a weapons stash we can borrow, yet you have no contact at the airport who'll look the other way so we can bring in weapons?" Beckett was only partially kidding.

"He's losing his touch," Oliver jested, which produced a small smile from Carter.

"We should bring Elaina and Emily with us to the safe

house," Beckett suggested, remembering their flight was arriving later that evening. "Once Liam arrives tomorrow, he can call the shots when it comes to his family's safety."

"Agreed," Carter answered. "We'll all stay there tonight. Tomorrow, five or six of us will head to the hotel where Jesse's staying." When Carter pinned Beckett with a look that asked, *You in on that?* Beckett nodded. "In the meantime, Camila's working to obtain the names of everyone who flew to Santiago with Miguel today. While Natasha does her best to identify the men who traveled with him three weeks ago. It's possible Miguel took the same guys today though."

"If one of them is somehow connected to Cora's time in LA, I'll recognize him. I remember everything from then." *Though most days, I wish I could forget.*

"Which means we need to be careful. If you can recognize this guy, then it's safe to assume he can identify you too," Gray pointed out.

That would impact Beckett's plans to stay at that hotel, but damn it, he didn't want to keep hidden and not be part of the op.

Beckett thought back to his time in LA. "I turned over the case against MS-13 and the cartel to another detective. I wanted to disconnect myself from it as much as possible before arrests were made to protect McKenna. But yeah, they'd most likely still recognize me as Cora's original mark at the LAPD."

"Let's not jump ahead of ourselves." Carter patted the air as if sensing Beckett's concerns. "We'll wait for intel from Natasha."

Beckett nodded, grateful he seemed to be calling the shots more so than Gray, who didn't exactly have any love for him at the moment.

"So, Cora must've called Ivy for help around the same

time she phoned you," Sydney said. Beckett shifted to the side to see her walking down the aisle. "Otherwise, Ivy would never have known the club was her best chance to get to Cora."

"You mentioned yesterday Ivy had no connection to the cartel or MS-13 in LA," Mya spoke up, "so she wouldn't run the risk of being recognized when trying to seduce Miguel. Also, since Ivy and Cora haven't seen each other for years, the likelihood of someone at Jorge's connecting them as sisters is far less."

Beckett nodded. "And I guess Cora decided to cover as many bases as possible and called me too." *Only someone stopped her mid-call.*

Were they already too late?

What if McKenna's mom was already dead?

*Blood doesn't make a mother.* A.J. had said something like that to him that morning.

When Beckett focused back on Sydney, he couldn't help but wonder what it'd be like for McKenna to have a woman like her for a mom.

"All I know is it feels like the universe has set us all on the same path for a reason," Mya whispered, and Beckett looked over at her.

"Yeah, well, it sure as hell feels like the universe has given us a deadline," Oliver chimed in. "And I get the feeling it's this billionaire asshole's birthday on Friday."

"I hate the word deadline," Mya said as Sydney sat alongside her. "Implies someone will die if we're not successful."

Sydney's gaze fell for a moment before she shifted her attention to Beckett, a sad look in her eyes when she spoke, "In our line of work . . . that's exactly what it means."

## CHAPTER TWENTY-THREE

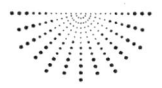

SANTIAGO, CHILE

"THAT WAS FAST. I'M GRATEFUL WE HAVE NATASHA IN OUR corner." Sydney swiped her finger across the iPad screen she and Beckett were sharing and scrolled through the files Natasha had sent shortly after they'd arrived at the safe house.

"You recognize any of the men who traveled with Miguel three weeks ago?" Gray asked Beckett, maintaining his distance by standing as far as possible from Beckett in the room. Like practically out the door and in the foyer.

Sydney handed Beckett the iPad for a closer look. "I know one of them." He pointed to the screen.

Carter stepped away from the rest of the team gathered in the living room and faced him. "Who?"

"Hector Lopez," Beckett shared. "He ran drugs between Mexico and California for the Sinaloas back when I worked in LA. He was one of the men arrested shortly after Cora left town."

"Looks like he got out a few years ago and moved to

Mexico after his parole ended," Carter commented while studying his own iPad. "He's one of Miguel Diego's cousins. This has to be the connection we've been looking for."

"Well, Hector has reason to hold a grudge against Cora. I'm sure he assumed she betrayed him since not long after she left town, he was arrested for drug trafficking. It's been thirteen years, but I'm sure he hasn't forgotten her." Beckett handed Sydney the iPad and folded his arms. "Was Hector on the flight with Miguel today?"

Sydney heard the concern in Beckett's tone. If Hector was there, it'd change everything for him. He'd have to hang back at the safe house and remain out of sight.

"The cartel used their private jet again, and flying private doesn't require a manifest, just an itinerary. Natasha's working on accessing the CCTV footage from earlier today," Gray shared. "The photos Camila took at the airport may be a quicker option." He turned to Carter, planting his hands on his hips. "Where are we on that?"

"Camila's on her way here, but let me see if she can text me the images now." Carter swapped the iPad for his phone and left the room.

"If Hector's—" Gray's ringing phone left his sentence hanging. "It's Natasha." He placed her on speaker. "Hey, we're all here. You have news?"

"Hey," Natasha answered. "I don't have the passenger information yet, but I can confirm Hector Lopez is not in Chile."

Sydney spied Beckett's shoulders collapse from relief at her words.

"He took a flight to Cancun this morning. My guess is he was sent there to track whoever was responsible for taking out so many of his cartel thug friends," Natasha explained.

"We should give Martín a heads-up that Hector's most

likely poking around Tulum," Oliver spoke up and Gray motioned for him to go make the call.

"So, if you all hadn't been in Tulum causing some trouble for the cartel," Natasha went on, "then my guess is Hector would be in Chile now."

All the pieces seemed to be fitting together to their advantage, but how long would that last? In her experience, nothing ever worked out "just right." No, there was always darkness around the corner.

"I have a call coming in from the director. I need to go," Natasha abruptly said. "I'll be in touch when I know more."

"Thanks, sis." After the call, Gray pocketed his phone just as Carter returned. "Hector's in Cancun. Well, probably Tulum by now. Oliver's warning Martín."

"Martín's men can handle Hector. I'm not worried." Carter quickly handed Beckett his phone. "Camila sent me the photos of who was on the plane with Miguel, Jesse, and Ivy today. Know any of them?"

Sydney stood closer to Beckett to check the iPhone as Beckett zoomed in on the screen.

"I don't know any of these guys. That means I can head to the hotel tomorrow, right?" Beckett asked as Carter accepted his phone back.

"As long as Hector doesn't show up, yeah, you're good to roll out to the hotel tomorrow." Carter looked back and forth between her and Beckett. "You two can stay together. Pose as a couple. That'll be your cover story."

Jack coughed a few times, drawing everyone's attention. What was that about?

And then Gray up and left the room, starting for the foyer.
*Shit.*

"I, um." Sydney shot Beckett an apologetic look, then followed Gray from the house.

Gray was pacing alongside the two SUVs that Camila had waiting for them at the airport when they'd arrived. "Go back inside," he barked out.

"No, we need to talk," she said while shutting the door behind her. She rushed down the three porch steps to get to him in the driveway. "I don't need to stay with Beckett."

Gray raked his hands through his hair, and his gaze moved to the home's only neighbor. The Andes Mountains. The safe house sat on a few acres of property with no other homes in view.

"It makes the most sense for you to stay together. Beckett wants to be there because of Cora."

"Then why are you pacing? Why'd you fly out of the house?" she called his bluff. When he didn't stop pacing or respond, she proposed, "What about Camila? Why doesn't she stay with Beckett? If she's Carter's friend and had a safe house like this on standby, she must have operational experience. She can do it."

But why the hell did that thought send chills racing across her skin?

"So, who would you stay with? *Me*?" A humorless laugh fell from his lips, but he finally stopped crunching his black boots over the gravel. "You think he can handle me staying in the same room with you without breaking down the door?" he asked in a low, deep voice. "Because I see the way he looks at you."

Sydney bit down on her back teeth as she tried to navigate this conversation without breaking his heart. "And would *you* break down the door? Because you didn't this morning when you were outside his bungalow." She had no idea why she'd said that, but too late now.

"I have self-control." He pointed at his chest as if wanting to throw down. But his target? Beckett, not her. "Mission comes first."

"The mission does need to come first, I agree." *Which is probably why I shouldn't be alone with Beckett.*

"Beckett came to Mexico risking a hell of a lot to find his ex." Gray's shoulders slumped, the transition from anger to defeat taking her by surprise. "And he found you instead."

Her heart skipped a few beats as she considered her next words.

"You feel something for him. I can see it in your eyes." She opened her mouth, prepared to remind him she and Beckett barely knew each other, but he held up a hand. "Time is insignificant, remember? It took me five minutes to fall in love with you the day we met at West Point. And it's been nearly a lifetime of me trying to stop."

Sydney's knees went weak at his confession. He must've noticed because he stepped forward, catching her arms.

"I'm not trying to hurt you. I know I need to find a way to move on. To put my feelings for you behind me once and for all." Still holding her, his eyes fell closed. "It's possible I spent twenty years loving the idea of us because that'd be easier than opening myself up to anyone new. Maybe it was all in my head. Fiction."

Like a romance novel. But was whatever she felt for Beckett a thing of fiction too? Unrealistic. Their passion and connection happened so fast, would it die just as quickly if she allowed herself a chance to explore "more" with him? Well, after the mission, at least.

"You deserve someone who would've fought for you after you said no to their proposal."

"You knew if I said no, it was a no. There'd be no changing my mind." She didn't need him kicking himself for his decision not to fight for her.

"Well, you should also be with a man who'd say fuck the mission and break down your door. And if you share a hotel room with any man other than him, I reckon he'd do that." It was rare for Gray's Texas roots to slip through, and he was wearing his heart on his sleeve tonight, which had to be why. He parted his lids and released a heavy breath from his lungs. "And maybe I'll never find someone who . . ."

"You will find her," she whispered, worried her voice would break. "I promise."

His lips drew into a tight line, but he kept quiet, then angled his head toward the house and let her go.

"But I still don't need to play the role of Beckett's girlfriend. We can all check into different rooms at the hotel tomorrow," she told him in a steady tone. "Let's talk to the rest of the team. See what we can come up with, okay?"

He looked past her, and at the sound of tires crunching the gravel, she turned to see an SUV on approach. It must have been Camila, and she was relieved for a distraction. Mission-focused was easier than feelings-focused. For her, at least. And knowing Gray, same for him too.

"So, um, what do you know about her?" she softly asked.

"Mid-thirties. Former spy for some agency. Not the CIA. And now she's more of a freelance do-gooder like Carter," Gray filled her in as they faced the incoming SUV. "Carter also mentioned her mom is Brazilian and her dad's American. Her father met her mom while serving in South America while in the Navy."

Camila's vehicle stopped a few feet away from them, and she killed the bright headlights.

"If I'm remembering correctly," Gray continued, "Carter's dad was born in Brazil, so maybe his father knew Camila's mom, and that's the connection between them?"

"Well, you know more about our boss than I do." She winced. "Sorry, you're our boss too."

Gray laughed, which somehow helped ease some of the tension. "We both know who's really in charge, but don't tell him I admitted that."

She smiled, hoping the two of them could go back to being colleagues again after all of this. Well, friends would be better. "And Camila happens to be here working a case, huh?"

Gray shrugged. "Lucky for us, I guess."

"Carter has a lot of 'lucky for us' contacts around the world."

"Looks like you found my place okay," Camila said after exiting the SUV. She was gorgeous, that was for sure. And Sydney's stomach somersaulted at the idea of Camila sharing a room with Beckett.

Maybe *Sydney* would be the one breaking down a door.

Sydney stole a look at Gray, who sure as hell took notice of the newcomer. She hid her smile at that fact, erasing the bit of space between her and the striking woman in dark jeans and a black V-neck tee on approach.

Camila's jet-black locks went to her breasts, and even with the sun having set, it was the glossiest hair Sydney had ever seen.

"Camila." Sydney offered her hand. "I'm Sydney Archer. A pleasure to meet you. Thank you for your help."

Camila took her hand and smiled. When her attention skirted to Gray, he accepted her palm and held on to it a bit longer than necessary.

*Stunned into silence, huh?* Sydney stole a look behind her to see Carter exiting the house.

"Camila," Carter said while heading for them. He pulled

her in for a hug, which was something Sydney rarely ever saw the man do.

"Camila's like a kid sister to me, so when I say you can trust her, you can," Carter said once he'd freed himself from the hug.

"And he's like an overprotective brother who usually finds himself needing more help than he can provide me," Camila teased, and Sydney loved this woman already.

"Everyone's inside." Carter motioned to the house. He began speaking fluently in Portuguese, one of the languages Sydney didn't speak, so she walked in silence alongside Gray.

"Thank you again for helping us out on such short notice," Carter said once they were inside the two-story brick house.

"You're lucky I was already here working my own case," Camila commented.

"Yeah, lucky us," Sydney said, trailing behind them.

Chills covered her arms as she thought about the last thirty-six hours and how they all managed to be together there in Chile.

"This is my friend, Camila Hart," Carter introduced her to everyone once they were all in the living room. The large space just off the foyer only had a few couches, but it did have a fully stocked bar.

Camila individually greeted the others, learning their names, and then she went over to the bar and poured herself a top-shelf scotch.

Yeah, a friend of Carter's for sure.

"My mother and his dad dated in college in Brazil forever ago. They remained friends after that, even when marrying other people," Camila revealed, her accent still noticeable but not quite as heavy as Valentina's when speaking English. It was just as sexy in Sydney's mind. "Anyhow . . ." She faced the room. "I didn't realize our cases were connected until the men you asked me to follow checked into the same hotel as the man *I'm* following."

Her announcement had Sydney nearly faltering in surprise. "Wait," Sydney whispered in shock. "*What*?"

## CHAPTER TWENTY-FOUR

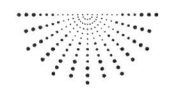

Camila's dark espresso-brown eyes narrowed as she looked Beckett's way. And yeah, no way would Sydney be able to handle this gorgeous woman alone with him.

*He's not mine. Ugh, he's also not Seth.* Beckett wouldn't sleep with her. *Why am I thinking about this?*

"Carter mentioned your ex-wife is in danger," Camila said to Beckett.

"We weren't married," Beckett quickly informed her. "But yes, it's safe to assume she's in danger. Or worse."

*Dead.* Goose bumps danced across her skin like memories of a nightmare. The kind that had her body trembling. She hated Seth. But dead? No, she couldn't handle that news.

Camila finally withdrew her attention from Beckett and focused back on Carter. Was she going to explain how their cases were connected? She was as mysterious as Carter.

"Carter only mentioned the cartel to me over the phone," she shared while lifting her glass in his direction. "Why didn't you tell me you're here for Jorge Rojas too?"

Sydney stepped forward, nearly lining herself up with Beckett.

"Jorge appears to be the common denominator between our two cases," Camila said. "I'm a private investigator, and I was hired to find the man *or* woman who murdered a Brazilian scientist. I managed to track down the main suspect to Santiago two days ago. He's staying at the same hotel as the cartel men you're after."

"Go on," Carter urged, his arms tight across his white dress shirt.

"My suspect met with Jorge at the hotel yesterday. And now your men are at the same hotel the week of Jorge's party this Friday. I'd planned to surveil Jorge's house tonight, and then you called in the favor." Camila set her glass on the bar before focusing on the room again. "But that's not the only reason I believe our cases are connected."

"You're a great storyteller," Mya chimed in, and Sydney looked back to see Oliver shaking his head. "What? I love a good story."

"Ignore her," Oliver grumbled, oblivious to the eye daggers Mya was sending his way. "Go on."

"Before my client's husband was murdered, he was working on an experimental drug. A drug that, in the wrong hands, could be used in nefarious ways. The suspect I've been tracking is also a scientist who worked at the same lab, and I believe he killed my client's husband for the formula."

"And you're thinking he did this for Jorge?" Gray asked. "Why would Jorge care about a pill? That's not his thing, or am I missing something?"

Carter went to the bar this time and snatched the scotch. His taut back muscles flexed as he poured himself a drink. "Your suspect needed funding for his lab after he killed the other scientist, so he went to Jorge. In exchange for funding, your guy had to share a secret. I'm guessing murder qualifies," Carter theorized.

"That's what I'm thinking, yes," Camila said as Carter faced the room. "I didn't realize this until my suspect and Jorge met." She peered around the room, her gaze landing on Gray last, and she kept her eyes locked his way as she added, "But what if Jorge decided to change things up from his normal MO?"

"Instead of bartering a favor for a secret this time, he just wants the formula for himself?" Gray clarified, and Sydney stole a look at him to see his brows slanting as if suddenly making sense of why.

"The cartel," Sydney whispered when it clicked. "Jorge wants the club, Capone, but it's not like the cartel is hard up for cash and needs to sell it just to appease some billionaire." She shifted to the side, catching Beckett's eyes in the process. "Jorge would need to entice them with more than just money. What if he's offering the Sinaloas a new drug in exchange for the place?"

"Why would Jorge want a club?" Camila's brows climbed, clearly unaware of the type of club it was in Mexico. "He's rich. He could build his own place."

"Because he's obsessed with Al Capone and all things nineteen-twenties," Gray told her. "And Capone visited there during Prohibition. There's an old black-and-white photo of him posing with the then-owner outside. And the cartel turned it into a tourist hotspot with a nineteen-twenties theme."

"Ah, yes, I've seen Jorge's estate." Camila nodded.

"So, you think he'll use the scientist's formula to get what he wants?" Gray crossed the living room to where she stood.

"I think it's possible, which is why he has everyone staying at the same hotel. He's arranging a deal that works for all of them," Carter suggested. "Jorge has a reputation to maintain, after all. He'll stop being known as The Guarded

One if he sells out a client that didn't break a deal with him."

"Jorge has a table reserved at the hotel's club Wednesday night. I guess this is also why he chose that hotel. Wednesday night is—"

"Let me guess, Roaring Twenties night?" Jack interrupted Camila, on his feet next to Griffin.

Griffin remained quiet as usual. Preferring hands-on field work, he let the rest of the team figure out the details leading up to a mission.

"No dress code from what I read, but yes, the music is from the nineteen-twenties," Camila answered Jack.

"The cartel will want proof the drug works before they make a deal." Carter added more scotch to his glass. "Maybe he'll use it on his own guests at his party Friday night."

"And what exactly can this drug do, especially if your guy may have modified it in a lab with Jorge's money?" Sydney asked.

"I don't know what it can do now," Camila began, "but the scientist's wife shared with me that before her husband was killed in a supposed random shooting, he was working on a pill that would alleviate social anxiety."

"Anxiety," Sydney said under her breath, not quite understanding why the cartel would want such a drug.

"Not the typical kind of prescription drug. Sort of like MDMA, or I believe it's commonly known as Ecstasy . . . but imagine that drug times five." Not the best picture to paint, but now Sydney understood the appeal. "His wife told me the pill was meant to help people lose their inhibitions. To stop people's fears from holding them back from getting what they truly desire in life. Make them more comfortable in social situations. Less anxious."

"But?" Mya broke her silence.

"His wife said there were problems with the drug initially. It made people a bit too lax. Too free. She said her husband had recently tweaked it to make it safe." Camila's long, dark lashes fluttered a few times. "If the murderer had the funding, he could reverse engineer the formula to its original design."

"MDMA on steroids," Jack hissed.

"I can't imagine the cartel having access to a drug like that. Men who've been trafficking women for . . ." Mya's voice trailed off, and Sydney had the same horrified stomach-turning reaction as her friend at the idea of what the cartel planned to do.

"We can't let this formula fall into the Sinaloas' hands," Beckett hissed, probably speaking as both a sheriff and a terrified father.

Camila opened her palms. "I guess it's lucky we're all here, then."

"Not lucky." Beckett stepped forward. "I'm certain this *is* why we're here. Not because of my . . ."

"We'll still help Cora," Carter interjected. "If we can."

Which Sydney knew meant, *If she's alive.*

"Emily and Elaina's flight will be landing soon," Beckett said in a somber tone. "I should head to the airport."

"I'll pick them up." Gray snatched a set of keys from the table. "They're like family to me."

Beckett pivoted to face him, a hand in the air. "What do you think they are to me?"

"They're here because of you," Gray snapped. What happened to the man who'd said he wouldn't break down a door for Sydney? Why was he trying to face off with Beckett now?

"Yeah, I'm well aware of that fact." Beckett didn't back down from what felt like an inevitable fight, one she highly doubted was really about who'd be escorting Emily and Elaina from the airport. "I'm going."

"You riding with me, then?" Gray swallowed the space between himself and Beckett, the keys dangling from his hand.

"I don't think that's the best idea," Sydney intervened.

"Am I missing something?" Carter came between them with outstretched arms as if to stop them from throwing fists, and Griffin quietly joined him. "What's with you two? You've barely looked at each other since Mexico."

"Nothing," both Gray and Beckett said at the same time, maintaining eye contact with one another.

*Well, this is just great.* "How about Griffin and I go instead?" Sydney did her best to keep her tone level, to not yell at them like they were her son.

"No," Gray and Beckett said at the same time.

"Gray," was all she managed, hoping to remind him of their conversation outside.

"Gray. Griffin. You two are going." Carter's deep voice was borderline authoritative, command or not. "Beckett, you hang back so we can talk about Cora and Ivy. I need more information."

That wasn't true, and Sydney knew it. But Carter was trying to defuse the tension the only way he knew how. Barking out orders.

"Fine. But if anything happens to them . . ." Beckett's warning trailed off as he took two steps back.

"Save the warning for yourself," Gray countered, motioning for Griffin to head out.

Beckett shook his head and took off for the back hallway leading to the stairs, but Sydney didn't follow, opting to give him some space to cool off.

"You seem to be at the center of whatever the hell just

happened," Carter cut straight to the point. "Is this thing with them going to be a problem?"

Sydney let go of a heavy breath and shook her head. Camila provided a short reprieve by pulling Carter to the side of the room to talk in private, saving her from an undoubted ass-chewing.

"A word," Jack requested, tipping his head toward the foyer.

"What's up?" she asked once they were alone by the front door, the engine noise from the SUV already retreating.

Jack set a palm to the door and studied her. "I've known Gray nearly my whole life, and I was by his side when he was at his worst." He set his free hand to his chest, his tone more serious than she was used to hearing from him. "He's been through too much. You need to be careful."

"The last thing I want to do is hurt him. I promise." And that was the truth. "But he told me outside before Camila showed up that—"

"I don't care if he told you he still believes in the Easter Bunny." Jack pushed away from the door. "Gray knows how to trick people into believing he's okay. He's a fucking expert at it." He pounded once on his chest. "He let everyone believe he was okay after the accident. Told people what they wanted to hear. But on the inside, he was dying. Actually wished he was dead, Sydney. Thought he could never operate again, so in his mind, what was the point of going on."

"I . . ." She set a hand over her heart, wishing so much that she'd had the nerve all those years ago to walk into Gray's hospital room when he'd been awake instead of only checking on him when unconscious.

"Considering you were wearing a man's shirt when I saw you at the bungalow this morning, I think it's safe to say you slept with Beckett, and Gray's messed up about it." He added in a softer tone, "We all thought you and Gray would end up together. That it was just a matter of time. That fate brought you two back together last October. Brought you to the team."

*Fate.* That word . . .

"I was the one there for Gray, helping pull him free from the hell he'd created for himself after that accident. But I can't have my best friend getting killed on an op because his head is elsewhere. I can't bring back the dead." His gaze fell to the scuffed hardwoods, the only indication someone had once lived there.

Was Jack right? Had Gray only told her what he thought she wanted to hear? Because seeing the way he'd faced Beckett minutes ago had her wondering if Jack was right. Was Gray faking it for the sake of not just the mission but for her benefit? Always putting others first, that was him.

"What do you want me to do?" she asked in defeat, and Jack worked his eyes to her face.

"Griffin and Savanna couldn't keep their hands off each other on that op despite orders to do so. And you know the story with Jesse and Ella. But if you care about Gray, you'll refrain from mixing business and pleasure with Beckett while operating together."

"Done," she answered. Zero hesitation. She and Beckett had already made the decision to do so. And considering she barely knew him, she needed time to process her feelings for Beckett. "You don't believe me?" She angled her head, trying to get a read on his blank expression.

"Carter asked you and Beckett to share a hotel room starting tomorrow," Jack began, "so no, I don't."

## CHAPTER TWENTY-FIVE

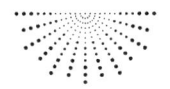

"I promise everything will be okay," Sydney told Levi over the phone an hour after Gray and Griffin had left the safe house for the airport. They'd be back soon, and she wanted to check in on her son before solely focusing on the mission.

"Alice had dinner here tonight," Levi whispered. "Dad's trying to turn us into a family. But Alice stopped being family the day she betrayed you."

Sydney dropped onto the bottom bunk in the bedroom, careful not to whack her head on the bed above her.

"We'll figure it out when I come home," she forced out in as steady a voice as possible. "Will you put your dad on the phone?" Seth had left five messages since his marriage announcement yesterday, and she hadn't had the stomach to call him back before now.

"Sure. Don't forget . . ."

"Stay safe, I know." She smiled even though she knew he couldn't see her. "I love you."

"Love you more," he said before calling for Seth.

She set her free hand on her thigh, bracing herself for the rest of the conversation.

"I've called you a half dozen fucking times, Sydney," Seth bit out the moment he picked up the line.

"Whiskey. Tango," Levi began, enunciating each word in the background in a low voice, "Foxtrot. Daaaad."

"That shit works with your mom, but not me. Get in your room," Seth snapped, his tone sharp. It had Sydney back on her feet, ready to go to bat for her son. All day. Every day.

"Give him hell, Mom. You have my permission," was the last thing Levi said, and she heard his angry steps fading in the background.

"Oh, you need permission to be a bitch to me now, huh?"

Who the hell was he right now? He never talked to her like that. Even when they fought in the past, he wasn't *that* much of an asshole. Was this Alice's doing? Was she trying to place an even greater wedge between them? Was she worried he might cheat on her the way he'd cheated on Sydney?

"Have you been drinking?" That was the only possible explanation for his insane behavior. Historically, he didn't handle his liquor well. Maybe he was anxious about having Alice over for dinner with Levi and had one too many.

"I've been on edge since I shared the engagement with you yesterday, and you hung up on me. So yeah, I'm drinking. Not your problem."

"It is my problem when my son is at your house and I'm relying on you to take care of him." She paced the length of the small room between the two bunk beds.

"He's *your* son now, is he? Never mind the fact I adopted him ten years ago. Raised him like my own. His biological father's only contribution was to knock you up during a one-night stand."

Sydney stopped walking and did her best to pull herself

together. "Levi's father never had a chance to be in his life. He died serving our country, so don't you dare disrespect him like that." Torn between rage and tears, she curled the fingers of her free hand into her palm and set her fist over her heart. Fighting hadn't been her intention, and she probably wouldn't have made the call if she'd known Seth had been drinking.

"I'm sorry," Seth surprised her by saying, his voice softer this time. "I shouldn't have said that. I'm just mad."

"And why exactly are you mad at me?" she asked, keeping her fist firmly to her chest. When he didn't elaborate, and she heard the swish of liquid, she realized he was drinking straight from the bottle. Perfect. "You're marrying my ex-best friend, the woman you cheated on me with. Hell, she's trying to take my life from me. Has the nerve to even wear my perfume. If anything, I should be upset with you."

"I bought her that perfume."

*Wait, what?* "Why would you do that?" Did he realize how insane he sounded right now, liquor or not?

"Because I . . . because I miss the way our home used to smell. How you smell." He'd gone from sounding angry to a wounded animal in a matter of seconds.

*Annnd I need to sit again.* "You hate me. Cheated on me. You're marrying someone else. Why do you miss how I smell?" She shook her head. "This is the alcohol." But had he been drunk when he bought Alice the Tom Ford *Lost Cherry* perfume too?

"The person you've become since we divorced is the woman I always wanted you to be." He sighed. "Why'd you become her now? Why not when we were together?"

*You've got to be kidding me.*

"I always thought you were cheating on me while you were traveling. Your dad had you working in all those exotic locations during our marriage, and I just assumed . . ."

"Not this again," she whispered. "I didn't cheat. And your *what-if* scenarios about me were no excuse for what you did." This conversation was way heavier than she'd anticipated it would be. She'd planned to say, *Marry Alice, I don't care. But make sure every decision you make is okay with Levi first*, but this . . . THIS? What was this conversation? What was happening right now?

"I miss you," Seth slurred.

A humorless chuckle fell from her lips, but her stomach dropped right along with the fake laugh. "That's the alcohol talking. You don't mean any of this."

Not that it changed anything. But first Gray and now Seth.

What were the chances?

He was quiet for a moment before adding, "I'm sorry for calling you a bitch, or well, alluding to you being like one." And then the line went dead.

Sydney stared at the phone in her hand, trying to grasp what had happened. From Levi yelling at his dad to Seth professing she'd become the woman he'd always wanted her to be.

So, she hadn't been good enough for him then? *But I am now?*

She wasn't sure how long she sat in a daze after tossing her phone on the bed, but at some point she'd found herself in the nearest bathroom to check her eyes. To ensure they weren't bloodshot before facing one more man tonight. The only man she wanted to see. *And he's off-limits. Well, for now.*

She went in search of the room Beckett had selected, unsure if he was still there, and found him two doors down, alone on a bottom bunk with his head in his hands.

"Mind if I come in?" She'd rather talk now before Gray

came back. She wasn't entirely sure what to say, but she assumed a conversation with him would go much better than it had with Gray and Seth.

Beckett lifted his head and looked over at her. "Of course." His voice was raw and raspy as if he'd been yelling, but she didn't take him for the type to have a shouting match with the wall.

"I know it's not easy for you to stay here instead of going to get Elaina and Emily. I'm sorry."

"I guess I should've expected some animosity from Gray." He remained seated, and she wasn't sure if she ought to risk joining him.

The last time they were together on a bed . . . well, the man had more than delivered. She didn't trust her body to *not* respond around him. She didn't have control over the feelings he provoked. But more than that, her guard kept crashing down when he was near.

"Gray's stubborn," she responded as if he hadn't guessed as much.

"That makes two of us," he tossed back with a self-deprecating smile.

She turned, giving him her profile as her nerves bested her. But at the feel of Beckett's fingers skimming the side of her hand, she faced him.

Beckett wrapped his hand around hers, and that firm, masculine touch had her eyes closing. He guided her to the bed, and she sat next to him, not ready to look him in the eyes. "This okay? Gray's still gone, but I'm not quite sure of the rules."

He kept hold of her hand as she opened her eyes and looked his way, but within a second, he understood she was on the verge of breaking into a hundred pieces.

He turned on the bed and palmed her cheek with his free

hand. "What happened? Did someone say something?" he said darkly, his pupils dilating a touch.

Dilated pupils, didn't Ecstasy do that? Impact mood. Desire. Mimic the natural emotions that were now on full display from Beckett.

*The case. I need to focus. That drug . . .*

Worry clung to his dark eyes as he asked, "Did someone hurt you?"

"Does emotional damage count?"

"That's the worst kind for me." His honesty and lack of hiding behind some manly concept of needing to be tough twenty-four seven was humbling. And appreciated. "What's wrong?"

"So many things." She frowned and let go of a sigh as he leveled her with a hard look, one that said he'd hurt anyone who'd so much as upset her.

He smoothed the back of his hand along her cheek, and her lids fluttered closed once again. The way he touched her, the way he seemed to know what she needed and how she needed it was just . . .

"When I'm confused or unsure about something, I call Levi's dad," she confessed, her body trembling as she shared something no one else knew. Well, no one aside from her therapist, who'd first recommended the idea two years ago. "Not Seth. I mean his birth father, Matt. The man who never had a chance to see Levi born because he died. Roadside bomb."

She scooched a bit closer to him, their knees bumping in the process. And he squeezed her hand with his other one, a gentle and reassuring, *I'm here for you.*

"I was a Military Intelligence officer and had tried out for one of the Cultural Support Teams. I made it and was later attached to a group of Green Berets. I deployed to

Afghanistan whenever they did," she slowly shared. "Matt was one of the guys I worked with, and we became friends. Totally platonic. It was never like that." She took a few breaths, working up to the next part. "One night, we were both feeling pretty shitty about life. The war. Everything. And we . . . you know." She didn't need to spell it out for him. "It was a mistake. Also, forbidden. And the next day, we both agreed it'd never happen again."

The fact Beckett was still holding her hand through this meant more to her than she could put into words. She felt his compassion in his touch and not a flinch in the way of judgment.

"Six weeks later, I realized I was pregnant. Matt barely had time to process the news because a day later, he was ordered to roll out on an op. A target package my team had put together was given the green light by the higher-ups. It was my intelligence that put him on the road that day." A sharp, stabbing pain filled her abdomen as she recalled the moment she'd learned an IED had killed Matt and severely wounded another guy on the team.

"You know this, but I need to say it anyway—it wasn't your fault."

She knew that, yes. But it didn't erase the horrible pit of guilt when that thought hit her at the start of each day. "Matt didn't have any family. He grew up in foster care. Never adopted."

"That's not true. He had family. The military. And now, he still has family. He lives on through Levi."

Her attempts to resist crying at his words failed. It was hard not to shed her emotions when Beckett framed her face with both palms, and a few tears fell freely.

"I leave him messages about Levi. Ask him for advice. I

pay to have a number in service so I can do this. I know that sounds . . ."

"You amaze me, that's all I know." Beckett's rough voice had her meeting his eyes, finding them glistening as if he might cry too.

"If I were amazing, I never would've married a man I didn't love." She still wasn't sure if she had said yes to Seth's proposal as one last act of rebellion against her father since her dad hated Seth. Or because she felt rushed to provide Levi with a role model growing up. "And I'm not sure if you heard Gray share this morning that he knows Seth cheated on me four years ago with one of my best friends."

"You tell me what you want and when you want to. No rush."

How'd she feel closer to Beckett in thirty-six hours than she ever had with Seth in all their years of marriage?

"Seth just told me he misses me. He wishes I was the person I am now when we were together. As if that'd have made a difference in our marriage. But he was drunk, so I'm sure he's just confused."

Beckett slanted his brows in surprise. "So, he proposed to your former best friend as a way to . . . what, make you jealous? Get you back?" He narrowed his eyes as if he didn't understand how two plus two made four in this case.

"I don't think so, but it wouldn't matter. We're done." She let that sink in for a moment. "And Gray," she began, realizing he needed to hear this one more time, even though she'd already told him as much. "He and I won't be getting back together either."

He quietly studied her, his hands on his lap now. She took the chance to rid herself of any remaining tears and stood. "Can I ask you something?"

She faced him, unsure what to do with her arms. There

was so much tension there. Everywhere for that matter. "Sure."

He slowly rose and removed his ball cap, a new one he must've grabbed from his suitcase since she was pretty sure he'd lost his other one in the jungle. "What do *you* want?"

"That's easy." She wet her lips and stared into his eyes, a sense of calm washing over her with his gaze pointed her way. "I want what I can't have."

## CHAPTER TWENTY-SIX

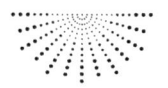

"What is it that you want but can't have?" Beckett wasn't so arrogant as to assume she meant him, but damn, he wanted exactly that.

Sydney's fingers danced along her collarbone while saying, "I want what Valentina and Martín have. I didn't need to spend much time with them to know they have the kind of marriage most people dream about. I could see and feel their love for each other in every look and touch."

He could sense her guard was still down, but was it temporary?

"I gave up on the possibility of ever falling in love again," she continued in a soft tone, "but seeing them together made me wish I could have that too."

"And why can't you? Why is it not possible?" He'd sworn off love and romance too, but then this blonde badass archer with a beautiful soul came into his life, and now he wasn't sure what to think from one minute to the next.

"Hey," a voice called out. Jack and his horrible timing . . . "Emily and Elaina just pulled up."

Beckett took a step away from Sydney at the sight of Jack's disapproving frown.

"Coming," Sydney told Jack, stealing a quick look at him still hanging back in the hall.

*Jack must know about us. But is there an us? Can there ever be?*

Jack nodded and slapped the doorframe once as if to say hurry, then left.

Beckett hated that their conversation felt unresolved, and he had no clue when or if they'd have a chance to pick things back up again. He followed her from the room, then paused at the top of the stairs, wondering if they shouldn't enter the living room side by side.

"You go first," Sydney suggested, sharing his thoughts. "I'll give it a minute and come down."

"Yeah, okay." At the sound of Elaina's voice, he shoved aside his emotions and maneuvered around Sydney to go downstairs.

"Beckett!" Elaina called out the moment he walked through the doorway to the living room. She shot straight for him, arms stretched open for a hug.

Elaina wrapped her arms around his waist, and the guilt at being there and away from his daughter struck him hard. "Hey," he said softly, meeting Emily's tired eyes from across the room where she stood between Gray and Griffin.

Aside from Jack on the couch, the room was empty, but he heard footsteps coming from the hallway.

"How are you?" He meant his question for both Emily and Elaina as Emily swapped places with her daughter for a hug.

"I'm here. That's all I know," Emily said into his ear and faked a small smile for his benefit after pulling back.

"I'm sorry," he mouthed, his head spinning, reality settling in with the two of them in Santiago.

"Mya." Elaina beamed and started for Mya, who'd walked into the room with Oliver.

"Wait, you two know each other?" Beckett pointed a finger back and forth between them as he tried to remember when and how Mya had met Elaina.

"I was at Julia and Finn's wedding in North Carolina last fall," Mya reminded Beckett, and then it clicked as Elaina fist-bumped Oliver in greeting. "Both of us were." Mya tipped her head toward Oliver as if this would jog Beckett's memory.

Oliver dragged a finger over his throat, and it came back to Beckett. Julia and Mya were friends. They'd been the ones to help keep Oliver from losing his head last year. And Julia was married to one of A.J.'s teammates, Finn.

Mya waved to Emily. "How are you?"

"I'm here," Emily repeated what she'd told Beckett and faked yet another smile. She looked exhausted and stressed, and she had every right to be.

As more guilt stabbed him in the chest, he crossed his arms and tried to steady his breathing so he wouldn't look so shaken up.

"I'm sorry I didn't tell you anything in D.C.," Elaina told him while striding back his way, and she pursed her lips apologetically. "It had to be this way."

"Right." Beckett nodded. "Mya," he shared. "She would've . . ." He closed one eye a second later. "Why'd you call her a dark-haired woman with dark eyes if you knew Mya's name?" he asked at the realization. "Why not tell your mom it was Mya that needed help?"

Elaina turned to look at Mya for a moment. "I didn't know Mya was in trouble." She lowered her head as if surprised by that fact. "I only saw the other woman in trouble. I'm sorry."

"Hey, it's okay. I'm fine." Mya approached Elaina and took a knee alongside her. "If Beckett hadn't gone to Mexico, I might not have been okay, so you saved me anyway."

"Wait." Now Beckett was really curious. "You said 'the other woman.' Who's the woman who'd die if—"

"Her." Elaina pointed to the hallway, and Beckett swiveled around to see Camila and Carter joining them in the room.

"Well, you must be the one I've heard so much about." Camila smiled and extended her hand while waiting for Elaina to approach.

Elaina took slow steps, studying her without accepting her palm. Was she nervous around her? No, that wasn't it. But the way Elaina observed her was—

"You were going to die earlier today," Elaina whispered, interrupting Beckett's thoughts. "But you didn't." There was a childlike quality to her tone Beckett hadn't heard from her since they'd met when she was around eight or nine.

Camila withdrew her hand and peered at Carter for clarification. She appeared as confused as Beckett felt.

"What do you mean?" Carter asked, and Beckett spied Sydney coming into the room from the corner of his eye.

Elaina frowned and took one more step toward Camila as if feeling the need to inspect her closer. "You were going to be somewhere else earlier. You would've been taken as a hostage. Tortured. And then killed." Well, that was blunt, even for Elaina.

"I, um." Camila's forehead tightened as she studied Elaina, and Mya pushed upright to stand by Sydney.

"Elaina, sweetheart." Emily came up behind her daughter

and set her hands on her shoulders. "Sorry," she apologized to Camila.

"It's okay," Camila began. "I was supposed to be somewhere earlier, but then Carter called, and I changed my plans. She may be right."

Beckett remembered now. Camila had planned to surveil Jorge's house, and fuck, that meant she would've more than likely been detained while there. Because Elaina was always right. And neither Mya nor Camila would be standing there now had . . . *Well, had Cora not called me for help.* Because either way, Mya would have been in Tulum to meet her contact. And Camila would have tracked her scientist to Santiago and to Jorge Rojas.

But Cora . . . she was the link that brought them all together. The reason these two women were still alive. *This is over my head.*

Elaina continued to observe Camila as if there were something else she wanted to share, searching for a thought that wouldn't quite materialize.

"What is it?" Mya asked, drawing the same conclusion as Beckett.

Elaina reached for Camila's arm instead of her hand. Closing her eyes, she whispered, "You're like me, aren't you? But not quite the same, I suppose."

Beckett watched the whole scene unfold in shock, not sure what to make of it. It seemed only Emily was at ease with her daughter's abilities. Of course, she knew Elaina better than anyone in that room.

"I don't know what you mean," Camila said while Elaina opened her eyes.

Beckett shifted to the side to better view Elaina as Emily offered her daughter an alternative explanation, "Maybe you just feel connected to her because of your vision."

"Honestly, it's starting to feel like we're all connected," Oliver spoke up, voicing exactly what Beckett was beginning to believe.

"If you're not ready for others to know, I understand." Elaina let go of Camila's arm and stepped back. Emily wrapped her arms around her. "Most people wouldn't believe you anyway." She peered around the room, remaining comfortably within the safety of her mother's embrace. "But they will." Her shoulders fell on a sigh. "Mom, my head doesn't hurt anymore. The headache is gone."

"Well, that's something to celebrate," Emily said, her eyes glistening as if she might cry at the news.

"But I'd like to go to bed," Elaina told her while squinting at Camila with that searching-for-a-memory look of hers Beckett had grown to know.

"I saved you a room with a queen bed instead of bunk beds," Carter said. "Griffin can show you where it is."

"Of course." Griffin stepped away from where he'd remained by Gray and swiped a hand along his jawline.

"Elaina?" Camila tipped her head and stepped forward when Emily released her hold of her daughter.

"Yeah?" Elaina asked in an almost wistful tone.

"Do you know anything else . . ." Camila let her voice trail off.

"Not yet, but I think being here will help me," Elaina said with confidence. "I think being near *you* will help me," she added, and Emily shot Beckett a puzzled, slightly worried look. "Goodnight." She tossed a hand in the air, doing a three-sixty to make sure she waved to everyone, and then Emily quietly followed her and Griffin from the room.

"That was interesting," Oliver muttered a few moments later, setting his hands on his hips while focusing on Carter.

"Her head was pretty bad when she arrived at the airport,"

Gray shared, speaking for the first time since returning with Emily and Elaina. He certainly had Beckett's attention. "The closer we got here, the less pain she was in."

*And now her headache is gone.* Beckett shifted toward Camila, who looked like she'd seen a ghost. Quite the contrast to the cool and confident woman he'd first met a little over an hour ago. *Is Elaina better because of you? Why?*

"I don't know why," Camila said, responding to the question no one had vocalized, but Beckett had definitely been thinking.

But knowing Elaina, Beckett had a feeling they'd all soon find out.

## CHAPTER TWENTY-SEVEN

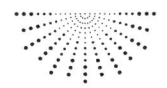

"Mason's at Martín's home." Mya tossed her phone onto the bottom bunk, walked to the small window, and peeked through the dusty blinds. "He didn't waste time . . . must've flown overnight." Mya stepped back and faced Sydney, wiping the dust on her hot-pink yoga pants. "Martín knows Miguel's cousin is poking around Tulum, right?"

"Yeah, Martín will be on the lookout." Sydney released her knee and went for the other one, stretching out her muscles. "But we just ran five miles to de-stress, and one text from Mason has your face looking all contorted." *Contorted? Is that a thing?*

"He's just frustrating me. Pissed about what happened." Mya leaned her back against the window in their bedroom and crossed her arms. "I know, I know. He kind of has a right to be." She shrugged. "Buuuut, he wouldn't be in Mexico now with the assistance of Martín's team to dismantle those human trafficking networks had I not been . . ." She freed her locked arms and used air quotes when finishing her sentence, "'Reckless.'"

Sydney let go of her other knee only to bend her leg

backward, holding the side of the bunk bed so she didn't wobble and fall. Her balance was off today. "Everything happens for a reason, remember? You've been saying as much since we were sipping mimosas on the beach on Sunday."

"True. But if I respond to his texts, I won't be so ladylike right now. So, I need to let him cool down. And well, I should too before I talk to him again."

"He just cares about you," Sydney reminded her.

"Martín's going to wait to make any moves against the cartel until we've completed our op here. Unless Hector causes problems before then," Sydney said, sharing what Carter had told her in private last night before she'd called her son.

"Which is why I don't get Mason's need to be in Mexico right now. He's not needed yet." Mya exaggerated her frown this time. "He just wants to be closer to me since he has orders not to come to Chile, I'm sure of it."

Sydney smiled at Mya's dramatics, then let go of her leg when the door behind her opened. Camila had slept in their room last night for a handful of hours, and she was gone before Sydney and Mya had risen for a run. She'd already showered and changed in that time too.

"You were up earlier than us," Mya commented as Camila shut the door behind her and went to her luggage alongside the bunk beds across from Sydney.

Camila grabbed what looked like a journal from her bag before facing them. *"Deus ajuda a quem cedo madruga."*

Sydney could only translate the first word, so she waited for her to share what she'd said.

"God helps those who wake up early." Camila clutched the black leather-bound book to her chest and tipped her lips into a friendly smile.

"Then I'm getting up even earlier from now on." Mya sat on one of the beds, careful not to hit her head in the process. "I need all the help I can get."

"Don't we all." Camila turned her attention to Sydney. "Does running help clear your head? I'm one of those women that if you see me running, that means someone is chasing me," she added with a light laugh.

*Did it help me? Not today.* No, her cyclone of thoughts whirled around uncontrollably on her run.

"Girl, you and me both," Mya responded before Sydney had a chance. "This one dragged me along to de-stress."

"I don't think it worked for you," Camila commented, her tone level. Her dark eyes were ringed with brown eyeliner and dark mascara, making them stand out even more. God, the woman was stunning. How did she and Carter never . . .

*Carter was once married*, Sydney remembered. So, there was that. But still.

"So, Carter's really like a brother to you?" Mya asked, sharing Sydney's brain.

"Is Carter attractive? Yes, I do have eyes." Camila angled her head, her gaze lifting to the ceiling as if in thought. "But we are too much alike." She balled one hand in front of her, focusing back on the room again. "Not the fiery, passionate kind of arguing that results in hot sex. No, no. We fight like siblings. Especially when he tries to boss me around. Warns me not to do anything dangerous." She freed her fist into an open palm. "Men." She shrugged. "You know how they can be."

"Oh, that I do." Mya playfully scowled. "I'd love to hear more about Carter though. He's such a wild card. A mystery. And if he's like you . . .?"

"Carter is . . . well, Carter." *And that was all they were going to get, huh?* Yeah, she really was like Carter, then.

Camila went for a quick subject change and said, "I'm surprised he didn't bring Dallas with him here. Doesn't he always travel with his dog?"

"Lately, he has someone back in Pennsylvania watching Dallas on ops, so he doesn't have to worry about something happening to him," Sydney explained.

"Ah, that makes sense. He loves that animal more than he likes most people." Camila grinned. "Can't say I blame him." She turned to leave, but then went still and released a deep breath. "How well do you know Elaina?"

*Ohhh. Hmm.* Now she was the one with questions. "Not well," Sydney shared. "Why?" Was she remembering Elaina's words to her last night? Did they spook her?

Camila's profile was to Sydney, so she couldn't get a great read on her as she said, "It's just interesting how we all managed to be here. How everything is connected. And she seemed to know it would work out this way."

"But she couldn't intervene. Not yet, at least," Mya said. "But I'm guessing Elaina felt the need to come to Chile now because she has to step in and help us at some point?"

Sydney peered at Mya as she waved a hand in the air as if still processing the last two days. *Meeee too.*

"And Elaina's visions, they're always accurate?" Camila slowly faced them, lowering the leather notebook to her side, eyes moving to Sydney this time.

"From what I know, but . . ." Sydney's eyes thinned as she studied her. "Was she wrong about you? Are you not like her?"

Sydney was pretty sure Camila's smile was the first fake one she'd seen. Her eyes didn't crinkle around the edges like all the other times. "No visions like hers, no."

*Why does that feel like a loophole answer?* But Sydney wouldn't prod. It wasn't her business.

"It just amazes me everything that has transpired because one eccentric billionaire is obsessed with Capone and the twenties. And had he never visited that club, your friend Beckett would never have come to Mexico . . ." Camila's words faded a bit into the air.

"A crazy string of events and all that jazz that brought us together," Mya added on while snapping her fingers.

"Yes." Camila nodded. "*Destino.*"

*Fate.*

"Wait . . . jazz." Mya nearly bumped her head on the bed above her as she jumped to her feet. "Sydney, remember your grandfather's eightieth birthday party? Your dad's dad."

"How could I forget? It was a month before he died. Why?"

Mya set a hand on the top bunk, her eyes going to the floor as if working through her thoughts. "Your grandfather asked you to sing at the party. None of us even knew you could sing. And you didn't want to, but you'd do anything for him, so you sang his favorites."

Sydney smiled at the memories. Her dad's parents were so different from her own, and she was grateful they'd had a hand in raising her while her father had been busy building his empire.

"The songs you sang that night," Mya said while circling her hand in the air as if Sydney was supposed to understand her point but was still not on the same page. "The ones you said your grandmother taught you were—"

"From the twenties," Sydney finished for her, starting to understand where she was going with this.

"Ah, I see," Camila said with a nod. "If we can find a way to get Jorge's attention, that might be our chance to get close to him without getting killed, like I apparently would have yesterday had I gone near his house."

Sydney pointed at her chest, still damp from sweat from their early morning run. "You want me to sing? What, at the club Wednesday night?" No, that was crazy. Give her a gun. A bow. A target to take out. Sure. Sing in public again? No, that was a one-time-only thing because she adored her grandfather.

"There's a twenties band that will be performing, and I'm pretty sure the event sign I saw in the hotel lobby advertised a female singer." Was Camila really agreeing with Mya's idea?

Sydney adamantly shook her head and folded her arms. "We're not going to kidnap the lead singer so I can take over for her. How would that even work anyway?"

Camila reached for Sydney's forearm, setting it there while looking into her eyes. "Money talks. Carter has plenty. He can buy this woman off. Ask her not to show up." Her eyes gleamed as if the plan was brilliant. "You happen to be at the club, and Jorge will be disappointed when the singer is a no-show. Then you stand up and offer to sing. This will catch Jorge's attention." She was nodding as if the scheme was already a done deal. "You seduce the man with your voice by singing his favorite songs."

"Right." Mya snapped her fingers. "And if he happens to invite you to his table after, that's our way in."

"But you'll say you're with your boyfriend and friends, and you can't leave them out, so you turn him down." Camila was smiling now. "A man like Jorge will love a challenge. A taken woman that saves his night by singing . . . he will want you. He'll insist we all join his group."

"So, I'm bait, huh?" Sydney laughed at the absurdity.

"It's worth a shot. Your teammate, Jesse, will be there. You'll have some of us with you as backup," Camila offered. "My four men are still staking out the hotel. So, we have them too." She nodded. "This might be our only way to get our foot in the door in the literal sense."

Sydney palmed her cheek, feeling the heat rise to her face. "Let me cool off and shower while I think about it."

Camila let go of her arm, and Sydney grabbed her shower kit from her luggage. "*Destino*," she said behind her. "There is no question now. It is all fate."

## CHAPTER TWENTY-EIGHT

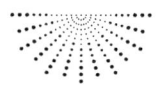

Flustered and still heated from her run, despite the fact it'd been barely fifty outside that morning, Sydney rushed to the closest bathroom in the hall. She clutched her shower kit to her chest while reaching for the door handle but nearly fell as the door opened inward.

"Whoa," Beckett said, grabbing hold of Sydney's arm as she almost crashed straight into his brick wall of a naked chest.

She stepped back into the hall and nervously looked around for Gray or even Jack. But they were alone. "Hi."

"Hi." He smiled, releasing her arm and setting a palm to the doorframe, his muscles on full display.

"I guess it's your turn to be half-naked around me lately, huh?" She swallowed, trying not to remember when she'd gone to his bungalow and found him showering that night. And now here they were, Tuesday morning in Chile, and he was shirtless, his body still wet from his shower.

She worked her gaze from his chest to his full lips, then on to his dark, slicked-back hair. Hair she wanted to thrust her fingers into and tug at, urging him to draw that mouth of his to hers.

"You go for a run?" He arched a brow, no concern in his eyes. It wasn't like they were being hunted. No danger for them. For now.

If she agreed to Mya's crazy singing idea, she'd be placing herself quite literally in the limelight for Jorge Rojas.

"I did," she managed.

"Did it help?" he asked, his voice a bit hoarse as his attention skated to her sports bra. She'd tossed her tee back in the room when they'd returned since it'd been soaked in sweat. And now, her cleavage was on full display for this man to see.

He'd caressed her breasts. Sucked her nipples. Taken his time to kiss every inch of her skin in that bungalow. He knew her body, but he was looking at her now as if seeing her again for the first time on the beach. Maybe he was practicing restraint, and that was why his jaw was locked tight.

She could relate. Her body responded to seeing this strong, tough man with only a towel barely clinging to his hips. She was desperate to reach out and trail her finger along his abs, follow the lines that dipped beneath the towel. She wanted to wrap her hand around his cock and stroke him. Help ease his tension the way she'd hoped running would do for her.

Clearly, it hadn't helped. And standing before Beckett now, she knew it'd take a lot more than running to unwind the sexual tension between them.

"What'd you say?" He'd asked her something, right?

She'd allowed her attention to remain on the towel a bit too long, and slowly worked her eyes back up to his face. The knowing smile he gave her said he knew exactly what was on her mind.

"I'm thinking you're still about as tense as me," he said instead of re-asking his question.

"Did you, um, at least get any sleep?" His eyes were bloodshot and exhausted, so she figured if he slept, it wasn't well.

He shook his head. "The only decent sleep I've had in weeks was . . ." He paused as if checking to ensure they were still alone. "With you at the bungalow."

She needed him.

Wanted him deep inside her.

*Not the time. Not the place. And I need to sing in public for the first time in fifteen years.*

"If you keep looking at me like that, I'm going to pull you back into this bathroom with me," he said, the warning clear in his tone. "Please," he added, a plea in his voice this time.

For the life of her, she had no clue why she whispered, "What would you do if you pulled me in there?"

Beckett angled his head, meeting her eyes. He leaned in so close she could smell his minty fresh breath. "Sweetheart, I'm two seconds away from showing you," he growled out in a low, raspy voice that went straight to her core.

"I, um." She wet her lips, trying to remember why she was there in the first place. "I should shower," she forced out. "Alone," she added around a swallow, remembering Gray was somewhere in the house. *And also, we're working. Focus.*

Beckett pushed away from the doorframe, taking a cue from her words to behave. But the desire didn't disappear from his heated gaze.

She lowered her shower kit from where she had it clutched to her abdomen and swapped places with him.

Once he was in the hallway, his gaze landed on her leggings. "The idea of other men seeing you in those . . ." His jaw strained beneath his facial hair, and his broad chest rose from a deep inhalation.

She wasn't sure if he'd meant to say that out loud, but she found herself drawn to his alpha-possessive need to keep other men from seeing her body. Would it stop her from wearing the fitted leggings? Probably not. But she wouldn't mind having him ravage her in the bedroom and—

"Touch yourself while you're in there. You need to," he commanded, completely derailing her thoughts. "You're going to be strung too tight to operate if you don't."

"And did you do the same?" She lifted a brow, imagining his strong hand around his hard length, getting himself off.

"What do you think?" His deep voice sent a ripple of heat cascading over her exposed skin.

She nodded her answer, and a small smile ghosted his lips.

"Now, be a good girl and do the same," he murmured darkly before walking away, leaving her breathless and horny.

All thoughts of responsibilities and singing were gone the second she was beneath the steamy water.

She replayed her time with Beckett from the other night in her head while sliding her fingers along the seam of her sex before thrusting two inside her pussy.

And then she couldn't help but create a new scene, writing it in her head as if she were the author of one of those books, while she pressed upon her swollen clit, which was almost too sensitive to touch.

*Beckett takes me over his knee and swats my ass three times while whispering, "Bad girl." Then he sets me face down on the bed.*

*My ass is still in the air, and he caresses and kisses my*

*flesh before reaching between my legs to cup my swollen, aching sex.*

*"Spank me there too," I beg.*

*He flips me around and runs his finger over my seam before sucking it, eyes holding mine.*

*He does as I ask, and my back arches off the bed at his touch, desperate for him to take me. To give me what I need.*

*"You want me to fill that tight cunt of yours, don't you?" he rasps before thrusting inside me and . . .*

Her explosive orgasm shocked her back to reality, and she came harder than she ever had on her own.

Sydney set a hand to the tiled wall, trying to find her breath.

"Where did that come from?" she whispered to herself while reaching for her soap a few seconds later, still trying to steady her racing heart.

But she knew the answer. It was all Beckett. Her desire to unleash and be sexually free around this man was like nothing she'd ever experienced.

Free and yet she wanted to surrender in the bedroom. Give herself completely to him in that way.

He was right. She had needed that. She'd never have made it through another conversation with the team otherwise.

And after the shower, she'd be able to focus.

To face the music.

The *actual* music.

*Do I still remember how to sing?*

\* \* \*

"I'm sorry, what?" Gray was the first to object to Mya's idea about seducing Jorge Rojas on Wednesday.

But it was Beckett that Sydney couldn't rip her focus away from, and the straining of his jaw as he stared at her as if piercing her invisible armor with his dark gaze. He didn't have to verbally object, she felt his over-my-dead-body in the way he looked at her.

"We're not considering this," Gray went on when no one else had spoken. He strode to Carter, holding his leg a bit as if in pain. "Not happening. She is not seducing that fucking psychopath."

*Well then.* "You realize that will make her want to do this all that much more, right?" Jack jested, tossing a thumb toward Sydney and smiling.

"Aren't you going to say anything?" Was Gray talking to Beckett about this now?

Beckett had his back to the wall, and he remained silently staring at Sydney instead of answering Gray.

"Am I missing something?" Camila asked, drawing Sydney's attention. "Ohhh," she tagged on to her question within seconds, her eyes thinning. "You love her?"

"What?" Gray blinked a few times, his gaze swerving to where he gripped his leg, and he let go. "No, I . . ."

"Don't be mad at Sydney." Mya stood from the couch. "It was my idea. She has a great voice. Happens to know songs from that time because her grandmother taught her. This might be our best chance to get close enough not just to Jorge and Miguel, but near Jesse without raising eyebrows too."

Sydney was the last to stand in the room. Her legs were a bit wobbly, her nerves getting to her the longer Beckett continued to only silently observe her. *What are you thinking?*

"Jesse's only been able to give you bits of information here and there however he's managed to communicate with you," Mya tossed out the reminder, doing her best to sell the seduction idea. "He might have more news to share if we can get close enough to him. Insight that'd help us."

"She has a point," Carter agreed. "Plus, I may not be able to get an invite to the birthday party. I'm working on a believable alias, but Friday's around the corner."

"A man like Jorge will want a woman like Sydney, I guarantee it." Camila strode past Gray to get to Carter, confidence in every step. "And if she's there with a man, he'll pursue her even more."

"It may not work," Oliver joined the conversation. "But I say it's worth a shot." He opened his palms. "I mean, what are the chances Sydney happens to know that kind of music and has a voice worthy of listening to?"

"You checked out three rooms at the hotel, yes?" Camila asked Carter, and he nodded. "Mya and I can go for support. We can stay in a room as sisters."

"Sisters . . .?"

Sydney looked over to see the owner of that small voice. Elaina hung back in the doorway to the hall with her mom at her side, her gaze fixed on Camila.

"Sisters," Elaina softly repeated, her brows pulling together.

Camila pointed to Elaina. "See, she agrees."

"I promised Mya she'd stay behind the scenes on cases. Having her at the hotel might place her in danger. And after what happened in the jungle Sunday, I think she should stay here," Sydney suggested, folding her arms over her gray tee, which she'd paired with jeans after her too-hot shower.

"I'll be fine at the hotel. It's not like anyone will shoot at us. Plus, I was always the lead actress in the plays in high school. I can perform. Put on a show for this Jorge guy," Mya responded. Sydney didn't hear any weakness or tremble in her tone, so maybe she was up for it.

"Yeah, that makes sense," Oliver blurted. "The acting thing, I mean. Your flair for dramatics."

Mya rolled her eyes without bothering to look his way. "Just as long as I don't need to play the role of your girlfriend, I'll be fine." She lifted a shoulder and smiled. "There's only so much acting I can do, ya know?"

Carter freed his hands from his pockets and strode closer to Emily and Elaina. "I need to hang back here and work. Gray and Jack can handle surveillance. Oliver, you'll go to the hotel with them."

He was going to stick Oliver and Mya together, wasn't he?

"Liam should be here soon. Is, um, this close enough for you to, well . . ." Carter fumbled with his words when speaking to Elaina, probably uncomfortable with taking his cues from a twelve-year-old.

"Here is good." Elaina gave him a small smile as Emily scooped a protective arm around her back.

"If Sydney's going to the hotel, I'm going," Gray announced. "Griffin can handle surveilling Jorge with Jack." The tight draw of his lips as he peered at Carter had Sydney's pulse racing, worried about another Beckett–Gray showdown. And in this case, who'd protect Sydney at the hotel.

Jack was right. Gray had said what he believed Sydney needed to hear, and how quickly he'd forgotten those lines.

"Okay, so it'll be Sydney, me, and Mya. And Gray, Beckett, and Oliver at the hotel." Camila looked at Mya and frowned. "The sister idea might not work. Couples all traveling together sounds more realistic." She waved her finger between Mya and Oliver. "I'm assuming Gray and Sydney will stay together?"

"No," Sydney spoke up. But shit, she promised Jack she wouldn't stay with Beckett, which only left Oliver. And regardless of what Mya said about that man . . . Mya staying with Oliver made the most sense.

"Beckett and Sydney," Carter repeated what he'd ordered last night. "Mya and Oliver. And Camila and Gray."

This had Jack on his feet, eyes on Sydney. Was he going to go against Carter? He really was loyally protective of his best friend, and it was something Sydney admired.

"I don't bite," Camila said to Gray. "If you're worried."

"There should be two queen beds in each room," Carter was quick to say. "No need to share a bed. *Any* of you," he added, focusing on Oliver. He'd clearly picked up on the fact their love-hate behavior could quickly spiral to a love-hate between-the-sheets kind of thing.

"Roger that," Oliver muttered sarcastically.

"Where are your men right now?" Carter asked Camila. "The four men you have on your team with you, they're still scoping out the hotel, right?"

Camila nodded. "Yeah, but we can pull two and bring them back here if you need an assist for anything."

"Have them stay put for now." Carter then addressed Sydney, "Do you need a place to practice singing before you head to the hotel?"

Sydney clutched her throat, worried her vocal cords might fail her tomorrow. "Hopefully, it's like riding a bike. Or, in my case, shooting an arrow." She forced a small smile, trying to stay optimistic with a twelve-year-old in the room. Plus, she had two grown men who were more than likely both unhappy she was going to try and seduce Jorge. Well, she assumed Beckett was on the same page as Gray, but he'd been silent.

"I'll get the name of the woman who's supposed to sing Wednesday," Carter began, "then pull her aside Wednesday night and make her an offer. She can fake being ill, so she doesn't piss off her band."

"That should work," Mya commented, but her tone was more tentative now than before, most likely considering the fact she had to "shack up" with Oliver all week.

"Dad's here!" Elaina abruptly announced, despite the fact Sydney hadn't heard anything outside, and then pulled away from Emily and ran toward the front door.

A minute later, Liam walked into the room hand in hand with his daughter. He was tall, with dark blond hair, and he looked eerily similar to the actor Chris Hemsworth. His Aussie accent made the resemblance even more fitting.

Emily hugged her husband, and then Liam redirected his attention to the room, his gaze cutting straight to Beckett.

Beckett visibly tensed as Liam unglued himself from his wife and daughter and ate up the space between them. "Elaina said her headaches are gone now that she's here," Liam shared in a low, raspy tone. "I don't quite understand what in the bloody hell is going on, but if my daughter says we're all supposed to be here, then so be it."

Liam surprised Sydney and probably Beckett, too, pulling him in for a quick one-arm hug. He slapped his back twice, then faced the room.

"So," Liam said while opening his palms, "tell me, who is it that I need to kill?"

"Daaaad," Elaina whispered in dramatic pre-teen fashion.

"Right. Sorry." Liam shrugged.

Elaina grabbed her dad's arm and tugged as if she were five, not twelve. "You will need to kill someone though." She squeezed her eyes closed. "But it's okay. It's to rescue a five-year-old boy."

## CHAPTER TWENTY-NINE

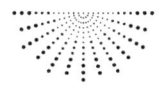

"I know you don't want me doing this. But would you say something? Anything? The silence is killing me."

Beckett crouched and picked up a stone by his boots, which thankfully hadn't been ruined from their river swim two days ago. He remained in that position for a moment, not prepared to face Sydney without sunglasses to shield his eyes.

And no, he sure as hell didn't want her seducing the psycho billionaire. But try and stop a woman like her from doing something? Better chance convincing his die-hard meat-and-cheese-loving father to go vegan.

"We're rolling out in five minutes. I want a chance to clear the air before we're all stuffed into one SUV together." Sydney's soft plea had him standing.

Hotel check-in wasn't until three, and the team had spent most of the day digging into both Jorge and Miguel's backgrounds.

Plus, there was the fact Elaina had shared that her dad would need to kill someone to rescue a kid. *But whose kid?*

"What are you thinking?" She reached for his arm, and he

forced himself to finally meet her beautiful green eyes. "Talk to me."

"No," he replied, allowing the word to roll free as he tossed the stone. "I don't want you in the limelight tomorrow singing for that fucker," he drawled, finally speaking his mind. "The idea makes me want to commit murder, and I don't like killing people. Not even bad guys." *There. But what now?*

Sydney squeezed his arm a bit tighter. And although it was barely sixty-five out now, a contrast to Mexico's harsh heat, he wanted to roll his sleeves to his elbows because it was hot beneath her stare.

"Do you have any other suggestions on how to get Jorge's attention?" She arched a questioning brow.

*Singing . . . fuck. It just . . .* "Carter's still trying to construct an alias and get a party invite. There's that plan. If he can get on the inside, at least we have him and Jesse there. The rest of us can infil that night."

"We need more of us on the inside if possible." Sydney let go of him. "I have no clue if he'll even notice me on Wednesday. It probably won't work anyway."

He looked up at her while busying himself rolling his sleeves to his elbows. "You're funny, sweetheart. A man *not* notice you?"

"If Cora's his type, I'm probably not." He spied her throat move with a subtle swallow she'd probably tried to hide.

Had Sydney seen Cora's photo? Read up on her when he wasn't around? Carter had probably pulled together a case file on all things Cora Barlowe, and there'd been no need to share it with Beckett.

"You're nothing like Cora." His arms fell, resisting the urge to reach out and palm her cheek. "And that's a good thing, I promise," he gritted out. "You're my type, by the way. Fuck Jorge's type."

"You loved Cora once upon a time," she murmured.

"I was young. Stupid. She was a weakness for me back then and—"

"A weakness?" she whispered. "So, you couldn't resist her?" She paused, then quickly tossed out, "I'm not jealous." She frowned, and her shoulders fell a bit in defeat. "Maybe I am? I guess the idea that this woman might still have some effect on you makes me a little crazy."

Yeah, he understood "crazy." He had a hard time stomaching the fact any other man had ever shared a bed with Sydney.

"Listen." He reached for her elbow, tugging her closer, not giving a damn who might be watching them from the house. "She manipulated me. A professional con artist. I should've recognized she was playing with me. It was my job to go undercover. To work a room. In a sense, I had to con people so they bought my story. And the fact she was able to turn the tables on me like that . . ." *Fuck, what am I trying to say again?* He was losing his focus with her green eyes on him. "I'm not the same person I was back then," he promised. "You have nothing to worry about when I see her again. *If* I see her again."

Sydney pivoted to the side as if searching for her invisible shield of armor. "You're not mine. I don't know where this is coming from."

He knew this blip of insecurity was Seth's doing. His affair. She had trouble trusting how absolutely amazing she was because of him. And now the jerk wanted her back. He was so stupid to lose her. Never deserved her.

"Well, you sure as hell feel like mine," he rasped, unable to prevent the truth from passing through his lips. "I don't have any self-control around you. *You're* the only one I can't resist." And he'd spend every second making sure she knew and understood that if it'd help her. He'd kiss away whatever insecurities still plagued her from the damage the men in her life had done to her. "I'd love nothing more than to have you see yourself through my eyes."

Sydney slowly faced him. Her green eyes held his in the most innocent way, and he'd swear twenty years had been peeled back as she quietly studied him.

With his free hand, he pointed at her heart. "You're everything I ever wish . . ." Fuck, his voice broke, and he was shocked to realize tears filled his eyes. "You're everything I wish McKenna had in a mother."

"I think that's the best compliment anyone has ever given me," she whispered, her lower lip trembling as tears filled her eyes too. "I don't understand how you know the real me when barely anyone does."

He brought his hand to her chin and gently held her face. "Easy," he said with a smile once she parted her lids. "Because you let me in."

"It's time to roll . . . out." Gray's voice shattered their moment, and Beckett let go of Sydney. She quickly erased the tears from her cheeks and turned away from the house.

Beckett cleared his throat and swiveled to peer at Gray hanging back on the small porch, his arms stretched out on each side of him, bracing the columns that held up the small overhang. Mya ducked under his arm to get to them when he'd yet to budge.

"Ready to go play couples in love and be all touristy?" Mya asked sarcastically.

Beckett frowned. "Why do we need to act touristy?"

Gray finally dropped his arms when the others attempted to come from the house, and he had no choice but to move.

But the expression on his face didn't read so much as, *I want to hit you.* More like he was conflicted. Maybe he realized he needed to let Sydney go, but it had to hurt. God, he couldn't imagine being in that man's shoes.

And after the op, if he did have to walk away from Sydney for whatever reason, how would he survive that?

"I think it'd be best if you all play the part of tourists instead of looking like you're private security scoping the place out, which might draw Miguel's attention if he sees you there before Wednesday night," Carter explained, walking alongside Camila toward the SUV.

"Do we have an update on Jesse's whereabouts?" Beckett asked Camila since it was her guys keeping an eye on the hotel.

Sydney sidestepped Beckett and grabbed the suitcase Mya had been carrying for her.

"Jesse hasn't made contact," Carter said, then tipped his head to Camila.

"But my team said he's with Miguel's crew at a restaurant down the street from the hotel. They arrived there for lunch around one," Camila shared.

Beckett turned his attention toward Elaina exiting the house with her parents, and she motioned to Beckett with a wave of her hand. "Can I talk to you before you go?"

"Of course." In a few quick strides, he moved away from the others off to the side of the SUVs. His heart made its way to his throat, worried about what she might say.

"Sydney will be okay. You don't need to worry about her," Elaina cut straight to the point, and he appreciated the good news. But with her small hand, she reached for his wrist. He'd swear he felt a small buzz of electricity pass between them. "She has you." She hid her brown gaze from him when her lids dropped. "But when you see the roses, be sure to stop."

"Stop what?" Beckett blinked in confusion. "Roses?"

"When you see the roses, you'll need to stop." And with that, she let go.

When she opened her eyes a moment later, Beckett sensed there was more she knew, but he had the feeling she was afraid to tell him too much. To change things. Some type of . . . what was it called in movies? The butterfly effect?

"And, Beckett," Elaina began, "he'll be okay too." She angled her head toward Gray without looking at him, but he was the only one off to her right.

"Do you mean . . .?" *He won't die on the op, or he'll fall in love with someone else?*

Elaina smirked, and he still wasn't sure how to read that, but she added, "You know exactly what I mean." And then, just like her father loved to do, she winked.

# CHAPTER THIRTY

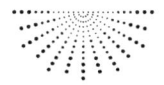

"Well, that sucks." Mya folded her arms as the six of them stood in the hotel lobby, her eyes on the keycards in Beckett's hands. "We going to draw straws to see who gets the honeymoon suite?"

Only two rooms had been available with two beds in each. And the only other room was the honeymoon suite on the top floor with one king-sized bed.

"You two take it." Gray reached for the keys from Beckett and handed them out as if that was that. Case closed. "Makes the most sense."

"Gray." His name came out like a small protest from Sydney. Or an apology? Beckett wasn't so sure, but either way, Gray shook his head.

"It's fine," Gray said nearly under his breath.

But was it fine? No, not even close. It was bad enough he and Sydney were sharing a room, and now Gray knew they'd be sharing a bed. The team didn't need Gray's thoughts derailed and not mission-focused because of their sleeping situation.

*Who am I kidding? We're all a bit fucked in the head on this one, aren't we?*

"Sooo," Mya cut through the awkward tension, God bless her. "Let's meet in the lobby in ten. We'll go do the tourist thing?" She pointed toward the elevators as if they'd lose their way. "I'd prefer to spend as little time as possible alone in the bedroom."

"Ten minutes is fine," Gray said, and Mya and Oliver led the way and began arguing about something as they all crowded into the elevator.

When the doors opened on the fifth floor, instead of exiting, Gray turned and peered at Sydney. "I need a word with Beckett in your room. Can you give us a few?"

"Oh, um, okay." Sydney squeezed between Beckett and Gray to join Camila and Mya in the hallway.

"Thanks." Gray quickly pressed the button to close the door before Beckett could protest. Not that he would've, but he sure as hell wasn't in the mood to be alone in the honeymoon suite with Sydney's ex-boyfriend.

They rode in silence to the top floor, and Beckett side-eyed the third suite they passed on their way to his room, recognizing the number as one of the rooms Miguel had booked. Sydney had hacked the hotel reservations before they'd left the safe house and found that Miguel had booked rooms all on the top floor. So, maybe it wasn't such a bad thing he'd wound up there today.

At least he was finally close to his brother-in-law again, and God willing, they'd soon be free from this mess.

It was one of the first times guilt didn't do a number on him. Now that he knew Mya and Camila were alive because of this insane trip, he didn't feel the need to keep berating himself.

Once they were both inside the suite, Beckett dropped his

bag by the door and pinched the bridge of his nose at the sight of a porcelain white tub sitting almost regally in front of a wall of glass, the Andes Mountains in the distance. But even the tub and view couldn't distract from the *one* bed, and he sure as hell didn't want to face Gray now.

"I know what you're going to say," Beckett began after hearing the door behind him click shut. "I can save you the trouble."

"Actually, you don't know what I plan to say." Gray's voice wasn't as harsh as he'd expected, so he slowly eased around, lowering his hand to his side in the process.

Gray had his eyes pinned to the bed, with its black leather headboard, gray comforter, and overabundance of white and gray pillows covering it.

"I'm sorry," Beckett apologized at Gray's forlorn expression, and in that moment, it was hard for him to remember Gray had once been an elite operator, a Green Beret. Because right now, he didn't look deadly. Just . . . well, defeated. And maybe he'd rather face the man's anger. He could deal with a pissed-off Gray better than a tough guy like him breaking apart.

"Since Sydney joined the team, she's been quiet. Reserved. Frankly, intimidating to most people, including the guys on Falcon." He paused for a moment. "The woman not only has walls up but barbed wire at the top just in case some idiot tries to climb over, if you get what I mean."

Beckett kept quiet, letting Gray work through whatever it was he was trying to say. He could hear his heartbeat in his ears as he waited. His pulse flying.

"And in the thirty-plus hours I've been around you two together, well, I've never seen her like this. Visibly wearing her emotions. Walls down. Barbed wire gone. And I get the feeling you're the reason. I don't know how you did it and so fast, but . . ." He let go of a deep breath and worked his gaze to meet Beckett's. "I won't stand in the way of that woman's happiness. She deserves the world, and if you're the one she wants to give her that world . . . so be it."

Beckett set a hand to his chest, worried his heart might break free as he grappled with how to handle Gray's words.

"What's that saying? If you love someone, let them go, and if they come back, it's meant to be? Well, she didn't come back to me." Gray shifted to the side, offering only his profile now.

"I don't know what to say," Beckett finally spoke, his words catching in his throat. "As soon as Oliver told me you two had a past, I declared her off-limits in my head," he admitted. "I promise you, I didn't plan for this to happen. I'm still trying to understand how it did, to be honest."

"I would die for that woman. In a heartbeat," Gray said while swiveling his focus back around, unable to shake that look of mourning in his eyes, which shredded Beckett to see. "Would you?"

"No question," Beckett answered without a second thought.

Gray nodded. "Then there's nothing left to talk about." He started for the door, pinning his shoulders back as he walked. "If I didn't make myself clear, though," he added while reaching for the handle, "you two have my blessing. Not that you need it, but it's there."

Beckett dropped onto the bed once Gray was gone and set his head in his hands, replaying Gray's words, ensuring he wasn't delirious, that he didn't hallucinate the conversation.

There was a knock at the door a minute or two later, and Beckett forgot Sydney didn't have the keycard to the room.

"Coming," he answered a bit gruffly, still working to

make sense of . . . well, everything that'd happened since walking into Capone last weekend.

"Hi," she said in a small voice after he'd opened up. "You're not bleeding, so that's a good sign."

"Did you talk to him after he left here?" He reached for her bag, taking it from her, then stepped aside so she could join him.

"No, he just told me you were waiting for me when he came to his room." Sydney shut the door behind them as Beckett set her bag alongside his. "Are you okay?" She looked around the room as if searching for signs of a scuffle, and her eyes fell on the tub.

"Yeah, I think so." He swallowed and waited for her eyes to meet his. "He wants you happy. And well, if that's with me, he said that I, um, have his blessing."

"He's great at telling people what they need to hear to make them feel better."

"So, you don't believe him?" He came closer to her, close enough to kiss her, but did his best to resist.

"I believe he wants me happy, yes." Her eyes thinned as she studied him. "But I'm not sure if—"

"If I'm the one who does that?" Where had that come from? Probably his fucking past. *Cora.* She was to him what Seth had been for Sydney, he supposed.

Sydney reached for his hand, and at her warm touch his body stiffened. "You do. It's just all unexpected, obviously. And fast." She was chewing on her lip. Another thing he assumed Gray would say was far from the norm for her.

*You do wear your emotions around me.* But he was the same around her. He let his guard down. She was the first woman he'd let in since Cora.

"So, maybe we should still wait until after the mission before we . . ." Sydney released his hand but didn't finish her train of thought, leaving him with too many possibilities about what she might've been thinking.

He was too afraid to press, knowing with absolute certainty how he wanted her to complete that sentence. And anything beyond that would have him feeling as broken as Gray had looked.

He'd told himself a few days ago he couldn't be with Sydney. And now? There was zero chance he could handle being without her.

# CHAPTER THIRTY-ONE

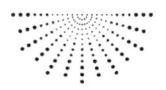

"So," Camila continued with her story, holding her red wine at dinner that night, "imagine Carter dangling from that rope without his pants . . . while this snarling Belgian Malinois whipped his jeans around in his mouth down below, tearing them apart."

"No, I actually can't picture that," Sydney responded, her stomach hurting from how hard she'd been laughing from all the "Carter Tales" Camila had shared that evening.

"Tell me the dog got his boxers too. Or is he a briefs guy?" Mya asked with a chuckle while going for her glass of wine too.

Camila leaned back in her chair and peeked at Mya sitting at her side at the six-person table. "He was buck-ass-naked. Well, the bottom half of him."

Oliver held a hand up and grinned, snatching his wineglass as well. "Please tell me I have permission to tease him at some point with one of these stories?"

They'd set out to keep up appearances by having dinner together at the hotel. Drinking wine. Eating too much food. Couples in love, yada yada yada. They'd easily fallen into their roles, and for Sydney, it hadn't felt fake all night. It helped to have Camila distracting them with her adventurous life.

"If you want Carter to kill you, sure," Camila finally answered Oliver.

"Well, what I need to know," Sydney began, "is how Carter got down from that rope."

"I saved his ass. Quite literally." Camila reached for the bottle of red on the table and added more to her glass. "Dogs seem to love me, so I came in for the rescue and calmed him down. With Carter's pants and briefs ripped to shreds, I had to give him my jacket so he could maintain what was left of his dignity in front of the ten guys out in that field working with us that day."

"And how many times have you two worked together since he left the Agency?" Beckett asked as he reached for Sydney's hand on top of the table and lightly squeezed. Was that for show? Or had he forgotten Gray was across the table from him and simply wanted to touch her?

Sydney had her answer in a matter of seconds when Beckett cleared his throat and withdrew his hand to his lap.

"We have teamed up a few times." Camila's dark brows lifted as she studied Beckett, and it was clear in her expression she understood the messy situation.

Oliver patted his stomach and yawned. "How long are we going to stay?" He checked his watch. "I don't think Miguel's going to eat here tonight after all."

When Sydney had hacked the hotel's system earlier, she'd discovered Miguel had made dinner reservations there for nine. No show yet. And it was well past ten.

"I'll text one of my men to get an update." Camila pulled her phone from her purse and began typing.

"I'm in no rush to go back to our suite," Mya commented once Camila set her phone on the table by her plate.

"This one," Oliver said while waving a hand Mya's way, "is crazy. Do you know what she did before we came here for dinner?"

While waiting for Oliver to share, Sydney thought back to what she, herself, had done before dinner.

She'd taken a shower and dressed *alone*. Because Beckett couldn't seem to stand being in the same room with her. He'd cleaned up and changed into his jeans and white button-down dress shirt in a matter of seconds before telling her he'd wait in the lobby.

Carter had provided him with a new phone, so he'd said he'd call his daughter and sister to check in while she got ready.

She knew him leaving their suite while she showered was the smart play if they were going to behave and reduce the risk of temptation.

Regardless of Gray's blessing, they were still on a mission, and they didn't need to further explore their feelings for each other there. It wasn't the time or place.

But that'd still left her feeling a tad disappointed his control hadn't snapped when they'd shared those handful of minutes alone before he'd taken off for the lobby.

"Well, are you going to tell us what Mya did that was crazy, or should we guess?" Camila asked Oliver, breaking through Sydney's thoughts.

Mya sipped her wine before saying, "He's shitty at stories, unlike you."

"I don't know where she got the string and duct tape, but she created a barrier between our beds," Oliver finally revealed. "Taped the string up on each wall, then draped one of the gray sheets over it as her protection from me."

"I don't need to run the risk you might try and check me out while I'm in my pajamas tonight." Classic Mya. And Sydney loved her for that.

"You also chose the bed that's next to the bathroom, and I have orders not to take a piss in the middle of the night." Oliver's tone was anything but angry though. "Are you really worried I might see you in your pajamas? You forget I saw you topless on Sunday."

"You did?" Gray cocked his head to the side and shot Oliver a puzzled look.

*And shit, you don't need to know I was topless too.* Sydney peered at Mya, hopeful she'd get the message to save her.

"I decided to be wild. Tossed my top," Mya explained. "Had I known Oliver would show up, I wouldn't have been so—"

"Brazen?" Oliver finished for her, and Mya shook her head and took a rather large gulp of wine.

"Are they always like this?" Camila waved her finger between the two of them.

"He brings out the—"

"Child in you?" Oliver once again cut off Mya.

In Sydney's opinion, Oliver was right. But Sydney rather enjoyed seeing this side of Mya. She'd spent the last few years hunting human traffickers, and the damage she knew that'd done on her psyche, well . . . Mya deserved to be young and playful again. And if Oliver brought that out, Sydney was happy to see it. In a brother-like or lover-like way, the jury was still out.

"Well, Gray, I don't think we need a wall between our beds," Camila began before searching Sydney's gaze, "unless you'd prefer us to?"

"Oh." *Ohhhh.*

"It's fine," Gray answered for Sydney, but she was grateful his tone wasn't clipped or angry. That was a start.

Camila reached for her phone when it buzzed on the table. "Looks like they're not coming here. They're at another restaurant in the city."

"So much for being seen as couples. I guess you can put your arm down, Romeo," Oliver joked to Gray.

Gray's wince at the word Romeo didn't escape Sydney's attention, but he quickly erased his expression while dragging his arm away from the back of Camila's chair.

*Romeo.* When joining Falcon, Sydney had learned Romeo had been Gray's Army call sign. And hers, ironically, had been Juliet.

"I guess we'll wait to get their attention tomorrow, then," Mya commented as if picking up on the tension rising again.

Tension Sydney hoped would soon fizzle since Gray had given Beckett his blessing.

And God help her, she wasn't sure if it was the wine or not, but she couldn't help but wish she could test that blessing out in the bedroom tonight.

\* \* \*

SYDNEY AND BECKETT EXITED THE ELEVATOR AND HALTED AT the sight three doors down.

Jesse McAdams stood outside his door alone, a keycard in hand. He peered at them from over his shoulder, sensing he wasn't alone, and the moment her eyes met his, relief washed over her. But were they safe to talk?

She discreetly looked around for a camera and spotted one overhead as she and Beckett started for their room.

Jesse made a show of fumbling his keycard and cursed under his breath as it fell to the carpeted floor. He squatted to grab it and whispered, "Meet me at the coffee shop at six a.m." Then he stood, swiped the card, and disappeared into his room.

"Maybe you should go alone tomorrow?" she asked Beckett once they were in their suite.

"If you think so." He slid the chain lock across the door and faced her. "It feels good to know we're near him."

"It does," she responded while mindlessly going for the knot of the belt of her red wrap dress.

"Sydney." Beckett's gruff voice had her fingers going still, conjuring memories of the orange sash from her dress in Mexico and how he'd bound her wrists with it.

"Oh." She blinked and refastened the knot so the dress remained on. One pull, and it'd fall open, exposing her strapless bra and matching satin panties.

Beckett removed the loafers he'd bought earlier when they'd played the role of tourists. He'd also picked up a few other outfits, same as her. The white button-down shirt and jeans were new as well.

His sleeves were rolled to the elbows, exposing his strong, corded forearms. The top two buttons of his shirt were undone. And his hair was styled and parted to the side. Well, it had been until he tossed a hand through it moments ago, as if annoyed by the stiffness of the gel there. And why'd that little act turn her on even more?

"How are we going to do this?" She slipped off the red heels she'd bought with the dress that day and toed them aside before taking two steps his way.

"Do what exactly?" He knew precisely what she meant. But did he want her to spell it out for him? Be the one to break?

And she would. Because she could barely share the same

air with Beckett without every part of her body begging to be touched by him.

Putting the two of them together in a room with one bed, a sexy clawfoot tub in front of a wall of glass and a view of the mountains . . . and for them *not* to make love? How the hell would they survive the week?

Gray already knew they'd slept together. He'd "okayed" their relationship. Not that she needed permission, but it did feel good to have it. And at the moment, the mission was on standby until she sang at the club tomorrow night.

So, was there anything truly stopping them right now from giving in to what they both desperately craved?

*I was the one to suggest we put on the brakes.* She was pretty sure that was the rational side of her brain coming in with that reminder, but she wanted to toss those thoughts free from her mind. To live and be present in the moment.

She nodded, deciding to cast fear and caution aside, and announced, "I'm going to take my clothes off." She went for the knot of the fabric belt. "Take a bath."

"Sydney," he said again, nearly growling her name.

But she ignored his warning the same as she'd done seconds ago with her own internal monologue. Once the belt was untied, the jersey-fabric dress parted. She shrugged the material back so it fell to her feet. Bra off next beneath his intense stare.

Her nipples hardened with him surveying every inch of her exposed skin while he quietly stroked his jaw.

To push the envelope a touch more, she traced her tongue along the seam of her lips while slowly lowering her satin panties.

She strutted to the tub, swaying her hips a bit before bending over to turn on the water.

"You're naked in front of the window." His growly tone

had her knees pinning together with desire. "What if someone sees you?"

"Let them." There were no other buildings in sight as tall as their hotel, which made it pretty damn difficult for anyone to catch a peek of her.

"Do you think I'm the type of man who'd run the risk of another person seeing his woman naked?"

*His woman?* She stood upright, then continued with the teasing act by smoothing her hands along the sides of her body. "Do you think *I'm* the type of woman to let a man stop me from doing what I want?"

At the feel of his hand sliding beneath her mass of hair to grasp the nape of her neck, she remembered the fantasy that'd inspired her orgasm earlier in the shower.

He held her gently, guiding her around with that one touch until she faced him. His brows were drawn tight, his eyes dark with arousal.

"You will *not* take a bath in front of a window with the curtains open, I can promise you that." He brought his face closer to hers, and she tipped her chin, preparing to be defiant. Why did this thrill her so much? Why did she love how he was a gentleman outside the bedroom, but in there, a dominant force to be reckoned with? And every part of her wanted to be controlled by him.

But resisting a little first would be more fun, so she couldn't help herself.

Because the woman she was tonight and really ever since he showed up in Mexico, was a far cry from the one she'd been since becoming a mother thirteen years ago. She'd buried that wilder, semi-reckless side of herself. And he was bringing her back to life. Hell, she felt more alive now than ever.

"And yet, the curtains are still open," she reminded him.

His jaw strained, as if angry at himself for allowing her to stand there as long as she already had. But still, he didn't budge.

"You're being awfully bratty tonight." He tipped his head, his wickedly sexy mouth nearly slanting over hers. "What is it that you want, Sydney?"

"I just want to be yours," she confessed a bit breathlessly. He groaned and captured her mouth, drawing her against him with one hand on her ass and his other still holding the back of her neck.

His tongue met hers with such a ferocious intensity that she nearly fell back into the tub, but he kept her upright with his firm grip.

After exploring her mouth with his tongue, he eased back and stared deep into her eyes. "I don't want you moving once I get you in position . . . you good with that?" He released her and stepped away.

"You can do whatever you want to me," she eagerly gave him her permission. "I trust you."

His eyes narrowed at her use of the word trust before he ran his hand over the length of her throat and down to her breast, clasping it a bit roughly. And damn, did she like that.

Still holding her eyes, he leaned in and nipped her lip. "Say stop anytime. Okay?"

Wasn't going to happen, but if he needed to hear it, sure. "Do I need a specific safe word, is that how all this works?"

"Honestly, I've never done anything like this. This has only happened in my head with you."

She ran her tongue along the line of her lips.

"So, what's your safe word?"

"Mmmm. I'm good with just saying stop, not that I'll need to."

"Stop," he repeated with a nod. "Okay."

He let go of her as his hand traveled to the buttons of his dress shirt, and she groaned at the loss of his touch. But with every button coming undone, it had her anticipation building more and more.

He finally peeled his shirt back, exposing his golden tan skin, and she reached forward, prepared to smooth a hand over his chest hair, but he shook his head. A reminder to not move. And he'd clearly meant that in every possible sense.

Beckett moved around the tub, his pants the only thing still on after he'd discarded his loafers and shirt. As promised, he drew the curtains together, but then he shut off the water and approached her once again.

"You can take a bath after. You'll probably be sore," he rasped while removing his belt.

She gulped, wondering if he planned to use it on her, but then he tossed it to the ground and quickly removed his pants and black briefs.

He surprised her by scooping her into his arms, then carried her to the bed. He set her on the edge and demanded, "Stay seated, sweetheart. And you're going to do exactly what I say. What do you think will happen if you don't?"

She set both palms alongside her, staring at him as he lowered to his knees on the floor. Her heart jumped when he grabbed her hips and nearly pulled her off the bed, drawing her pussy closer to him. "You won't give me what I want?" she whispered her answer. "Or . . ."

God, this was new. She didn't know how to navigate it all. Did she tell this man she wanted him to torture her a little, but in some type of pleasurable way? *That's a thing, right?* God, she wished she'd read more than that one romance book to know what to say or do.

He winked. "I guess you'll find out if you misbehave."

She chewed on her lip, curious what was going to happen next.

He ran his finger along the inside of her thigh before drawing her leg up, positioning her foot above his pec, and then did the same with the other. "Stay like that."

Her back was arched a bit, and she rested her forearms on the bed.

"I'm guessing you're going to want to move. So, push your feet against me instead." He ran his finger over the lips of her sex, and she flinched with excitement from the gentle touch. "I'd rather find something to hold you down, but this is the best I can do for now."

"Oh? And what would you like to do if you could?" She inhaled a shaky breath and let it go. "Tell me."

He angled his head, drawing his gaze from her wet center to meet her eyes. "Cuff your ankles to something to keep your legs spread open for me. Bind your wrists." His dark eyes looked nearly haunted by his need for her, and she had a feeling her eyes were but a mirror of his.

She was desperate for this man to do anything and absolutely everything to her. Whatever he desired. She wanted it. All of it.

"That's how I imagined you in my head during my shower this morning," he said like a confession, but in her mind, he needed no absolution.

"And what happened next? What would you do to me? Your words, they're . . . making me even wetter." She'd never known words could be so . . . sexually powerful?

He smirked and surprised her by bringing his mouth near her sex, his tongue peeking out between his lips without yet touching her. She shifted closer with desperation to have his mouth on her, but he pulled his face back as a reminder "not to move."

"Mm. Now I understand the need to tie me up." She smiled, and the dark hint of a smile from him was all she got in return before he ran the flat part of his tongue over her sex. She followed his order, only pushing against his hard body with her feet in response to what felt like eternal bliss from one stroke of his tongue.

And then his mouth was gone again.

*Torture, all right.*

She was already panting from just this moment alone.

"I want you to watch. The whole time. I need you to see how beautiful you look," he ordered in a low, deep voice.

She bit down on her back teeth while watching him touch her most sensitive part, worshiping her. Then he set a small kiss there, and when he looked up, he withdrew his mouth. *Oh, God. Yesss.*

"I want you to see how fucking delectable you are. I need you to watch yourself while I'm between your legs. Don't watch me. Look at *yourself.*"

God, that was going to be hard. Refrain from looking at his long, dark lashes? Or peer into his brown eyes? To not study his granite jawline as it flexed when he went down on her?

She *did* need to be restrained.

"I'll obey." *Try to.*

"Good girl." He smiled. "But where are your eyes supposed to be?"

Right, she shouldn't have seen that gorgeous smile of his if she'd been obeying. Her heart hammered in her chest with anticipation as she walked her focus back to her own sex. He pushed two fingers inside her, which had her almost bucking up off the bed, so she clenched her teeth in an attempt not to move.

His fingers glistened with her arousal when he removed

them, and he slid his index finger over the swollen part of her again. This had to be the most erotic thing she'd ever watched.

He slowly licked her sensitive flesh again, then added two fingers inside her once more, pumping in and out with every flick of his tongue.

And when his mouth sank over her, eclipsing her view of her pussy, she released a shuddery moan, on the verge of coming. Her eyes went to the ceiling and he must've noticed, because he withdrew his face.

"Sorry." She quickly returned her attention where he demanded it to see him lightly swat her sex, just like he'd done in her fantasy in the shower earlier. Then he gently set his mouth on her again as if kissing away any possible sting.

And when she witnessed his tongue swirl over her swollen flesh just before sucking, she came undone. The pleasure had built too much to hold back any longer.

She trembled as she began rocking her hips faster and faster, unable to stop herself from nearly grinding against his face. And this time, he didn't command her to stay still.

"Fuck me, please. While I'm still coming," she begged.

Beckett had her on her back and farther up the bed in a heartbeat, and in the next breath, he sank inside her in one hard move.

He hissed while staring into her eyes, and she grabbed hold of his biceps while continuing to ride the longest orgasm of her life.

His brows dipped. "I'm not going to be able to walk away from you after this, you know that, right?"

## CHAPTER THIRTY-TWO

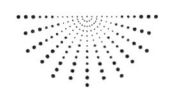

BECKETT PULLED ON A PAIR OF JEANS AND GRABBED A T-shirt from his bag, moving quietly around the hotel room that morning, careful not to wake Sydney.

They'd only fallen asleep around two a.m. after a night of lovemaking, and he was supposed to meet Jesse at six. He wanted Sydney to rest since she'd be singing that night. The idea of her seducing a psychopath made him crazy, but what could they do? He sure as hell didn't want her lack of sleep throwing her off later.

He slipped on his shoes, his gaze lingering on the beautiful path of her spine that led to the slopes of her ass. The covers were shoved to the bottom of the bed, and her arm was draped over her head, her face turned to the side.

God, she was beautiful. And last night had been . . .

He didn't have words to describe it. She was one of a kind, that was for sure.

Hell, she'd asked him to spank her on their second go at it. *Harder*, she'd begged, and it'd been almost too hard for him to do that. He didn't want to hurt her. But she'd whimpered from pleasure at the contact. His handprint had remained on her ass cheek after he'd taken her pussy from behind and plowed deep inside her.

Beckett quietly approached the bed and did his best to cover her without rousing her from sleep. Satisfied he'd done so without disturbing her, he turned toward the bathtub, which had triggered his slightly crazy, possessive behavior last night.

He had no idea if she'd be his for just this trip, and that they'd only made love because of their forced proximity. And the thought had his heart feeling like it was going through a meat grinder as he started for the door.

But he needed to focus. Shove his emotions to the back corner of his mind, something he used to be great at doing. Until now. Until this woman.

Beckett tossed one last look at her sleeping, his heart aching at the mere sight of her, then he grabbed his wallet, new phone, and keycard and went downstairs to the coffee shop.

He spotted Jesse by the window that looked out onto the street. He had a newspaper in front of him and a steaming cup of coffee on the bar attached to the window he was facing. His back was to the coffee shop, and while Beckett stood in line to place his order, he looked around for cameras.

There was one in the ceiling behind the register, but he was pretty sure Jesse was just outside the camera's line of sight.

After getting his black coffee in a mug, he removed his phone from his pocket and joined Jesse at the standing bar area. He kept a little space between them and set his cup down before scrolling through the phone Carter had provided him back at the safe house, ensuring it was on silent and wouldn't ring.

"Good to see you alive," Beckett said once he held the phone to his ear, faking a phone call.

"You too." Jesse folded the sports section of the paper and placed it by his coffee before opening the stock market section, feigning interest in Wall Street. "Sharing a room with Sydney? Hope she's not being too rough on you," he mused.

"No, she's quite . . ." *Soft?* He decided not to finish his line of thought. It'd be too complicated. Instead, he quickly filled him in the best he could on what had gone down and their plans for the night leading up to Jorge's party Friday.

Jesse casually looked over his shoulder toward the cafe before returning his focus to flipping pages.

"Ella knows you're safe," Beckett added. "Well, as safe as you can be. She's strong."

Jesse set down his paper and sipped his coffee, keeping quiet for a bit as he processed the information Beckett had shared along with his mention of Ella.

When Jesse discarded his coffee on the narrow bar counter, exchanging it for the paper again, Beckett asked, "Did you have a chance to talk to Ivy alone?"

Jesse stole a quick look from the corner of his eye at Beckett. "Yeah, I have news I didn't want to share over the phone. And I wanted it to be with you first."

Beckett's heart shot up into his throat at his words, and he ended his fake call and set the phone down in preparation for the news. "Mind if I have a look at the sports section?" He pointed to Jesse's paper.

"Sure." Jesse slid it over to him as he shared, "Cora wasn't dating Jorge."

*Wasn't?* But he tried not to jump to conclusions at his use of the past tense. "So, then, who?"

"She lives at his estate, but it's because she targeted someone from his security team who's been with Jorge for a decade. Easier prey, Ivy had said. While still acquiring her desired life of luxury." Jesse paused to let the news sink in. "A man like Jorge is too cautious to be conned."

"Too guarded," Beckett translated, and the nickname made sense yet again. "Are we right about the club and drug swap theory?" he whispered, then did a quick check behind him to ensure they were still alone aside from a few businessmen in line for coffee. "Did Ivy mention the name Hector Lopez to you?"

"Yes, to both," Jesse confirmed. "Three weeks ago, Cora called Ivy in a panic when she saw Hector at Jorge's place in Santiago. She overheard he was there with his cousin, negotiating a deal to sell Jorge the club. She'd planned to steer clear of him, worried he'd remember her, but I'm guessing he spotted her, and that's when she called you. But that was the last call she made."

"Has Miguel mentioned Cora? Do we know if she was turned over to the cartel? Is she still alive?" he rushed out the questions in as low of a voice as possible.

"Yeah, um."

*Fuck that um. Damn it.* What was Jesse worried about sharing? *Is Cora already dead?*

"Ivy knew Miguel would be going to Chile to finalize the sale of the club, so she's been waiting for her chance to come down here. To find out if Cora's alive."

"And *is* she still alive?" Beckett asked, willing himself to remain calm even as his stomach felt all fucking weird.

"Yes, she's still alive. I heard Miguel mention her, but Miguel is clueless Cora and Ivy are related," Jesse shared, and Beckett tipped his head to the ceiling at the news. There was still a chance to save McKenna's mother. Not that he knew what to do with that woman after all of this, but he owed it to his daughter to try. That was why he was there, right?

"But there's something you should know before I share more. Something Ivy told me. The *other* reason she wanted to come to Chile. There's someone *else* here she's worried about."

"Who?" He couldn't help but focus on Jesse with his pulse jockeying so fast.

"Cora has a kid. A five-year-old son."

*The kid Liam will save on Friday is . . . Cora's kid?* Beckett felt the blood draining from his face in shock.

"Beckett . . ." Jesse slowly began, "is there a chance he's yours?"

\* \* \*

"Beckett, I've been calling. You've been gone for two hours. What happened?" Sydney asked the second he walked into their hotel suite.

"My phone was ruined in the cenote," he replied, still in a daze.

"Carter gave you a new one. You called McKenna from it yesterday." Sydney stood before him and reached for his arm. "What's wrong? Talk to me."

"I'm sorry." He pinched the bridge of his nose, trying to think straight. "I needed to take a walk." He'd thought he'd only been outside the hotel for thirty or so minutes. Had it really been hours since he'd met with Jesse?

"You're worrying me. Please." She motioned for him to sit on the bed, but he couldn't get himself to move, so he leaned against the door and lowered his hand so he could peer into this beautiful woman's eyes.

She let go of him and tightened the knot of her white silk

hotel robe. Her hair was in a messy bun with a few loose strands framing her face. She was . . . perfection.

*Miles. Cora has a five-year-old son named Miles.*

Closing his eyes, Beckett thought back to the last time he'd seen Cora six years ago. He'd dropped McKenna off at his parents' ranch after Cora had called and begged him to meet her at her hotel to talk about their daughter.

He knew she must have had an angle, another con in mind, but he'd decided to hear her out for McKenna's sake. But her pleas for another chance to start over as a family were insincere, and her words were hollow. How could he trust her? Bottom line, he couldn't.

And why in the hell wouldn't Ivy have reached out to him, regardless of his threat to arrest her two years ago, if she knew a five-year-old was in danger too?

*Cora instructed Ivy to tell you about Miles only upon her death. So, when Cora failed to call on their agreed upon day, Ivy decided her best bet was to head to Mexico and cozy up to club Capone's owner since Cora told her about Jorge's desire to buy the place. Since Ivy had never had any dealings with the cartel and hadn't seen Cora in six years, she figured she'd be safe. Before contacting you, Ivy wanted to go to Chile and confirm Cora and Miles were alive*, Jesse had told him when Beckett had raised that point. Because yeah, Ivy was as stubborn as Cora, but he knew Ivy didn't have a death wish and wouldn't go into battle alone. But the damn woman could've given him some type of heads-up.

*Miles is McKenna's brother.*

God, he was going to puke. McKenna had always wanted siblings. Hoped for a brother or sister. And Beckett had never delivered. Not only that, he'd opted to have a vasectomy a few years back.

"Beckett." Sydney reached for his bicep this time and

squeezed. "What's wrong?" The sound of fear and concern in her voice compelled him to face her.

Beckett's hand slid from his chest to his abdomen as he tried to make sense of it all.

"Please talk to me," Sydney pleaded.

"Cora and Jorge aren't an item," he managed out in a hoarse voice. "She pulled her seduction con on an easier target. One of his security guys who lives on-site. But we were right, Hector Lopez recognized her when he traveled with Miguel to Chile three weeks ago." Beckett's mind replayed the rest of what Jesse had told him at the coffee shop, his eyes falling closed.

"What is it?"

"The cartel's not only getting the drug formula in exchange for Capone on Friday. The transaction also includes Jorge handing over Cora. Once he learned she was a con artist, Jorge was worried Cora had infiltrated his organization, so he requested time to interrogate her first, which is why, um, he chose this Friday for the . . ." He swallowed. "Deadline."

*Deadline.* He thought back to Sydney's words on the jet the other day. In her line of work, a deadline meant someone would die if they weren't successful.

"So, she's still alive. We have time." Sydney's optimistic tone had him peeling his eyes open again. He probably looked drugged to her. He knew his eyes had to be red or his pupils dilated.

How could he keep this news from McKenna? *A brother.*

"Isn't this good news?"

"The cartel wants to make an example of her once he turns her over, and . . . they want her son too. That's part of the deal."

Sydney released him at his words and stepped back. "She

has a son?" Her chest lifted and fell with a deep breath. "The five-year-old Elaina said her dad needs to save? Elaina was adamant that she and Emily come here," Sydney whispered, "because she knew Liam, the world's best sniper, would follow. She must have been so tied to this vision because he's McKenna's brother. Family."

Beckett slowly nodded.

"He's five," she softly said, her eyes glossy with tears. "Is there a chance she was already pregnant when she met Jorge's bodyguard? Did she make him believe the baby was his when it may have been—"

"I may have been an idiot to go to Cora when she called in the past for help," Beckett began, realizing Sydney was wondering the same thing Jesse had, "but sleep with her six years ago?" He shook his head, remembering Cora's bullshit performance that night and the warning he'd delivered afterward for her to stay away from him and his daughter. "Hell no."

## CHAPTER THIRTY-THREE

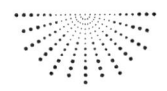

"WE'RE GOING AHEAD WITH THE PLAN," CARTER INSTRUCTED via speakerphone. Sydney looked over at Beckett sitting on the couch inside Gray and Camila's suite, where they had gathered along with Mya and Oliver. "The only reason we'll change course is if Hector Lopez hops on a plane for Chile."

Beckett looked like he'd been to hell, his elbows on his thighs and his head cradled in his palms, and well, he hadn't come back yet. A fiery inferno of fear, anger, and doubt was eating him alive. Because his daughter had a brother, and that kid was now in the hands of a dangerous Mexican cartel.

Sydney knew Beckett would do absolutely anything for his daughter, evidenced by the fact that he'd come to Chile to save a woman who'd screwed up his life ten times over. It was only natural he'd risk his life for Miles too.

"Is that clear?" Carter asked in response to everyone's silence. Per Beckett's request, Sydney had shared all he'd learned from Jesse, and everyone, including their co-leader Gray, appeared to still be reeling.

"Roger that," Oliver piped up.

"Maybe Beckett should steer clear of Jorge tonight," Gray

offered his opinion for the first time, grabbing Beckett's attention. "Jorge is willing to give up Cora and her boy, his bodyguard's son, in exchange for a club. It's clear Jorge is either not working with a full deck or just plain evil. Maybe both," Gray continued.

"I won't risk losing our chance to attend that party Friday." Beckett stood, eyes on Gray. "I'll play nice tonight if that's what you're worried about."

Gray held his hands up in surrender, clearly understanding that Beckett would knock down anyone who stood in his way of rescuing Miles.

"Have we learned anything from Martín about Hector Lopez's movement in Tulum? Any chance Hector has plans to make a move against Martín prior to Friday?" Oliver asked.

Beckett returned to the couch, and Sydney ignored the urge to join him. Offering comfort wasn't her forte, and she knew he needed her, but the team was discussing their mission, so this wasn't the time nor the place.

"Martín believes Hector might attempt to come after his men since the cartel learned they took out their guys who were after you in the jungle on Sunday," Carter shared. "If that happens, he'll be ready. Plus, Mya's Marine friends are there for extra support. I'll let you know if anything changes. Just focus on the plan tonight."

"Any luck using an alias to get tickets for his twenties-themed birthday party on Friday?" Camila asked Carter.

"I'm still working on it," Carter answered, then added, "Beckett, Elaina asked me to remind you—"

"The roses," Beckett cut him off. "I remember."

*Roses?* Sydney stole a look at him. His arms and body were tense as he shouldered the weight of the news, and it was taking all his strength to do it.

Carter went over a few more details, more like *orders,* then he ended the call.

Gray pocketed his phone and swiped a hand through his hair. "Jesse took a chance by meeting you down in that coffee shop," he began, "but I guess I understand why he couldn't relay all of that information to Carter." He cleared his throat as if about to ask something uneasy, but only said, "Are you, uh, okay?"

There was still some awkward tension between them. But he could see Beckett was in pain.

Beckett peered at Gray, realizing the question had been meant for him. "Would you be?"

"No," Gray answered without hesitation.

"Miles will be fine." Camila sat next to Beckett. "Elaina said Liam has to kill someone to save a kid. It's Miles. He'll be saved." She looked around the room, her gaze falling on Sydney last. "If you truly believe in Elaina's gift, you all need to remember her words right now. Let them put your minds at ease."

Beckett nodded, letting go of a deep breath.

"We can do this," Mya said, but Sydney picked up on the slight tremble in her voice.

When Sydney's gaze met Beckett's, a memory of something he'd said down in that cenote came to mind. *I used to hang out at one specific place regularly, and that's where I met a singer.* Her stomach lurched at the thought. *Shit.*

Mya was right. They'd pull off their scheme, but they'd need to deviate from the original plan. "Mya, can I talk to you alone for a minute?"

"Um, sure." Mya stood, a look of confusion on her face about the sudden need for privacy. "In my suite?"

Sydney nodded. "We'll be back soon," she said, then hurried from the room before anyone could question her.

"Wow, you really did make a sheet wall between your beds, huh?" Sydney asked once they were alone, and Mya plopped down on the bed. "You did that to annoy him, right?"

"What do you think?" Mya's smirk quickly faded when her eyes met Sydney's. "What's up?"

"I can't sing tonight," Sydney revealed. "I can't do that to Beckett." She crossed her arms and leaned against the wall behind her, tipping her eyes to the ceiling. "He wasn't just upset because I'll be offering myself up as bait to seduce Jorge." Why hadn't she remembered sooner? "It's *how* I'll be doing it." Not that he'd said as much, but after the day he'd had today—learning McKenna had a brother—how could she do that to him?

"What do you mean?" Mya asked. A heartbeat later, her mouth formed an O when she remembered Beckett's confession in the cenote. "Oh, fuck."

"Cora studied up on Beckett back in LA before conning him. She knew he loved music and got a job as a singer at the club he frequented. First, she seduced him with her voice before she pulled the damsel-in-distress act."

"And you don't want him to have to witness you seduce Jorge in a similar way. Use your voice to draw his attention." Mya stood from the bed. "I get that, but I'm sure he'll understand. That was over thirteen years ago when she did that."

"After what he learned about Cora and her son this morning, those wounds are as fresh as if they'd happened yesterday." There wasn't a chance in hell she'd inflict more damage upon that man by having him relive his past watching someone he . . . well, cared about, sing for another man tonight.

Mya nodded. "Not only does McKenna have a brother she never knew about, but her mom didn't abandon him like she did McKenna," Mya whispered. "Different circumstances. But I can't imagine how that news might translate to a thirteen-year-old girl if McKenna were to hear it."

A possibility Beckett was more than likely grappling with—how to tell McKenna about everything.

"Beckett's just had so much thrown at him. Regardless, I think it'd be a bad idea for him to see me up there singing for Jorge. He told Gray he'd be okay, but I don't think we should take the chance. He may snap. He's . . ." *Protective of me.* "Besides, you're the one with the theater skills. High school musicals and whatnot. You should do it." She pointed to her chin. "See my face. People think I'm a cold-hearted bitch six out of seven days a week because of how I always look. I can't fake-seduce Jorge. He won't buy it."

"First of all, you don't have resting bitch face." Sydney opened her mouth to protest, but Mya waved a dismissive hand. "And second, you've gone undercover before. I don't buy you can't swing anything you put your mind to." Mya held her palms open this time. "But I do see the way Beckett looks at you. He will probably lose his shit if Jorge so much as sets a hand on your arm, let alone tries anything else."

"Beckett will go to the ends of the earth for Miles no matter what since he's McKenna's brother. But that doesn't mean he won't break Jorge's jaw in a split second, considering all the stress he's under." She allowed that horrific scene to unfold in her mind and winced. "So . . . will you do it? Take over for me tonight?"

"One small problem. I don't know any songs from the nineteen-twenties."

Sydney lifted her watch and checked the time. It wasn't noon yet. "You have all day to learn. And those songs don't have that many lyrics. You can do this."

She'd beg if she had to. She already cared about Beckett

so much, maybe more than she should've in such a short period of time, and she'd do anything to safeguard him when or if possible.

Mya turned away from Sydney and peered out the window toward the gorgeous Andes Mountains. "Syd, of course," she responded, and Sydney circled her to make eye contact. "You're my best friend. I've got your back. You know that." She reached for Sydney's hand and squeezed. "Always."

"I promised not to put you on the front lines for ops, and here I am asking you to risk your neck."

"I won't be in danger." Mya sent her a soulful, expressive look. "Because you've got my back too."

## CHAPTER THIRTY-FOUR

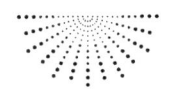

"You're wearing *that*?" Oliver pointed at Mya, shooting her a disapproving glare as Sydney joined the two of them in the hallway. She'd opted to get ready in Mya's suite, so they'd kicked Oliver out an hour ago.

"As opposed to wearing nothing?" Mya asked, clearly loving to goad this man.

"You may as well be wearing nothing," Oliver accused as Sydney closed the door and leaned against it while observing their back-and-forth.

"Those dresses make you both look like exotic backup dancers. Every man in the place will"—Oliver waved a hand in the air—"well, you know."

"No, I don't think I do. You should tell us," Mya said, batting her lashes innocently. When he only scowled, she gently patted his chest twice as though to say *there, there,* then stepped away.

Oliver had on black slacks and a white button-down shirt. His brown hair was styled and slicked back, and he looked part mafia, part businessman tonight.

*Then again, none of us are supposed to look like*

*ourselves.* Sydney lowered her focus to the gold metallic knit dress, with its plunging cowl neck. She was tempted to do a little twirl in her gold rhinestone heels, showing off the open back of the bodycon silhouette. But she'd leave the teasing to Mya for tonight. Plus, it was Mya's job to be the temptress, which was why her matching dress was siren-red.

"I get it, I get it," Oliver said when Mya spun around like a ballerina with her arms over her head. "You're—"

"Sexy? Hot? Gorgeous?" Mya smoothed a hand over her glossy mane of dark hair. She and Sydney had gone vintage glam with their hairstyles, sporting tight curls pulled over one shoulder.

Oliver had yet to close his mouth or use it to assemble words and form sentences after Mya had cut him off.

"Cat still got your tongue?" Mya stepped over and playfully jabbed Oliver in the side with her elbow, freeing him from whatever spell he'd fallen under.

"My tongue is just fine," Oliver said, his voice strained and deeper than normal. "I'm hoping not to have to kill some asshole sooner than necessary. And you two in those dresses are going to attract a lot of attention."

"As opposed to the garbage bags we normally wear?" Mya poked back. "Damn, who knew rhinestones made us suddenly so attractive."

"Sure, sure." Oliver rolled his eyes.

Sydney fished her phone from her matching clutch and checked the time as they headed to Gray and Camila's room.

"You rehearse all day?" Oliver asked, tossing a look back at Sydney, who trailed behind the two not-so lovebirds.

"Yeah, we did." Not quite a lie. Sydney had helped Mya learn the lyrics for a handful of songs, and Mya was a natural. Her voice was better than Sydney's anyway, as were her acting skills. Between Mya's seductive renditions of songs from Jorge's favorite era and that bombshell dress, she was sure to garner the man's attention. As well as every other guy in the place.

Oliver rapped at Gray's door, and when he opened up, he looked as dapper as Oliver. Black pants and a black button-down shirt. Hair styled as well instead of hidden beneath a backward ball cap as per the norm for him.

Gray stepped into the hall, letting the door shut behind him. "Camila's getting dressed in the en suite. She should be out shortly."

Stowing her phone back in her clutch, Sydney wished for the hundredth time it contained a weapon, but at least Camila's men were on watch in the hotel. The fact she hadn't clocked their locations meant they were good at their jobs.

"You two look beautiful," Gray said with a polite nod.

"See, that's what you were supposed to say. Not that we look like strippers," Mya chided, nudging Oliver again.

"Do that one more time, and I just might put you over my knee and—" Oliver left the sentence unfinished and clenched his jaw instead.

Sydney bit back a laugh at the thought of Oliver administering a well-deserved spanking to her friend. Although, Mya might benefit from that. Sydney had thoroughly enjoyed Beckett's firm palm connecting with her ass cheek last night.

"Yeah, good move shutting your mouth and not crossing that line," Gray warned.

But so many lines had already been crossed since Beckett and Oliver had shown up on Sunday and crashed her and Mya's vacation. And now here they were on Wednesday night with an impending deadline and a five-year-old to save.

"Ready for tonight?" Gray asked, redirecting the

conversation to the mission at hand, forcing Sydney to discard her emotions and get back on track.

"I think we are," Sydney replied.

"Can Beckett really handle this? *Truly* handle it?" Gray caught Sydney's eyes, a worried look there. "I'd lose my mind if I were him."

"Same," Oliver agreed as the elevator doors chimed down the hall, and Sydney turned to see Beckett stepping out.

*Mine.* That was the first word that popped into her head at the sight of him in those black slacks with a thin gray sweater-type shirt that showed off his broad shoulders and barrel chest. God, the man was handsome, and she loved his sexy, distinguished look. A gentleman, but one that screwed her like a . . .

As Beckett's long legs carried him their way, he swiped a hand along the side of his dark hair, which was as slick as Oliver's and Gray's tonight.

Beckett stopped alongside Oliver, and he tipped his head in greeting. That worn, sad look that clung to his brown eyes was all it took for her to snap back to the reality of their situation.

"Ready?" Camila's soft voice and the closing of the suite door had Sydney turning in her direction, eager to see what she'd opted to wear tonight. But before she could really appreciate the stunning outfit her new friend was wearing, Gray's reaction snagged Sydney's attention.

The man looked like he'd just seen a beautiful woman for the first time in his life as he devoured her with his eyes. Camila was a vision in her black satin wrap dress that hit mid-thigh, and the crisscross style dipped low in front, revealing an ample amount of cleavage.

She'd styled her long hair to hang over one shoulder, exposing one dangly earring. "You're a knockout." Sydney didn't want to get overly optimistic that another woman was catching Gray's attention. But she could certainly hope, right?

She wasn't sure if Gray was quite ready to fall in love, but he deserved a little desire and passion in his life. *We all do.* And she hadn't realized that until Mexico.

"Let's do this." Camila motioned for them to get a move on.

Carter had texted the team twenty minutes ago that the headline singer was considered a no-show, so the plan was falling into place. At least, so far. And one of Camila's teammates confirmed Jorge's arrival at the club ten minutes ago and that he was now with Miguel and Camila's scientist. Jesse and Ivy were at Jorge's table as well.

Sydney hung back as everyone started toward the elevators, then reached for Beckett's arm. "You okay?" she whispered.

"No," he said while turning her way. "But I'll get through this," he added in a rougher voice that time.

"I've got you," she promised and gave his arm a quick squeeze.

"Not sure if I deserve that." His words had her pausing. She caught Mya's eyes down the hall and waved her off, telling her to head down without them.

"Be there in a second," she told the others, and Gray nodded before disappearing into the elevator last.

"Why wouldn't you deserve me?" She assumed that's what he'd implied, and his hands diving into his pockets and the tight strain of his jaw had her worry catching back up with her. His dark gaze met hers, and she sucked in a sharp breath.

"Because we're in this situation because of me. Because I was stupid enough to let myself get conned by Cora and—"

"I hate her for hurting you. For hurting McKenna. But

she's your past." Sydney reached for his hand and set his palm over her heart. "I'm here. Your present." *Your future?*

He smoothed his thumb in small, back-and-forth motions where his hand lay near her breast.

"I'd never hurt you like that," she found herself promising because, in a matter of days, this man had revived parts of her that'd been dead or lying dormant for years.

"Same," he whispered, the look in his eyes saying so much more than that one word.

They both nodded in silent understanding and made their way to the club.

Sydney spotted their team two tables away from Jesse's before her gaze moved to Ivy sitting between him and Miguel. But before Sydney had a chance to truly assess the con artist, the billionaire was on his feet cursing.

*What do you mean the singer didn't show?* Jorge hollered in Spanish at a man Sydney assumed was the manager standing next to him.

Sydney sat opposite Beckett, her eyes riveted on Mya sitting next to him. "You ready?" she mouthed. Mya tipped her head in a nervous nod, but she didn't waste time and stood.

"Wait, what are you doing?" Oliver grabbed Mya's wrist and tugged, but she ignored him.

"There's been a change of plans." Sydney peered at Beckett. "Mya's going to be singing tonight instead."

"Excuse me," Mya called out toward Jorge's table. "I'd be happy to sing with the band."

Jorge and the club manager swiveled their focus her way. "Who are you?" the manager asked.

Miguel was on his feet now alongside Jorge, whispering something into his ear as they both studied Sydney's table.

"You can sing twenties music?" Jorge asked Mya in English.

"Why don't you be the judge of that?" Mya asked, already playing the role perfectly and sauntering a bit closer to his table.

Jorge said something to the manager, then nodded at Mya. "Go for it, beautiful. Win me over." He flashed her a smile before taking his seat again.

"Give me a few moments to talk to the band," Mya requested.

"*Cinco minutos*," Jorge told her.

"What the hell is happening?" Oliver hissed. "Why is she doing this?"

Before Sydney could explain, Beckett was on his feet and circling the table. He held out a hand for her. "A word, please."

Sydney stood and accepted Beckett's palm. He guided her down a dimly lit hallway and pinned her against a door, the wood cold against the exposed skin of her back.

He cocked his head, studying her. "Why?"

"There are several reasons, but honestly, I just couldn't bring myself to be like Cora," she whispered. "To sing and seduce. To con."

Beckett continued to gaze at her silently.

"After the hell you've been through . . ." She freed a harsh breath from her lungs before continuing, "I promised I wouldn't hurt you, and if I were to do that and—"

Beckett dropped his mouth over hers, stealing her words. He held her face gently while kissing her hard and with so much passion she forgot where they were.

"You," he said between kisses. "I don't know what to say." Another quick kiss before pulling back slightly. "You're everything to me."

The sincerity of his words shot her straight in the heart, and her mouth went still against his lips.

Beckett leaned back to catch her eyes as she searched for what to say, but at the sound of the saxophone playing, she turned her head toward the music coming from the dining room.

"We should head back." He pushed away from the wall. "They were playing this song at Capone last weekend," he commented as Mya began singing the lyrics Sydney taught her earlier for "It Don't Mean A Thing."

The band behind Mya crooned "Do-op, do-op, do-op" just as Sydney and Beckett re-entered the room, and Sydney focused on Jorge, who appeared already enamored by Mya.

Sydney caught Jesse's eyes as they neared his table, his gaze quickly falling so they didn't reveal they knew each other. Although, it was hard not to eyeball Ivy, wedged between Jesse and Miguel, and shoot daggers her way.

Beckett placed his palm on Sydney's back, and his touch helped steady her nerves. He pulled her chair out for her at the table and scooted her in.

When Sydney looked up, she spied Camila tapping at her mouth, and oh . . .

*My lipstick. Probably smeared.* She quickly dragged a finger beneath her bottom lip in hopes of erasing the evidence of her make-out session with Beckett and nodded her thanks.

When the song ended, Jorge was on his feet applauding enthusiastically, then gestured for Mya to continue. But when he lowered to his seat, his gaze averted to Sydney, sending chills up her spine at his undivided attention. He raised his wineglass her way while talking to the club manager hanging by his table. The manager's focus fell to Sydney before nodding as if Jorge had given him a directive.

"I think the plan is working," Camila said when the

manager approached their table with two bottles of wine and six glasses.

"Compliments of Señor Rojas." The man began uncorking one of the two bottles.

Mya was on her second song now, and her performance was stellar. Thank God for her drama skills. But now Sydney had to get into the undercover groove herself. She wasn't a fan of drinking on an op, but what choice did they all have right now? Jorge had sent them wine, and if they refused, their plan would quickly fall apart.

"Tell him *gracias*," Sydney replied with a nod to the manager while accepting the glass. She took a small sip of the red, and it was smooth in her mouth. A hint of cherry, which no longer triggered her. She and cherries were good again. She was pretty sure she had Beckett to thank for that. He'd managed to free her mind of any lingering emotional strings still connected to Alice's betrayal.

"Easy there," Gray remarked when Oliver polished off half his glass in two large gulps. "You nervous or something?"

Oliver jerked a thumb toward the stage where the band played. "*Mya's* up there, and I'm supposed to be her guy, right? And now there's a room full of men staring at her like they want to eat her up. I may have to play fisticuffs soon."

Camila chuckled, the noise barely audible over the music. "Fight, you mean? Defend your manhood if anyone tries to go after your girl?"

"I mean, if I'm playing her boyfriend, shouldn't I do that?" Oliver knocked back the rest of his wine like it was a tequila shot.

"Men," Camila said under her breath. "We do want Mya to catch a certain man's attention," she reminded Oliver.

"But do we really?" Oliver grimaced and focused back on

Mya. "I just have a bad fucking feeling," he added too low for anyone aside from their table to hear.

And when Sydney looked past Beckett, finding Miguel focused on her again, her stomach squeezed. "Yeah," she whispered. "Maybe I do too."

## CHAPTER THIRTY-FIVE

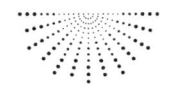

Beckett was two seconds away from killing a guy. Any damn guy. Every man. Every which fucking way. They all seemed to be closing in on him and Sydney on the dance floor. *They're going to try and steal her away. Take her from me.*

"Something's not right." Beckett held Sydney tight to his body while they danced to the Spanish music now playing instead of the nineteen-twenties jazz.

After Mya had sung a few more songs, Jorge requested they all join his table, and a DJ took over at the snap of the billionaire's fingers.

Now they were crowded on the dance floor playing their role as couples, but something was wrong. He couldn't possibly be drunk. He'd barely finished a glass of the wine Jorge had sent over to their table.

"Tell me there aren't really a ton of guys swarming us right now," Beckett said as Sydney swiveled her hips, grinding against him to the sensual beat of the music.

"What guys?" The music was loud, but still, did she sound as "off" as he felt? Drowsy or loopy, maybe. Sydney peered left and right, gripping hold of his shoulders as though she might lose her balance. "No, there aren't any guys. Well, not a beehive of them or whatever you were saying," she slurred.

*Sydney slur?* "Something's wrong," he mumbled again, trying to make sense of the odd sensations flowing through his body.

He sure as hell shouldn't be hallucinating from a glass of wine.

Beckett closed his eyes and shook his head, grateful to see the "swarm of men" were gone when he reopened them. No one was trying to get to Sydney and take her away. Instead, he spotted Gray and Camila dancing nearby. Camila appeared to be moving as erotically as Sydney, and he doubted she was acting.

*Where are Oliver and Mya?* He searched the dance floor without losing hold of Sydney and spotted Mya with one leg pinned to Oliver's hip as he dipped her back and slowly dragged a palm down between her breasts. *Damn.*

When he forced his attention away from the dance area and over to the tables, he saw Jesse there, a reminder they were undercover. Jesse mouthed something to him, but he couldn't read his lips. He was too fucked in the head to even know what was going on.

"Welllll, I feel fantastic," Sydney declared, cupping the back of his neck and drawing his face back to hers. She wasn't lust-drunk. The woman was drunk-drunk. "I want you to make love to me. Take me back in that hallway," she murmured into his ear. "Hook my panties to the side and thrust your cock into me and slam me against the wall. Cuff me. Spank me. Fuck me," she rasped. "Whatever you want, *I* want."

Beckett's knees buckled at her words, and his dick went

hard. *Or maybe it was already hard?* He was so damn confused.

"Take me. Now," she begged, then set her mouth to his and shimmied against him.

"Sweetheart," he said, unsure where he was going with that line because he was growing lightheaded and dizzy again. Desire planted roots in his mind. It was taking control of his body. And he was tempted to take her into the hall and fuck the naughty from her. Make her behave. Be a good girl for him.

"Damn, you're beautiful," he overheard Gray telling Camila, which momentarily distracted him from taking his bad girl over his knee and putting his palm print on her ass as he drove into her hard like he'd done the other night. "Something's not right," he remembered, trying to focus. To switch from bedroom mode to sheriff mode. Regain his senses. All five. *Or are there six? Shit, I'm losing it.*

"There's something wrong," a deep voice announced nearby, and Beckett found Jorge at his nine o'clock, a cigar dangling from his lips like he was Tony Montana in *Scarface.*

*Wasn't Capone nicknamed Scarface? Half my brain is working, at least.* "What's wrong?" Beckett asked Jorge as Sydney continued dancing in his arms, grinding her pussy against his cock as if they had no clothing barrier between them.

"We're at this club when we should all head to my place. That's what is wrong," Jorge shared once he removed the cigar from between his teeth. "We shall take the party there. More privacy if you get my drift." He smiled, his gaze cutting to Sydney.

*To my woman.*
*No.*
*You can't have her.*

He protectively held her against his body, ready to throw down and blow the plan . . . there'd been a plan, right? What was going on right now? Why was the room so upside down and sideways?

Jorge smiled, and he really did resemble a young Al Pacino. "I won't touch her," Jorge promised, not that his promise held any weight to Beckett. And then the prick leaned closer and whispered, "But I'd love to watch."

*Watch?* Beckett closed his eyes when another weird, roiling sensation traveled up his spine and had him feeling so damn strange. "Watch what?"

"Baby." Sydney's voice had him opening his eyes, struggling to hang on. To not lose consciousness, which was what he'd swear was about to happen. "He wants to watch us make love."

"Good girl." Jorge's comment had Beckett letting go of Sydney, his attention snapping to the man's jaw he was about to break.

The desire to hit this fucker now trumped his desire to have sex.

*Desire?*

He went still as he thought about the bottles of wine. They'd been unopened, but . . .

*Ohhhh, fuuuuccck.*

The "desire" drug. It was all coming back to him. Did the scientist use them as test subjects to show the cartel the effects of his formula? Had the bottles of wine been drugged before being corked?

He felt like he was inside a nightmare. Surely this wasn't how an "Ecstasy on steroids" drug would feel.

"You okay?" Jorge studied him as his grin stretched. And in Beckett's mind, he was transforming into that freaky cat from *Alice in Wonderland.* His daughter had good taste.

She wasn't a fan of that movie. He officially hated it now too.

When Sydney reached for Beckett like she might fall, he secured his hands around her hips. But the room was spinning again.

Sydney had two glasses of that wine, and if only the one was having such an impact on him, damn it . . .

More imaginary men, now with those Cheshire Cat smiles, appeared. But this time, they were real. Reaching for them. For Sydney. *His* woman.

And then everything became one big blur.

## CHAPTER THIRTY-SIX

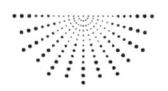

BECKETT STARTLED AND PULLED HIS MOUTH FROM SYDNEY'S at the sound of breaking glass echoing throughout the room. It felt as though he was moving underwater as he twisted his torso and found the source of the noise—a large vase lay shattered on the floor, bloodred roses scattered among the debris.

"Roses," Beckett muttered as he took in their surroundings and worked like hell to rid his mind of the fog clouding his memory. "Where are we?"

Beds and couches were randomly situated in the massive room. High ceilings. No decorations on the walls aside from the . . . *chains?* What in God's name was going on?

His attention snapped back to Sydney, pulling her upright when she began wilting in his arms. She was totally out of it, her eyes closed and her hips still swaying to music only she seemed to hear.

*We were drugged.* He remembered now. Jorge had brought them all back to his estate in one of his SUVs. But when was that? How long had they been there? *Hours? Minutes?*

"I need you to make love to me. Please," Sydney begged, grinding against him again like she was catching her second wind.

"Roses," he repeated, suddenly recalling Elaina's warning. Ordering himself to snap free from the stupor, he gave Sydney a quick shake, then brought his mouth to her ear. "We need to stop. We can't do this. We're drugged," he said urgently. "Someone may be watching."

And why was it as hot as a sauna in there?

Strands of Sydney's hair clung to the rivulets of sweat sliding down her neck and disappearing into her cleavage. Thank fuck she was still wearing her dress.

"What are you talking about?" she murmured, her eyes fluttering open only to fall closed again.

"Gray. Mya. The others," Beckett said, his memories slowly floating to the surface. Everyone had been in the SUV, so they must be there somewhere.

Maintaining his hold of Sydney, he slowly turned in a circle and searched the . . . sex dungeon? Velvet couches and club chairs, lavish beds, huge potted plants, bondage equipment, and furniture that would have most likely rivaled the high-end clubs he knew existed in LA.

And was that Oliver and Mya leaning against a red leather wall making out?

No sign of Gray and Camila yet, but they could be hidden by one of the many six-foot-high privacy partitions sectioning off the room.

"I need to stop them before they do something they'll regret." Drugged or not, he knew Gray and Oliver would never be able to forgive themselves for having sex while under the influence.

"I'm so confused," Sydney said as she struggled to find her balance, then he lifted her into his arms.

"Baby," he said, brushing his lips over hers as she hooked her arms behind his neck, "I need you to fight this. Snap out of it. They drugged us at the club. We're at Jorge's."

He carried her to a nearby black leather sectional and set her down before noticing a wall composed of one giant mirror twenty or so feet away.

*Test subjects. They're watching us, aren't they? Seeing what the drug does to us.*

Beckett peeled Sydney's arms from around his neck and examined her eyes. Her pupils were fully blown.

She was so much smaller than him, and the wine had hit her hard.

"Stay here," he ordered, even though her eyes were closed and her head lolled to the side.

Beckett hauled ass over to Oliver, every movement causing intense dizziness. Despite the nausea, he had to keep going.

Oliver had Mya pinned to the wall, her arms stretched above her head, and was holding her wrists together with one hand as they kissed.

"Oliver. Snap. The. Fuck. Out. Of. It," Beckett hissed, his words falling on deaf ears. "Oliver," he barked, yanking his arm this time, then discreetly looked over at the mirrored wall. Once whoever was observing noticed Beckett was no longer under the influence of the drug, they may come into the room. In which case they'd all be screwed. "Stop." He pulled Oliver's arm harder, forcing him to release Mya's wrists.

"What the fuck?" Oliver asked, and although confused and still slightly drugged, he had the presence of mind to grab on to Mya as she began to slide down the leather wall.

"The wine was drugged," Beckett explained, hoping he didn't need to elaborate with possible eyes on them.

"Fuck." Oliver blinked and looked at Mya as she grabbed his shirt, drew him back to her, and planted her lips on his. *Shit.* The drug still seemed to have a solid hold on Oliver, who was eagerly kissing her back.

"Damn it." Beckett cursed while forcing them apart like two teenagers at a high school dance. They both resisted, trying to keep hold of each other. "I don't have time for this." He had to find Gray.

Beckett was on the verge of knocking Oliver unconscious to pull him away when Oliver finally "woke up" again and held his palms in surrender between himself and Mya.

"Shit, this stuff is powerful," Oliver said. "Why are you okay?"

"I only had one glass. You had—"

"More," Oliver finished for him, then helped Beckett guide Mya to the couch.

"Stay put. I gotta find Gray," he ordered as Mya snuggled up next to Oliver, and he pulled her tight to his side. "Don't touch her."

"I'm not. Just holding her," Oliver said, dragging his free hand down his face and nodding. But would he fall victim to the drug again? Beckett wasn't so sure, so he had to hurry. "And don't touch her." He pointed to Sydney. "Or I will kill you."

Oliver tipped his head and closed one eye. "Roger that," he said with a nod that wasn't all that convincing.

Beckett raced through what felt like a maze of debauchery to find Gray and Camila. There was another mirrored section of the wall off to his left and still another one farther down. Jorge needed visual access to multiple vantage points during whatever sex shows he must've had performed for him while he watched.

Relief pounded through Beckett at the sight of Gray

around the next partition, and the fact he was trying to stop Camila already.

"You're drugged. We can't. Stop," Gray said, struggling to pin her against his frame to stop her from stripping.

"Need a hand?" Beckett called out on approach.

"You still possessed or good?" Gray asked.

"Mostly good," Beckett returned, thankful Gray was as lucid as he was. He needed all the help he could get.

"Is Sydney—" Gray's words cut off when Camila lunged forward and kissed him, her hands reaching for his zipper.

Beckett went in for the assist and gently held her wrist, stopping her mid-zip. "Camila," he began, "you need to try to remember . . ." Was he wasting his words? She looked as possessed as Mya had been. "I have the others on one of the couches. Let's just bring her there. We can keep an eye on them until we figure out how to get out of here," he suggested to Gray. "I think I had less wine than you. I'll carry her. You just keep hold of her hands, so she doesn't hit me."

"It was in the wine? That's how they did it?" Gray cursed as Beckett lifted Camila, who thankfully didn't try to kiss him. Did that mean the drug only woke up desires already within a person? Did she want Gray?

"I'm assuming so," Beckett said as he set Camila on the couch beside Sydney, who appeared to be asleep.

"Do you remember what happened tonight?" Gray asked, a hand circling his neck and a haunted look in his eyes.

"Just dancing. I think they were hoping we'd all have sex in here while they watched, but fortunately, that didn't happen." Beckett tipped his chin toward the mirrored wall, assuming they still had eyes on them. "Elaina's instructions to me were to stop when I saw the roses," he added while gesturing toward the roses lying amid shards of broken glass on the floor.

"Thank God for that," Gray remarked, dropping alongside Oliver, who was fast asleep with Mya snoozing, her head on his shoulder. "If Miguel's on the other side of that mirrored wall, then Jesse is too." He lowered his voice, adding, "He would've stopped us from doing something unthinkable if he had to."

"True." Beckett sat and pulled Sydney against his exhausted body. "I guess we wait until they decide to come in. But keep our eyes open. I don't want anyone coming near them."

"That drug is potent," Gray whispered a few quiet minutes later.

"Back at the club, I kept thinking someone would take Sydney from me. I wasn't expecting paranoia to be a side effect." The fact he shared that with Gray meant the drug was still very much in his system.

Gray's gaze cut to Camila. "And I can't believe . . ."

*You were making out with her?* Before either could continue, a set of double doors leading into the room parted.

Jorge was the first to enter the room, Jesse in the hall behind him. "Nothing to see tonight. Too bad. I was hoping after hours of dancing in here, something more exciting would have transpired. But my men just came to let me know you all seemed to be sleeping instead."

*Dancing for hours?* No wonder his body was fatigued. And hell, what time was it?

"Perhaps you'll all join us for my birthday party tomorrow night. I think you didn't have quite the right amount of wine to"—Jorge stroked his jaw—"loosen you up enough."

Jorge wanted to up the dose of the drug and test it on them again? *Yeah, fuck you.* But if Jorge was going to let them walk out of there alive, that was all that mattered.

"Get some rest. Plenty of beds in here. My men will be back in a few hours to take you all to your hotel."

*How cordial of you*, he thought bitterly, as Jorge turned and left without another word.

Jesse caught Beckett's eyes from the hall before the doors closed, a slight nod from him confirming his, "I've got your back." Beckett trusted his brother-in-law with his sister's life, so he'd trust him with his own.

Beckett forced himself to stay awake after that, but he was clueless how much time had passed between when Jorge had left, and Oliver woke up.

With Oliver starting to come around, Beckett decided to attempt to revive Sydney while Gray did the same with Camila.

"Sydney," Beckett said into her ear. "Wake up." He smoothed the pad of his thumb over her cheek. She moaned and turned her face into his palm and kissed his hand.

"I could love you." Beckett's eyes widened at Sydney's words.

"Sweetheart," Beckett said after a hard swallow. He leaned in to kiss her like that might break the spell, hating doing it in front of Gray, but at this point, he doubted it mattered.

"Mmmm." Sydney's tongue slid between his lips. Yup, she was still in "desire mode."

"Sydney," he whispered into her ear again. "You've been drugged. We're at Jorge's."

When she went still in his arms, he followed her eyes to the roses on the floor. "Elaina," she muttered. "She said to stop on the phone today. Or was that yesterday? Did she mean for us to stop? To not . . ."

*Have sex. Yeah.* Poor kid for having to tell them that too.

"Oh my God." Mya's voice snapped Sydney's attention her way. "Did we . . .?"

"No. None of us did," Beckett answered, shutting down her alarm.

"Thank fuck." Oliver shook his head.

"Ah, I see you're all awake," a man said a moment later, joining them in the room. Probably one of Jorge's guards. "Your car is ready."

Once Sydney was on her feet, he slid a hand around her waist to help her walk. He barely paid attention to their surroundings as they left the room. The damn place was too big. Too bright. Too much gold everywhere. Overall, it was just too Gatsby-like for him to look around without squinting, feeling like it was the sun obstructing his view. But no, it was just gold and glitzy shit everywhere.

Once they were outside, the fresh air was another wake-up call he hadn't known he needed.

He spotted a black SUV with special tires, the kind that could take a bullet and keep driving. Armored vehicle most likely.

"That's not your ride. Another guest just pulled in," the guard told Beckett before pointing to a six-car attached garage. One door lifted, and a similar all-black SUV pulled out a moment later.

Gray helped Camila in the back before taking shotgun. Oliver and Mya climbed into the third row, which left the middle for him and Sydney.

Once he tucked Sydney inside, he turned at the strange feeling of being watched. Eyes were on him, and not from Jorge's guard.

Beckett looked up at a window over the garage and grabbed the side of the SUV at the sight.

A kid was in the window staring at him. He couldn't make out much more than that, but . . .

*Miles?* The idea of driving away from the boy right now was unbearable.

"Hey, I know you."

Beckett shifted for a better look at the man leaning against the other SUV. Dark hair. Ink covering his exposed skin, forehead as well.

And he wasn't just any man.

Hector Lopez.

*You remember me. Great.* His shoulders fell, and when he looked toward the window again, the boy was gone.

"You're here for her, aren't you?" Hector asked.

"Get them out of here," Beckett whispered before he slammed the door shut and turned his attention to the new problem at hand. "I don't know what you're talking about," Beckett answered Hector as casually as possible, hoping to buy Gray some time to knock out the driver and take over the wheel.

Hector waved his finger in the air and reached for his gun at his hip. "I never forget a face. Stop the others!" he shouted as the SUV started to move.

Hector rushed Beckett, setting his gun at Beckett's temple while demanding he lower himself to the ground.

Beckett followed orders, his heart in his throat when he stole another look at the window to see the boy there watching again.

"What's going on?" he overheard someone ask, coming from the direction of the house. When Beckett forced his gaze away from the boy, he found Miguel and Jorge exiting alongside Jesse.

"Stop them at the gate. They're getting away," Hector shouted before switching to Spanish and barking orders to one of the guards already speaking into his comm unit, most likely to one of the guard towers near the exit.

An unexpected explosion rocked the ground, and thank God, the SUV hadn't been hit. From Beckett's vantage point, it was the first guard station by the main gate in the distance.

Then the second tower burst into flames a moment later.

*Carter.* He had to be out there. He must have had them followed from the hotel to Jorge's last night. *Sydney will be safe.*

"They must have backup. Who the hell are they?" Jorge asked, approaching where Beckett remained on his knees, hands behind his head. He crouched before Beckett, and Beckett knew this was going to be hard for Jesse to watch, but as long as Sydney and the others made it out safely and someone could save Miles . . . he'd take every punch or bullet he had to.

When Beckett remained quiet, Jorge ordered two of his men to secure Beckett's arms. "Who am I?" Beckett finally asked, faking a laugh after another one of Jorge's men clocked him across the jaw. Maybe it was the drug. Or he was just pissed. But Beckett rasped, "*El Diablo*. And I'm here to take you back to Hell."

## CHAPTER THIRTY-SEVEN

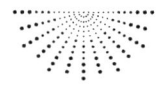

"BECKETT, WAKE UP."

Beckett groaned and clutched his ribs, trying to remember what happened and why he was in so much pain. "Sydney?" He reached out in search of her, eyes still locked shut. Why'd his face hurt so damn badly? "You okay? Tell me you're okay."

"It's me. It's Cora."

The voice. The name. Beckett fought through the mental fog and opened his eyes.

He squinted against the harsh sunlight streaming through a window opposite where he sat. *I'm on the ground. Where?* "Cora?"

"Yes, it's me. Did Ivy find you?"

His stomach turned as he sought to visually locate the woman who kept screwing with his life. "Cora," he repeated.

He felt a hand on his shoulder. He'd need to turn his head to see her, but every part of his face hurt after Jorge's men had punched him repeatedly on the driveway to the point of blacking out.

*And now I'm here with Cora. Or am I dead? Is this purgatory? My hell is to be stuck with her.*

"Please tell me you brought help. I—I heard the explosions outside. Saw the two guard towers blow up. Tell me you have friends out there who will rescue us," she rushed out.

"Not alone," he mumbled, grabbing hold of his side again. Squinting through the pain, Beckett opened his eyes and took in Cora for the first time in six years. The black eye and swollen cheek were a clear indication she'd not been living in the lap of luxury, at least not lately. "I'm not dead, right?"

"No, but we will be if we're not rescued soon. When Jorge dumped you in here, he informed me I'm being traded to the cartel tomorrow," she explained in a shaky voice, brushing her long, dark hair away from her face, exposing more bruises on her throat.

He may have hated Cora, but no woman, regardless of circumstance, should ever be abused, and it pained him to see her bruises. "How long have you been in here?"

"A few weeks, I think. Ever since they grabbed me from my bedroom the day I called you. Hector told Jorge he knew me from LA, and I was a con artist. That I betrayed their guys, and it was why Hector went to prison."

"You didn't betray them," Beckett bit out. "Just betrayed me." When she kept quiet, he asked, "Why'd they put us together?" He coughed up blood and spat it to the side.

"Probably to torture us."

"Yeah, putting me with you is torture," he drawled, unable to stop himself from speaking the truth. Maybe that was still the side effects of the drug talking, or he really was just done with her bullshit.

"I meant that he'll probably send someone in here to beat you in front of me. Make me watch."

"Tell me they didn't . . . hurt your son?"

"No, but I was forced to watch while they tortured and murdered his father, Daniel." She pointed to the blood-stained wall across the room. Beckett looked up at the chains hanging from the ceiling. "Wait, Ivy told you about Miles?"

"Yeah, Ivy said something." *To Jesse, not me.*

"Jorge blamed Miles's father for allowing himself to be duped by me. Letting me in their lives for nearly six years. And as part of his security team, he believed Daniel should have vetted me more thoroughly."

"Men have a habit of doing that around you," he bit out, letting go of his ribs with a wince.

Beckett dragged in a deep, painful breath and slowly expelled it through his nostrils, then tried to get his brain to work. Figure out his next steps. Carter and Camila's men had to have been outside Jorge's estate that morning, clearly prepared for shit to go down if they took out the guard towers at the front gates.

Beckett hoped he wasn't wrong to assume Sydney and the others escaped.

"You didn't want me to know about Miles. You didn't want McKenna to know she had a brother, did you?" he accused.

Cora leaned back and stretched her legs out in front of her, eyes going back to the blood-stained wall. She was wearing a khaki jumpsuit like prisoners wore, and Beckett wondered if that'd been Hector's suggestion. A little payback since Hector incorrectly assumed she'd helped put him behind bars thirteen years ago. "You'd want Miles in McKenna's life. I know you. And that wasn't a possibility given my situation."

Beckett swallowed, which hurt given someone had almost choked him to death earlier.

"Why'd you really send your sister to my house two years ago?" He wasn't sure where that'd come from, but he'd blame the drug for his desire to know the truth too.

Cora turned to meet his eyes. "She was telling the truth. I had no new pictures of McKenna. It made me sad every time I looked at my son that he'd never meet his sister. So, I asked Ivy to check on her again. Get photos and try to learn more about her for me."

He wasn't sure if he bought that story, but why lie at this point?

Tears filled her eyes, and if she weren't such a manipulative liar, he'd believe they were real. Now? How could he ever know what was fiction or reality when it came to her? "After the last time you rejected me, I learned about Jorge and his inheritance. I decided it was time to settle down. Try and start a real life somewhere. You'd said to never bother you again, and for some reason, I felt that you were serious that time. More so than the previous warnings you'd given me."

And he had been serious. *Yet, here I am. But it's meant to be*, he reminded himself. "So, was Jorge your original target?"

"No, a man like him would be too cautious. I chose someone close to him that'd been with him for years. I searched for the weakest link on his security team."

The woman had always been spot on with her research. She'd known everything about Beckett before going after him in LA.

"Did you get pregnant on purpose?"

She nodded. "I was getting tired of moving around. I rarely stayed with a mark for more than a year. My sister was living with some guy in France, and it seemed permanent. I wanted that too." She paused for a breath. "I thought a pregnancy might buy me more time in one place and in the lifestyle I prefer. The only drawback was not being able to see my sister during all of this. I was worried they might put two and two together somehow. We tend to get in trouble when we're together."

Beckett replayed her words. The sickening selfishness of her situation.

"When I was pregnant with McKenna, that wasn't planned, and I wasn't ready to settle down then. Plus, you found out the truth about me, and I wasn't sure what you'd do, so I had to run. You see the difference between her and Miles, right? It's not that I chose one child over the other."

"Are you fucking kidding me?" he rasped, angry on McKenna's behalf. "I can't . . . it's not worth the air in my lungs to explain to you how bad this all sounds."

She shook her head. "Her life wouldn't have been better with me in it, and you know it."

"That's the one damn thing you've said that's a fact." He growled at the sharp stabbing pain in his side before adding, "You let your son live in a house with a psychopath so you could have a nice car? Expensive purses?" He scooted himself to the side, needing to get as far away from Cora as possible in the small space. "I hate you."

"I'm sorry."

"Your apology means absolutely nothing to me." He was only grateful he'd opted to come after her despite his inner voice telling him she'd only use him again because otherwise, Mya and Camila would be dead, and McKenna's brother handed over to the cartel. "I really hate you," he tossed out again with more venom this time.

Cora remained quiet for a moment before saying, "I really

did miss out on McKenna's life. I understood that more as Miles grew up. I still don't think I'm fit to be a mom, his nanny does most of the work. But McKenna's my daughter, and if I survive this, I want to get to know her. Visit her, at least."

Before Beckett had a chance to respond, the door swung open.

"My turn to question you, *pendejo*." Miguel stepped inside and gestured to Hector and another man to grab Beckett, and he didn't bother to resist as they bound his wrists with rope.

"Please don't hurt him." Cora's weak protest went unnoticed.

Hector and the other guy secured Beckett's arms over his head with the chains. "Payback time."

"Tell us about your friends," Miguel began, casually folding his arms over his white dress shirt. "How many people are you with, and what are you here for? This bitch? The drug? Jorge? What's your deal?"

Beckett hadn't answered any questions from Jorge's men between blows on the driveway, so did they really think hanging him by the wrists before swinging at him in that room would make a difference?

Hector strode around Beckett and cocked his head. "You ruined my life."

Beckett shook his head. "Being a bad guy. Doing bad shit. *That* ruined your life. Your own choices."

*"Un comico."* *Comedian.* Hector *tsk*ed as he unbuckled his belt and slid it free from the loops.

"Wait." Miguel held up his hand. "Let's give our new friend a go at him. See if he's really cut out to join us."

Beckett tugged against the binds at his wrists as he shifted his focus toward the door.

Jesse entered the room and walked up to Beckett, and when their eyes met, Beckett knew Jesse had no other choice but to follow orders.

"Go ahead." Miguel leaned back against the wall next to Cora and motioned for the other man to stand back.

Jesse moved in fast, grabbed the back of Beckett's head, and leaned in close as he punched him hard in the abdomen. "Please don't make me do this," he whispered, then struck him again. Beckett groaned loud enough to cover Jesse's words. "For the love of God, don't make me," he added the moment his fist connected again, and Beckett growled in pain.

"Fuck you," Beckett barked out, making it clear Jesse had better throw everything into this act. "That all you got?"

Jesse released Beckett's head with a shove and stepped back, then began rolling up his sleeves.

Beckett knew what his brother-in-law was capable of, and Jesse couldn't pull his punches without tipping off Miguel.

Beckett caught his breath before saying, "Just do it." He shut his eyes, knowing it'd be too hard for Jesse to look at him while he punched. "Do it," he repeated, urging Jesse not to try and play hero right now. It wasn't the time. He felt that in his bones. "I ain't talking, so, show me what ya got."

## CHAPTER THIRTY-EIGHT

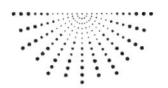

"We left him there. I'm just . . ." Sydney paced the living room of the safe house, unable to erase the image of Beckett on his knees with a gun to his head.

"We didn't have a choice. We didn't anticipate Hector would change plans and come to Chile. And you weren't answering your phones for obvious reasons when we tried to warn you." Carter blocked her path and set his hands on her shoulders. "Griffin and I followed you all from the hotel to Jorge's, but—"

"No way could you go into his estate without a plan. You were heavily outnumbered. You'd suffer casualties." Her shoulders slumped. "But damn it, it's killing me we left him behind."

"I'm sorry." Elaina's voice redirected everyone's attention her way. "I didn't know more. Just the roses."

"This isn't your fault," Liam told her, dropping to one knee while clasping her hands in his.

Tears rolled down Elaina's cheeks as she squeezed her eyes shut, and Liam held his daughter in a tight embrace. "I wish I could have done more."

"Your warning about the roses helped us," Gray said. "As soon as Beckett saw the roses, he was able to pull himself together. See, you saved us."

*That's what happened?* Sydney was still disoriented from the effects of that drug, but the entire ordeal had done a number on her—their SUV racing away in a flurry of gunfire moments before Carter blew up the guard towers was little more than a blur. But leaving Beckett behind to face God-knew-what stood out crystal clear and was the most disturbing memory.

Elaina pulled free from her dad's embrace and peered at her mom standing beside her. "Something's wrong. I—I think. Maybe I made a mistake." She set a palm to her head and squeezed her eyes closed. "There's so much pain." Elaina began crying, and Emily sheltered her in her arms this time while Liam stood tall, appearing torn between operator and dad mode.

"Your head?" Emily asked. "Liam, get her some medicine."

"No." Elaina pulled away. "It's Beckett. I think I'm feeling *his* pain." She looked at Sydney and began sobbing.

Elaina's gut-wrenching news hit Sydney hard, and she felt as though her world had been pulled out from under her. Like a vital piece of her had suddenly gone missing. And then Levi's voice appeared in her head. *You're a warrior, Mom.* Her son was right. She had to stay strong and hold it together for Beckett.

"He'll be okay." Mya stepped forward, and she looked like she'd been through the wringer too. The drug was still in her system, and Sydney wasn't sure if her friend remembered anything from last night. But Oliver had apologized about kissing her, so *he'd* recalled some of it. "Beckett *will* be okay, right?"

"This is too much for her." Emily shook her head. "Too much stress."

"It's not that, Mom." Elaina frowned, tears still falling down her cheeks. "I'm upset because I can't see what will happen to Beckett. I only know Dad saves the boy." She turned and ran from the room.

After Emily and Liam followed Elaina from the room, Sydney gave in and fell to her knees.

"We need a new plan," Carter spoke up. "Making our move at Jorge's birthday party, even if it's still scheduled to happen, is out. We need to move in sooner."

"Beckett and Jesse may be on the inside, but they can't take down everyone," Griffin pointed out. "We're going to need an army, but do we have the time to assemble one?"

"We already have an army," Mya said, still appearing pale and shaky. "We have Marines in Mexico. Martín and his men." Mya scanned the room, her gaze falling on Camila last. "And we have you."

"Me?" Camila set a hand to her chest.

"Elaina can't see what will happen, but . . ." Sydney rose from her knees. "Elaina's never been wrong, so was she right about you?" she asked, guessing Mya may have been grasping at straws, but they'd take all the luck, fate, whatever it was called they could get. "Can you see things like Elaina does?" She swallowed as their eyes connected. "Can you help us? Help Beckett?"

Camila turned her back to the room. "The last time I tried helping," she began, "people died anyway. Seeing things, as you put it, has only ever been a curse for me."

"*Camila.*" The normally stoic and composed Carter sounded shocked, but he quickly recovered and calmly walked her way while the rest of the room fell back to give them space.

Sydney remained rooted in place. They needed help. And she needed Beckett alive.

The universe hadn't put her on this path with Beckett only to steal him away now, damn it.

"Camila, if you can help," Sydney said, unable to rein in her emotions, "I'm begging you."

Camila turned her way. "I don't have visions like Elaina. I have dreams. And they're messy and hard to interpret." She closed her eyes. "More like nightmares."

"But did you have a dream about this trip? About Beckett?" Sydney crossed the space between them, her heart racing.

"I accepted the murder case because of one, yes," Camila confessed. "I'd have to try to remember the details. Maybe sketch what I saw in the nightmare to make sense of it." She paused and released a shaky breath. "What if I misinterpret it and make things worse? What if it changes the outcome and someone who should've lived dies?"

"We need all the help we can get right now," Sydney pleaded.

"The party planners and band will be setting up at Jorge's tomorrow," Carter said. "Too many civilians. Plus, unlike our original plans, they'll see us coming."

"Right." Sydney worked through the problem in her head. "But do we have time to get Martín's people here and map out an infil plan to strike tonight?"

"Not tonight." Camila looked up, rubbing her forehead the way Elaina had done as she tried to remember the nightmare. "We must go now. Beckett doesn't have time." She squeezed her eyes closed and drew a hand over her heart. "The details aren't very clear, but I can see your friend Jesse, the one from the club last night. He'll try to stop them from killing Beckett today." She gave Sydney a grave look. "But they both die."

"Well, that ain't gonna happen, I can promise you that." Sydney recognized that deep voice and Southern accent and turned just as A.J. dropped his duffle bag in the doorway.

"What are you doing here?" Carter asked.

"Caught a flight yesterday. I couldn't let my brother do this without me." A.J. removed his ball cap and ran his fingers through his close-cropped hair as Liam joined them. "The terrorists aren't going anywhere. They can wait," A.J. gritted out. "But from the sounds of it, Beckett and Jesse can't."

## CHAPTER THIRTY-NINE

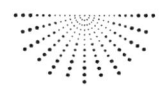

"This will work. It has to." Sydney looked up from the map displayed on the iPad screen, meeting Carter's eyes across the table.

"It's the only plan that makes sense, and they won't expect a daylight rescue. We draw as many men away from the estate as possible." He pointed to the road on the screen where some of the team planned to position themselves on high ground several klicks away from Jorge's estate. "Our bait vehicle will fake an attack, then retreat. Jorge will send a team to pursue. Our guys will wait to take them out as soon as they get"—he zoomed in on the road on screen, repeating the plan they'd already agreed upon—"here."

"They'll send another team of men out when their boys don't answer their calls." *Hopefully.*

"And then we'll light up the next team," Carter finished for her.

"The second y'all blow those fuckers sky high," A.J. joined the conversation, heading toward the table, "we quietly breach the estate. Once we free Beckett and Jesse realizes he can switch to Team Good Guys, there should be enough of us to handle the stragglers left inside Jorge's home."

"After you let us know Miles, Jesse, and Beckett are safe, the rest of us will converge on the property and join the party," Jack tossed out. "Plus, we have the world's best sniper here," he added while looking at Liam. "And Griffin ain't half bad."

Griffin rolled his eyes. He and the rest of the guys were checking their weapons and prepping for the op. Everyone except Oliver, who would be staying back to keep an eye on Elaina, Emily, and Mya at the safe house.

"Luckily, we did recon on Jorge's place this week with the drone. Thermal imaging showed twenty people on-site any given day. Some of those are more than likely staff. So, heads on a swivel for innocents," Carter noted, probably for A.J.'s sake since he hadn't been clued in on the details. "We also now have Miguel, Hector, and the scientist at Jorge's too."

"My guy watching the place right now just texted that four more heavily armed men rolled up, which we anticipated after this morning," Camila shared.

Carter nodded. "Let's run through this one more time before we roll out." He pointed to Jack. "You're driving the bait vehicle. Griffin and one of Camila's guys are handling the first pursuit team. If another pursuit team is dispatched, I'll handle that with Camila." He looked to Sydney. "And you said the boy was in the room over the garage?"

Sydney thought back to that morning when she'd followed Beckett's gaze as he'd stood on the driveway. "Yeah, I think it's safe to assume that's where Miles is living right now."

"Then he's your target," Carter told Liam. "Get Miles out of there. Don't worry about anything else."

"Roger that," Liam confirmed.

"Sydney will disable the security cameras. Then, Sydney, A.J., and Gray will infil the home. First mission is to find Beckett and Jesse." Carter let go of a deep breath, seeming reluctant to say the next part. "Save Cora and Ivy too."

*The ones who got them into this mess.* But yeah, Sydney would do what she could. "Once Beckett and Jesse are safe, we'll alert you to advance."

"We should get going," Camila abruptly announced. "They're running out of time."

"And don't go down the tunnel when you're inside," Elaina yelled out, startling Sydney.

Liam turned toward his daughter in the doorway. "What tunnel?"

"That bad man has a tunnel. Just don't go in," Elaina said in a steady voice, her eyes wide as if she were seeing events unfold in real time. It was so beyond Sydney's comprehension, but she was grateful for anything that'd help rescue Beckett and Jesse.

"A billionaire obsessed with Al Capone having tunnels is not surprising," Mya joined the conversation. "Capone had a bootleg tunnel he used at his home in Chicago. I did my research on him this week."

"Just don't go in," Elaina whispered.

"Okay," Sydney responded with a firm nod, letting her know she understood.

"Dad." Elaina turned to Liam and launched herself into his arms.

Liam stroked her back. "I'll be okay."

"I know." Elaina pulled away. "That's my *thank you for saving my best friend's brother*." She chewed on her lip. "I know it hasn't happened yet, but it will."

\*  \*  \*

Sydney adjusted the wireless comm in her ear and waited for Carter's green light, her heart beating faster than during previous ops. Out of range of Jorge's perimeter security cameras, she prepped her urban assault CarbonLite ladder kit, designed for special operations to aid in combat situations.

Once she had the go-ahead, she'd use the app on her phone, which was highly advanced software her family's company had created and had yet to sell to the U.S. government, to scramble Jorge's security cameras. At that point, she'd head to the twelve-foot security wall and scale it with her assault ladder as planned.

"This is Alpha Four," Jack announced over the radio. He was too far away to be on comms with her and the rest of Bravo Team, which also consisted of A.J., Liam, and Gray. The others would join the line once they arrived on-site. Sydney dialed down the radio to keep Jack's voice low as he added, "They're hot on my tail. The bait worked. Two vehicles en route to Alpha Three's position."

"This is Alpha Three. That's a good copy," Griffin piped up. Two minutes later, he said, "I have visual. Preparing to engage in three, two, one."

Thankfully, Griffin's designated "kill zone" was far enough away that no one at Jorge's estate would feel the vibrations.

"Both vehicles down," Griffin shared. "What's your status, Bravo One?"

"Four more men just exited the gates in one vehicle," Gray informed them over the radio.

A few minutes later, Carter announced, "This is Alpha

One. Target vehicle down. Bravo Team, you're a go. Disable cameras and move in."

"Roger that," Sydney responded, then opened her app and quickly handled the cameras. "Surveillance cams are now down inside and outside the property. We're clear to infil," she alerted the team. "Advancing now."

"That's a good copy," Gray said, and Sydney pocketed her phone, grabbed the assembled ladder, and hurried for her target location.

Within seconds, the ladder was up, and Sydney scaled the wall. Once at the top, she stayed low and peeked over the ledge, finding an armed tango ten meters away with his back to her.

She was moving in from the east side of the property. A.J. and Liam were taking the entrance, which was closest to Miles. And Gray was entering from the west. The place was too big to mount an offensive from the back, and they didn't have enough of them to cover the ground, so they'd have to make do.

Sydney anchored herself to the wall and reached for the Glock, suppressor already attached. She wouldn't be able to send an arrow from her position, which she would've preferred to do.

She quickly fired two shots. Bullets weren't truly "silenced" by a suppressor like in the movies, but since they were outside, she doubted anyone on Jorge's team inside the property had heard. "One tango down."

"This is Bravo Three. Roger that. One guard down here. I'm advancing to higher ground to get a vantage point of the garage," Liam shared.

"This is Bravo Two," A.J. spoke up. "Covering your movement, Bravo Three."

Sydney silently approached the guard she'd taken down, swiped his radio, and hooked it to the side of her khaki cargo pants to keep tabs on Jorge's team.

She remained crouched and alert as she moved, ensuring there were no snipers in the windows as she advanced.

The second-floor balcony off to the side of the home was her point of entry based on the blueprints Carter had managed to secure a few days ago. But an armed guard walked the length of the balcony, so she'd have to make a run for it.

The man spotted her as she hauled ass across the wide-open expanse of lawn and toward the house. Bullets struck the ground around her, but luckily, the man was a lousy shot.

*Made it.* Breathing hard, she pinned her back against the wall beneath the balcony overhang and watched as more shots tore up the grass.

"*La puta. Perra. Dónde estás?*" the man called out.

*Bitch? Whore? Well then.* She stowed her Glock and went for her bow, prepared to send this man to meet his maker in two seconds.

"This is Bravo Three," Liam came over comms as she tried to get into a position to take down this asshole from the balcony. "I've secured the package. Exfiling now."

*The package.* Relief overwhelmed her at the news. Miles was with Liam. Now they just needed to get the others and not die trying.

Sydney closed her eyes, said a quick prayer and pictured her son. Her light to the dark inside her. Her everything. She'd make it out alive for him.

"This is Bravo One," Gray popped into her ear a moment later. "Alpha Team is en route to join you now."

Sydney peeled her eyes open, readying herself to move away from the cover of the balcony to take down the shooter, but before she had a chance, the guard's radio at her hip squawked to life. Her stomach sank at the orders barked out in Spanish. "*El hombre. Mátalo, ahora.*"

*The man. Kill him. Now.*

## CHAPTER FORTY

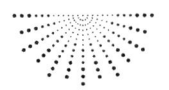

"Holy shit, Beck." Beckett tried to focus on the man standing in the doorway, the voice familiar but entirely impossible, unless . . .

"A.J.?" Beckett whispered in disbelief.

A gunshot rang out close by and Beckett flinched, but he was still hanging from the ceiling by the chains and too banged up to do anything.

Another gunshot and a body hit the floor.

"This is Bravo Two. I have eyes on the prize."

*Bravo Two? Prize?*

"A.J., that you?" Beckett repeated, blinking away the blood dripping down his face and thanking God that it really was his brother.

"Yeah, it's me. Let me get you down."

As soon as A.J. freed Beckett, he collapsed into his brother's arms, then slid to his knees.

"We need to get you out of here. They'll send more people." A.J. wrapped an arm around Beckett's torso and assisted him to his feet. "Take his other arm and help me with him," he said to Cora, who was on her way out the door.

"Don't go out there by yourself, damn it," A.J. rasped.

Cora whipped around. "I have to get to my son."

"He's safe with my team," A.J. said, and Beckett breathed a sigh of relief.

Before Cora could respond, one of Miguel's men appeared behind her and deftly wrapped an arm around her neck, using her as a human shield.

Beckett closed his eyes, willing his body to remain upright on its own so his brother could deal with the asshole.

A.J. popped off a headshot, nailing the guy with precision and splattering blood across Cora's face. "Not sorry," A.J. bit out. "You deserved that. Now, help me get Beckett out of here."

"No. There's too many of us. We'll draw attention." She grimaced and wiped at her face, then crouched and took the pistol from the dead man. "I'm going out on my own." But she was blocked by another obstacle.

Jesse and Ivy this time, and Ivy flung herself at Cora.

"A.J. and I got split up while I was handling Miguel and Hector," Jesse explained, maneuvering around the family reunion. "Glad you found the room."

"Thanks to your directions," A.J. replied. "Not that I wanted to leave you alone with those animals."

"Taken care of. I meant to leave Miguel and Hector alive, tied up and unconscious, but they weren't very cooperative. So, I put them down for good," Jesse said, then quickly snatched the pistol from Cora.

"Is Sydney here? I'm assuming she took down his security cams?" Beckett asked, and the idea of her being out there alone had his stomach turning.

"Yes and yes." A.J. assisted Beckett to the doorway, which was blocked by two dead bodies and the women who kept fucking up Beckett's life.

"Can you radio her to join us?" He knew Sydney could handle herself, but that didn't mean he wanted her out there on her own.

"Sydney knows I'm with you and that Jesse was working his way to meet us." A.J. nodded. "She's handling a few fuckers on the second floor. We're still trying to find Jorge and the scientist."

Beckett tested his legs to see if he could stand alone. "I'm good," he reassured his brother before A.J. unholstered the sidearm strapped to his leg and handed him the Sig Sauer P226. "We can't drag them along with us while we search for Jorge." He tipped his chin toward Cora and Ivy. "One of you should escort them out of here. But I'm not leaving without Sydney."

"I'd like to be reunited with my son," Cora begged. "Please, get us out of here."

"Sydney's my teammate," Jesse said. "I'm staying."

"I really hate leaving you," A.J. began, peeking into the hall to check if it was clear, "but I know I won't convince you to walk out the door with me. Too damn stubborn."

"Where do you think Jorge may be hiding?" Beckett asked Jesse. "You spent some time with him."

"One sec. I have Sydney over comms," A.J. announced, and Beckett secured his hand against the wall near the doorway for support.

"This is Bravo Two. That's a good copy. Sending backup to you," A.J. said over comms before directing his attention on Beckett. "She's heading to the room you two were in this morning. With the roses? She interrogated one of his men, who said there's a hidden room down there. She took a remote control off the guy to open the door."

"That room?" *The mirrored wall?*

"I know how to get there," Jesse said as A.J. handed him

the earpiece to stay connected to the team.

"Get out of this alive, brother," A.J. ordered.

"See you soon." Beckett motioned for his brother to get a move on, and A.J. rattled off the call signs for Bravo and Alpha Teams to Jesse.

According to A.J., Sydney and Gray were still inside, and the others were preparing to infil.

A.J. reached for Cora's elbow, urging her to stay with him and her sister. "I don't like you, you know that, right? And if something happens to my brother while I walk your asses outta here, we're gonna have much bigger issues."

"You're clear." Jesse motioned for A.J. and the sisters to leave.

Cora took one last look at Beckett and followed A.J. with Ivy tight to her side.

"Gray's in my ear," Jesse said, peering into the hall again. "The scientist tried to escape, but Camila and Carter intercepted him just outside the gates. We're down to our last HVT and an unknown number of potential tangos inside."

"Copy that." Beckett followed Jesse away from Jorge's "torture room," or whatever the hell it was called. So far, the place was eerily quiet, and no sounds of gunfire nearby.

"That sex fuckery room is down this hall," Jesse said a moment before an armed guard appeared. Jesse nailed the guy in the head before the man had a chance to raise his weapon.

"You think he ran into Sydney before he turned down this hallway?" Beckett asked once they were on the move again.

"No, he would have been stumbling our way with an arrow in his heart if that were the case." Jesse hesitated, then added, "I'm really fucking sorry for earlier."

"You had no choice," Beckett remarked. Jesse didn't need to beat *himself* up about the beating he'd been forced to give

Beckett. *Hell no.* They had a mission right now, and they needed to see it through.

"There." Jesse glanced back at Beckett with a smirk on his face. "See what I mean."

On the floor just outside the open doors of the sex dungeon lay a dead tango—his throat slit and an arrow in his chest. Overwhelmed with a mixture of awe, pride, and fear, Beckett pushed his battered body forward toward the room.

Sydney whirled around, bow raised and ready to fire another arrow, as Beckett hobbled in holding his ribs. The look of surprise and relief on her face hit him hard.

"Beckett," she cried as she took in the sight of his banged-up face.

"I'm okay." He reached for her wrist. "Let's get this bastard and get the hell out of here."

She pressed her lips together and shook her head, on the verge of tears, but quickly shook it off and reached for a remote control on a nearby table.

Jesse kept watch near the double doors as Sydney aimed the remote at the mirrored part of the wall and pushed a button. The mirror shifted and began to slide sideways, revealing another corridor.

Sydney swapped her bow for the rifle slung around her neck and gestured for Beckett to get behind her.

"You're not my shield, sweetheart. Sorry." He peered at her. "But we can go in together. Side by side."

She let go of a breath as if prepared to argue but then gave him a hesitant nod.

"I've got y'all's six," Jesse said. "Go ahead."

The three of them slowly entered the space, finding a safe and precisely what Elaina had predicted they'd find—a tunnel. A bookshelf as the "cover" for the tunnel was off to the side of it.

"Jorge left it exposed on purpose." Sydney turned in a three-sixty, ensuring the room was empty before advancing to the tunnel entrance. "This thing could be miles long, and we have no idea where it dumps out. But regardless of Elaina's warning, we'd be crazy to go in there."

"Not just crazy. Dead." Jesse pointed to something on the wall just inside. "Jorge's got the place rigged with explosives. He wanted us to follow, and once he exited, he'd blow the whole thing."

"We'll find him another way, then." Beckett glanced at the bookshelf and saw a framed black-and-white photo of Al Capone. He started to turn away, but a reflection in the frame's glass caught his eye. Jorge. *He's been hiding in the dungeon waiting for us.*

Beckett shifted around and blocked Sydney's body while raising his gun at Jorge. With his injuries, his shot was garbage, only striking Jorge in the shoulder, but Jesse finished him off with a bullet to the head.

"He's down." *That was almost too easy.* But he'd take easy every day of the week. When he whirled to face Sydney, she was frowning. "What's wrong?"

And then he felt it.

*He'd* been shot too.

"Hey, you good?" Jesse asked on approach, not looking all that worried.

"I'm fine. It's just a flesh wound," he said, but Sydney didn't seem to agree it was nothing.

She unstrapped her vest, tossed her bow and rifle, then ripped her shirt off and began wrapping the fabric like a tourniquet around his arm. "Bullet points only," she hissed. "You're not supposed to take an actual bullet for me."

Beckett lifted his face to find her angry eyes focused as she continued to tighten her shirt around his arm.

"Hey, I sent word over comms to let everyone know our final HVT is down. They said all other threats have been extinguished. We should be safe to walk out," Jesse informed them. Now Beckett could relax and let Sydney finish taking care of his arm.

But as she did so, his eyes lazily fell to her black bra. And he couldn't help but tease, "This really is becoming a habit, Miss Archer."

\* \* \*

"Damn it, Cora. Don't do this." Beckett jerked his arm free from Griffin, who was attempting to patch up his flesh wound outside on the driveway of Jorge's estate.

Cora was crouched before Miles, wiping tears away from her cheeks with one hand while holding his arm with the other. "I'm sorry, but I need to go. Thank you for bringing him back to me so I could say goodbye," she said to Liam, who stood there with a confused look on his face.

Beckett knew Liam sure as hell hadn't wanted to reunite a mother and child, only for them to separate. And like this, after what this poor kid just witnessed . . .

"*Te quiero mucho*, Miles." Cora now pointed at Beckett as tears filled Miles's eyes. "This man will take care of you," she dropped the news on them all in English, so Beckett assumed Miles was bilingual.

"Cora, do *not* leave him," he begged again. "You chose to stay in his life. Don't walk away from him like you walked away from McKenna."

Cora shook her head, a sob catching in her throat when she said, "You were right to keep me away from her. I'm not cut out to be a mom."

Beckett caught sight of Sydney talking to Gray at a

distance, her profile to him. Gray had given her his T-shirt to cover up. Beckett blinked and returned his attention to the problem at hand.

Cora leaned in and kissed her son's cheek before standing. "Ivy and I are going. We'll find a new home. A fresh start. Maybe I'll check in? But please, be the one to take care of him."

Ivy was behind the wheel of a sports car she'd driven from the garage a few minutes ago, waiting for her sister to bail on her child. *Again.*

"*Mamá, no vayas. No, por favor!*" Miles threw his arms around her leg and dropped his weight, nearly tugging her down to the ground with him. "No go. No, please," he repeated in English, breaking Beckett's heart.

What in the hell was he supposed to do? He couldn't force Cora to stay with her son. Hell, even if she took him with her and Ivy, Beckett wouldn't put it past her to hand him off to some stranger next month.

"You will be better without me, *mi amor*. You have a sister. Remember I told you about her. Showed you her pictures. Go be with her."

*Photos? You weren't lying about that?*

"*Mamá, no vayas,*" Miles cried again, holding on tighter. Beckett looked around at the others still outside, but they'd all turned away, whether to give him privacy or unable to handle the heartbreaking sight.

Carter, Camila, Jesse, and a few others had gone inside Jorge's estate, hoping to crack his safe and find the scientist's formula and records of the secrets Jorge had traded for favors.

"*Cora, vamos!*" Ivy yelled out the window and patted the side of the car, urging her to get a move on.

What the hell was wrong with these women? Did neither of them have a soul? Beckett lifted his good arm to set a hand to his aching chest, finding the emotional damage worse than any of the beatings he'd taken today.

"I'll check in when I'm settled and safe." Cora tried to pry Miles's arms free, but he wasn't relenting. "Help me, please." She looked up at Beckett.

"You're going to leave and start a new life. Just like that?" Beckett frowned. The woman was the devil in his eyes already, but this? This was cruel even for her.

"Take him, damn it," she begged.

He cursed under his breath. "I'm so sorry," Beckett said to Miles, then asked Liam to pick the boy up, worried he didn't have the strength to handle a five-year-old's resistance in the shape he was in.

Miles flailed in Liam's arms while watching his mother run for the car. She stood outside the passenger door, gave her son one last look, and then they took off.

"Wait," Sydney called out a second later. "Stop her."

"She's made up her mind." Beckett looked back to see Sydney covering her ear while going for her gun.

"No, Jorge must've called for more reinforcements before we took him out," Sydney yelled as Griffin and Gray drew their weapons in preparation for whoever was coming for them.

"Cora!" Beckett called out, limping after the car in vain, his sidearm now in hand. "It's not safe! Stop!"

Cora turned on her seat and peered at him out the back window, but Ivy only pressed down on the gas pedal harder.

"How far out is the armed vehicle?" Beckett stopped running, realizing it was pointless. He couldn't outrun a Mercedes even if he were uninjured.

Sydney didn't have a chance to answer because a moment later, just as Ivy drove through the destroyed gated entrance, an SUV T-boned the little convertible.

## CHAPTER FORTY-ONE

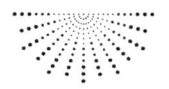

TWO HOURS LATER

Beckett sat on the bunk bed in the bedroom at the safe house, his head in his hands. His body was numb, but not from the morphine. Apparently, Oliver was the medic for Falcon, and when they'd returned an hour ago, Oliver had a syringe waiting for him.

He had a feeling he was more mentally numb than anything after watching Cora abandon Miles only to have her killed right before his eyes.

He hated that damn woman. Hated her for everything she'd done. But watching McKenna's mother and aunt die like that, unable to get to them in time . . .

After the collision, the assholes in the SUV had riddled the car with bullets before turning their sights on Beckett and the others. The four men were taken down within a matter of seconds and, thankfully, Liam had managed to shield Miles from the scene.

But how would Beckett tell McKenna what happened?

With Miles more than likely returning to Alabama with him, he had no choice but to share the truth now.

He groggily lifted his head to find Sydney in the doorway, leaning against the interior frame. "Can I sit with you?" she asked.

He nodded, and she joined him on the bed and linked their hands together.

After they arrived at the safe house, he'd taken a sixty-second shower and changed into clean clothes, worried about Miles seeing him covered in blood. Not just from his own injuries but the blood of the men he'd killed. And Cora's too. Beckett had dragged Cora's body from the wreckage. She'd most likely died upon impact, but her body had also been punctured by two bullets.

"I should be mourning her, but I fucking hated her," Beckett hissed. "What she did to that boy today. The second she had a chance to run, she took it. No hesitation. Who does that?"

"It's normal to be angry. There are stages of grief."

"I don't want to grieve that woman," he admitted, but it was the truth, wasn't it? "But I do grieve McKenna's loss even though she didn't know Cora. And Miles's loss as well."

"It's okay for *you* to be upset too. I know you feel like you shouldn't be after what she did to you, but you never wanted her to die. Or you wouldn't have come to Mexico in the first place when she called." Sydney swept her thumb in small, circular motions over his hand. "You need to allow yourself to grieve for *you*."

He wasn't sure how to interpret his conflicting emotions. He hadn't shed a tear for Cora yet, and he wasn't sure if he was capable. He'd come close while watching her son beg his mother not to leave, but that sorrow was for Miles. Cora was responsible for everything that ultimately led to her death.

"Am I supposed to convince myself that if Cora had stayed, something worse would have happened instead? Possibly to Miles? Or maybe her actions would come back to impact my daughter in some way?" He swallowed the lump in his throat. "Is that the deal with all this universe and fate stuff?"

"I don't know," Sydney whispered. "Maybe Elaina or Camila would have an answer for you. Or maybe there isn't one, and we just have to trust that it was meant to be?"

"I'm glad you're okay." He needed to focus on something else right now. Focus on *someone* who had become so important to him in the last five days. *Wow. Five days?* That was all the time they'd spent together.

"You're the one who had to get beat up by your brother-in-law. I can't imagine how hard that was for the two of you." She turned and smoothed her free hand over his cheek, studying his face. "Then you took a bullet for me."

"Technically, I didn't take the bullet. It only ripped a piece of flesh from my arm."

"Still. I was wearing a protective chest plate, not you. You shouldn't have taken that risk for me."

"Act first. Think later. Kind of a guy thing." That had to be the morphine talking. Not to mention he'd been drugged the night before, and that drug could still be in his system.

"Well, mister, don't do it again. Think first. Okay?" Sydney pressed a soft kiss to one of the bruises near his eye.

Beckett shrugged his good shoulder. "Mm. Your safety will always be first on my mind. Sorry, sweetheart. Non-negotiable."

"Always, huh?" She kissed another bruise.

"Hey, sorry to interrupt." Griffin stood in the doorway, and Sydney gave him her attention. "I hate to say this, but we're leaving Santiago." He checked his watch. "Right about now. Martín and Mya's Marine friends are en route to Juárez to meet us there. They think we should strike against the rest of the upper echelons of the cartel while they're scrambling to make sense of what went down with Miguel."

Beckett stood, but his legs gave out, and he fell back onto his ass.

"Easy," Sydney remarked and motioned for him to stay put as she stood. "I don't think Beckett should go."

"He's not. He'll be returning Stateside today with Miles, Liam, Emily, and Elaina. A.J. has to hop on a flight overseas to wrap up his op. But Gray's making arrangements with his government contacts to get clearance for Miles to travel under Beckett's supervision."

*Miles. Am I adopting him? I'll have a son. And is Cora really dead?* If he hadn't held her body in his arms, he might believe he'd hallucinated it all, and she'd simply faked her death. Another con. A tactic to escape and begin her next con, find a new mark.

"Jesse is talking to Ella now, deciding what to do. He may sit out this op. He doesn't want to stress Ella out anymore this week," Griffin went on. "And I support that idea."

"Will there be enough of us to handle the cartel?" Sydney folded her arms. "*And* dismantle their trafficking network?"

"Not enough of *us*. But Martín has an army. So with our help, plus Mya's Marine friends, I think we're solid. And you know if Carter had doubts, he wouldn't risk our lives." Griffin stroked his jaw, eyes falling to Beckett. "Camila wants to come, but Carter's insisting she leave and wrap up her case. Turn over the scientist so the wife can get some justice for her husband's murder."

"Right. I almost forgot about that with everything that's happened." Beckett tried to stand again, and Sydney offered him her forearm instead of demanding he sit.

"Give us a minute?" Sydney asked Griffin, who nodded and left.

"I hate that we're going—"

"Separate ways?" Beckett finished for her while setting a hand to the bed frame for support. When she remained quiet, he cupped her chin with his free hand and peered into her eyes. "I hate not being at your side when you go."

"You need to be with your daughter," she said softly. "Miles too. I'll be fine in Mexico. You don't need to worry about me."

"Impossible." He kept hold of her chin, not ready to lose her.

Her small smile quickly faded. "After Mexico, I need to head home. See Levi. Figure things out there."

Why'd this feel like the "we'll take some time and think about things" kind of talk? To decide if the last five days were real? It was for him. He didn't need time to confirm that. "I understand."

Bottom line, he had a life in Alabama. She couldn't leave her son in D.C. since she shared custody with her ex. Was it possible to make a relationship like that work? Did she even want something long-term with him? The questions buzzed through his brain, but the reality of what happened that day washed over him again.

The drugs had his thoughts diverging in too many directions, and he hated not being sharp.

"Can I kiss you before I go? Or will that hurt?" Sydney tipped her head, and he offered his mouth as an answer, slanting his lips over hers.

And did it hurt? Yeah. But more like in the heart, worried this would be their last kiss.

Sydney's soft mouth responded to his, and her tongue

slipped between his lips, caressing his in sweeping, sensual motions.

Beckett eased his mouth away from hers, hating to break contact, but they were short on time. "They're waiting."

Her eyes held his captive as she silently studied him with parted lips.

"Tell me your walls aren't going to go back up while we're apart?" he asked, unable to stop himself.

"If anyone could knock them back down," she began with a nod, "it's you."

\* \* \*

"D!D YOU KNOW CAMILA IN SPANISH MEANS 'MESSENGER OF God'?" Elaina's question to Camila drew Beckett's attention as they stood outside the safe house, prepping to part ways.

Camila reached for Elaina's forearm. "Similar in Portuguese too."

"You have a gift, Miss Hart. Don't be afraid to use it." Elaina wrapped her arms around Camila in a tight hug.

"I have a feeling I'll be seeing you again soon." Camila let her go and smiled. "I'm sorry for your loss," she told Beckett.

"You didn't do anything to make her . . . die," Elaina revealed, peering at Miles sitting beside Emily in the back of the SUV, the door still open. Emily seemed to be working her motherly magic on the boy, calming him down, and thank God for her.

Beckett wanted to cling to Elaina's words. To believe he hadn't somehow played a role in Cora and Ivy's deaths.

"There are many other lives you'll be able to save now. All of you." Elaina pointed to where Carter stood talking to

Jesse and A.J. "Those secrets you found at the bad man's house will help more people."

*The Guarded One and his secrets. Right.* And the formula for that drug would hopefully never see the light of day again.

"Ready?" Liam strode up to his daughter and hooked his arm behind her back.

Elaina hugged Camila one more time, and when Camila shielded her eyes with sunglasses, Beckett had to wonder if she was tearing up.

"See you around." Camila patted Beckett's arm, then went over to Gray, saying her goodbyes.

The goodbye Beckett dreaded saying was to Sydney. He knew she was a hell of an operator, and if they were to find a way to make a relationship work down the road, he had to accept her work was dangerous. And to not freak the fuck out whenever she went out on a job.

"See you back home when I'm done," A.J. said on approach. "I gotta roll back out now."

Beckett nodded. "Stay safe. Kill some bad guys."

A.J. winked. "Roger that."

"And, uh, thanks for saving my ass this morning," Beckett added in case he'd forgotten to say that.

"We're family." A.J. fist-bumped him. "I got you." He gave him a one-arm hug, careful not to hurt him, then tipped his hat at Beckett before heading toward one of the vehicles so he could fly back to wherever he'd been before.

Once A.J. was gone, Beckett went over to Carter and Griffin. "Stay safe in Mexico."

"Of course." Carter faced Beckett. "Also, you should know we're having Cora and Ivy's bodies flown to New Mexico, where they were born. Their parents are buried there as well."

"You did your homework," Beckett remarked. "Thank you."

Carter nodded, then twirled his finger in the air, motioning for the others to get going.

"You okay?" Griffin asked him, his gaze cutting to the SUV with Miles inside.

"I have no damn clue." When Beckett turned his focus back on Sydney speaking with Camila now, their eyes locked. "But I'll have to find a way to be."

# CHAPTER FORTY-TWO

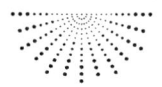

WALKINS GLEN, ALABAMA

"No word from your team yet?" Beckett asked Jesse.

"They're infiltrating the compound at nightfall," Jesse shared from behind the wheel of his Dodge Ram as they neared the Hawkins Ranch. "I'm sure Sydney will call you as soon as the op wraps up."

"And they'll be okay without you?"

"They'll be fine. I'm needed here." Jesse tossed him a quick look before asking, "What can I do to help make today easier for you?"

"I don't think anything will make it easier." Beckett opened the vanity mirror to check out the damage Miguel and his assholes had done to his face. He didn't want to scare McKenna. But instead of catching sight of his reflection, he spied Miles in his car seat.

The boy, a spitting image of Cora with his dark hair, eyes, and dimples, stared at him with a sad expression while clutching the teddy bear Emily had bought him at the airport in Santiago. They'd all taken the same flight to Miami, then

Liam, Emily, and Elaina flew home to D.C. while Beckett, Jesse, and Miles caught a flight to Birmingham.

"I didn't tell anyone about the boy, like you asked," Jesse said. Beckett had yet to grieve Cora's loss. He wasn't sure when her death would genuinely hit him, but he had to get through today first. Face his daughter and share the truth about her mom. Tell his family that with Gray's government contacts, he'd be expediting the process to adopt Miles.

*Miles and McKenna Hawkins. My children.* His eyes fell to his hand, finding it trembling on his jeaned thigh.

There was no way he'd separate McKenna from her brother or place Miles in foster care in Chile or the U.S.

He released a shaky breath. "You said Ella took a half-day today?"

"Yeah, and she texted me thirty minutes ago that she picked up McKenna early from school. Everyone's at your family's ranch." Jesse turned down the back road that would have them there within minutes.

"Will McKenna hate me for not sharing the real story about her mom?" Beckett squeezed his hands into fists, his nerves getting to him. The idea of causing his daughter any type of pain was too much to handle.

"I think McKenna will be sad to learn what happened," Jesse said, glancing in the rearview mirror, "but she has a brother to focus on now. That girl has a huge heart, and she'll do her damnedest to comfort him and make him part of the family."

*God bless her.* She was nothing like Cora on the inside. But her looks? Yeah, they were all her mom. McKenna would spot those similarities when seeing her brother today too.

"Here we go," Jesse said at the sight of the Hawkins Ranch sign. "You've got this. And I've got your back."

"I can't thank you enough for everything you've done."

Beckett's voice caught with emotion this time, and his pulse raced the second his parents' house came into view.

Ella's and Savanna's cars were parked out front. His brothers, Shep and Caleb, were there too.

He looked back at Miles once Jesse parked and unbuckled. "*¿Estás bien?* Are you okay?" Miles quietly clutched his bear, his eyes darting every which way to take in the property. "Your sister's here," he added. "Would you like to meet her? *Tu hermana*. McKenna. She's my daughter." He pointed a finger at Miles, then at his own chest. "*Somos familia*. We're family."

This caught his attention and Miles locked his gaze on Beckett. "*Familia?*"

Beckett nodded. "*Soy tu familia ahora.*" Fuck, he was going to cry. Why the hell now? He did his best to pull himself together as he repeated in English, "We're family now."

"*Mi familia*," Miles said in such a small voice that Beckett would've collapsed if he weren't already sitting.

"You've got this." Jesse nodded. "And there's my wife, so I'm going out there." Jesse's feet had no sooner hit the ground than Ella was in his arms, her legs wrapped around his hips and kissing him.

*Love.* Beckett wanted that. Now more than ever. But there was only one woman he wanted it with. Although they'd both been drugged, he recalled Sydney's words back in that freaky sex room. *I think I could love you.*

"*¿Listo?* Ready?" he asked Miles, then hopped out of the truck. Before he could open the back door, Ella was at his side.

"How about no more boys' trips for a bit?" Ella went to hug him but froze, her arms mid-reach. She'd spotted Miles.

Beckett tore his focus away from his sister when he

noticed McKenna on the porch, a hand over her mouth, clearly fighting back tears.

"Jesse, can you help him out?" Beckett rasped before moving as fast as his legs would carry him. Meeting McKenna halfway, she threw her arms around him. To hell with his injuries, he'd take the pain from her tight embrace all day long. "Sweet girl," he said, holding her head to his chest.

Beckett looked up to see his parents, brothers, and Griffin's wife, Savanna, filling the porch, their attention fixed beyond where Beckett stood.

Miles was in the spotlight now.

Beckett finally let go of his daughter, and they both swiped the tears from their faces.

"Who is that?" McKenna pointed to Miles.

Beckett took a deep breath, reached for her hand, and gave it a squeeze. "I'll introduce you." When they neared and Beckett heard Ella talking to Miles in her soothing teacher voice, he knew he'd be relying on his sister yet again. She'd always been there for him with McKenna, but what if . . . what if Sydney . . .

He shook the thought from his mind to focus on the present situation. Introducing his daughter to her brother.

"McKenna, this is Miles." He exhaled a shaky breath. "Um."

"He's my brother," McKenna said, beating him to it. "Right?" She placed a hand over her heart, and tears filled her eyes again. "I can feel it. I—I just know." She looked at her dad. "He's why Elaina . . ."

Beckett nodded, overwhelmed by emotions.

"She's gone, isn't she? My mom?" McKenna asked, nearly choking on her words as she said them.

"Yeah," Beckett whispered.

McKenna blinked back some of her tears and held her

head high. So strong. Tough. A Hawkins woman. She knelt before Miles and offered her hand. "I'm your sister. It's so nice to meet you."

Miles's eyes grew wide, the bear falling to the ground as he threw himself into her arms. McKenna let out a laugh when he nearly knocked her over.

The sob Beckett had held at bay since holding Cora's lifeless body in his arms yesterday tore free, and he fell to his knees alongside his family and cried.

## CHAPTER FORTY-THREE

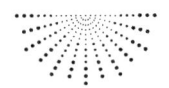

JUST OUTSIDE JUÁREZ, MEXICO – SEVENTEEN HOURS LATER

"We can take it from here. We appreciate your help," Martín said, reaching to shake Carter's hand as Sydney unstrapped her vest.

Their mission was declared a success after four hours of fighting. The Falcon Falls team came through unscathed, and there were only minor wounds for some of the men on Martín's and Mason Matthews's teams. Nothing a little rest and some stitches wouldn't fix.

"Are you sure you don't want us to hang around?" Sydney asked Martín. "You're planning to hit another one of their locations soon. We can go with you."

Martín shook his head. "We have the cartel scrambling. Running scared. We cut off the head of the snake tonight, and yes, someone else will take over by tomorrow. It will be an endless fight. But it's my people's fight." He nodded at Sydney. "And it is a fight we will win. You have done enough for us, and we thank you."

"I'd be happy to roll out with you tomorrow," Carter offered while Sydney looked around at the desert landscape. Their military-style tents were scattered around a wide area that served as their headquarters for the op. It reminded her of the time she'd spent in Afghanistan forever ago.

"And if we need you, we'll call." Martín patted Carter on the shoulder. "You have other work to handle now if I'm not mistaken."

*Right.* The secrets they'd discovered "The Guarded One" had protected back at his estate in Chile.

Sydney abruptly turned around at the sound of voices arguing. Mya stood between Oliver and Mason, her arms outstretched, keeping them apart. *Oh jeez.* "If you'll excuse me."

Martín smiled and tipped his head goodbye as she hurried toward Mya for an assist.

"Would you two stop it?" Mya yelled just as Sydney arrived at their team's camp area.

"What's going on?" Sydney grabbed Oliver's arm and yanked him farther away from Mason. "We're supposed to be on the same side."

Mya had lowered her arms when Sydney arrived, but quickly reached out and slapped a palm against Mason's chest when he took a threatening step toward Oliver. "Stop it. It wasn't his fault."

"I don't care if you were drugged. You stuck your tongue in her mouth," Mason snarled at Oliver. "You shouldn't have ever touched her."

How the hell did Mason find out about that? Damn, word traveled fast.

"I'm not yours," Mya reminded Mason.

"You're sure as hell more mine than his," Mason seethed.

Oliver cocked his head and clenched his jaw, but before he could launch into a rebuttal, Sydney jumped in.

"We were all drugged at the time, Mason. It was out of our control," she provided, hoping to defuse the situation. "Look, we just handed the cartel a major loss and screwed up their trafficking routes. We had a major win tonight. Can we focus on that?"

"No," Mason and Oliver rasped simultaneously, their eyes locked. Ready to do battle.

"Mya told me she's considering joining your team, but let me make myself very clear," Mason began, his voice eerily calm. "Not fucking happening."

"Not your choice," Mya snapped. "And I can freelance for the both of you."

"Falcon Falls," Mason muttered. "What the fuck kind of a name is that?"

"At least we have a name. You all call yourselves The Agency. Ripping off the CIA, huh? How original," Oliver shot back.

*A love triangle. Perfect.*

"Our name makes sense," Oliver defended. "Our headquarters is hidden by a waterfall, and there are, well, falcons flying around . . ." Oliver trailed off and Sydney half expected him to end the statement with a childish *so there!* She and Mya traded a smirk and bit back a laugh. At least some of the tension melted away.

"Bottom line, this is my life. I'll work where I want. Kiss who I want. And you both can just kiss my ass if you think you can tell me what to do." Mya lowered her palm from Mason's chest and eased herself to Sydney's side, no longer standing between the men. "If you want to fight each other, then fight. I'm done."

Mason's shoulders sagged, and when Oliver's resistance seemed to falter, Sydney let go of his arm.

"I'm sorry," Mason said with a sigh. "I'm still a bit worked up that you lied to me about why you went to Tulum in the first place. You nearly died."

"You really had no clue what she was up to?" Oliver asked, seemingly shocked by this fact.

"I trusted her." Mason held his palms open. "You really think you can juggle the two of us?"

Mya folded her arms. "You mean work with both Falcon and your *team*? I'm not juggling two men."

"Shit, that's not what I meant." Mason removed his ball cap and swiped a hand through his brown hair before fixing it back in place.

"You know me, man," Oliver said, sounding less like a jealous boyfriend this time. "You can trust me. I'll keep her safe when she works with us. And I'm assuming you'll do the same."

"Of course, I will," Mason quickly responded. Sydney now felt like a "fourth wheel" in this situation, and if they weren't going to slug each other, she'd retreat.

"I've got this," Mya said, reading Sydney's thoughts.

Sydney's gaze flew to Gray and Jack talking next to a nearby tent. "Behave, boys," she tossed out and headed toward her teammates just as Jack parted ways with Gray.

Since Martín didn't need any further help, they'd most likely be flying Stateside within a matter of hours.

"Hey." Sydney shoved her hands in her khaki pants pockets, and Gray startled her by leaning forward and brushing his thumb across her cheek.

"Blood." He cleared his throat as he pulled his hand away.

"Not mine."

"You okay? It was a long night." Gray scratched the side of his head, his eyes shifting to look at something behind her, most likely the "love triangle" situation since they'd already started arguing again.

"I'm good. You?"

"As good as can be, I guess." He forced a smile. "Have you, uh, talked to Beckett?"

*Beckett.* She let go of a deep breath. "I need to call him. Let him know we're all safe. It's still early though."

"Pretty sure the time of day won't matter to him." Gray set a hand on her shoulder. "I'm happy for you. You know, if things happen for you two. Genuinely, I mean that."

A fluttery sensation filled her stomach at his words. "Really?"

"Really." He angled his head toward the tent. "Call him." He let go of her shoulder and started Carter's way.

Sydney hoped Gray wasn't lying to himself about being happy for her. She still cared about him. They had history, and they worked well together at Falcon. They just weren't a good fit as a couple.

Shoving away the nerves that tried to take hold once she'd made it to her tent, Sydney dialed Beckett's new number, still wary since it wasn't even six a.m. Sure enough, he picked up on the second ring.

"Sydney?" He sounded alert, but that was no surprise once she remembered Alabama was an hour ahead.

"Hey," she whispered, unsure why tears were springing to her eyes. "We're all okay. Mission success."

He was quiet for a moment before a long, deep breath cut across the line. "I'm relieved to hear that. I was waiting to sleep until I heard from you."

"You stayed up all night?"

"You think I could sleep with you going up against the cartel?"

*You need to get used to me doing dangerous work. You can't have sleepless nights every time I . . .* "Well, we're okay. You can sleep now," she said instead of rambling off her thoughts. "How's McKenna? Miles?"

"Miles warmed up to McKenna right away. And my parents are spoiling him rotten already." He paused. "McKenna took the truth about her mom better than I thought. She's tough."

"Like father, like daughter." Sydney cleared her throat. "I'm happy she's okay. And are *you* okay?" *Have you realized you need to grieve for Cora, even if you don't want to?* But she didn't manage to get those words free either.

"I'll be better when I see you again."

She closed her eyes, her heartbeat quickening. "I don't know when that will be," she said. "I need to head home and see Levi. And you have a lot on your plate too." Beckett's silence had her worried he was misreading her, so she quickly added, "When things have settled down, will you call me?"

"Call?" was all he said, and there was a pinch of heartbreak in that one word. "I guess we did move pretty fast," he added.

Sydney opened her eyes and set her free hand to her chest. "Everything, um"—she hesitated, searching for what to say when all she wanted to do was beg him to be with her—"happens for a reason. And if things are meant to be, they'll be, right?" She was channeling Mya now. "*Destino,*" she said at the memory of the word Camila had used. "Fate."

Beckett remained quiet for a few agonizing moments before saying, "I'm glad you're all okay. And I guess if it's fate, we'll find our way back to each other."

Tears began to glide down her cheeks at his words, at his

unsettling tone that nearly gutted her. *Screw distance.* This man already meant too much to her to let something like that stand in the way. "I didn't make myself clear," she said, her voice nearly hoarse. Damn it, she didn't want her walls up. To guard her heart. "I want you." She sniffled. "And we *will* find our way back to each other."

## CHAPTER FORTY-FOUR

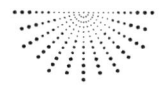

WASHINGTON, D.C.

"They're not getting married. Dad called off the engagement," Levi announced Sunday night as he helped load the dishwasher at Sydney's condo.

One week ago, she'd been sunbathing on a beach in Tulum when Beckett barged in and turned her world upside down. Well, some of that was Mya's doing. But during a week's time, they'd been chased through the jungle by the cartel, drugged by a crazy billionaire, and had witnessed the death of Beckett's ex, who left behind a five-year-old son that Beckett was adopting. Time was weird like that.

"I know," she admitted. "Your dad called while I was cooking dinner to let me know he broke up with her."

"Did you know Dad wants to work things out with you instead?"

Sydney turned off the faucet and did her best to calm herself at Seth's attempt to place their son in the middle of his insanity. Why in the hell would he tell Levi that? Why offer him any type of hope at such a reconciliation?

But before Sydney could reject the notion, Levi added, "I told him Hell would have to freeze over before you'd take him back. You know, something Grandpa likes to say when he's handing out a firm no to his clients."

Sydney reached for her son's arm and pulled him in for a hug. She was so grateful for him. For his understanding and maturity.

When she let go of Levi, she wiped a few tears from her cheeks. He gave her a puzzled look because he knew damn well those tears weren't on account of Seth. "What's up, Mom?"

She went over to their French country kitchen table and dropped down on the cushioned bench. *Where to begin?*

He sat next to her and sniffed the air. "And are you wearing your cherry perfume again?"

"I dug it out of the trash when I got home this morning. Alice isn't worth not wearing my favorite scent."

"Good for you." He smiled, showing his pearly whites. Naturally straight teeth that wouldn't require braces. "But what else is going on? Did something happen on your work trip? Bad? Good?"

Sydney thought back to the whirlwind of a week she'd had. "Bad guys were handled. Good guys won."

"Ha. Well, I figured as much with you being involved. But . . .?" He tipped his head, brushing his longish strands away from his eyes while waiting for her to share the part of the story she was still withholding.

She shifted on the seat to better face him. "Do you remember the sheriff at Savanna and Griffin's wedding in April? Beckett Hawkins?"

"The one you were checking out?"

"What?" She fake-gasped and dramatically slapped a hand to her chest. "Was I?"

Levi sent her a shy smile along with a nod. "Oh yeah, I noticed."

"Well then, I didn't realize I'm such an open book."

"Only to me. Well, and to Aunt Mya."

*And now with Beckett.*

"Oh, and quick subject change, but is Mya going to work with you?"

She thought back to the tug-of-war between Mya and the two men in Mexico. "She's going to help out from time to time when she can." *And maybe pick a team, or a man, eventually.*

"Cool." Levi waggled his eyebrows. "But back to the sheriff."

"Your Aunt Mya is rubbing off on you," she said with a laugh. "But um, well, Beckett and I worked together on my last case. Had a chance to get to know each other better."

"And you like him?" Levi's smile stretched from ear to ear. "That's the best news I've heard in forever."

"Really?"

Levi reached for her hand and squeezed. "I want you happy, Mom. You know that."

"He lives in Alabama."

"And we live in modern times," he reminded her. "You can find a way to make it work if you really want to." He winked, reminding her of his biological father, Matt. He let go of her hand and checked his watch. "Lucy's dad is picking me up for the movie tonight in five minutes. Still okay if I go? I mean, if you want me to stay, I can."

"No, no. Go. Be a kid. Enjoy life." They stood, and she pulled him in for another hug.

Levi left the house a few minutes later, and Sydney went to her bedroom and dialed Matt's number, waiting for the voicemail to connect.

"Hey, it's me," she began, sitting on her bed. "I wanted to tell you I met someone. And well, I think you'd like him . . ."

\* \* \*

THIRTEEN DAYS LATER

"This place is kind of loud for chatting over cocktails," Sydney had to practically shout over the band performing at the bar. "Open mic night and all."

Mya lifted the umbrella from her drink and set it on the bar. "It has its charm, though, don't you think?"

Sydney swiveled on her stool to scan the place. "I guess so," she said, looking at the variety of license plates nailed to the walls as decoration.

Returning her attention to her old-fashioned, she took a sip, and thoughts of Beckett sprang to mind. Not because anything about this evening reminded her of Beckett, but because the man was on her mind constantly.

It was now June, and it'd been two weeks since she'd called him from Mexico. They'd exchanged a few texts here and there. But only quick check-ins. Nothing too serious.

He'd flown Miles and McKenna to New Mexico last weekend so they could attend Cora's and Ivy's funerals, and that'd been rough on all of them. She wanted to give him as much space as possible to process the changes in his life. To not push. But God, she was ready to see him again.

"So, you're not taking any new jobs with Falcon until August, right? You're still taking part of the summer off to be with Levi?" Why did this feel like small talk from Mya? She already knew the answers, and she wasn't forgetful.

Sydney set her drink down and peered at her best friend, curious what her endgame was because knowing Mya, she had one. "Levi's last day of school is June sixteenth, and we leave shortly after that for England."

"Your family's place in the Cotswolds is amazing. It's straight out of *Downton Abbey*," she said with a smile, "or *Bridgerton*."

"Well, my parents are going to be with us the first week, so that should be fuuun," Sydney responded sarcastically. "You're welcome to join. The house has like a million rooms and bathrooms."

"I would love to, but I promised Carter I'd help cover for you while you're on vacation. And I'm happy to do so. I want you to enjoy yourself. When was the last time you got away and spent some quality family time?"

"Levi will miss Lucy, so we won't stay there for more than two weeks, but thank God for Wi-Fi, so he can FaceTime her every day." *Young love.* "So, are you only helping Falcon for the summer, or . . . ?"

"Playing it by ear. Mason decided to stay back in Mexico and assist Martín with dismantling more of the Sinaloa cartel. But I think he's decided he wants more than friendship." Mya rolled her eyes. "He must think Oliver's interested in me, so he's being all weird."

"I think Oliver *is* interested, but you two fight a hell of a lot, so I don't know what to say."

"True." Mya shrugged. "Despite being, um, drugged," she started in such a low voice Sydney had to read her lips over the drummer's solo, "I remember our kiss." She fanned her face. "And his massive cock. I mean, I didn't see it with my own eyes, so the jury is still out, but I was sitting on his lap, and these hips don't lie. I can say that, right? I haven't started working with the team officially yet, so we're not co-workers. But still, don't tell Carter."

Sydney laughed. "I think you're fine. And only Carter?

Aren't you worried about your other boss knowing you gave your soon-to-be teammate a lap dance?"

"Please, we all know who's in charge there. But back to Oliver. A man that can kiss like that can surely use his mouth six ways to Sunday." She lifted a hand between them. "Not planning to find out. All work and no play with both guys. Period."

"Sure, sure." Sydney let go a breath of relief when the music stopped. Her back was to the stage, but from the sounds of it, a new group or singer was taking over. Hopefully, they'd be better than the last one trying to croon the lyrics to a U2 song and failing miserably. "It just dawned on me you've yet to bring up Beckett all night. Why? I thought for sure when you asked me out for drinks, you'd start right there with the twenty questions."

Sydney started to shift on her stool toward the next performer when Mya snatched her arm, redirecting her focus. Sydney lowered her gaze to Mya's death grip.

"I didn't bring him up because I thought it'd be tough for you to talk about him."

Sydney was two seconds away from calling bullshit, but the guitarist began to play, effectively cutting off the conversation. When a man started singing, goose bumps peppered her body beneath her black silk tank top at his voice.

The song was familiar. She didn't know many country songs, but . . .

"Cody Johnson, 'On My Way to You,'" Mya told her, reading her thoughts. She let go of her arm, a smile crossing her lips in the process.

"Yeah, but this is . . ." Sydney closed her eyes, her heartbeat pounding as her thoughts went wild. It couldn't be him. Could it? She was too afraid to turn and look, too worried she was wrong. But no way would anyone else cause such an intense reaction other than *that* man.

Sydney composed herself before opening her eyes. She spun around on her seat, and the most intense butterfly sensations of her life struck her abdomen when she set her eyes on Beckett behind the microphone, his gaze trained on her. And was that A.J. on the guitar alongside him?

Beckett's lips curled into a brief smile as A.J. strummed the guitar like a pro.

*I come from a music-loving family*, Beckett had shared down in that cenote in Mexico nearly three weeks ago. He had left out the fact he could sing.

She refused to break eye contact, but from her peripheral view, she spied women on their feet, crowding around the stage, clamoring for his attention. But the man surely didn't give it to them.

In dark jeans, cowboy boots, a white shirt, and his Stetson, he looked every part her country cowboy from that romance book brought to life. *In my life.*

And the lyrics . . . Perfection.

"You set this up?" Sydney asked Mya.

"Beckett called in a favor. I may have helped with a covert assist in getting you to this spot." Mya nudged her side. "He's quite the guy."

"I'd say so," Sydney whispered, the swell of emotions nearly trapping her words that time. The song was ending, so she worked her way through the crowd, and as soon as the song ended, the audience went wild. But Beckett was already on the move, making his way to her.

He rushed down the three stage steps, and the women parted for him.

When he stood before her, he dropped a simple, "Hey, you."

Her body was trembling, and she restrained herself from jumping into his arms as if he'd just come home from a six-month deployment. "You're here."

"I never had a chance to tell you during our last phone call that I want you too."

"You do," she responded, not as a question but as a fact. She felt that truth deep in her gut. "Soooo, you can sing."

"A.J.'s the best of us all, but I can hold my own. Been decades since anyone's heard me publicly." A smile played across his handsome face. "I thought maybe I could seduce you with my voice. Did it work?"

"Seduce me, huh?" She pulled her bottom lip between her teeth and stared into his deep brown, soulful eyes. "Oh, it worked."

Maybe it was the lighting, but she'd swear that eye-twinkling thing she read about in the *five* other romance novels she'd devoured to occupy her time in the last two weeks was happening right now. "So, you see, it's my birthday tonight, and Miles and McKenna are at Liam and Emily's for a sleepover. And I heard your son is at his dad's. Maybe I'm being a bit presumptuous, but maybe we could have a sleepover too?"

"A sleepover, hm? I think that can be arranged." A soft chuckle escaped as he set a hand on her hip and pulled her closer to him. "And happy birthday, Sheriff Hawkins."

He flicked the brim of his dark brown hat with his free hand.

"No birthday suit for me? I'm kind of disappointed," she teased.

"Now see, I'll do just about anything you ask. If you want me to strip down to my birthday suit here for you, I will. So, sweetheart, what would you like me to do?"

She shook her head and walked her fingers up his chest.

"I don't share. Let's save the you-being-naked for my bedroom tonight."

Beckett leaned in and brought his mouth near hers. "As long as you plan on being naked too."

"Ohhh," she began while arching her back to draw her lips closer to his. "You can count on it. You know how hard it is for me to keep my clothes on around you."

EPILOGUE

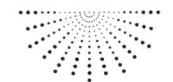

WASHINGTON, D.C. – FOURTEEN DAYS LATER

"I'M SOOOOO READY FOR THIS TRIP." SYDNEY SMILED AT Levi's words as he tossed his hands into the air, pumping his fists. "I'll miss Lucy, but I'm looking forward to the next two weeks. Especially since you guys are coming." Levi peered at McKenna and Miles on the couch at their condo, where McKenna had just finished reading a book to her brother.

"You sure you don't mind we're crashing your family trip?" McKenna rose from the couch and smoothed her hands down the sides of her pale pink sundress.

"Hey, I mean," Levi said with a shrug, "I feel like you're kinda on your way to becoming family already. It makes sense we test out the whole traveling-together thing."

"And if I fail the test?" McKenna smirked, a bit of sass in her tone that Sydney admired.

Levi laughed. "Eh," he responded while swiping a hand through the air, "I'll tutor ya on the flight over. Teach you how to navigate dealing with my grandparents." He peered at

Sydney. "Mom is totally cool. No need to walk on eggshells around her."

"Well, thank you." Sydney playfully tipped her head, grateful at how fast her son was taking to the idea of having McKenna and Miles in his life. "Beckett should be here soon, and we can head to the airport."

"Did he decide yet if he's going to work with Metro PD or Arlington?" Levi asked.

"Because Dad is Dad, and he's super overprotective, he chose Metro," McKenna answered before Sydney could. "Since I'll be going to school in D.C., he wants to work near my school," McKenna added, tossing in a perfectly timed teenage eye roll.

"I don't blame him. If I had a daughter, I'd want to . . ." Levi shook his head and squinted. "Did I just say that? Where'd that come from?"

Sydney laughed. "Channeling Beckett already, and you've spent less than two weeks with him."

The past two weeks were giving her one week in Mexico a run for its money in the massive-life-changes department. After their X-rated sleepover, Beckett had told Sydney about his plans to resign as sheriff of Walkins Glen and move to D.C.

McKenna would be able to go to school with her best friend, and Miles would be there with her since their private school covered kindergarten through twelfth grade.

Sydney had been worried about all he'd be giving up just to be with her, but Beckett reassured her that he was gaining *everything* instead.

A.J. and his wife had a second house near Quantico, where she taught a few times a year, so Beckett and the kids spent the last two weeks there.

*And now we're all going on a family trip together.* She almost had to pinch herself to believe it all.

They'd had dinner with her parents a few nights ago to warm them up to each other, but her dad was stubborn, which made her wonder how the trip would go. Fortunately, her parents were only staying the first week. Her dad was too much of a workaholic to take more time off.

"Must be him now," Levi said at the sound of the doorbell. "But why is he ringing the bell?"

Sydney followed Levi to the door and checked the security app on her phone because no, Beckett wouldn't ring. She'd given him a key. Not that they'd spent the night together when Levi was at her house, but during the school days, he'd popped in for some good-morning and good-afternoon sex.

"Oh. It's Elaina," Sydney said once the feed loaded.

McKenna joined them with Miles glued to her side. "She must want to say bye before we leave."

Levi opened the door at Sydney's okay and froze, blocking everyone's view of Elaina. What was that all about?

"I'm Elaina. I think I saw you at Savanna and Griffin's wedding, but we didn't officially meet."

Sydney peeked over her son's shoulder—due to a recent growth spurt, he was now a head taller than her—to see Elaina offering her hand while Levi stood speechlessly staring. Maybe Levi wasn't as "in love" with Lucy as Sydney had thought.

McKenna nudged him in the back and muttered, "Dude." Sydney grinned, happy to see how quickly McKenna was adapting to the role of sister to two brothers. "Elaina." McKenna maneuvered around Levi and hugged her friend since Levi was still in a trance.

"I wanted to see you before you left." Elaina tossed a

thumb over her shoulder where Emily was walking up behind her, holding her son Jackson's hand.

"Liam and A.J. had to spin up this morning, as I'm sure Beckett told you, so it's just us," Emily shared.

"Hey, nice to see you as always." They'd hung out a few times since Chile, and Sydney had a feeling she'd become fast friends with Emily. It'd be nice to have another close friend besides Mya.

Sydney gestured for everyone to gather inside, and the kids all hung out in the living room while she and Emily found space to chat alone in the kitchen. Jackson was younger than Miles, but when they'd introduced the boys last week, they quickly took a liking to each other. Miles was doing surprisingly well, given everything that had happened, but she'd suggested counseling when they returned from their trip, and Beckett had agreed.

"Beckett should be here soon. Not sure what the hold-up is. He said he only had to run an errand first before we left for the airport." Sydney went to her Nespresso machine and popped in a capsule, assuming they were both in need of caffeine.

"I just can't tell you enough how happy I am that Elaina will now have McKenna here," Emily said with a sigh. "Have you two thought about where you might live? Together or wait a bit?"

"Levi's okay with us all living together. I know that seems super-fast, but he likes Beckett and the kids. And he wants me happy." Thank God for that. She couldn't begin to imagine Levi not liking Beckett. Then again, the chance she'd fall for a man Levi wouldn't approve of now that he was "so wise" at thirteen was slim. "Maybe we'll have something built somewhere between Arlington and D.C."

"And that's not fast, by the way." Emily shrugged. "Liam

and I drunk-married in Vegas. So we skipped right past all the dating parts. Who accidentally gets married like that?" She pointed a finger at her chest. "Me, that's who. But it more than worked out. It will for you two as well."

"Beckett's here!" Levi announced, walking into the room, spinning his finger in the air like the blade of a helo. "Time to roll out."

Sydney caught Beckett's eyes when he showed up behind Levi. He hooked his sunglasses in the collar of his black tee as she spoke her thoughts aloud, "You have a mischievous look there, Sheriff."

"Not a sheriff anymore," he reminded her before drawing her in for a hug, then winked. "And mischievous? No clue what you're talking about, Miss Archer."

\* \* \*

WILTSHIRE, ENGLAND – ONE WEEK LATER

"Now that they're gone, we can loosen up. Relax a little." Levi turned up the music the second his grandparents' limo pulled away from the sprawling castle-like estate. They were all gathered at the back of the property, and she was pretty sure her parents leaving was about to become a celebratory party for the kids.

*Meeee too.* Not that she didn't love her parents, but they were a lot to handle. And they didn't see eye to eye on much. But overall, the trip had been amazing. She'd always loved Castle Combe, the village and parish within the Cotswolds area where they were staying.

McKenna had also adored the English countryside. They'd spent most of the week traveling around, and Sydney had loved showing Beckett and his kids everything the

Cotswolds had to offer, from the honey-hued stone architecture to the quaint pubs.

But now, Sydney had her own plans for the day. She had the archery targets set up and a custom-made bow for McKenna inside a large gift box tucked under her arm. She wasn't sure if McKenna was interested in learning, but she was about to find out.

Beckett began throwing the football with Levi, and Sydney spied Miles tuckered out, fast asleep on the hammock, shielded from the afternoon sun by an umbrella overhead. He was curled up with one of their staff's cats, a chubby, gray, and surprisingly vocal cat with a round, flat face and the softest fur she'd ever felt.

Raising a five-year-old hadn't been on her agenda at this stage in her life, but she'd quickly grown attached to him, and she knew Beckett had as well. Miles didn't need to share blood to become a son. Family didn't work like that.

Sydney paused for a moment, her nerves getting to her, and she lifted her eyes to the sky, wondering if Matt was watching over them now. Savanna believed her husband, who'd died in the line of duty in 2015, had guided Griffin to her as a second chance at love and life, and maybe Levi's father, Matt, had been pulling a few "fate strings" to work Beckett her way?

She smiled at the idea and found her confidence renewed in her mission to share her passion for archery with McKenna.

"Hey, uh, Mom?" Levi stopped her on her way to McKenna. "Question." He tossed the ball back to Beckett and held up a finger, requesting a second. At that, Beckett went over to check on Miles in the hammock.

"Sure, what's up?" She kept hold of the gift and shoved

her sunglasses into her hair to look her son in the eyes in case this was a serious question.

Levi scratched his chin, pursing his lips as if he was toying with how to share what was on his mind, a look she knew all too well from him. "Do you think you can get me into McKenna's new private school too? I was thinking it'd be better if we all go to school there."

"Don't you love your school in Arlington?"

"I only go there because of your job. So I can be right by Dad's," he reminded her. "But if you and Beckett are planning to live together, then I'll have him if you're traveling. I think it's best if I'm in school with McKenna and Miles to keep an eye on them. Plus, McKenna's a young thirteen for high school like I was this past year. She could use a big-brother type watching out for her."

"Levi." God, her son was so sweet. "But what about Lucy? Sure, you can see her anytime, and she lives near your dad's place when you're there, but I—"

"I feel bad about this, but we broke up. Last night over the phone. I should've waited and done it at home, I suppose. But how can I date her when I'm thinking about someone else?"

"What? You broke up?" She almost dropped the gift. And yet, he seemed completely okay. "Wait, who are you thinking about?" And why did his words remind her of something Beckett had said back at that bungalow in Mexico. He hadn't gone home with his date from Savanna and Griffin's wedding because he'd been thinking about Sydney. "It's not McKenna, right?" Her eyes widened, a wave of panic about to set in.

"Whiskey-tango-foxtrot, Mom. No, just no." Levi shook his head. "I've always wanted a sister, and if you and Beckett become family, like, on a permanent basis, I think it'd be awesome to have her in only that way."

"Phew." She let go of a sigh. "Okay, then who?"

"Don't worry about it." He smiled. "So, will you try and get me into the school?"

"I won't have to try. I can get you in, no problem. I'll have to ask Seth first, but if it's what you want, he'll be on board."

"It's what I want." Levi tossed a look toward Miles and then over to McKenna. "I always wanted a big family." He returned his focus to her. "Thanks, Mom."

She shielded her eyes with her glasses before she ruined her mascara with tears. Levi was already on the move when Beckett yelled, "Go long," and Levi made the catch.

"McKenna," she called out once she managed to move again. "I have something for you, and since you're eyeing the archery targets, you probably know why I asked you to meet me here."

McKenna accepted the gift with a broad smile and opened the box.

"I had it custom-made for you. It's a starter bow, and we can upgrade you if you enjoy archery and want to—"

"I love it!" McKenna nearly smashed the gift box between them when she went in for a hug. "You'll teach me to be a badass like you, right?" She slapped her free hand over her mouth. "Sorry. Language."

"It's okay. And yes, I will absolutely teach you to be a badass archer." Sydney's heart squeezed as she went through the motions of helping McKenna set up and frame her stance. "My grandfather taught me right here when I was young. I'm honored to have a . . ." *Daughter?* Not officially, true. And maybe she and Beckett were still in the dating phase, but her gut told her everything would work out. That McKenna would become her daughter one day. And Miles her son. "I'm happy to pass down this tradition to you."

"Thank you." McKenna nodded with tears in her eyes. She shook them free and declared, "Okay, let's do this."

After an hour, McKenna really had the hang of it. Beckett and Levi had gathered to watch McKenna send arrow after arrow. And once Miles awoke, Beckett brought him over to watch as well.

"You're a natural, sweetie," Beckett said to McKenna, who looked to Sydney and declared, "I want to be like you when I'm older."

"Well," Sydney said, too choked up to manage anything else.

"She's kinda cool, right?" Levi smirked, coming in for the save.

"That she is." Beckett hooked his arm around Sydney, pulling her to his side as Miles chased the cat, and Levi took over for Sydney in helping McKenna learn.

Was this what it felt like to be part of a family? She didn't remember having such a complete feeling when she was with Seth. Not ever. And her parents weren't the warmest of people. In a matter of weeks, Beckett had changed her whole life.

"Dad, I think you should go ahead and do the thing," McKenna said about ten minutes later, and Beckett slapped his free hand to his chest as if he were choking on the fresh air.

"What thing?" Sydney quirked a brow and turned toward him.

"The *thing*," McKenna said with an exaggerated nod. Yeah, she'd get along well with Levi, that was for sure.

"Well, um, McKenna thinks this house," Beckett began, pointing toward the massive gray-brick mansion in the distance, "is like a castle."

"And you're the princess of the palace," McKenna spoke up, rolling her wrist and twirling her finger like an urgent reminder to remember his lines. "And he should be your prince," McKenna went ahead and said. "What do you think?"

Sydney chuckled and played along. "I mean, sure, that works for me. But does that make you kids the mice? And which one of you will turn into the pumpkin?"

Beckett scrubbed a hand down his face, then looked up at the sky for a moment before returning his focus to her. "How about we do this my way?" He peeked at McKenna, and she smiled, then he shoved his sunglasses into his hair. "I'm old fashioned, what can I say?" He slid his hand into his pocket, then lowered to one knee.

*Oh my God.*

"Sydney, I'd be honored if you'd spend your life with me as my wife," Beckett began, his voice rough with emotion. "It's fast, I know. But will you marry me?"

Sydney glanced at her son. Based on the huge smile on his face, she had a feeling he already knew this was going to happen. Because, of course, a man like Beckett would ask him first.

*And oh wow, this is real.* "Absolutely," she whispered when finding Beckett's eyes again. "Yes." She dropped to her knees, and he slid the simple but perfect solitaire diamond, set in a thin white gold band, onto her ring finger.

He brought his lips to hers and kissed the hell out of her as the kids cheered. "I love you," he said. "I think I skipped that part. A little nervous."

*Right.* They'd never even said that before. "I love you too," she cried before kissing him again, doing her best to keep it PG-13 given the audience.

Beckett helped her to her feet and kissed her once more.

"This is why you were almost late for the airport last week?"

He nodded. "I already had the ring. Bought it in Bama before my birthday. Levi had to use his stealth skills and help me get your ring size, so I was waiting for it to come back from the jeweler. Almost didn't get it before our flight."

"You had this planned since Alabama? The proposal?" She stared at him, a bit stunned.

"When you know, you know, Mom," Levi spoke up, and Beckett smirked.

"Kid has a point." Beckett tipped his head her son's way. "He gave me his blessing back in D.C., but you're going to have to be a rebel one more time."

"Just the one?" She narrowed her eyes. "And why is that?"

He winced. "Your dad told me no when I asked him for your hand two days ago."

"He's just seeing if you're man enough to ignore him and do what you want," Levi answered for Sydney that time, and she couldn't help but laugh.

"The kid has a point," she repeated what Beckett had said, and Beckett gathered her back into his arms and brought his mouth to her ear.

"And am I man enough for you?" he whispered, lighting her body up with the need for him. *When's bedtime?*

"You know the answer to that," she murmured, then turned her face, drawing her lips near his. "But I'll let you show me just how much tonight," she teased before he slanted his mouth over hers again.

"Okay, okay. Let's leave these two alone," Sydney heard Levi say, and she allowed Beckett to continue kissing her.

When their mouths finally parted, they were both panting like they'd sprinted a 5k. And just when she grabbed his hand to start dragging him inside, her phone rang. The one ringtone she didn't want to hear.

"I'm not answering that," she told him. "It's work."

"And what if it's an emergency? Like that time you got pulled away from your girls' weekend to save my ass?" Beckett placed a quick kiss on her cheek. "It's okay. Answer."

She blew out a frustrated breath, knowing Carter wouldn't disturb her unless it was important. "Horrible timing. He better have a damn good reason to call." Sydney went for her phone and placed Carter on speakerphone. "Did someone die? Or will they die? Otherwise, I'm hanging up."

"No to the first question. Yes to the second. But we're on your side of the pond," Carter shared. "We're in London, and we need you. Just for tonight. Someone needs saving connected to one of those damn secrets that fucker, Jorge, was guarding." He cleared his throat. "Also, sorry to interrupt. I should have led with that."

*Elaina said we'd save more lives because of those secrets. But the timing.* "Beckett just proposed to me. I can't leave."

"Ohh." Carter went quiet, and she wasn't sure what he'd say next, but Beckett set a hand over the phone and held her eyes.

Beckett gestured toward the kids playing catch in the distance. "I've got this. I'll be with our family, and we'll celebrate when you get back."

*Our family.* How could she leave them now? "No." She shook her head.

"Carter, she'll call you right back." Beckett took the phone and ended the call. He angled his head and studied her. "The timing does suck, but if someone might die without your help, you won't forgive yourself. That's who you are, and I need the love of my life happy." He reached for her cheek with his free hand. "I need my woman to go be the hero she is and not feel bad about that," he rasped. "I've got your back while you're gone. I have them with me, and we won't do anything *too* fun without you, I promise." He grinned and pulled her in for a soft kiss.

God, she was already so overwhelmed by emotions, and now for him to say that? For him to support her. Love her. Stand by her in every possible way.

But he *just* proposed. "I can't—"

"I won't take no for an answer. I can be stubborn too." Beckett eased his face away from hers and winked. "Trust me, okay?"

"I do trust you. But I love you and our family, and I don't want to walk away."

"You're not walking away. You're stepping out for a second. You'll be back." He gave her a stern look along with a nod. "I will spank your ass when we're alone if you keep arguing with me. Go save the day."

"Okay," she agreed. After a few more passionate kisses, she phoned Carter for the details, and then they made their way to the kids to share the news. "I'm so sorry," Sydney added at the end of her explanation of what was going on. "Do you hate me for leaving?"

When McKenna began to run away, Sydney slapped a hand to her heart at her reaction.

"She'll be fine," Levi said. "Don't worry, Mom. I'll tell her about some of your heroic stories when you're gone. She'll understand." He patted her on the shoulder.

"Beckett, I can't go now. Not when she's so upset." She faced him, and he was scratching his beard, his eyes on McKenna.

"She's not upset," he said matter-of-factly.

"She took off," Sydney reminded him, but when she

followed Beckett's gaze, her heart skipped a good five beats. What was McKenna doing?

McKenna's cheeks were red and flushed by the time she returned. "Here." McKenna extended Sydney's bow. "A badass needs her bow. Just didn't want you to leave without it. We need you to come back safe, you know? We just found you."

Sydney couldn't stop the tears this time, and she handed the bow off to Beckett before pulling McKenna in for a hug. She squeezed her probably too tight, and they were both wiping away tears from their cheeks once they parted. She spied Beckett turning his head to hide the fact he was doing the same.

"See, told you." Levi lifted Miles into his arms and hoisted him up onto his shoulders. Miles threw his hands into the air with little adorable fist pumps of excitement.

Beckett handed her the bow and swatted Sydney's ass when the kids had turned their backs. "Go, sweetheart. Go be that hero *our* daughter admires." He grinned from ear to ear before gently tugging her wrist, drawing her close, holding her captive with his dark, deep gaze. "Go be mine too."

CONTINUE TO LEARN MORE ABOUT OTHER CHARACTERS FROM *The Guarded One. Plus, there is a music playlist, reading guide, and more.*

# FALCON FALLS CROSSOVER INFO

**Next up?**
Falcon Falls, book 4, releases Fall 2022.
*Be sure to check out the "bonus scene" tab on my website in case I release any bonus content before then.

### *Previous Falcon books*

*The Hunted One* (Falcon Falls, book 1) is Savanna and Griffin's story.

*The Broken One* (Falcon Falls, book 2) is Jesse and Ella's book.

### Where else have you seen some of the secondary characters?

**Elaina, Liam, and Emily** - Their book is *Finding Her Chance*. These characters appear in a few more books from the Stealth Ops Series as well. This book can easily be read as a standalone.

**Mya Vanzetti** is a journalist in the contemporary romance, *My Every Breath*. And she is Julia Maddox's friend in *Chasing the Storm* (where she helps save Oliver's life).

**Mason Matthews** (brother to Connor). Connor's book is *The Hard Truth*.

**Gray Chandler** was in *Chasing the Knight* and the epilogue of *Chasing the Storm*.

**Jack London** was also in *Chasing the Knight*. *Chasing the Knight* stars Gray's sister, Natasha.

In *Chasing Daylight*, we first meet the Alabama crew (Jesse, Beckett, McKenna, etc). This is **A.J.'s** book. We also discover the tension between Ella & Jesse in this book, and that tension continues in *Chasing Fortune*, which is **Rory's (Jesse's sister's)** book.

Aside from the Falcon Falls Series - **Carter Dominick** was also in *Chasing Fortune* and *Chasing the Storm*.

**Oliver** and **Griffin** are briefly in *Chasing the Storm* as well. But in *Chasing the Storm* - Griffin is only referred to as "Southern sniper guy.

Publication order for all books
Books by Series

Be sure to join my newsletter, Facebook groups, or follow me on Insta, TikTok, or Facebook to learn more about the upcoming releases. Plus, get access to teasers, giveaways, and more.

The Falcon Falls Pinterest muse/inspiration board.

**Continue** for a *music playlist*, reading guide, and Stealth Ops/Falcon Falls Family Tree!

# MUSIC PLAYLIST

*Never Go Back - Robin Schulz Remix* - Dennis Lloyd, Robin Schulz

*Don't Blame Me* - Taylor Swift

*Broken Arrows* - Avicii

*It Don't Matter* - Alok, Sofi Tukker, INNA

*OK Not To Be OK* - Marshmello, Demi Lovato

*Revival* - Sigala, Cheat Codes, MAX

*Bam Bam (feat. Ed Sheeran)* - Camila Cabello, Ed Sheeran

*Feel Me* - Selena Gomez

*One of Them Girls* - Lee Brice

*DAKITI* - Bad Bunny, Jhay Cortez

MUSIC PLAYLIST

*Titi Me Pregunto*- Bad Bunny

*Holy* - Hogland, Charlie South

*'Til You Can't* - Cody Johnson

*Independent With You* - Kylie Morgan

*On My Way To You* - Cody Johnson

*The Archer* - Taylor Swift

                Spotify

*Note: Spotify adds "suggested" songs to the end of my list, so you may see other songs there.

# FAMILY TREE: FALCON FALLS & STEALTH OPS

**Falcon Falls Team members:**

Team leader: **Carter Dominick - Army Delta/CIA**

- A widower (lost his wife)
- Dog: Dallas

Team leader: **Gray Chandler - Army SF (Green Beret)**

Family:

- Admiral Chandler (father)
- Natasha (sister)
- Wyatt (brother-in-law)

**Jesse - Army Ranger**
Family / Friends -

- Wife: Ella Mae (now pregnant)
- Sister: Rory

# FAMILY TREE: FALCON FALLS & STEALTH OPS

- Parents: Donna and Sean
- Brother-in-law: Chris
- Friends: AJ, Beckett, Caleb, Shep Hawkins
- Beckett's daughter: McKenna
- AJ & Ana's son: Marcus (Mac)

**Griffin Andrews - Delta**

- Married to Savanna

**Jack London - Army SF (Green Beret)**

- Divorced (Jill London)

**Oliver Lucas - Army Airborne**

- Tucker Lucas - brother (deceased)
- Tucker was engaged to Julia Maddox before he passed away.

**Sydney Archer - Army**

- Engaged to Beckett / Son: Levi
- McKenna and Miles Hawkins*

\* \* \*

**Stealth Ops Team Members**

**Team leaders:** Luke & Jessica Scott / Intelligence team member (joined in 2019): Harper Brooks

**Bravo Team:**

Bravo One - Luke
Bravo Two - Owen
Bravo Three - Asher
Bravo Four - Liam
Bravo Five - Knox (Charlie "Knox" Bennett)

**Echo Team:**
Echo One - Wyatt
Echo Two - A.J. (Alexander James)
Echo Three - Chris
Echo Four - Roman
Echo Five - Finn (Dalton "Finn" Finnegan)

## ALSO BY BRITTNEY SAHIN

Find the latest news from my newsletter/website and/or Facebook: Brittney's Book Babes / the Stealth Ops Spoiler Room /Dublin Nights Spoiler Room.

Publication order for all books

Books by Series

Pinterest Muse/Inspiration Board

\* \* \*

### Falcon Falls Security

*The Hunted One* - book 1 - Griffin & Savanna

*The Broken One* - book 2 - Jesse & Ella

*The Guarded One* - book 3 - Sydney & Beckett

### Stealth Ops Series: Bravo Team

*Finding His Mark* - Book 1 - Luke & Eva

*Finding Justice* - Book 2 - Owen & Samantha

*Finding the Fight* - Book 3 - Asher & Jessica

*Finding Her Chance* - Book 4 - Liam & Emily

*Finding the Way Back* - Book 5 - Knox & Adriana

### Stealth Ops Series: Echo Team

*Chasing the Knight* - Book 6 - Wyatt & Natasha

*Chasing Daylight* - Book 7 - A.J. & Ana
*Chasing Fortune* - Book 8 - Chris & Rory
*Chasing Shadows* - Book 9 - Harper & Roman
*Chasing the Storm* - Book 10 - Finn & Julia

**Becoming Us:** *connection to the Stealth Ops Series (books take place between the prologue and chapter 1 of Finding His Mark)*

*Someone Like You* - A former Navy SEAL. A father. And off-limits. (Noah Dalton)

*My Every Breath* - A sizzling and suspenseful romance. Businessman Cade King has fallen for the wrong woman. She's the daughter of a hitman - and he's the target.

## Dublin Nights

*On the Edge* - Adam & Anna
*On the Line* - follow-up wedding novella (Adam & Anna)
*The Real Deal* - Sebastian & Holly
*The Inside Man* - Cole & Alessia
*The Final Hour* - Sean and Emilia

**Stand-alone** (with a connection to *On the Edge*):

*The Story of Us* – Sports columnist Maggie Lane has 1 rule: never fall for a player. One mistaken kiss with Italian soccer star Marco Valenti changes everything…

## Hidden Truths

*The Safe Bet* – Begin the series with the Man-of-Steel lookalike Michael Maddox.

*Beyond the Chase* - Fall for the sexy Irishman, Aiden O'Connor, in this romantic suspense.

*The Hard Truth* – Read Connor Matthews' story in this second-chance romantic suspense novel.

*Surviving the Fall* – Jake Summers loses the last 12 years of his life in this action-packed romantic thriller.

*The Final Goodbye* - Friends-to-lovers romantic mystery

Printed in Great Britain
by Amazon